PRISONERS OF FATE

CRAIG A. GODFREY

Black Rose Writing | Texas

The author grants the final approval for this literary material.

First printing

ISBN: 978-1-68433-792-7
PUBLISHED BY BLACK ROSE WRITING
www.blackrosewriting.com

Printed in the United States of America
Suggested Retail Price (SRP) $19.95

Prisoners of Fate is printed in Traditional Arabic

*As a planet-friendly publisher, Black Rose Writing does its best to eliminate unnecessary waste to reduce paper usage and energy costs, while never compromising the reading experience. As a result, the final word count vs. page count may not meet common expectations.

For Warren and Penny

PRISONERS OF FATE

PROLOGUE

The dictionary tells us a prisoner is a person committed to prison confinement as a punishment for a crime against another. *Fate* is believed by many to be a development of occurrences uncontrollable in a person's life, a future mapped out in advance and controlled by a supernatural power. Some suffer from *greed*, an avaricious egocentric compulsion to possess something, be it wealth or power.

There are those who are vain; conceited narcissistic types with an excessively high opinion of themselves. *Thieves*, well we all know what they do, taking another's property, in particular another's treasures. To steal without using violence, mostly, like a burglar entering another's property for the sole purpose of taking their possessions.

Then there are those who commit fraud; wrongful deception to deceive for personal gain or *desire*; a strong feeling of wanting. And one of the worst of all, *revenge*; hurting someone as payback for a wrong committed against themselves ... even to the extent of murder.

The human race has endless traits, many good, some bad, but most of us are honest and hard working. Many people are living outside of what is normal. These sorrowful souls are the prisoners of fate ...

The fated characters in this saga of greed, fraud, desire and revenge

In order of appearance:

Meredith Kendall – Sex Worker (Barbie)
Stanley Smart – Tasmanian Museum and Art Gallery Curator
Signor Jacopo Moretti – Antique Restorer
Stella Bathe – Assistant Curator/Conservator
Max Shreeve – Cray Fisherman, owner of *Infinity*
Mason Swinburne – Deckhand
Verity Shreeve – Max the fisherman's Estranged Wife
Ryan – Villain
Christian Yardley Winterbourne – Magistrate
Alfred Kenning – Conman
Rory Benetti – Simpleton
Susan Kirby – Assistant to Mr Alfred Kenning
Sergeant Ray Highlander – Police Interrogator
Ivano Stipanov – Burglar to/of the rich
Charlotte Fysh – TMAG Director
Neville Goldman – Art Dealer
Mareike – Bordello Madam
Phoebe Crow – Mareike's Rival Madam
Chastity – Sex Worker
Maggie – Max the Fisherman's Sister
Maddison Lovett – Police Inspector
Jock Birdwhistle – Antique Dealer
Landon Finch – Senior Detective
Seraph – Killer
Luke Farrell – Rookie cop/ Forensics expert, Coroner's Assistant
Dr Barrett 'Tiger' Griffin – Coroner
Sophie Smart – Daughter of museum curator Stanley Smart
Dr Jennifer Macintyre – Police Psychologist
Ronny Smith – Killer

CHAPTER ONE

Cremorne Beach Summer 1995

B arbie woke to stillness. Her mouth felt dry, her head a little overcast. With pleasant dreams fresh on her mind it took a moment to recollect she had slept in an old shack at Cremorne Beach last night. She didn't have to open her eyes; her ears pinpointed her position like GPS. The serenity of the beach. Benign shallow waves barely making a sound, rolling ashore in a perfectly spaced, eternal rhythm of peace.

And damn it was hot.

Barbie kicked off the single satin sheet that had covered her body, now tangled about her feet. She was naked. The sliding doors to the balcony over the beach were wide open. But there was no breeze. This was a rare hot and balmy morning in Tasmania and Barbie was starting to register her preference for a more temperate climate when she realised she was alone. Now she opened her eyes. Max's indentation in the cheap mattress was still evident; a shape a little like a Madeleine cake mould without the grooves, Barbie fancied.

Ah, Max.

The good-looking fisherman with the body of a pro Aussie rules footy player. She liked everything about him; he was stocky, rock-chested with a handsome six-pack, mature for his early thirties. She liked his short dark slicked down hair and trimmed beard. And best of all he was good company and extremely charming.

Barbie's sense of smell was acute. *Ah, Frangelico.* The sweet nutty aroma of hazelnuts drifted by Barbie, wafting towards the open patio doors, the liqueur's scent an invisible reminder of a wonderful evening. She glanced at the bedside table and the sticky dregs of melted ice and the caramel-coloured dregs brought back pleasant memories of their love making less than half a dozen hours earlier.

'Max,' Barbie called out. An unwavering slap of water on sand answered.

'Max.'

She sat up and listened for the clanging of a frypan, the smell of frying bacon, toast maybe. Nothing. Just Frangelico scenting the salt of the sea and the sundried seaweed at low tide.

Barbie pulled on panties and bra and took short measured steps down the narrow hallway to the kitchen. 'Max.' Nothing. Outside his Ford Pickup was gone. Barbie cupped her hands under the tap and took a long drink of water and thought how pure the tank water tasted rather than the town water in Hobart.

'Nice of you to say goodbye,' Barbie muttered at the tap, when she saw the envelope on the sink.

Barbie.

She opened the package and folded the two one hundred-dollar bills, securing them in her bra, before reading the note.

Sorry, had to leave for work. Thanks for a great night, we'll do it again soon. Lock the doors on your way out.

Max xxx

Three kisses! That's nice. Clients rarely leave kisses, the escort smiled at the message. She knew Max was about to go through a nasty divorce with the woman he only referred to as *the bitch.* Last night had been the second time in the one week that she had had the same all-night client and, truth be known, she was keen on the man. He was honest, up front and a listener. Not to mention the great sex. Barbie, although a novice at this ancient profession, had mastered the art of faking an orgasm. But with Max … well … there was no need. Barbie wore a wide smile in the mirror, splashing water on her face. Sure, they drank too much and went at it like rabbits, but hey … *ah, Max!*

Barbie destroyed the note, tidied the shack, made the bed, put the rubbish out and locked the doors behind her. It wasn't the first time she had done this and prided herself as being professional.

Barbie sat behind the wheel of her white '91 Ford EB Falcon. A bit of a boy's car but hey, it was cheap, a bargain from a car salesman client. She pulled down the visor to use the mirror and waxed her lips. Bordeaux brown. Pinching her lips together to spread the lipstick, she couldn't stop thinking of Max. The memory of lying with him only hours before sent prickles through her body. Three times they had made love. Why wasn't he there this morning? Barbie twisted the key in the ignition and the car started immediately. She wound down the driver's window, engaged gear and crumbled over the gravel and sand onto the bitumen. Home was twenty-five minutes away.

Twenty-two-year-old sex-worker Barbie, real name **Meredith Kendal**, had been a call girl for seven months now. She was studying at the University of Tasmania – for her Bachelor of Arts degree – and needed the cash for university fees. She wasn't alone in this caper either. A few other students had confessed to the same income source, usually young women from less fortunate backgrounds wanting a higher education. And there was nothing wrong with it, was there? Anyway, who cares? Meredith made no excuses. Besides she liked the sex. She enjoyed the work. The only downside was overly fat men, unhappily married. Max however … well, he was a treat.

Turning right off Cremorne Avenue onto South Arm Road driving north towards Hobart twenty minutes away, Meredith took passing notice of the fire engine red XJ-S grand tourer Jaguar – only to observe the speeding sports car fishtail in the gravel on the beach road turnoff. The two drivers had little reason to recognise each other as Meredith had never met *the bitch.*

Verity Shreeve – the fisherman's wife – corrected the skid, dropped back a gear and booted the Jag's accelerator back to the floor. Three seconds later she was back in top gear, the six-cylinder motor hurling her towards the Cremorne Beach shack. Verity, a wannabe blonde with long hair dyed with peroxide, slim, pretty and bitter, parked the sports car fifty metres away and hurried between sand dunes to the beachfront property. But there was no sign of life. Inside she could smell Max. She just knew she could. Ralph Lauren Cologne, Polo Eau de Toilette. Max loved the stuff, but Verity always hated its *masculine blend of tobacco, wood and leather energised with the refreshing scent of brilliant herbals,* whatever the hell that was! At least that's what it said on the pretty green bottle with the faux gold stopper. Verity stormed through the shack to the bedroom overlooking the bay. If she wasn't so angry, she would appreciate its beauty. Instead she yanked back the bedclothes. It smelt like Max. *Max and some slut.*

Right … she said under her seething breath. *I'm taking the shack as well. I want the house, the shack and your fucking boat.*

Max Shreeve, fisherman, hefted the last cray pot onto the deck of his cray boat, *Infinity*. He had fetched ten new tea-tree cray pots in his pickup and the green wood made them heavier than usual.

'Christ it's hot,' he told his deckhand Big Bill.

Bill, notably big, as his sobriquet suggested, used an old t-shirt to wipe his brow. 'If it wasn't so early, I'd crack a beer eh?' The six foot six Maori was a gentle giant in reality. Max nodded agreement. He fancied he could smell last night's Frangelico seeping from his pores.

Big Bill read his skipper's manner like a book. 'Big night boss?'

'You could say that!'

'Did yer get lucky?'

'You could say that too.'

The Maori had no control over a huge grin, distorting geometrical tattoos on his face. 'So?'

'So, what?'

'Yer gunna kiss an' tell?'

'No mate, I'm not that kind o' bloke.'

'Bullshit!'

Truth was Max didn't want to confess to paying for sex. As he didn't want to be seen hanging around Hobart's bars, he had picked up the phone. Now he didn't want to confess to his deckhand that he had phoned an escort advertised in the classifieds of the Mercury newspaper, under *Adult Entertainment*. *Salon Rouge* was a call girl service operated from an upmarket brothel in Liverpool Street and this had been the second time Max had used this service. Sure, he was married, but the marriage was on the rocks and besides, Max was now certain there was someone else in his wife's life. Either way it didn't matter, Max had decided to move out to his shack at Cremorne. Now Meredith occupied his thoughts. The young university student whom he first met as Barbie was unlike anyone he had ever met. Admittedly she was nearly ten years his junior and a sex-worker, but something deep was happening in his life. He had spent two wonderful nights with her and found her so open, so virtuous in many ways, and the more he thought about her the more he fancied he could make an honest woman of her. They just clicked; compatible in a crazy way

Max never thought possible. Mainly she satisfied Max's sexual needs. He could be insatiable, especially when he was drunk.

'Hey boss!' Bill's mood shifted from jovial to astute. 'Those bastards are back.' The big Maori alluded to an unmarked sedan pulling into a parking space three cars from Max's pickup further along the docks.

'Jesus!' Max looked past the New Zealander discreetly. 'Will they never leave us alone?'

'They was here an hour ago eh, but when they seen your pickup wasn't there, they buggered off.'

Max went about his work as if he was unaware the fisheries inspectors – *who stood out like dog's nuts by the way* – were watching him. It had been well over two years now since they caught him selling poached abalone to Tom Chung, the owner of The Smiling Dragon Chinese restaurant in the northern suburb of Moonah. All had been quite lucrative and safe until Mr Chung started sending frozen boxes to Hong Kong. Max knew he should have served time behind bars for this indiscretion, but a friend of a friend had introduced him to a magistrate with a snobby name, Christian Yardley Winterbourne. Not only did the man have a snobby name and act high and mighty, but he also had a passion for antiques, in particular colonial antiques connected to early Tasmania. And this passion was known to tempt this particular magistrate into the path of corruption by accepting a choice collectors' piece for legal favours. So, for the price of a model ship made of whale bone by a 19th century seafarer, a very rare piece left to Max by his grandfather, Max was able to broker an exchange: a moderate fine for the model ship. And stay out of prison. Tom Chung however, received six-month gaol sentence, serving only three with time off for good behaviour.

'All I can say Bill is that I hope this cray season's a bumper,' Max told his deckhand, while shaking his head towards the fisheries officers. 'Cos mate, I need all the money I can get my hands on, otherwise the bitch's going to get *Infinity* and then guess what? She'll be your skipper.'

'Bullshit! That'll never happen boss.' Bill helped secure the last cray pot before noticing Max had also bought some new spear fishing gear at the chandler. 'Nice.' Bill whistled. 'You bought a Saumarez speargun.'

'Not bad huh?'

'Bloody ripper; open muzzle railgun, stainless steel mech, fibreglass parts. Nice one boss.'

'You know your spearguns then?'

'Yeh well, I've had a few in me day. Where do yer want it skip'?'

'In the locker next to the hold. Chuck the weights in there too will you.' Max watched the fisheries observing him from the docks. 'Look at the bastards, subtle as dogshit.'

'What'ya gonna do skipper?'

'Tell you what Bill. Let's slip the mooring and we'll motor upriver. We've caught our quota for a few days so we can't go out anytime soon.' Max stepped into the wheelhouse. 'I'll moor at Lindisfarne and stay on board there a few days I reckon,' Max spoke of his Lindisfarne Motor Yacht Club membership. 'You can go ashore there.'

'Sure thing.'

Both men heard a car door slam two cars from the fisheries inspectors. A younger man, average height, strong build, wearing shorts, deck shoes, wife beater and a backwards cap stepped onto the floating jetty and walked towards *Infinity* with purpose. It was Mason, another deckhand, whom Max had fired for drunkenness two days earlier. Max wasn't pleased. 'What's that prick want now?'

'He's come to fetch his kit,' Big Bill said. 'I'll piss him off boss.'

'Yeh,' Max scowled through the grubby wheelhouse window. 'You do that.'

Max had had an awkward altercation with the twenty-one-year old and it didn't end pleasantly. Truth be known, he had a decent-sized bruise on his left pectoral where the bastard kicked him when he fell to the deck fighting. Big Bill saved his arse.

Clearly Mason had not seen Max in the wheelhouse. 'Where's dickhead?' Mason spat.

'He's below deck, so take yer kit an' piss off, alright.' Big Bill had gotten along fine with the younger deckhand, but the crew member had crossed the line two days ago and Bill knew which side of his bread was buttered.

'Hidin' from me is he?' Mason persisted. He raised his voice. 'Bloody wimp.'

Big Bill smelt beer on the young bloke's breath. 'Look Mason, there's yer kit.' And he pointed to a duffel bag sitting ready for collection on a hatch cover. 'So, take me advice and bugger off, eh.'

'Hey Bill,' Mason persisted. 'I heard one of the lads talkin' at Shippies …'
Big Bill's patience was being tested. 'Said Captain Max Arsehole is fuckin' some whore, gone an' fallen in love with 'er an all.'

Max flew out of the wheelhouse, incensed, fists balled.

'Get off my boat,' he screamed. 'Now!'

Mason stood, one foot on the jetty, one on the deck. He came to stir up a hornet's nest and succeeded. 'Isn't that right Maxie?' Mason yelled back. 'Fuckin' some whore that …'

Bill shoved Mason back onto the jetty and threw his kit after him. 'Piss off Mason. You're not welcome here.'

Mason knew better than to anger a six-foot-six Maori. Bill stepped onto the pier shoving his chest out like a prize cock, blocking further attempts as Mason stubbornly stood his ground. But Mason knew the Maori's history. Big Bill had been done for assault a few years back and another public fight could see him arrested.

'Just bugger off Mason.' Bill's eyes reddened. He was like a bull being flagged in the ring. He shoved the deckhand backwards with his chest, a chest hard as an iron ram. Max managed to look around the giant torso. 'Weak as piss Max, gotta get Bill to save yer pathetic arse.'

Max lost it. He mounted the gunwale and cleared the jetty with arms flaying. The first punch slammed Mason's mouth and blood squirted from a loosened tooth. The second punch floored the deckhand onto his back where Max dropped to finish him, one knee into his chest. Max managed one more punch to the throat before Big Bill pulled him away. 'Boss, boss. No.' Bill thought Max had lost it completely, and maybe he had. 'He's not worth it boss.'

Gasping for air from the punch to the throat Mason picked up his duffel bag and backed away along the jetty. 'You're crazy,' he yelled out when he thought he had reached a safe distance.

'Piss off,' Max called out. 'I never want to see you around here again.'

'Oh, you'll see me again, don't you worry, when you haven't got that bloody gorilla to save your arse.'

Gorilla!

Big Bill made to chase after him, but Mason was already in his car and squealing tires as he reversed away …

Meanwhile, across the docks at the Tasmanian Museum and Art Gallery (TMAG)

Museum Curator Stanley Smart patted his unruly shock of grey hair into place, aware that his baby-soft locks looked like a wig if he didn't attend to it. At five-foot-five he was a short man, but what Stanley lacked in stature he made up for in canny intelligence. He was also frugal and extraordinarily savvy. A seven times radio quiz show champion with a remarkable memory for storing facts; whether it be geography or trivia. At fifty-nine Stanley walked with a slight stoop; his face narrow, his small mouth downturned and his pointed nose separated by loose jowls. Paired with hooded eyes and large ears, gave Stanley the semblance of a basset hound; if, that is, one had to compare the shrewd man with an animal.

Yet, to older women the man was charming, personable even. But beneath the façade was an incurable anguish.

Stanley was sharp and, many would suggest, bordering on paranoid. However, he had never been diagnosed as such; although he had battled mental illness all his working life. But this ailment blessed him with extraordinary intelligence. He had a photographic memory with a thirst for knowledge, especially in his chosen favourite subjects; archaeology, history, geography, antiquities and antiques of the western world. He was particularly attracted to coins, medals, tokens and banknotes; a passion that saw him take on the position of numismatist at the TMAG. He was revered by academics in similar fields around the globe, with whom he corresponded regularly. Outside his employment he maintained few acquaintances. Besides, his profession kept him in the bowels of the museum, where he felt most at home, researching, cataloguing collections, conserving artefacts and antiques and creating exhibits for the museum.

Anti-depressants kept him in check. Outwardly friendly and polite, a rare few saw another side to the man, especially after drinking, a daily habit he kept hidden from most, when he drank alone at night. Red wine only, and out of a cask.

Stanley's expertise saw him offered higher positions over the years, particularly in the larger institutions in cities like Melbourne and Sydney. However his lack of personal confidence saw him reject every one of them. Another reason was a trail of past discrepancies he preferred to keep hidden.

As curator of the Tasmanian Museum archive, Stanley was responsible for taking care of all the museum's collections; be it maintenance, preservation, archiving, cataloguing and display. Occasionally museums traded objects from their collections with other institutions.

With limited staff Stanley occasionally wore another cap, aiding conservation when required. What kept Stanley in good rapport with the museum director was his work ethic. He spent many hours more than his expected thirty-eight-hour week doing unpaid overtime. He was dedicated. So dedicated, he took his work home with him …

And therein lies the problem. Take *it* home he did, but often failed to return *it*.

Yet the museum was Stanley's life. Of course, being a lonely widower afforded him this extra time, living alone and motivated by his enthusiasm for the museum's collections. Stanley's wife of thirty-eight years, one must understand, had died of pancreatic cancer at the age of fifty-nine, several years back, and the only way the curator could move forward in life was to indulge his passion for history and museums. Stanley's only child was his daughter Sophie. Twenty-five-year-old head-strong Sophie Smart – whilst not the most attractive portrait in the gallery – had an alluring personality and an affable disposition. She had a shock of red hair, gorgeous green eyes and a curvaceous figure. And she had youth on her side, although she was yet to meet *Mr Right* and settle down. Sophie worked as assistant manager at Menzies Menswear – men's clothiers – in Collin's Street in Hobart's CBD, and did not share her father's interest in history or the arts, preferring her social life with like-minded twenty-five-year-olds.

***

Stanley had one friend and confidant, **antique restorer Jacopo Moretti**. It was Stanley's role as conservator at the museum that introduced Stanley to Jacopo, a talented Italian cabinetmaker and perfectionist. Jacopo had already entered his sixth decade when he met Stanley. That was eleven years ago now, and the two men discovered they shared a kinship; a keen interest in history, antiques and a talent for twisting the truth and bending the rules, ever so slightly. Now at sixty-one, Jacopo showed no sign of slowing down in his North Hobart workshop, where he restored antiques for more affluent

Hobartians. And charged handsomely in the process. But perfection came at a price, right? Jacopo – short, slim-faced, large nose (sprouting hairs) sunken eyes and shovel-brush moustache – was one of those men who could eat pasta, pizza and tiramisu every day in any quantity and never gain weight. Except for a neat round pot-belly from wine, like he had a small balloon under his cardigan; an inherent attribute, especially for an Italian. Like his pleasant manner, Jacopo was never without his herringbone plaid woollen flat cap and fur collared coat, when not clad in carpenter's overalls in his workshop. Jacopo's affable demeanour rarely waned. Only when he thought of Eleonora, his wife of forty years and now suffering dementia, did he let down his amiable front. Besides cunning, the two rascals, Jacopo and Stanley, had loneliness in common.

***

Stanley's introduction to museum life had started with work experience back in the early '50s. An uncle had a friend who was the taxidermist at the TMAG, a naturalist by the name of Kenneth McRae, who took the fifteen-year-old Stanley under his wing.

'Plucking penguins Jacky,' Stanley told his Italian mate one night, reminiscing over several glasses of cask red wine and a plate of Italian sausage. (Compliments of Jacopo's butcher mate, Mario.) 'Have you ever plucked a penguin?'

'Pluck a penguin?' Jacopo manoeuvred macerated sausage from one side of his toothless gums to the other. 'No, my friend, never.'

'Well this taxidermist,' Stanley leant closer to elaborate on the services of a taxidermist. 'In case you don't know my Italian friend, taxidermy is the art of stuffing and mounting animal skins, so they look lifelike.'

'Si, si.' Jacopo leant back evading a mist of spittle.

'Well this taxidermist thawed penguins out from the freezer, and they didn't half smell. They were caught down Antarctica I think, or maybe Macquarie Island.' Stanley had a sudden thought, a common habit during his intoxicated ramblings. 'You know, he told me there are seventeen species of penguin and they're all found in the Southern Hemisphere, with the Emperor Penguin the tallest at four feet.' Stanley put his hand out to estimate this height, amazing even himself. 'Anyways, he turned them inside out.'

'The penguins?'

'Yes. What else would I be talking about?' Stanley studied his old friend a moment as Jacopo swallowed hard, washing his food down with wine and pouring them both another. 'Ever seen a penguin turned inside out, Jacky? Like a sock? And a smelly sock at that.' Stanley grinned; his lips stained red from the wine. Jacopo shook his head trying to imagine the sight. 'No? Well, when inside out, all the feather quills pop up like porcupine spikes and there's fat between them that needs to be plucked out with tweezers.' The curator mimicked the plucking and poking with invisible tweezers. 'Otherwise the fat goes rancid and rots the stuffed bird when it's finished. It's a laborious job, time consuming and most unpleasant. I only lasted one day.'

'One day!' Jacopo shook his head.

'Yes. One day too many. Anyhow I made friends with the museum numismatist instead and ended up working with him … and now here I am … the rest is history.'

And indeed, it was. Stanley left school after completing grade twelve to join the museum staff. He spent three years in the numismatic department before moving into conservation. Meanwhile he completed a degree and then studied with conservators in Sydney for two more years before returning to Hobart. He was immediately employed in the museum's archive section. Now, close on forty years later, Stanley was a senior curator, trusted numismatist and conservator. He was at the top of his game, in a position of trust, rubbing shoulders with the likes of the Lord Mayor, the state's Premier and Tasmania's leading authorities in the arts.

But this trust was about to be tested.

***

A new museum director, a new chapter

Newly appointed **Ms Charlotte Fysh** – CEO of the TMAG was a breath of fresh air, selected by the TMAG board of directors recently, after an extensive national and international recruitment process. Originally from Hobart, she had been Assistant Director at the Powerhouse Museum in Sydney. Charlotte had over twenty-five years of experience. She looked the part too, with her teased curls, tortoise-shell glasses, conservative blue skirt suits and wide collared business shirts. She had studied at Cambridge and the University of London. At forty-eight Charlotte had the full experience required to take the position of chief executive officer of the Hobart. She was now accountable for daily operations, long term plans, any research required in all areas and responsible for the museum's finances. Although supplemented financially by the government, the museum was expected to make money where possible and this, Charlotte was more than capable of achieving all this. She had excellent supervisory skills and had mastered the art of delegation. Charlotte was also fiercely competitive and expected everyone to pull their weight. She was definitely a career woman, savvy in business and an achiever. Being gay she'd toughened during adolescence and pity help anyone who criticised her work, or her sexuality.

***

Stanley sat silently on his stool, his grey dustcoat with its repairs and frayed stitching hanging loose about him. In years gone by his wife would have made repairs. But nowadays Stanley was a widower with frugal habits. Out on the street the mercury hit twenty-five, but here in the museum coin vault it must be over thirty. Stanley opened his coat even further hoping to benefit from a single wall fan while trickles of sweat moistened under his arms. *Damn it's hot today.*

Floating the jeweller's loupe over the silver *Macintosh and Degraves Tasmania, one shilling* token, Stanley was unaware he was salivating, until he almost dribbled on the rare coin. Minted in 1823 for use in colonial Van Diemen's Land, the token was valuable and highly sought after by private coin collectors. Stanley was well aware that one sold as recently as six months ago at a Sydney auction house for fifteen thousand dollars. The museum's specimen, one of two in the collection, was certainly a handsome coin; desirable to collectors, and would easily fetch five figures, should it ever reach the open market. Stanley waited. He listened, his large ear tuned to the corridor.

Stella Bathe, one of two assistant conservators, had been talking to the new director in the passageway outside the coin room - this small vaulted lockup in the museum basement where filing cabinets were situated, storing the museum's priceless currency collection.

Now all had gone silent. Stanley had heard the whispers. If Stanley didn't know any better, he thought there was a possibility the two women were attracted to each other. *Was there romance afoot?* Stanley shook the image from his mind. That's their affair. He had more pressing business to attend to.

With the deft move of a magician Stanley slipped a hand into his dustcoat pocket, plucking another Macintosh and Degraves silver shilling token free. Stanley replaced the museum's extremely fine specimen from its acid free plastic sheath with his less fine condition coin, which was taken from his own collection. With the swap successful, the museum's numismatist replaced the token in its museum storage, locked the cabinet, switched off the light and locked the door. In the corridor he checked his breathing and straightened his dustcoat. Of course, he had done this plenty of times over the years, but it never became any easier. The exchange took only minutes and Stanley Smart's personal coin collection just increased in value to the tune of several thousand dollars.

Stanley had exchanged dozens of coins in this way, maybe as many as a hundred. Swapping rare coins of poorer condition with the museum's prized mint condition samples had become an addiction, and as he was the museum's numismatic expert, and only numismatist, who would ever know?

***

So how did Jacopo Moretti wind up mates with such a rogue as Stanley Smart one might ask? It happened a few years back, over a decade by now. 1985. With the aid of (wealthy) *Friends of the Museum* funding, Stanley had orchestrated the purchase of the now famous *Bothwell Inn Sofa*. This extremely rare jewel of Regency period colonial furniture, made by an anonymous cabinetmaker around 1825, was discovered in a local woodshed and put up for sale at auction. The final price was well into six figures. The sofa was now on display at the museum. Many of the friends of the Museum were invited to inspect the Australian red cedar, eucalypt, peearwood and mahogany treasure, which Jacopo restored for them. The wily old Italian seemed out of place at the cocktail party celebration honouring the acquisition of the unique sofa. Especially since he wore an open neck shirt and cheap suit while rubbing shoulders with dinner-suits, gold Rolex watches, diamonds and pearls. Stanley sympathised with the Italian man's discomfort and struck up a conversation. Both men soon realised they had much in common including no great fondness for mingling with the establishment figures of Hobart.

They met at the museum café days later where Jacopo was amused to watch his frugal new friend pocket the sugar sachets to take home. The following weekend Stanley accepted an invitation to visit Jacopo's workshop/studio. The studio was a 19th century stable. Inside, grubby window panes offered a view out into what was once a manicured garden. Since Jacopo's wife Eleanora had taken ill the vegetable, flowers and fruit garden had fallen into disrepair. However on this warm afternoon the sun filled the workshop with golden light, highlighting the equipment and the craftsman himself and immediately reminding Stanley of Giuseppe, the old Tuscan toymaker who modelled the famous marionette, Pinocchio.

Jacopo could see Stanley was interested and showed him around the studio. The walls, made of handmade brick, had been rendered at some stage; otherwise the stables were much as they were when built a hundred and seventy years ago. Only the stable stalls had been removed to accommodate three heavy wooden workbenches, each gnawed and chipped by saws and chisels over the years. The cabinetmaker's tools – hammers, mallets, chisels, squares, drill bits – were displayed on wooden panels fastened to one wall in what looked to Stanley to be organised chaos. Along the back wall were his lathes, table-saw, mitre-saw and drilling jig. A pot belly stove kept the workshop warm in winter.

'Oh Jacopo,' Stanley said with a reverence that brought a serious smile to the old cabinetmaker's face. 'This is stunning my friend.'

Stanley ran a gentle hand across the beautifully polished top of a Huon pine chest of drawers. It was perfection. Jacopo was in the process of polishing the chest with its final coat of oil. Stanley eyed the piece a moment – almost as tall as he was – admiring the famous bird's eye knots in the timber that made Huon Pine so desirable for furniture. Stanley caressed the carved pilasters flanking either side of the seven drawers to the short stubby turned legs at the base. He opened the top hat drawer, sampling the Victorian cabinet maker's craft. 'Here.' Jacopo showed Stanley two dog-eared polaroids of the chest as it was when it was brought into his workshop.

'You have done well my friend. It is truly a beautiful piece of furniture.' The curator stepped back stroking his chin in thought. '1870s?'

'I'm think-een a little more old,' the Italian nodded sagely, his red ringed eyes blinking from the sawdust. 'Maybe 1860.'

'You're probably right. Who's the lucky owner?'

'A magistrate. He live in Battery Point,' the cabinetmaker spoke of Hobart's historic suburb.

'Well I'm certain he will be a happy man.' Stanley picked up a handful of Huon pine shavings, fingering their coarse blonde twists and curls before allowing them to drop back to the flagstone floor of the old stables. 'Do you know these shavings are a good pest repellent?'

'Si, my wife Eleonora, she sew them into cloth bags and she put them everywhere, in the wardrobe, drawers ... even Figaro's bed.'

'Figaro?'

'Si. Figaro my dog.' The old Spaniel rose from his siesta in a patch of sun at the open doorway, limping into the stables when he heard his name mentioned. 'The shavings keepa da fleas away, si.'

'Ah. Well that would make sense.' Stanley suddenly caught movement in the shadows. 'Oh god!' He jumped involuntarily.

'Eleanora!' Jacopo was startled also. His elderly wife had been standing silently in her red velvet dressing gown watching the men. 'Cosa fai?' Jacopo said automatically in Italian. 'What are you doing my love? You frighten our visitor.'

Eleonora stood expressionless, the world of dementia confusing her tired brain further, and Stanley noticed she was holding an old Zippo cigarette lighter, thumbing its flint wheel until the fuel-soaked wick ignited. She stared into the flame, hypnotised by its dancing performance fuelled by a draft in the workshop. Jacopo relieved her of the lighter, took her by the elbow and she was led obediently back to the house.

'I'm so sorry my friend,' Stanley said when Jacopo returned. 'It must be exhausting for you?'

Stanley now remembered Jacopo telling him of his sick wife earlier.

'Si. Each day she more bad, bit by bit, more bad.'

With the chest of drawers ready to be delivered, Jacopo explained the set of cedar backed dining chairs lined against the wall were next on the list. Stanley eyed the chairs – they were in sad disrepair, their horsehair stuffing spiralling loose through tears in the tapestry covers like they were about to spill the beans on risqué dinner parties of decades past.

'But you only have five chairs Jacopo,' Stanley observed.

'Si, I must make a sixth. One is missing.'

The early Victorian chairs, Stanley knew, would be worth only a fraction of their value without the complete set of six. 'And you are confident you can build a reproduction to match these five, precisely?'

'Si, si my friend,' Jacopo face flushed with pride. 'Thees ees what I do best.'

'It won't look out of place?'

'No. Jacopo is master craftsman. What I make, no man can tell. No expert even.'

And that was music to the curator's ears, and the beginning of a lasting friendship.

CHAPTER TWO

That evening in Sandy Bay just before the Aussie television show *Blue Heelers* finished, Max the fisherman's wife, Verity – *the bitch* – replaced the phone in its cradle. She missed the end of her favourite show. But something worse was afoot. She twisted her face in disgust, anger and in a sickening way, a kind of relief. Pammie, her best friend since leaving her elite private school, Fahan back in '84, couldn't wait to call Verity and spill the latest goss on her estranged husband Max.

'Maxie's been fucking a prostitute!'

'What?'

'Yes darling. That husband of yours has been paying for sex.'

Verity was aghast. Pammie explained how Mark Chester, one of Maxie's fishing mates, had told Garry Phillips who then told Pammie's husband that Max had fallen for a younger woman. And when the boys dug further, over several beers at the Royal Yacht Club, Maxie let it slip that they met over the phone, before confessing she was a prostitute.

'Disgusting!' Verity listened, horrified. Angry, and in the knowledge their marriage was over, Verity told Pammie for the first time how in the past year, before the marriage collapsed, Max had become more demanding in the bedroom, especially after drinking. And when they did make love ... *no not make love, had sex* ... he became increasingly rough with her, forceful and deviant. Excessive alcohol was aggravating his sexual appetite; he became insatiable and behaved like an animal – so Verity claimed – but the straw to break the camel's back came three months earlier when he put his hand around her throat trying to throttle her as he climaxed, This, of course, was also only Verity's story.

'Nooo!' Pammie was bursting to share this juicy titbit to her clique of dim-witted followers. She had never liked Max, ever since the wedding six years earlier. But if one was to dig deeper, this stemmed from Max's rejection of Pammie's earlier advances. More than once Pammie had said to her friend Verity, 'It's so lucky you didn't have children.'

Little did she know that Max actually wanted kids. Verity couldn't, adding to the anguish in the relationship (She had never told Max until it was too late). Max told his mates, 'Verity is Jill Frost in the sack. It's like she's gone off me.'

'You need to talk about it. Face to face,' came the advice. But Max had affairs instead. And now Verity wanted revenge. Oh, dear god, did she want revenge. She had already had a fling a few months back, but Max didn't know about that, she hoped. It had been with their insurance broker, Teddy Wilder. *He was wilder alright,* Verity felt a warm shiver from the memory course through her body, starting below and terminating in a flush. Wilder than Max *the strangler,* but with finesse. Now ... now that Verity knew what the bastard was up to, she had no intention of holding back. Hell, she was only in her thirties, she was in good shape and maintained a pretty face, when she wasn't so goddamned bitter. *And now that the marriage was turning to shit, and Max was fucking a whore* .... Verity wanted the lot and made this clear. The house was worth \$300,000, the shack \$180,000, *Infinity* \$280,000. They had investments of \$670,000, and Max was worth more dead than alive. He had taken out an insurance policy for one million dollars. One million!

But Verity knew Max too well. He was going nowhere without a fight. *It would be a godsend if the bastard had a fatal accident.*

Now there's a thought.

***

In the past ...

Museum Curator Stanley Smart's home in Harrington Street had been a morgue, or an undertaker's residence really. Either way it serviced the dead. That's why Stanley purchased the title for ten thousand less than its true market value of sixty-thousand-dollars back in '79. But Stanley fell in love with the four-bedroom double-storey Georgian home the moment he stepped into the hallway. And central! It was almost in Hobart's CBD. The only negative was the nightclub in the laneway behind. It could be noisy some nights out in the street. But Stanley, true to his voyeuristic nature, on occasion took advantage of the situation. Standing alone in the dark, masked by the night and hidden behind curtains, Stanley would observe amorous couples canoodling in the dark corners of the side street. And every so often his patience paid off when drunken fornicators, throwing caution to the wind, gave the old man a thrill.

***

Tonight was a weeknight, and a balmy summer night at that. The nightclub was closed. Stanley sat in front of the telly watching the news, a tray on his knee, soaking up the remains of his runny poached egg yolk with toast. It was an old favourite with the bachelor; poached eggs on toast, heavily buttered toast cut into strips. '*Soldiers*' his old mum used to call them. He'd finished off the third glass of red wine from its cardboard coffin and was deciding whether to pour another when the doorbell shrieked.

'Jacopo!' Stanley greeted his friend at the door. 'Well, this is a surprise.' Stanley stood in the doorway in singlet, boxer-shorts and socks. He grinned. 'Warm night.'

'Si, si … all day, so hot,' Jacopo said. 'I justa deliver a writing bureau to a customer in Davey Street si, and thought, Jacopo, you should visit your friend Stan.'

The skinny Italian stood on the front step holding a bottle of wine. No label. Stanley recognised this as local Italian home brew that wasn't as palatable as the cask wine he was used to, but it had the desired effect.

'Come in.' Jacopo entered. 'Who's with Eleonora?' Stanley asked, knowing how difficult it was for Jacopo to leave the house.

'Mrs Benetti, she neighbour, she come sit with Eleonora when I ask.'

'You're fortunate to have a neighbour like that.'

'Si. Eleonora and Mrs Benetti old friends, si. Soon, Eleonora, she go to nursing home.'

'Oh.' Stanley stood in thoughtful silence a moment regarding the situation. Clearly his friend needed cheering. 'Then it's for the best my friend. Come, I was just having a glass of wine after dinner.' Then as an afterthought he added, 'You hungry?'

'I eat pasta already.'

Jacopo was no stranger to Stanley's home, but each visit was as fascinating as the others. Stanley was a hoarder, there was no other way to label him. He lived alone with an eclectic collection of antiques, accumulated over decades. Some of dubious provenance. Antique magazines piled to the ceiling in the front passage, teetering next to pillars of Millers Antique Guides and other reference books from antique jewellery to collecting Japanese ceramics. And Jacopo knew his friend had read them all; his knowledge of history and the arts was so vast.

Stanley lead his friend to the living room through a narrow path well-trodden, between cabinets of antique tin toys, bookshelves crammed to the ceiling, a Georgian dresser out of place in the hallway stacked with china, porcelain, pewter and plated silverware and crate after crate of collectables stacked against each wall. But Jacopo loved antiques also and the *odeur de histoire* that accompanied the chaos was, to the Italian, as pleasant as the bouquet of his awful wine. Stanley caught Jacopo sniffing the air. 'Sometheen, she burns?' the Italian asked.

'Burn!'

The suggestion of a fire loose in Stanley's home was as terrifying as a doctor's diagnosis for cancer. Suddenly the curator laughed. 'Toast! I burnt toast earlier.'

Stanley propped open the living room door with a brass artillery shell case, a soldier's souvenir brought back from the battlefields of the Great War seventy-eight years earlier.

'It's so darned hot.'

They both agreed. Jacopo knew better than to suggest opening a window as he knew they were all kept firmly locked. Besides they were seized up with decades of hardened paint.

'I think I prefer the cold.' Jacopo agreed, looking for a spare glass. He negotiated the clutter and squeezed through to the kitchen where he had a quiet chuckle to himself. Even the stove top was littered with utensils, pans and pots. It was a wonder his friend could even poach an egg. Jacopo fetched a Vegemite jar from the bench, wiping the inside with his shirt tail before returning to the television room. Jacopo filled their glasses while Stanley cleared his friend an armchair.

'Salute.'

Both men drank.

Stanley screwed up his face and slapped his leg with a spontaneous *yeeha*!

Jacopo looked affronted. 'You no like wine?'

'It's an acquired taste Jacky, I've got to say.'

The Italian took a second mouthful and made a show of smacking his lips. 'It ees better vino than vino in box,' he said defiantly.

'You reckon?'

Twenty minutes later Stanley stood and stretched his legs; he had been sitting far too long and his muscles agreed. 'Come. I've got something to show you.' Jacopo stood also. 'And bring that moonshine with you Jacky, we may as well finish it.'

***

That same evening a few kilometres away …

Seventy-year-old magistrate Christian Yardley Winterbourne prepared for a new day. Christian was happy with his lot. He still managed a full head of hair; a soft ash-coloured mop, unruly in a stiff breeze. Body wise he was portly, not overly tall at five ten. Clothes weren't an issue and he drove a 1978 Mercedes-Benz S Class, thistle green, brown leather interior. He would rather spend his money on fine antiques rather than say, a Hugo Boss pinstripe suit. Winterbourne was also a creature of habit, lunching alone with a book or magazine at his favourite steakhouse, *The Ribeye Grill*, at Salamanca Place, at least twice a week; more often when he was sitting at the nearby courts. Christian was a common figure amongst the antique shops of Battery Point – Hobart's historic village and popular tourist attraction. Although Christian appreciated a handsome Georgian period portrait or a Victorian seascape, he didn't like collecting paintings because he didn't know much about art works.

Investment. Yes, it had to be a shrewd investment. This fact alone made it all the more surprising to his few friends – more work colleagues really – when he boasted of buying a William Dobell portrait, oil on cardboard, titled Lady with flowers, and a signed Tom Roberts oil, titled The Miners, along with six other works of art, including an unsigned sketch of Sir Robert Menzies by William Dobell.

***

Back at Harrington Street …

The museum curator and the antique restorer climbed the stairs to the first floor of Stanley's home, their old bones creaking along with the wooden treads. Jacopo noticed even the stairway acted as a repository for Stanley's collection and he never tired of the novelty. From the top of the landing the full length of the corridor separating the four bedrooms reminded the Italian of a second-hand shop. The passageway was a confusion of curios nestled on columns of books piled to the architraves. Mangy taxidermy specimens in glass cases from 19th century Africa guarded shelves of pottery and glass. Off the passage the spare bedrooms were each an Aladdin's cave filled with antiques. The main bedroom was a repository for Stanley's surplus books. Stanley led Jacopo around cardboard boxes coded with scribbles only he could decipher, leant down on his knees awkwardly and pulled an old blanket wrapped parcel from beneath his bed.

'Here.' He placed it carefully on the bed. 'See what you think of this.'

Jacopo folded back the woollen blanket and sucked in a short breath. He knew his colonial artists well and recognised Benjamin Duterrau's work immediately. The Anglo-French, London born artist's work was distinctive, rare and highly sought after by collectors. Jacopo knew Duterrau had painted a series of Van Diemen's Land natives in the mid-1830s and his most famous work hung in the Colonial Galleries in the Tasmanian Museum – *The Conciliation*, a large oil of George Augustus Robinson meeting with Tasmanian aborigines in an attempt to negotiate with the natives during the dark period in Tasmanian history, namely the Black Wars.

'I don't know what to say,' Jacopo said in a respectful whisper. The oil painting of a native man wearing a shell necklace and kangaroo skins and holding a spear was titled in the artist's hand, *Wild man of Van Diemen's Land. Woureddy.* Jacopo gazed at the painting with reverence. The Italian so desperately wanted to ask how his friend came by such a gem but as Stanley often jested, '*if I told you I would have to kill you.*'

'That painting disappeared from a private collection in Sydney twenty-five years ago,' Stanley offered unexpectedly.

'Si?'

'But the thief's name I do not know.'

'Oh.'

'He wanted that painting for a bargaining chip for another dodgy enterprise. A much larger enterprise that fell through.'

'Who? This thief?'

'Yes. In the meantime, he had asked my contact to have the painting meticulously copied, which he did.'

Jacopo looked despondent a moment.

'This, I might add, was before I knew you, Jacky. Then after a year or two he put the copy on the market with false provenance papers. He took it to

Shadlocks see.' Jacopo knew of Shadlocks, the fine art auctioneers in Melbourne.

'But thees painting, it not sell as a Duterrau,' Jacopo wondered aloud. 'I mean it couldn't?'

'No, it was handled as a very good contemporary Duterrau copy.'

'Ah ... 19th century copy, si?'

'Yes my friend. Done by a 19th century student copying Duterrau's work. But someone vigilant in the police art squad recognised the painting as stolen years earlier from the collector in Sydney and confiscated the painting from Shadlocks. It subsequently was returned to the wealthy collector in Sydney.'

'You mean the copy?'

'Yes, the copy. The collector was none the wiser and now presumed he had bought a copy in the first place, that he himself had been conned years earlier. So now the original was hotter than ever.'

Jacopo looked at the painting and shook his head.

'The thief,' Stanley continued, 'a man I don't know by the way, asked my contact, a man I only know as Ryan, to take the original and hide it for a while, as the police were keeping an eye on him knowing he was the one who tried to sell it.'

'Why they no arrest him?'

'They didn't have enough evidence that he stole it. He said he originally purchased the painting at a church fete, thinking it was a copy. Told them he paid a hundred dollars for it.' Jacopo sipped his wine, his eyes fixed on the portrait. 'However, the police kept him under surveillance. So, my contact, Ryan, had the painting, when blow me down if the original thief doesn't drop dead of a heart attack a year later.'

Jacopo coughed a laugh. 'How ... how you say... convenient?'

'Yes convenient, but the story gets even more interesting.'

'Oh.'

'You see my contact ...'

'Ryan?'

'Yes. Ryan, suspecting that the police were now onto him also, brought the painting to me. He and I are the only two who realise it is the actual original masterpiece. Now Ryan knows of my passion for Tasmanian history and, dare I say, my clandestine collecting habits, asked me to look after the painting, hide it for a few years until things cooled off.'

'Mamma mia, you take a big risk my friend.'

'Yes I know, but look at it Jacopo, what a magnificent painting. I couldn't sit back and see it damaged, or worse, destroyed.' Stanley took a fortifying sip of wine and grimaced. 'Well,' he went on, 'suspecting his time was up for a while in Australia, Ryan went back to his confidence trickster ways. Originally from London, and on dual passports, British and Australian, Ryan made several trips to Cairo from London where he purchased top quality Egyptian antiquities from his black-market contacts. At an undisclosed workshop in the suburbs of Cairo, Ryan, who was also a master restorer of all artwork, dipped the original antiquities – like carved alabaster and bronze statues – in a clear plastic resin, and then covered them with a cheap gold and black paint to look like gaudy tourist souvenirs.'

'Reproductions?'

'Yes, you know those awful souvenirs you can buy.'

'Si, si. Same in Italy. Plastic statues of Michelangelo's David or goddess Diana.'

'Exactly. But these were tourist copies of antiquities found in the tombs. The Customs officers wouldn't look twice at the *cheap* kitsch. He made several successful trips I was told, selling to dealers in London with false provenance papers saying the pieces came from a long dead great uncle's collection – the William Walton collection I think he called it. He would spin a story of how this uncle travelled the Mediterranean back in the 1930s.'

Jacopo smiled at the deceit. 'Thees man ... thees uncles, he not real, si?'

'Of course not, he never existed. Ryan even forged labels to be stuck or tied with old string onto the antiquities. And he soaked the labels in cold tea to stain them with *age* and forged the details with quill and ink.'

'So what happen to thees Ryan? Was he caught?'

'Yes. He got greedy. He was caught by the Egyptian authorities and sentenced to fifteen years with hard labour.'

'Fifteen years in Egypt prison,' Jacopo tutted at the thought.

'I heard from a contact in London he got out of gaol six years ago, but he has disappeared. So he's now out of the picture. Pun intended.'

'Pun?'

'Never mind.'

'So it's ...ah ... hot as you said.'

'Yes well. I've had it for years Jacky. I'm positive it's a genuine Duterrau and that the private collector in Sydney thinks he had a purchased a copy originally, that he had been conned. By another artist maybe. I'm certain this one is an unrecorded Duterrau that has slipped through the radar, so to speak. Trouble is I can't display it or sell it. It just sits under my bed and I take it out once in a while to admire it.'

'Why you no re-invent painting?' Jacopo's kindly old Italian face turned crafty.

'Have you been reading my thoughts?'

'You thinking same as Jacopo?'

'If you are suggesting the painting suddenly turns up in a house auction, at an old deceased estate for instance, then yes, we are on the same page.'

'I am thinking great Italiano thinking meet great Australia thinking,' Jacopo grinned.

'Yes. We will re-invent her ...'

'We?'

'Yes. You and me. You touch up the painting with water-based paints to cheapen it. Paints that can be removed carefully later. You put the painting into a house and contents auction.'

'Me?'

'Yes Jacky, I can't be seen selling things at auction. It's too risky, you know that. I work at the museum for god's sake. No. You consign it with half a dozen other bits of rubbish, old damaged lithographs, other framed garbage, as a boxed lot. Auctioneers are always happy to take extra items to toss in with house lots. It's all income to them.'

'Then what we do?'

'Not we Jacky, you. You attend the auction. Buy the lot for whatever it takes, shouldn't be much, and make certain you get a receipt for the sale. Then we have our legal provenance.'

'And then?'

'We will send it to Shadlocks in Melbourne for their next fine art auction.'

'What ees my cut?'

'Because we are mates, twenty per cent.'

'Fifty.'

'Jacky, Jacky. I'm the one who has kept this picture safe and sound all these years, taken the risks, kept it hidden ...'

'Forty!'

'Twenty-five.'

'Thirty per cent. Not a lira less you old … what you say, furfante … ah … scoundrel.'

'Thirty per cent it is then. What's ten per cent between old mates, eh?'

The two chinked glasses and Stanley rewrapped the painting in its blanket, slipped it into a garbage bag and gave it to Jacopo.

***

Ten days earlier …

Magistrate Christian Yardley Winterbourne met Mr Alfred Kenning. The shrewd … no, shrewd is not the word … the *wily* magistrate, was enjoying his usual fare at The Ribeye Grill – filet mignon medium rare with béarnaise sauce and baked potato with sour cream and chives and a glass of Argentinian Malbec – when he was approached by a tall dark and handsome stranger. A man dressed in a style that one would say, *he was flush*, or successful at least. He was, maybe, half a decade younger than Christian, spoke like a true gentleman and radiated a most amicable personality.

'Afternoon,' the man said. 'Would you mind if I join you?'

Winterbourne looked about the busy restaurant. It was nearly a full house, nearly, but the magistrate was feeling generous and in good spirits so welcomed the stranger.

'Alfred Kenning,' the stranger introduced himself.

The magistrate remained seated but shook the man's hand warmly, 'Christian Winterbourne.'

'Nice to meet you. I hope you don't mind me asking to join you, but I've been here before and noticed you seem to be a regular and always dine alone.'

'You're observant Mr Kenning.'

'Alfred, please.'

'Alfred. I can't say I have noticed you; then again I'm usually wrapped up in a book or magazine.' Almost as if to prove a point Christian nodded to his magazine sitting open across the table. The *Antiques Monthly*. He closed the periodical to make space.

'You're interested in antiques I notice,' Alfred said.

'Yes. Are you?'

'I'm a painting man myself. Collect Australian artists.'

'Interesting.'

Winterbourne took an instant liking to this fellow collector, whom he learnt was an accountant. They seemed to have much in common, although Alfred Kenning had lost his wife to cancer and Christian himself, had left his wife after forty years of marriage. Not for another woman mind, Christian Winterbourne's mistress was his antique collection. He simply woke up one morning after years of unhappiness and said to his wife, '*You know what, I don't love you anymore, I'm moving out.*' And he had the finances to do so, whilst leaving his sixty-seven-year-old wife (he had left her three years earlier) with the family home and an income from his other business interests. One of the most successful being shares in an oyster farm on Bruny Island.

The two men talked for hours over steaks and a shared a cheese platter with port, something Winterbourne never did. They discussed their chosen occupations, although Christian thought he had had a far more interesting life as a magistrate. They discussed cricket, football – discovering they both barracked for Geelong – and of course compared notes about antique collecting versus the accumulation of paintings. They discovered they were both in the army. Winterbourne had reached the rank of lieutenant colonel, although he never saw service overseas and Alfred ranking as sergeant major after serving time in Vietnam. The magistrate enjoyed Alfred's company so much they agreed to meet the following week, Wednesday, 1PM, for another lunch together.

***

After a second long lunch Winterbourne invited Alfred Kenning to his home in Mona Street Battery Point; a delightful double-storey, red-brick home built in the 1890s and on its original title with established fruit trees at the back. At five bedrooms it was somewhat large – more a mansion really – for the single older man but the magistrate was a self-confessed magpie when it came to collecting. Clearly, he had a passion, with each room themed, as in Georgian antiques, Victorian, maritime and so on. It was also pleasantly obvious to Alfred Kenning that his new friend was quite well heeled.

Armed with crystal tumblers of Glenmorangie 18-year-old single malt poured from a Georgian cut glass decanter, Christian gave his guest a tour of the house and his collections. Alfred noted that, although the rooms were well displayed with fine antiques, the walls of some rooms were rather sparse, and as the tour wound up in the maritime room, Kenning noted few paintings. The collections, however, were well worth the visit.

'That ship,' Alfred said of a model ship made of whale bone on the mantelpiece. 'Scrimshaw isn't it?'

'Yes. Lovely don't you think?'

'Superb. Rare as hen's teeth I should imagine.'

'Yes, I acquired it about a year ago from a fisherman.'

'Family heirloom?'

'I don't know. He didn't say and I didn't ask. But it needs some repair work done. I've yet to ask a restorer I know to have a look at it.'

'Repair work?' Kenning examined the model a little more closely. 'Oh yes, the mainsail yard's broken and the rigging's fallen off.'

'Plus, there's some damage to the hull planking on the starboard side.'

The accountant pointed with his tumbler of scotch to the mantel where the model ship looked rather lonely with an empty chimney behind it.

'You need some artwork Christian,' he said casually. 'A seascape for example on the wall behind the ship.'

Winterbourne agreed, but confessed he knew little, if anything about paintings. This was music to Alfred Kenning's ears. Kenning's observations of the magistrate were about to come to fruition.

***

Fuelled with his third tumbler of Glenmorangie scotch, Alfred Kenning leant forward in his early Victorian upholstered gentleman's chair and fixed the magistrate with the eye of a sharp businessman. 'Look Christian, I have an acquaintance who collects art but recently got himself in a fix.'

'A fix?'

'Horses. He has a gambling problem. And, well, truth be known he needs a cash and fast. He owes the bookies you see.'

'Oh.'

'Yes. Now I happen to know he has a Dobell to sell, it's titled *Lady with flowers*, he also has a Picasso.'

'Picasso?'

'Yes my friend. It's quite large and colourful and would not look out of place in your main living room.'

'Oh, I don't know,' Winterbourne was more uncertain than naïve. He was certainly trusting, as he had no reason to distrust Alfred. *The man had been in the army for Christ's sake.* They were brothers in arms.

'Look,' the accountant persisted. 'I have a friend who is an interior decorator; she's helped many of my friends. I'll get her to bring the paintings over and you decide if you like any of them. No stress. No pressure. But I'm telling you now, my collector friend is desperate for money and you will get a bargain.'

'No obligation?'

'No obligation.'

***

Directly after this conversation, Christian phoned Alfred Kenning a City Cab and while the two men waited in the front garden – the evening was balmy – the two men chatted. The magistrate was feeling good about himself. If he was shrewd, he could possibly make money out of this new area in collecting, whilst at the same time adorning his mansion walls with a few pleasant eye pleasing artworks. He would just have to wait and see.

The cab arrived. The men bid each other farewell and Christian stepped back onto the veranda as a 1980 Ford one-tonner flat tray pick-up scraped its diff on his driveway with an awkward crunch. Christian smiled. His day was getting even more interesting. The antique restorer Moneta … Moretti … whatever his name was, was finally delivering his restored Huon pine chest of drawers. Christian looked at his watch. Good god, it's 6.30PM already.

Jacopo sat low behind the wheel looking quite comical to the magistrate; the Italian's little round yet happy face grinning back through the windscreen.

'Mr Mon … Moneta,' Christian greeted.

'Moretti,' Jacopo corrected in his rich Campania accent. 'Signor Winterbourne. My name … ees Jacopo Moretti.'

'Ah yes … Moretti. My Huon pine chest is finished at last eh?'

'Si.' Jacopo smelt the brandy on the man's breath before he climbed from the car. 'Thees is Rory,' Jacopo introduced his male passenger. 'Rory Benetti.'

Had Christian been a little more observant he would have noticed twenty-eight-year-old Rory was special, slightly mentally handicapped.

'Rory ees my neighbour's boy. He help old Jacopo on deliveries sometime.' Jacopo had spoken of his neighbour's *boy* before. He told Christian the lad was a bit slow, *lento, mentale,* were the words Jacopo actually used as he tapped himself on the head.

Christian studied the younger man a moment, fancying himself as a good judge of character, after all he should be in his profession. The man with the baby face and slim body was in his twenties, clean shaven, with a small mouth, and longish unkempt hair brushed back and over his ears. He seemed reticent, although Christian sensed he was smarter than he let on. Dress wise, Rory was influenced by the punk movement; leather coat over black t-shirt, torn black jeans, chrome chain around his neck with a small padlock pendant. Rory's passion was punk rock, and amongst his prized possessions was his collection of 80's tapes for bands like *Jawbreaker, Rancid* and *Green.*

Christian was certain he noted signs of makeup, especially around Rory's eyes. But he was loath to stare.

'Say ciao to Mr Winterbourne,' Jacopo told Rory.

'Ciao.'

Christian nodded a grunt.

Rory bounced from the one-seater cabin full of verve and energy. Jacopo had told Rory earlier that this man was a magistrate and the title seemed to unnerve the simpleton. 'Had he been in trouble with the law?' Christian pondered. *If one was to judge him by his dress one would wonder.*

Christian's observations shifted to the blanket covering his restored chest strapped to the rear of the Ford flat tray.

'Well come on then,' he tried to disguise a slur in his words. 'Don't keep me waiting.'

Jacopo put the magistrate's rudeness down to enthusiasm. Rory leapt onto the flat tray with the agility of a monkey, loosened the ties and slipped the blanket free.

'Oh … oh yes … lovely,' Christian ran a hand down one side of the chest. 'Lovely, lovely. You've done well Mr Moneta.'

'Grazie,' Jacopo ignored the name discrepancy.

Christian inspected the piece of furniture in detail, admiring the bird's eye knots of the Huon pine, caressing the carved pilasters flanking its sides. He had bought the chest through an advertisement in the local paper for a fraction of its value. Sure, he had to pay this little Italian for restoration, but his patience was finally rewarded. *Yes, Christian Winterbourne*, he congratulated himself, *you've done it again.*

'Well don't stand there man,' Christian snapped from his reverie at Rory. 'Get it inside.'

Whilst he and Jacopo were of similar age, Christian was happy to lead the way, brandy balloon in hand, and watch the old cabinetmaker struggle to keep up with Rory as the two delivered the piece of furniture up the stairs and into the master bedroom.

'Not there,' Winterbourne muttered when the two took a breather. 'Between the windows.' And he pointed with his glass to the far wall facing Mona Street. 'Lovely. Yes, you've done a lovely job. Excellent.'

'I gave it one last oil two days ago,' Jacopo said. 'The wood, she now last another hundred years.'

'Excellent.'

Jacopo took a handwritten statement from his pocket. He removed his reading glasses and wiped the sawdust clean with his handkerchief to check it was the right paperwork.

'Here Signor Winterbourne. The bill, si. Eet take longer I think, but I tell you one hundred and ten dollar, so I ask no more.'

Christian stood staring at the chest of drawers a moment before leading his visitors back down the stairs. Jacopo's observant eyes darting every which way, inspecting the old mansion, the collection. Clearly, he was a wealthy man. 'Your home, eet is bellissimo Signor Winterbourne.'

'Yes, it is.'

'You could use some nice paintings I am thinking.'

Christian didn't suffer criticism lightly, or was the man just being politely honest. 'Yes, well. I'm working on it.'

Rory whispered something in Jacopo's ear. Jacopo pulled a face.

'What's he saying?' Christian asked.

'Ah …' Jacopo looked awkwardly at Rory before asking. 'I am sorry signor … ah … Rory, he ask if he can use your … gabinetto … ah lavatory.'

'Hmm,' Christian harrumphed. *If he were honest, he would prefer the man piss out in the garden.* 'End of the hall,' he said, not happy with the request. 'Turn left before the kitchen.'

Christian looked at the statement once more. 'Right then,' he said, watching Rory a moment wandering off down the passage. 'Wait here will you,' he ordered Jacopo. Jacopo watched the magistrate stagger slightly entering his office off the passageway. From where Jacopo stood – the office door ajar – Jacopo could see the magistrate's shadow clearly where the desk lamp threw out a warm light. Christian removed something from his top drawer. A key. The shadow shifted to the wall behind the desk, a family portrait was swung aside on a hinge and an old fashioned key safe revealed. Moments later the magistrate returned, handing Jacopo the cash. 'You can be assured Mr Moonachie I am very pleased with your work.'

'Grazie. Anytime Mr Winterbourne.'

Christian was showing the men to the front door when he remembered. 'Oh, I nearly forgot. Take a look at this will you.'

He led the restorer into the wood-panelled dining-room with its 18th century tapestry, Persian carpet and Georgian extension table complete with sterling silver, four-pronged candelabras and a set of eight Regency chairs. Jacopo was impressed. 'Bellissima.' Jacopo ran a hand along the tall back of the closest chair. At each end of the table were earlier Jacobean carvers, heavy solid oak.

'Bellissima,' Jacopo repeated.

'Aren't they?' Christian agreed. 'But this one has a broken back.' Christian nodded to one of the carvers. 'A guest leant back in it, idiot. Can you fix it?'

Jacopo inspected the back in the chair. 'Eet need new piece to replace broken cresting rail,' the Italian instructed with a professional hand. 'And thees,' he alluded to the base of the back, 'thees need a rebuilt shoe.'

'Can you repair it or not?'

'Si, si.'

'Good, then take it with you.'

'I busy Mr Winterbourne, but maybe two week I finish.'

'Fine.'

The chair was heavier than the sixty-year-old restorer expected, and Jacopo was glad he had Rory to help secure the chair onto the back of the pickup. Task done, they were about to leave when Christian summoned the

Italian back into the house. 'I've something else I would like you to look at while you're here.'

'Certainly,' Jacopo checked that Rory was busy before following the magistrate back down the passageway to the maritime themed room.

'That ship Jacopo,' Christian stood before the whalebone model ship, carved by a 19th century sailor and taken as a bribe (*no, no, payment Christian reminded himself. Bribe was such a dirty word.*) from the fisherman Max Shreeve whom he had kept from a gaol sentence. 'That ship, it needs repairs. Is that one of your capabilities? I mean, have you done that kind of thing before?'

Jacopo inspected the damage to the rigging and hull. *Easy money* he thought. 'Si, si. Jacopo fix … easy, nessa problema.'

'I rather love looking at her on the mantelpiece, she is rather grand, what?'

'Si.'

'But she does need a little work.'

'Then I take now signor, Rory can nurse ship in car for safe journey. I fix and have back for you in few days, before I fix chair, si.'

'Excellent.'

***

Days later …

Christian had another visitor. Forty-two-year-old Susan Kirby, Alfred Kenning's *art dealer* acquaintance, had been an art teacher at Sydney College and now worked with people who hired her for professional art assessment, people like Kenning. She was also a delight to the eye in her short black skirt and gold jewellery; keeping her figure trim at the gym. But seventy-year-old Christian had to contend with her aesthetics alone. Not that she wasn't a flirt. She held the magistrate's eye and said, 'Fifty thousand for the Picasso.'

Is this a joke? Christian flinched.

Christian studied the cross-eyed portrait that looked more simian than human *and* with three eyes not two. 'To be honest I don't even like Picasso,' he said.

'Fair enough,' the art dealer didn't flinch. She skipped paintings like she was choosing a chocolate from a box of Cadbury's Roses. 'The Dobell, do you like that?'

'Yes, I do. But I wouldn't know if that was a genuine Dobell.'

'That's no problem, you can have them appraised before you purchase, naturally.'

'Yes, yes … of course.' Christian wasn't that gullible, and he wanted her to know it. But what really caught the man's eye was the seascape. A maritime scene of Royal Navy ships of the line painted on canvas by Australian artist Haughton Forrest.

'You like that one,' Kirby said. 'I can see it in your eyes.' Kirby smelt success. 'I could imagine a big strong gentleman like yourself as ship captain. An Admiral maybe, out on the ocean mastering one of those great ships.'

Don't push your luck girl. But a little bullshit can go a long way.

Christian tried to be blasé. *Don't show too much interest.* But he wasn't the greatest actor to tread the boards. 'Yes …' he croaked. Cleared his throat, 'Yes, it's quite nice.'

'It's by Haughton Forrest. It's not too expensive either for a Forrest.'

'Oh, how much are we talking?'

'I know the owner would take five thousand for it.'

Immediately this seemed doable. 'Five thousand huh,' Christian cast an artful eye over the other canvasses carefully rolled in professional storage cylinders and placed deliberately, each beneath a vacant space on the various walls. 'So what else do we have?'

The art expert revealed a William Dobell portrait, oil on cardboard, titled Lady with flowers, and an unsigned sketch by Dobell of Sir Robert Menzies. Christian was instantly interested. Then came the signed Tom Roberts titled The Miners, an Arthur Stretton, two Frederick McCubbins and a Sydney Long, of whom Christian had not heard; however, the panoramic painting of a naked nymph playing a flute amongst a flock of cranes was most pleasing to the eye. It all seemed too good to be true and had Christian Winterbourne listened to his conscience, it probably was. But the thought of owning such beautiful artworks by such reputable artists overwhelmed him.

'The Dobells, the Roberts, the Stretton, the McCubbin and the Sydney Long I have no doubt are genuine,' Susan Kirby told Christian. 'No doubt in my mind whatsoever. But to be honest I'm only ninety-five-per cent certain about the Picasso.'

'Oh, and why is that?'

'I simply have not had enough experience with his work. I'm pretty certain, but I would not bet my life on it,' she continued. Kirby crossed her arms and eyeballed Christian with a seriousness difficult to ignore, almost as if she was assessing the magistrate. 'You are in an enviable position here, Mr Winterbourne, to be offered such delightful works by some of Australia's finest 19th and early 20th century artists. Very fortunate indeed.'

Christian stepped back to take in the collection, massaging his chin with rolled lips. *Decisions, decisions.*

However, he would not be rushed. He was a strong willed, shrewd, and considered himself a savvy investor. Admittedly he was more comfortable around fine antiques. From where he stood in the front hallway of his mansion, he cast an eye over the Georgian extension table in the dining room, complete with its Regency chairs, Jacobean carver and four-pronged sterling silver candelabra. He admired his colonial cedar hall table supporting a French bronze of a hunter and his quarry and the Georgian hall clock, a mahogany grandfather clock; value five thousand. But art? He certainly had the wall space and he had the cash to invest.

'I would like another appraisal,' he said calmly.

'Of course. Do you know anyone? Would you like me to recommend someone?'

Christian would be happier with a totally independent opinion and said, 'No, that's fine. I have contacts.'

'Who may I ask?'

If Christian was taken aback by this question, he didn't let on. But he had run a finger through the Yellow Pages of the phone book before Kirby arrived. 'Neville Goldman of Goldman Galleries.'

'Wise choice.'

'You know him?'

'Yes, I'm familiar with him.'

Each canvas was carefully rolled back into their respective plastic cylinders. Whether Christian didn't think to ask or the fact that he was so transfixed on the masterpieces, tht it did not occur to him to ask why none were framed.

'They have been in storage some years now,' Kirby answered the unasked question. 'Hence the cylinders. The collector has other financial commitments and has decided to sell some of his works.'

'Some?'

'Oh yes, there are others if you are interested.'

CHAPTER THREE

While all this was happening in Christian's busy and nefarious life, over in Melbourne (Toorak to be exact) Ivano Stipanov – *Burglar to the Rich* – took a brief moment to admire the view. Well, it was not so much a view, as an aesthetic expression of the wealth of this six-bedroom, five-bathroom 1930s mansion. From where he stood in the shadows of the first-floor balcony, he could barely see the mansions across the street for mature trees. This property was private. Very private, that was for certain. Off to his right he could just make out the family pool; exactly where he would like to be right now on this balmy warm summer's evening. From the porch he had a sweeping view of a manicured garden with a rose-lined pathway in full bloom. It led through classic pillars to a two-metre-high stonewall with a decorative iron front gate. Designer hedges grew parallel with the perimeter wall.

Offering privacy for the owners and cover for a cat burglar.

Ivano wiped pearls of sweat gathering beneath his balaclava with his gloved hand. *Damn it's hot under here,* he thought to himself. *Maybe I'll invest in a pair of dark stockings next time.* The sweat was black from the boot polish he smeared over his face an hour earlier, and he noticed it staining the white balcony rail.

Bugger them. The hired help can clean up after him.

Ivano had cased the home known as *Stoneville* earlier. He knew there was a private tennis court at the rear along with a glass conservatory and a four-car garage. He knew the Rowlandsons, importers of Italian leather and shoes, were away. He also knew that their alarm system was Harriet the housekeeper and Saunders the groundsmen. It was Saturday and these two – close friends not lovers – were creatures of habit who walked to nearby Chapel Street each

Saturday to Alfonso's, their favourite Italian restaurant. Ivano had an hour plus to do what he knew would only take twenty minutes.

Ivano padded across the veranda and punched his elbow through the glass panel to the master bedroom. The window shattered, but the neighbours were some distance away, too far to hear anything untoward. Besides, *Stoneville* was well hidden behind all the grandeur of its generous grounds. Ivano waited in silence a moment. He knew from experience that if, perchance, a neighbour did imagine they heard the sound of breaking glass, they always stopped to listen for a repeat. After a moment's silence they shrugged and went about their business like nothing happened. It was human nature. Satisfied all was clear, Ivano slipped his arm through the broken panel and unlocked the door. He stepped deftly into the bedroom. Although it was dim, there was sufficient light from the streetlights. *Good thing my mother made me eat my carrots so as I can see in the dark,* he smiled to himself. He moved to the bed and smiled again. *Another king size!* He had been in the bedrooms of many of Melbourne's socialites and celebrities the past several years. *They did like their king size beds.* But Ivano was a professional. For nine years he had continued as cat burglar to the rich and famous. Yes, he liked that title.

Cat burglar to the rich and famous.

It should be mentioned Ivano had legitimate employment as well, to allay any suspicions. When the work was offering, he was a stuntman in the movies; having worked on such films as Mad Max, Gallipoli and The Light Horseman. In the two sequels to Mad Max his likeness to Mel Gibson came to the attention of George Miller the director and for this reason he doubled for the star in many scenes.

Average height, film star good looks, dark and handsome.

But free-lance stunt work wasn't consistent. Burgling could be. Through filmmaking he befriended Molly Yves, a makeup artist and prosthetics master, and through her he could be whoever he wanted to be. Tonight, any witness to his illegal activity would swear an oath to the police they saw a Chinaman. A Ninja warrior maybe. Thirty-one-year-old Ivano was physically fit, with enormous upper body strength. He was in the prime of health; slim, average height, short cropped dark hair, sharp features and good looking. He had no fear of heights and regularly scaled the outside of ten or fifteen storey apartment blocks. For tall buildings he climbed barefoot, often stealing runners or slippers for an exit back down the fire stairs.

Ivano learnt at an early age the workings of modern architecture, how to move within the building. From garage to basement to rooftops to fire exits. He cut his teeth as a kid in an old suburb where several houses were unoccupied. Here he would sneak out at night *breaking and entering* and explore the layout of these empty houses, preparing himself for a future in crime. Tonight, however, the Rowlandsons' old-style wall safe was easy to find; behind a portrait over the bed.

Pathetic.

And for an experienced thief the key lock was easily picked. Ivano picked up the albums of rare stamps At a glance in the poor light he recognised a *ten-shilling kangaroo & map essay* stamp, value $10,000 thereabouts, a sixpenny Queen Victoria pair, 1902, value $3000 and several other Australian rarities. Good start. Ivano slipped the three albums into his backpack.

These people are unreal, he thought. *They haven't even locked their jewellery away.* Taking a gold pinchbeck bracelet with five amethysts, gold broach set with emeralds and a pair of silver and gold earrings set with diamonds, he moved to the chest of drawers. Here Ivano managed to locate $2150 in cash amongst men's socks and underwear and a 1940s Longines Lindbergh aviator's watch in a bedside table drawer. Highly collectable and street value a grand at least. In the lady's wardrobe he snatched a Faberge gold mesh evening bag, the clasp set with rubies; value several thousand dollars. It would be difficult to fence but the picking was too good to resist.

Downstairs he hurried through the dining room collection of Georgian silver, a rare 18th century Irish silver sauce boat was left behind. *Too specialist, too hard to fence.* But the six antique miniature portraits on the drawing room wall, all colonial and compact. Perfect. He had a ready buyer for those in a dodgy dealer in Geelong.

Alongside the tennis court, well into the shadows, Ivano looked at his watch. He had been eighteen minutes. He re-arranged his treasures in the backpack, wrapping some pieces in newspaper so as not to be damaged, or rattle for that matter. He checked on his mountain bike. The *black beast* he called it. His escape vehicle of choice. Resting between the hedge and the perimeter wall, the bike had been easy to hoist over the wall in the darkness of the side street, off Toorak Road.

***

Ivano was confident, unshakably so and the police were frustrated. They hadn't a clue what this persistent thief looked like as he was scarcely ever seen on the property of any homeowner. Besides, rare sightings conflicted; suggesting the burglar was a Ninja style warrior, in a black roller-neck sweater and black jeans or some even swore they saw Spider Man. *Spider Man for Christ sake!*

One woman who did come face to face with Ivano in her garden told the police it was an old man with a nimble body. Ivano laughed when he read the report in the Melbourne Age. This was the masterful work of his make-up artist friend Molly Yvres and her prosthetics. What the police did know was that the total of loot stolen to date was well into the millions. They suspected his *modus operandi* was working alone.

The police never found a fingerprint and try as they did to trace him through the underworld of stolen property buyers – 'fences' – he could never be identified. Ivano was smart enough to conduct his dealings in disguise. He was also smart enough to fence much of his loot by travelling interstate.

And here lay a clue, if only the police had stretched their enquiries a little further. Ivano Stipanov was the son of Filip Stipanov who, as tradition dictated in Yugoslavia, named his son Ivano after his own father. Born in Perth, Western Australia, Ivano was in trouble with the law from age eleven. Always on stealing charges. He celebrated his 21st birthday in Fremantle Prison, charged with felonious entry of a home in Nedlands, Perth. After eight months in prison, where Ivano was tutored by the best, he went underground. He had learnt the hard way and was determined never to be caught again. It was in Sydney that he acquired a passion for antiques, absorbing knowledge like a giant sponge. He found work with an antique restorer, a fellow Yugoslav, in Paddington, who took a shine to the young Ivano. He also learnt the art of deceit; modifying antique furniture, creating hybrid pieces from antique scrap and selling to gullible collectors; a Victorian refectory table for example, as 17th century. Now at thirty-one-years old he was a pro. In his prime. As good as they come.

***

It was time to leave. The backpack was moderately light, although Ivano estimated the value of the contents was up around the twenty-thousand-dollar mark. But something bothered him. He had missed the opportunity to search Henry Rowlandson's study at the rear of the house on the ground floor. He knew he had the best part of half an hour remaining and would only regret this oversight tomorrow.

Leaving the backpack Ivano stole around the tennis court making directly to the back door. As he didn't want to climb the terrace a second time, he broke a back-door window in a repeat of upstairs. Knowing the layout, he hurried down the hall and tried the study door. Locked. A set of lock picks soon sorted that. Ivano couldn't help but smile as he picked the old-fashioned door lock with only its three internal pins. He had been taught the art by a cop, of all people, a neighbour – way back when he was fifteen. The kindly neighbour, who took a shine to the innocent kid up the road, had no idea what he had inspired in his student, who practised tirelessly until he mastered six pin locks by the age of sixteen. He even taught Ivano how to make his own picks from ordinary objects like the underwires from bras or discarded windscreen wipers. *But the best material of all,* the cop told Ivano, *is the bristles from the brushes of a street-cleaning truck. They occasionally fall off and are perfect.* Ivano took this advice seriously and would follow the street cleaners, sometimes for hours, watching for the odd bristle knocked loose by the gutter.

Ivano had learnt that the types of lock picks appeared endless. The most common being picks for pin-tumbler locks. Otherwise he carried a selection for the more popular locks. Picks like rake picks, snake picks, hook picks and ball picks. Some doubled as rakes, like the diamond rake; a pick with a flat half diamond shape at the end. Then there was the long reach hooks and slant hooks good for locks with a not too complicated a set of bittings in the tumbler. Bitting being the pattern of cuts on a key matching the internal components in a lock, for locking and unlocking. The suitable pick selected, pushes up the internal locking pins above the shear line and the lock can be turned. In other words, the lock has been picked.

The standard Yale lock of Rowlandson's office door clicked open.

Inside the spacious office the leather-topped oak desk was tidy and organised. The drawers proved uneventful. The top right was locked. Another set of picks tweaked the lock. The first item to catch his eye was a pistol.

You're kidding me? A pistol? This ain't America pal.

Doubting Rowlandson even had a licence for the Browning Hi-Power 9 millimetre, Ivano lifted the nickel plated beauty from the drawer. It felt great in his hand. It looked great and felt heavy. *I'll have that thank you very much.*

Ivano found a full box of bullets as well. He took the lot, pocketing the shells and stuffing the pistol into the back of his jeans, just like he'd seen done in the movies. Four hundred dollars in cash was better than nothing, but all in all the pickings in the study were lean. Ivano relocked the drawer and made to leave when he felt a creak underfoot.

Safe?

Sure enough a floor safe was hidden under a very average Persian carpet. The owner had expensive taste in many things, but carpet wasn't one of them. Ivano dropped to his knees, rolling the rug back to inspect it. The combination safe was neatly hidden beneath a hinged floorboard trapdoor. But it was firmly set in concrete. He would need his stethoscope, graph paper, pencil and several hours. None of which he had. Ivano made a mental note to return, maybe in a year's time …

ISuddenly the hallway filled with light. Hard shadows appeared in the study and Ivano heard a man's voice down the passageway. 'The study door's open!'

***

A few hours earlier back in Hobart …

Twenty-six-year old assistant conservator Stella Bathe had been ambitious since adolescence. Ambitious and astute. Most importantly she was an expert conservator, learning her trade working with Tasmanian Parks and Wildlife Service and the Queen Victoria Museum in Launceston in the early '90s, alongside conservationists excavating the underwater site of the *Sydney Cove*. The 250-ton *Sydney Cove* was a merchant ship lost off northern Tasmania in 1797, whilst sailing to Port Jackson from Calcutta. Stella had worked with archaeologists at the camp on Preservation Island, where hundreds of artefacts were brought to the surface packed in wet sand for transport to the Launceston museum. She was an integral part of the team, preserving artefacts the moment they were exposed to fresh air, as Stella learned dehydration affects the stabilisation of many retrieved relics.

Stella learnt how timber artefacts had to be soaked in polyethylene glycol before being freeze-died to extract all moisture. Organic material like leather had to be stabilised immediately. Glass and ceramics were soaked in fresh water to leach out the salts built up in the material over the two hundred years of being submerged. She was taught to X-ray concretions to identify their contents and soak larger metal objects like cannon and anchors in chemical solutions to remove the salts; which she knew took years.

Now at twenty-six Stella Bathe was an undisputed expert. So, it was only natural she resented being subordinate to Stanley Smart, whose work ethics definitely did not match hers.

It was also at this time in her life that Stella questioned her sexuality. There was no denying she was attracted to other women and had even experimented with Zoey Marshal, an older conservationist on loan from the Melbourne

University. They worked together on Preservation Island. It was lust not love, but Stella knew to which pathway in relationships destiny was directing her.

Stella had told Stanley, not of her sexual preferences, but of the position on offer at the Queen Victoria Museum in Launceston, to work on the new travelling exhibition the Federal Government was financing, marking the bicentennial of the loss of the *Sydney Cove*. 'And I've been offered the appointment,' she said.

'That's nice,' was all Stanley managed. Stella wondered, *Was he being condescending?* She had wanted to leave for some time now. Promotion seemed unlikely whilst Stanley Smart still ruled the roost in the museum's basement. But recently changes were afoot. Stanley Smart's colleague, Museum Director Mr Adam Sawyer, had retired, and the new Director, Charlotte Fysh, had started, just weeks earlier.

***

Back in Toorak that evening, in Melbourne

Burglar Ivano Stipanov froze as light from the hallway spilt into the study. He heard voices down the passage. 'The study door's open!' Immediately the voices lowered to a whisper. Ivano heard floorboards squeak. He ducked behind the door. A moment of silence …

A hand appeared around the corner feeling for the light witch. The study light flooded the room. Ivano caught an approaching shadow from the hall. The shadow of a large man wielding a poker.

Saunders the groundsman.

Ivano slammed the door closed on the man's hand. Saunders yelled in shock, dropping the poker. Ivano leapt from behind the door the moment Saunders bent to re-arm himself. Ivano saw his chance. He kneed the groundsman in the face. Saunders cried out as Ivano fled. In the hallway Harriet the housekeeper was already on the phone to the police. Ivano snatched the receiver jerking the cord from the wall and made his escape into the yard.

With backpack hitched and secure, Ivano threw the bike over the wall and mounted the two-metre barrier with the agility of an alley cat. On the nature strip he straddled the pushbike. Saunders leapt through the front gate. The man was angry, face bloodied, screaming and armed with the poker. He was also fast. Ivano pushed away on the bike but Saunders closed the distance with astonishing speed. He swung the hook-ended poker down hard as Ivano gained speed. But the poker slashed the pack and several contents fell free. Ivano didn't look back. He peddled hard and Saunders finally dropped back.

He was free. Just.

That was too close. What the hell happened? They were supposed to be dining in an Italian restaurant for Christ's sake.

From Grange Road Ivano took the bike track alongside the Yarra. Black Jeans, black skin-tight pullover, dark balaclava and black gloves on a black BMX against the dark of night, Ivano pedalled like he was competing with a world pro. At Alexandra Avenue he continued following the river, before cutting across King's Domain … when the first spotlight hit him.

'You on the BMX,' the cop called over the police PR. 'Pull over immediately.' The police car raced parallel. Ivano skipped off the park path onto the grass when he came to the Botanical Gardens enclosure. He was trapped. The cops parked and came after him on foot. They were closing fast. Ivano pedalled to the gates.

'Stay where you are,' one cop shouted. 'I repeat. Stay where you are.'

Ivano mounted the wall using flowerbeds on the outside for leverage. He tossed the bike into bushes on the other side and clambered easily over the wrought iron barrier. The two policemen threw themselves against the gates. They were stunned. What cheek … *And why?*

One radioed for assistance but Ivano couldn't help himself. He faced the cops briefly to taunt them. Said nothing. And pedalled away.

Exiting the gardens on the South Melbourne side, by the same method he had entered, Ivano kept to the back streets he knew so well. He had planned for such an occasion with great care, mulling over just such a scenario. Now it was real. He was pumped and bloody pleased with himself.

An hour later he pedalled calmly into St Kilda where he lived alone in a rented cottage in Neptune's Lane. Ivano ditched the black pullover to reveal a yellow T-shirt. He hid the balaclava and pedalled through the streets of Saint Kilda, careful to avoid the main roads. Although he had the option of a dynamo headlight on the bike, he opted to leave it switched off and dismounted four blocks away, pushing the bike home. Turning the corner from Robe Street into Neptune's Lane, Ivano froze. He recognised two police cars at the end of the lane and saw plain-clothes police on the footpath near his cottage.

Shit! After nine years. Why? How?

Ivano crept as close as he dared. The lane was narrow and dark but he heard voices carry in the quiet street. Neighbours were being interviewed by uniform police. Then he identified the shapely figure of his friend Molly Yves, the makeup artist. She was being ushered from his cottage and led to one of the police cars.

What's she doing here?

There was little Ivano could do. The game in Melbourne was up. He would have to execute his escape plan. Hiding the bike in a neighbour's front garden, Ivano watched and waited. It was now 2AM but still one surveillance car remained parked fifty metres away on the opposite side of the street, in the shadows. There was no choice but to abandon any attempt to return to his cottage to gather personal items. It was time for that one last job he had planned for the Victorian capital, and then it was Plan B.

***

Earlier in the same day at the Museum in Hobart

Director Charlotte Fysh pondered the struggling air condition unit rattling on her office wall and made a mental note to have maintenance look at it. She removed her coat, hooking it behind the door. It must be nearly thirty degrees outside already she thought. Charlotte felt overdressed in her navy-blue suit. She checked herself in the mirror. Although loose-fitting, the coat failed to disguise those extra middle-aged kilos. The skirt though, was more flattering, knee high in length showing off shapely legs.

Yer still got it kiddo! Okay, so you're a tiny bit overweight. But Charlotte loved her teased dark curls to the shoulder. She shared a cordial smile with her reflection, when she heard a tap on her door.

The director suddenly remembered she had an appointment with Stella Bathe, assistant conservationist, to discuss the new indigenous exhibit. And the thought thrilled her.

'Stella,' Charlotte tilted her head slightly, peering over her tortoise-shell spectacles. 'Come in, come in.'

Charlotte shuffled papers and photographs on her leather topped desk making room for Stella's folder.

Stella liked the new Museum Director the moment they first met a few weeks back. Ms Fysh was also attracted to Stella instantly. Stella liked the professional, enthusiastic feminist, a woman of strength of character and power, while forty-eight-year-old Ms Fysh liked the intelligent conservator, a pretty young woman she felt she would like to know better. Resolute that relationships should not take place at work, Charlotte knew she would be breaking one of her own rules. Yet she was attracted to this young woman immediately and made little attempt to disguise the fact.

Stella closed the office door behind her, and the two women stood before each other a moment. 'Director,' Stella finally greeted her superior with a subtle hint of insubordination, her voice a husky purr as she placed her folder on the desk.

'Enough of the Director, okay. I'm Charlotte.'

One of Charlotte's traits was the ability to extract the most from staff with the personal approach, whilst maintaining her professionalism. Although the new director had been settled in for weeks now, Stella had only experienced three brief one-on-one conversations with Charlotte, occasionally in passing, in the corridors. But with Mrs Wilson the head conservator away on holidays, this would change.

Stella re-addressed her boss. 'Alright then … Charlotte,' Stella smiled. Almost a cheeky smile. The room was warm. The air-conditioner on the wall faltered like a reluctant chaperone. Holding the director's gaze longer than she intended, Stella sent an unexpected warmth through the older woman. *I had better tread carefully here.*

'So,' Charlotte reluctantly switched to formality. 'What have you got for me Stella?'

Stella hesitated. Her initial thought was to answer something on the lines of *what would you like from me, Charlotte? But that would be playing with fire.*

Stella opened her folder. She spun the manuscript about for the director to read.

'The indigenous shell necklaces are ready to be displayed,' Stella said, matching Charlotte's professionalism. 'We had some fun re-stringing them, but they look fantastic now.'

Stella turned pages to present *before* and *after* photos. While Stella was pre-occupied, Charlotte cast a discreet eye over the twenty-six-year old. She had to admit Stella looked cute in her flannel shirt over turtleneck sweater, denim skirt and Birkenstock leather sandals.

'The new exhibit, complete with an aboriginal bark shelter and a full-sized bark canoe, build by aboriginal descendants, will be certain to draw the people back to the museum,' Stella said. 'The art department have almost finished the stone tools exhibit, and they are well under way to be completed by the end of the week.'

'Excellent. So, are we on schedule for the advertised opening? I need to send out invitations.'

'Sure. Go ahead, I'll see it's finished, if I have to work overtime.'

'You've been putting in a lot of extra time already I noticed,' Charlotte saw an opportunity to fish for information. 'Hope this isn't a strain on your love life,' she said, sounding positively reticent.

'What love life?' Stella huffed.

'What? A pretty little thing like you,' Charlotte held Stella's gaze. Stella simply smiled. 'The museum'll miss you here when you move to Launceston.'

Stella was tempted to say, *I'll miss you too.* But said, 'I'll miss it here as well.'

***

Later that day...

Stella stood in the doorway to the coin vault and watched Stanley a moment. He was perched on a stool in front of his IBM computer, studying a coin through a magnifying glass. Spaced out on the bench before him were four albums and three cigar boxes of loose coins and medals. 'Is that the Noble collection?' Stella asked.

Stanley harrumphed, deep in concentration. Stella knew the Noble collection to be a recent addition to the museum's collections, bequeathed by Anthony Noble's widow a month earlier. Little was known about the hoard, suffice to say the initial inspection by Stanley and the then director Adam Sawyer was one of pleasant surprise. Stella and other staff had been present, and many rarities were mentioned, although the widow had been adamant that her husband had not made an inventory of his collection.

'Do you need a hand?' Stella asked, already knowing the answer.

'What?'

'Do you need a hand to do the inventory? It's a big job.'

'No!' Stanley wheezed, almost too readily. 'I'm fine.' Stanley slipped a coin into an acid free plastic sheath. 'Haven't you got the indigenous exhibit to complete?' he muttered. 'Or a couple of skulls to clean?' he said of the aboriginal remains recently returned from the British Museum. The thought of the skulls alone annoyed the young conservationist. She had walked in on Stanley holding an aboriginal skull whilst mimicking Hamlet to the janitor. 'Alas, poor Yorick! I knew him Horatio, a fellow of infinite jest …' And Stella had reprimanded him for his lack of respect. This altercation, one of many, caused a rift between them.

'I'm waiting on conservation supplies,' Stella lied. 'I have a couple of hours to kill.'

'I'm fine,' Stanley muttered rudely, tapping denomination, numerals and pertinent information into his keyboard with one clumsy finger 'I'm certain you can spend your time usefully elsewhere.'

Stella stood silently staring back a moment when Stanley added, 'Close the door on your way out.'

Not surprised by Stanley's attitude, Stella walked off down the passage. She was on a mission. Stanley listened until he heard the laboratory door open and close, and locked himself in the coin vault.

***

Days later in Melbourne…

Ivano Stipanov, burglar to the rich, planned one last job in the big city. It seemed the right thing to do, Stipanov had convinced himself. One final hit to complete before leaving Melbourne where the cops were surely onto him. One final job to top up the coffers before changing cities. The hit was a high rise in South Yarra, a thirty-storey block aptly named *Highview.* Ivano had been casing the place for a month now, meticulously planning the job, as he always did, doing research on the occupants, their habits, checking the underground residents' carpark where, stupidly, the car spaces were numbered the same as the apartment numbers. If the car space was empty, then there was a good chance the owner wasn't home. The mark was the owner of a ladies' handbags franchise, a multi-millionaire, Andrea Mancini. Mancini was a high-profile single gay man, a socialite fond of the limelight. He lived alone in his penthouse, but was an energetic entertainer who spent a lot of time at home from where he also ran his office.

Ivano had been watching the building at night. The light was always on in Mancini's apartment, even when he knew the man went out. But the apartment next to his had been in darkness three weeks now and subsequent enquiries proved the owners were overseas. Research also showed that five evenings out of the seven, Mancini would dine out, always late and usually he was away for at least two hours, sometimes up to four – if he was meeting others. Ivano knew he had a two-hour window. Ivano had followed Mancini's progress in the social pages of magazines and newspapers, noting in particular that the jewellery he wore to these occasions varied. Meaning the wealthy man had plenty of it. And the good news was that when he popped out for a casual dinner, he wore little jewellery, leaving the rest at home.

***

Ivano was no stranger to high rise burglaries. He had managed several over his career and at thirty-one he was fit as any Olympian. One fact made rich people living in high rises vulnerable. Because of where they lived, they assumed no one could rob them. In all of Ivano's experience they often left their safes unlocked and valuable jewellery lying about, in the bathrooms and bedrooms particularly. However, Mancini's apartment was more of a challenge than most. The building had security and a doorman. On the positive side Mancini's apartment faced a public park which was in darkness at night and no one looking up at the building would expect to see a man climbing along a narrow ledge over one hundred metres up. Shaped like three towers staggered one next to the other, an open stairwell ran from the second floor all the way to the roof. Iron bars encircled the second-floor landing but for a man of Ivano's talent they were easily negotiated.

Three days of hiding in a motel after the bungled Toorak robbery Ivan struck again. It was a weeknight. He had waited until nine and was rewarded with the sight of Andrea Mancini vacating the building. Ivano waited another fifteen minutes like he always did, just in case the owner had forgotten something and returned. Darkness had fallen forty minutes earlier and the sky was overcast, masking the moon, a bonus. On the negative side a strong wind had picked up. Double checking he was alone, Ivano, dressed completely in black, entered the grounds from the park. He heaved a grappling hook to the second-floor ledge between two conjoined towers and hoisted himself up. Here he re-hooked to the third-floor landing above the iron bars and climbed the stairs silently to the roof. Once on the thirtieth floor, Ivano located the apartment in darkness one floor below and next door to Mancini's apartment. As he had no guarantee Mancini's apartment was empty, he would have to lower himself over the edge from the roof and onto the neighbouring balcony, and then crawl along the thirty-centimetre ledge that ran around the entire building to the Italian's balcony. As the ledge was so narrow Ivano had no choice but to negotiate the sliver of a ledge with his back to the wall and the toes of his runners sticking out over the ledge. Strapped to his waist was a bag of tools including glass cutters, lock picks and other necessities of his trade. The only positive about this terrifying stunt was the fact his escape route would be down the internal fire escape, even if it did mean tripping the alarm as he vacated the stairwell at ground level.

Twenty-nine floors up Ivano stepped out onto the narrow ledge.

Only centimetres supported him from the 97.6 metre plunge to his death. He sucked in a deep breath …

When the rains came.

***

About the same time, across Bass Strait, and down to North Hobart …

Antique restorer Jacopo Moretti listened to his suffering wife Eleanora's breathing. She lay in a comatose sleep in her favourite armchair before the telly, feet up on a crochet-covered Ottoman, a legacy of her own needlework in more fortuitous times. He cleared their used soup bowls and bread board from off the table and made room for magistrate Christian Yardley Winterbourne's damaged model ship. It certainly was a fine model, and all carved from whale bone. Folk Art, he had heard his friend Stanley call similar pieces in the past. The model was of the fully rigged barque *Aladdin*, a whaling ship of 264 tons built in Plymouth in 1825. Jacopo took a moment to inspect the workmanship before embarking on its restoration.

Entirely created from whale bone, Jacopo studied the pan bone decking with its fine cut caulking over a bulwark of more hand-cut bone; taken from the jaw of a sperm whale captured somewhere out on the Tasman Sea a hundred and fifty years ago, Jacopo fancied. A moment of reverent sadness for the beautiful creature came over the Italian.

All the pieces were present, they just needed restructuring, gluing the damaged hull planks back in place, resetting the topgallant yardarm on the main mast and re-rigged where necessary.

Four hours, Jacopo imagined, *sixty dollars. Easy money and I get to do it in the comfort of my living room. I might even charge a bit more.* Money always seemed a problem lately with his wife's being ill. Jacopo started with the starboard hull. The damaged planking came away easily, it looked like the model had been dropped at some stage. With the planks removed Jacopo lifted the model with both hands, the better to see inside the hull, when he noted an envelope …

***

Back at Melbourne's South Yarra's Highview apartments …

Burglar Ivano Stipanov was balanced precariously on the outer ledge of the penthouse 97.6 metres up, when the rains came.

He had his back to the wall; the wet and slippery ledge was barely wider than his shoes and he stared dead ahead towards the horizon. The wind came from the north but Ivano was facing west. Yet still the rain lashed his face. With his gloved hands flat against the wall at his back, Ivano looked out across a sea of lights that was Melbourne. He didn't take his eyes off the skyline. Ivano dared not look down. This was crazy. Probably the craziest thing he had ever done. At the halfway point, some five metres he seriously wanted to return ... But Ivano *was* halfway.

Guts and determination along with his disciplined mind forced him to continue. Never had Ivano been so relieved to drop onto the neighbouring balcony. Here the curtains were only partly drawn. Carefully, he peeped into the apartment. Yes! It was empty. Ivano unzipped his bum bag and was about to take out the glass cutters when he had presence of mind to try the sliding door first. It wasn't locked. Typical of the arrogant rich living in high rise buildings, they always assume no one is going to break into their home from a twenty-nine-storey balcony. Stepping inside he waited and listened ...

To be certain he was alone.

All was going to plan. Good planning included leaving the property just how the owners left it. Hopefully then, it would be some time before they realised they had been robbed, giving the burglar extra time to put distance between himself and the robbery. Looking about the apartment Ivano admired many expensive items; antique bronzes and ivory carvings, but this was a jewellery heist, in and out, snatch and grab, escape light. Ivano hurried to the bedroom ... Yes. Typical.

The jewellery box was left out on the dresser. Inside was a collection of gold watches, diamond studs, a hefty gold and ruby ring with some fancy insignia, but Ivano knew he could separate the stone and melt down the gold. He counted four gold fob chains, all antique and 24 karats. In a drawer beneath the box he found a diamond necklace, it looked old; an heirloom maybe. Either way he had done well. Taking a pillow slip from off the bed he tipped his haul into the bag. A hasty check in a chest of drawers next to the bed revealed a small carved box of collector's commemorative gold coins in their display sheathes; about twenty in all. Ivano tipped them loose into his pillowslip and tucked the heist under his sweater. Ignoring the rest of the apartment Ivano escaped by the front door. The passageway was clear. With his face hidden behind his balaclava Ivano rushed to the fire stairs and descended three steps at a time. At ground level Ivano tackled the panic bar on the fire-door, slamming the door open. The alarm tripped. Ivano ran off into the blackness of an ugly wet and miserable night. He had succeeded. In and out in less than twenty-five-minutes.

Now it was time for PLAN B ...

***

That same evening in Hobart, where the weather was pleasant …

Antique restorer Jacopo's rough carpenters' fingers unsuccessfully fished about inside the model ship for the mystery envelope. Taking up pinch nose plyers he finally juggled the old envelope free. It was brown with age and the brittle paper folded over double. But it felt thick and, dare Jacopo let his imagination run away, it felt valuable. Thinking of the magistrate's property, Jacopo prised the envelope open, carefully. He sat back releasing a loud whistle. Eleanora stirred. Jacopo remained silent and looked at the old banknotes, stunned a moment. Eleonora's gentle snoring continued. Jacopo spread the notes on the table. There were dozens and dozens of them, mostly Commonwealth of Australia blue five-pound or red ten-pound notes and a dozen or so green one-pound notes. Jacopo stared at the cache, his mind racing. Does Mr Winterbourne know they are there?

Of course, he doesn't. Why would he let you take the model away if he did?

Being an immigrant Italian Jacopo had no clue as to the existence of the pound notes. He guessed it was old Australian currency; well it was engraved Commonwealth of Australia. He quickly counted 109 five-pound notes, 98 ten-pound notes and 137 one-pound notes. One thousand, six hundred and sixty-two pounds. He whistled a second time.

Jacopo didn't wrestle with his conscience; he could be as underhand as the next man. The magistrate? Well Jacopo had heard stories and they all hinted that the man was immoral. But it was being caught that bothered him; and what if he was to be arrested for stealing and to come before the almighty Magistrate Winterbourne himself. *Mamma Mia,* so much money. Jacopo folded a pound note neatly into his wallet and hid the remainder beneath a pile of Italian women's magazines Eleanora once read in healthier days …

And settled in to repair the model ship.

***

The next day at the Tasmanian Museum and Art Gallery (TMAG)

Young Stella Bathe, the assistant conservator, had one objective at the museum, to instigate the removal of Stanley Smart. He was stealing, she just knew it. With her rapport with her new boss, Stella sought out Charlotte Fysh for the second time this week. She knocked on her office door. 'Sorry to bother you Charlotte, but can you spare a moment?'

'For you, any time. Come in.'

'That Noble collection,' Stella told the director of the recently bequeathed coin collection, 'was never catalogued by the late owner.'

'Yes, I'm aware of that, the wife said as much.'

'And it is being catalogued as we speak.'

'Yes, Stanley's onto it I believe.'

'Do you think he should be cataloguing alone?'

'What are you suggesting?' Charlotte asked, knowing exactly what her young colleague was thinking.

'Well, you know.'

'No, I don't know Stella. Be specific.'

'Well it would be easy for someone to, you know, take a coin or two.'

'That would be a violation of trust. A prison offence. Are you suggesting Stanley Smart is misappropriating coins?'

Stella felt herself flush slightly. It was almost as if the director was protecting Stanley.

Surely not!

Charlotte stood and walked around her desk to the door. Taking a glance into the passageway, Charlotte pushed the door closed and faced the young conservator. Charlotte took both Stella's hands in hers. '

I appreciate you coming to me with this matter,' Charlotte voice softened, it was almost conspiratorial. 'Do you have any proof?'

Charlotte continued holding Stella's hands, yielding to the chemistry between them. She was certain the conservator felt the same way. Stella's heart raced, she flushed even more. She had always fancied older women. Her last lover was thirty-eight. But this was crazy. This was her boss.

Charlotte shook Stella's hands gently. 'Well then?'

'Well ... well what?' Stella's voice was breaking. She cleared her throat.

'Do you have any proof?'

Stella's mind fogged. 'About Stanley?'

'Who else?'

'Well he … he never lets me assist whenever he's cataloguing or doing an inventory.'

'Of the Noble collection?'

'Of any collection; coins, medals, banknotes, tokens.'

'You had better be certain of your facts if you are to accuse a colleague of stealing.' Charlotte released her hold.

Stella swallowed hard. She had been one second from crossing the line, when her nerve deserted her.

***

Now the seed of doubt had been planted in Charlotte's mind she was like a dog with a bone. Later that afternoon she phoned the retired director, Mr Adam Sawyer, at home. Demanding utmost discretion, Charlotte put the question to Adam.

'Have you at any time in the past had cause to mistrust Stanley Smart?'

'Good god Ms Sawyer, what are you suggesting?'

Charlotte went on to explain her misgivings stopping short of involving Stella Bathe.

'Hmm.' Adam Sawyer was silent a moment on the end of the line. 'Stanley has been at the museum decades Ms Fysh.' Adam had decided it best to keep titles formal due to the nature of the call. 'Several decades in fact.'

'Yes or no Adam.'

'My, you are to the point, aren't you?'

'A woman in my position needs to be. Well?'

'There was an incident several years back.'

'Oh?'

'We had a collection bequeathed to the museum, only a small collection but it included thirteen sovereigns and one in particular was rare … worth several thousand dollars.'

'Yes.'

'Well there was a discrepancy with the rare coin. It was from the Melbourne mint and dated 1886. But what was unique about it was that it had a tooth mark right in the centre of the Queen's head where someone during its history had bitten the coin to determine whether it was real gold or not. It wasn't a big bite mind, just subtle, but particularly noticeable under magnification'

'And?'

'Well sometime later the coin was noticed in a catalogue by a colleague. It was amongst other gold coins for sale in an upcoming auction at a coin auction house in Sydney. You see coin catalogues have exceptional photography and the tooth mark was noticeable.'

'Surely biting gold coins was a common practice in the 19th century, could it be a coincidence … I mean a tooth mark and same date?'

'Certainly. It could, yes. But when I discreetly inspected the museum's collection in the coin vault the specimen had been switched for a similar rare coin, same mint and date, but in poorer condition, less the tooth print.'

'Was Stanley Smart the numismatist then?'

'Yes.'

This thought alone gave the meticulously honest museum director the shivers. Stanley Smart had had two decades of carte blanch.

***

Several days after art expert Susan Kirby visited Magistrate Christian Winterbourne…

Art dealer and proven art expert, Neville Goldman, was wary. The wealthy art dealer of Goldman Galleries in Hobart's up-market tourist area of Salamanca Place did not acquire wealth and reputation from being gullible or making shaky deals. At least not ones that were traceable back to him. And he knew Magistrate Christian Yardley Winterbourne came with baggage. Not baggage over art mind. He had a reputation as a magistrate who succumbed to baksheesh and hints of corruption. It was known that Winterbourne enjoyed gambling, especially on the horses, and this vice alone needed fodder.

It should be explained that Christian Winterbourne did not come from a privileged family as one may have thought, and he hadn't always been corrupted. Born in Bothwell in 1926, Winterbourne was only five years old when his father, a farmhand, died of tetanus from a farm machinery accident. Christian grew up wanting to be a teacher and travelled to Hobart to enrol in Teachers' College only to end up sitting for a public service exam instead. It seemed he had found his vocation and soon found employment as a clerk in the courts.

He enlisted in the army at twenty-one, spending most of his service in administration. After he was discharged, he studied law and was finally appointed a magistrate in the late sixties.

Art dealer Neville Goldman had heard the magistrate's problems started in the seventies. His colleagues, other magistrates and judges, soon noticed Christian's huge ego. He enjoyed the power his situation afforded him. He was seen more frequently at the races and in particular in the company of certain affiliates of the underworld. This made him an easy target for bribes. Neville Goldman also knew, more recently, the magistrate had imposed a small fine for an abalone poacher, Max Shreeve, when the man should have received a custodial sentence. A questionable result that, for some reason, had avoided the legal microscope.

However, a Chinese restaurant owner Tom Chung of The Smiling Dragon, who was affiliated with the fisherman wasn't so lucky – a different magistrate – and served a few months in prison for his dishonesty. Hobart was a small place, rumours persisted and it was said a deal had been brokered.

**

'The signed Tom Roberts is of particular interest,' Neville Goldman told Christian.

'That would do exceptionally well at say, Shadlock's in Melbourne.'

'Oh. How much are we talking about?'

'Twenty to thirty thousand, easy. The Dobell Lady with flowers, five thousand.'

Christian hoped his sudden twitch went unnoticed. His plan was to keep the paintings as an investment, enjoy them on his walls, then sell them in a few years at a handsome profit. But twenty to thirty thousand dollars was too much to resist. The fact was he had been offered the Tom Roberts for ten thousand all because the owner needed the cash immediately.

'Naturally I need to inspect the signatures on the paintings,' Goldman said.

'Oh?'

'Yes. I need to put them under a strong light with high magnification to be certain the artist's signature has soaked into the pigment of the canvas. This is a feature no reproduction can replicate.'

'Very well.'

'If everything is kosher, I would like to send the Tom Roberts to Shadlocks in Melbourne first. To test the water, you understand. My commission is ten per cent of the net take after Shadlock's commission.'

'And you think it could fetch as much as thirty thousand.'

'In today's healthy market, easily. All going well we will place the others in upcoming auctions.'

'Oh, but I wish to keep the Dobell and Sydney Long's *Nymph Playing Flute with Cranes.*'

'Fine. But the Stretton and the Forrest need restoration.'

'Restoration?'

'Yes, they have scratches and are dirty, they need professional cleaning. And obviously they all need to be framed.'

'Can you organise that?'

'Naturally. You'll be looking at five hundred to a thousand per painting. But it will enhance their value tenfold.'

Christian ordered the framing but for the moment declined the offer to send them to Shadlocks.

***

Days later...

On the strength of Neville Goldman's recommendation, Christian purchased the Dobell and the sketch immediately. Six thousand eight hundred dollars the pair and another twenty-four thousand for the remaining paintings days later. For cash of course.

'The owner is in deep trouble with the Australian Taxation Office also, you must understand,' Kenning told Christian. 'So, for this reason he can only accept cash.'

Everyone was happy; especially Alfred Kenning who promised to deliver more paintings, and Christian couldn't be more obliging. He fancied he had a new purpose as a middleman art dealer where the profit was easily made. It was time for celebration ...

CHAPTER FOUR

The following Friday night Christian indulged himself with another of his passions. He was also a regular at *Salon Rouge*, a well-established exclusive bordello run by a rather large proportioned madam who only answered to the name Mareike. Madam Mareike's bordello was situated at the top end of Liverpool Street, only a kilometre from Hobart's CBD. Since leaving his wife of forty years Christian satisfied his fantasies with fortnightly – occasionally weekly – visits to this long-running professionally operated brothel. Being a regular and especially being a magistrate, the madam, a self-made woman, pampered the portly lawman with his fetish for large boned women. He was content with being mature and choosing women in their late forties; unlike his fellow clients chasing younger women. But Mareike kept her girls of age – at least she tried to – and clean, after all it would not do if the governor's aide, a criminal judge or, god help her, an archdeacon, caught the pox.

***

The Liverpool Street address was a large family home converted to ten bedrooms. Designed by Henry Hunter in the 1870s, the sandstone erection was a handsome affair, two storeys with an east and west wing. Perfect for a brothel.

Mareike herself was retired from the game, that is, the actual pleasuring side of the business. She was fifty-four now – a madam and her own boss, retired from the degradation of gratifying over-sexed men for money. She had made her riches the hard way and built an empire. Well, maybe not exactly an empire, but the address was paid for and her goodwill strong. *And* she had cash stashed away for that rainy day. This gave Mareike time to visit St Mary's Catholic Cathedral in Harrington Street, ten minutes from her place of work to place of worship. Mareike had not always been the religious type, but something about approaching the winter years of life, and her past of less than moral behaviour, caused her to embrace the Lord Jesus. Now church gave her strength, she felt her dedication cast a protective eye over her and prepare her for such a time, hopefully years away, when she would meet her maker.

Mareike was born to an impoverished family in 1942. Her father was a bricklayer and her mother waited on tables when the work was available, but the bottle saw her mother die of cirrhosis of the liver, and she received nothing but neglect and abuse from her father.

These were the dark years when she deserted god, for god only knew he had deserted her.

Mareike scrounged a meagre income cleaning. She was an intelligent soul who appreciated the arts. She loved to go to the museum and galleries and visited the theatre whenever she could afford the ticket. But with a petite curvaceous body it was a given that she would be lured into prostitution. Besides, nature had gifted her with green eyes, long curls of soft black hair, an insatiable sexual appetite and a complete lack of morals.

Mareike left home at fifteen to start walking the streets in the late 50s but soon ended up under the wing of Ma Dwyer in her parlour on the Hobart docks. Mareike grew up tough. Sure, she could act the lady when she wanted to, but pity help anyone who riled her. By the age of twenty Mareike had had a falling out with Ma Dwyer and nursed a black eye for her trouble. It was time to move on.

Not long after, she met and married a smooth-talking, heavy drinking, charismatic American, Joe Dunhill. But it soon became evident Joe was more interested in acting as pimp than husband. However, Mareike went along with Joe's plan, and their teamwork flourished. Joe bought a second-hand Desoto and drove Mareike around the streets where there seemed no end of customers happy for a romp in the back seat of the big black car.

Joe became more demanding. His beatings more regular and Mareike hardened to the booze. She became well known around the streets as a whore who could drink any wharfie under the table and swear harder on the way down.

At twenty-five she had lost her pretty young looks and the booze affected her physique. But Mareike was a smart lass, and primarily a businesswoman.

Realising it was time to lift her game or be lost in the gutter, Mareike sent Joe packing before opening her first brothel – a three-bedroom weatherboard cottage in Campbell Street, close to the docks. The year was 1968. It was an instant success. At age thirty Mareike ran two brothels around the city, quietly hoarding away her hard-earned money. This of course came at the expense of the wrath of first Ma Dwyer and later, after Ma Dwyer fell off the perch, of Madam Phoebe Crow, who rose through the ranks of deprivation to become another self-made brothel keeper.

***

Phoebe Crow – Rival Madam

Mareike and Phoebe Crow became arch enemies. Their public fights were legendary.

Not content with brothel keeping, Mareike dabbled in crime. She acted as a fence for stolen property, moving it onto Melbourne via contacts on board the Abel Tasman's Devonport to Melbourne ferry service. But this brought her to the attention of the police.

Meanwhile her brothels flourished, especially when Mareike took advantage of a loophole in the law – the law that stated men could not operate brothels, while there was no clear law that declared women could not. As a legal precaution she let one room in each bordello to a legitimate tenant, on the pretext that her bordellos were lodgings and that she, Mareike, was no less than an innocent landlady. Naturally everyone knew differently but no one dared suggest otherwise, not to her face in any case.

It was also 1968 when she met the charismatic, sexually hypnotic Charles Ray. Charles, eight years older than Mareike, grew up in Queenstown, western Tasmania. A footy star as a youth, he was much loved and a wandering Lothario by the time he met Mareike. Their liaison – they met when he crashed one of her legendary parties – was one of the rare times Mareike fell in love. So in love the young brothel keeper let her guard down and became pregnant. Although she was not a religious person, not in those early days, an abortion was out of the question. Adoption, however, was not. The six-pound baby boy was taken from her within minutes of being born. If anything, this hardened Mareike. Of course Charles Ray had many affairs during his relationship with Mareike and by late 1969 she told him *to bugger off* as well.

Mareike went on to enjoy the trappings of wealth, and why shouldn't she, having grown up in poverty. She started wearing expensive furs, adorning her fingers with gold and diamonds. She exhibited all the style of the nouveau riche. But her vulgarity defined the book inside the cover. She drank heavily and chain-smoked. As time passed, any traces of her youthful beauty vanished; she suffered heavy jowls, angry, intransigent eyes and her luscious hair was lost to the ravages of time. She cropped it short and tucked it under a toque. Besides her vices and telling hacking cough, Mareike managed to stay fit during these earlier years, and was proud of the fact she was deft with her fists and could fight like any man.

On a more genial note Mareike loved to throw parties and anyone invited knew they were in for an outrageous time.

***

Chastity – Sex Worker

It was on a summer evening in the eighties, a Friday, when Christian Winterbourne came under Mareike's radar. The magistrate had been visiting the Liverpool Street brothel for close on twelve months at this stage. Christian had fallen for Chastity, an English lass with hazel hair, huge breasts, button nose and blue eyes. Chastity was thirty-five when they first met, but with the maturity Christian enjoyed. She was also someone with whom he could converse, content to pay for extra time while sitting in her room, post 'romance', and chat freely; usually about himself. Naturally all titbits were relayed to Mareike the next day, albeit unwittingly, and this often included magisterial business. By now Christian had separated from his wife and it was about this time that he began to be invited to Mareike's parties, which she held at regular intervals.

When at her parties, Mareike would ply the magistrate with his favourite cognac, and from time to time she would ingratiate herself with her life stories while he enjoyed Chastity at his side; his *date* for the night. For Christian's part, he enjoyed the madam's company and whether he knew of her criminal activities outside of the brothels or not, the subject was never discussed.

Mareike would inevitably drink too much. She would then hold the floor in a singalong next to the piano, belting out the vaudeville tunes she so enjoyed in her earlier years visiting the theatre. Occasionally some drunk would flirt with her but any man foolish enough to think he could lay her met a swift assault, fists first.

Yes, Mareike loved a fight, and the profanity that poured from her lips was legendary.

***

Mareike was exceptionally shrewd and went to great expense and care to compile a portfolio of discreet photos of her more influential customers. One room, known as *One night in Paris*, and decked out with outrageous Parisian décor from the 1890s, was also fitted with two cameras. Now, she could take compromising photos of her leading men nakedly trysting with her ladies of the night. The ace up her sleeve should she need it.

It was about this time that Mareike and rival Madam Phoebe Crow came to be at loggerheads. Phoebe had controlled the waterfront bordellos, usually small cottages in side streets off the waterfront and catering to lonely seamen. In other words, the bottom end of the market. But Phoebe decided, unwisely, to move in on the more lucrative upmarket scene. But Hobart was a small place. One madam to pamper the affluent was enough. Phoebe's one advantage was that she was as tough as Mareike. Like Mareike she carried pepper spray in her handbag, just in case she was being bettered in a brawl and, as acquaintances who had crossed her were well aware, she also had the punch of a mule. With both women employing thugs, street fights at night between them were not unknown.

Phoebe also dabbled in stolen property, namely booze stolen from various warehouses. So when she was raided and caught with four cases of whisky and gin receipted to Chancellors Wine Merchants, Phoebe had no doubt who had warned the cops. Phoebe was fined five hundred pounds and the crime recorded.

The gloves were off.

Phoebe Crow confronted Mareike about the affair in Elizabeth Street one weekday afternoon. The profanity and abuse quickly deteriorated to a fistfight and Mareike smartly had the older and also overweight Phoebe on her back on the footpath. Mareike straddled her opponent and was viciously punching her in the face when she was arrested. This wasn't the first time Mareike had been charged. She already had thirty other charges against her name over the past years and the magistrate fined her seven hundred dollars and put her on a good behaviour bond, before threatening her with gaol time should she come before the courts again.

But this did not satisfy Phoebe and she had her thugs slash the face of one of Mareike's most profitable workers, a young red head with exceptional prowess in the boudoir. For this Mareike sent her thugs to one of Phoebe's cottages, setting it alight. But Mareike could not contend herself with merely ordering the dastardly crime, she wanted to witness it for herself. Unfortunately, several witnesses noted Mareike's presence and her giving orders. She was arrested for arson and bailed. For this, Mareike knew she would definitely be imprisoned. Now it was time to use her trump card, the ace up her sleeve.

*****

For now, though ...

Fisherman Max Shreeve was enjoying sex gratis. *On the house*, or at least, *in the cabin.* Max was happy with his new mooring. He had motored his fishing boat *Infinity* away from public attention on Hobart's docks, anchoring off the foreshore from the Lindisfarne Motor Yacht Club, over on Hobart's Eastern Shore. Away from snooping fisheries inspectors and definitely out of reach of estranged wife, Verity, *the bitch.*

'You okay Maxie?' Meredith Kendall peeled back the wrapper on a Chokito chocolate bar and took a generous bite before offering it to Max. 'You're a bit quiet today.'

Max hadn't realised his pensive mood; staring vaguely out the galley porthole towards the club car park fifty metres across the bay. 'Maxie, darling?'

Max hated being called Maxie, especially by his *bitch* wife Verity, but Meredith could get away with anything. Max was in love. The two had been together nearly every night this week, since Max met the escort the weekend before.

'Sorry.' Max took the chocolate bar and bit into the sweetness of caramel fudge and crisp rice. 'Yeh babe, I'm fine.'

'What were you thinking about?'

'Us.' Max held the bar with his lips and drew Meredith close. The two shared the Chokito bite for bite until their lips touched and passion overcame the two lovers once more. Their lovemaking was intense. Early thirties Max felt early twenties once more, and in the arms of a twenty-two-year-old why shouldn't he.

Meredith rolled from Max's body in a lather of sweat. It was uncomfortably hot below decks. She lay naked on her back, her long spirals of black curls fanning across the pillow. Sated, Max propped himself on one elbow to look into the young lady's green eyes. He couldn't believe his luck in meeting Meredith, but like any man, or woman for that matter, the fact she was a sex-worker tugged at his emotions. *It can't last*, he kept telling himself. *She's an escort for Christ's sake.*

Struggling with negative thoughts – *Meredith having sex with men for money* – Max endeavoured to balance the positive. *She has only been doing this for seven months and she's only doing it to put herself through university.* Max recalled earlier conversations when he broached the subject. *I don't enjoy it*, she assured Max, *I just close my eyes and think of the money.*

'Is that what you do with me?' Max asked on their second night at his Cremorne Beach shack earlier in the week. Meredith had looked Max in the eye and told him how she felt about him.

'But we just met,' Max said cautiously.

'But you're different. You're not like the others.'

'Like how?'

'You're funny, you're fun to be with, we have a lot in common, like Aussie Rules footy and you don't treat me like shit because I do what I do.'

The third night was free. Meredith didn't charge for sex and Max felt a semblance of sincerity blossoming. *Call it romance if you like.* Max tried to tell himself his insecurity was ill-founded. However, he had one major regret. After his second encounter Max had drunk too much at the Royal Yacht Club and when pressured to spill the beans, he told a *yachtie* mate (well he thought he was a mate) Mark Chester about Meredith …

All about Meredith. Now it was common knowledge Max was fucking a prostitute.

Immediately a piercing whistle disturbed the serenity and Max heard his name travel across the bay. Slipping on clothes he poked his head from the companionway looking across at the jetty. Someone was waving to him. A woman. *Maggie?*

Max focussed, reminding himself to go visit his old mate Bruce at Total Eyecare in Liverpool Street. The second shrill whistle and the calling of his name once more left no doubt that the soft-focused figure on the jetty was none other than his older sister Maggie.

'Maggie!' he shouted across the flotilla of luxury craft. Maggie waved back frantically.

'Who's that?' Meredith heard the commotion and popped her head above the companionway, only to have Max's firm palm planted on her head. 'Stay down.'

'Why?'

'It's my sister, Maggie.'

'Is she coming on board?'

'No, I'll go see what she wants.'

'I didn't know you had a sister.'

'Well sometimes I wonder myself. I rarely see her.' Max dropped over the side into the tender and rowed ashore while Meredith dressed and watched Max's progress through a porthole in the galley below.

***

'Maggie,' Max called out on the approach, rowing rather sluggishly after having enjoyed a lazy champagne-fuelled afternoon with his new lover.

'Max,' Maggie said. 'I wasn't sure you'd be here. I went to the docks in town first and the guys said you'd moved here. Why's that?'

'Long story.' Max's dinghy bumped against the jetty. Max looked up at his sister, her portly figure silhouetted with the sun directly behind her. 'What's up?'

'Grandma's dying, that's what's up.'

Grandma Berenice Shreeve, their father's mother, was well into her nineties; a frail and sickly old woman who, quite frankly, was in the right frame of mind to die. Max wasn't surprised or, for that matter, sorrowful. He had never been that close to either grandparent on his father's side; their own mother Louise had seen to that.

'Is she still at Vaucluse?' Max asked of the retirement home for the affluent in Macquarie Street.

'No, she's been moved to palliative care.'

'Oh! That serious.'

'Yes, oh, that serious!'

That was a typical response from his sibling and another reason he kept his distance from her. Come to think of it the only time Maggie was pleasant was when the crayfish season was operating, and she wanted a free feed of the delicacy. Max jammed the port oar into the pier and shoved off. 'I'll go change, won't be long.'

'Wait! I'll come out with you.'

Max kept rowing. 'I'll be two minutes.'

'Max!' Maggie hooked her hands onto her hips, not happy. 'Who's out there with you anyway?'

'No one.'

'Bullshit. I saw someone's head.' Max kept rowing, thinking *thank god I'm not docked.*

'Max, it wasn't Verity's head.'

***

Maggie had had twelve minutes to stew as she waited by her car. Max walked towards her across the car park. Her vision tapered. 'I thought you'd have learnt to keep it in your pants by now.'

'Jesus Maggie,' Max opened the passenger door. 'Leave off will you.'

'No wonder Verity kicked you out.'

This hurt. Maggie didn't know half of her sibling's troubles, or the fact that if Max continued living under the same roof as Verity much longer he would end up on a murder rap.

'You're sounding like your mother,' Max spat.

'Well you should listen to her. Which trollop is this one, anyhow?'

Max made to open the door. 'Stuff it Maggie, I'll take my own car.'

'Settle petal, can't you take criticism?'

Truth was Max had been drinking and knew he would be over the limit. 'Just leave it, okay?'

'Sure.' Maggie twisted the key and the canary yellow Holden Commodore sparked to life. 'Put your belt on.' Maggie hit the accelerator spitting gravel, out of the car park onto the main road. 'I'll give you a lift back also,' Maggie said as she slipped lanes to head back to the Tasman Bridge towards Hobart's western shore. 'Maybe your bit of fluff will have gone by then.'

Max shook his head. It was going to be a long day. 'How long's she got?' he asked of their grandmother.

'Days, Mum reckons.'

'I hope she's ...' Max thought to choose his words carefully.

'Hope's she what?'

'Well, last time I saw her she had shit on the liver.' Max thought back to the last time he saw his grandmother. The woman was always criticising, quick to judge, moody. 'No wonder grandad carked it years ago. Off to the pearly gates for some peace and quiet.'

***

Grandma Berenice Shreeve was in good spirits. 'It's the morpheme,' the palliative care nurse said quietly, adding a conspiratorial wink. She fluffed up the pillows and left the grandchildren alone with their grandmother. Grandma was in death's waiting room, however she seemed happy enough and keen to chat; mostly about herself, family and trivia like her pet Scottie dog Alfie, who died nine years earlier. She went on to talk about her own son's early years, that was Max and Maggie's father Douglas Shreeve, who would be back soon.

'He spent the night here last night,' Berenice crowed. He could never do anything wrong, not her Dougie. 'Slept in that chair he did.' She nodded to the comfortable convertible bedsit Maggie had sunk her corpulent body into. 'Must have thought I was about to pop off.'

Berenice let out a weak laugh, but the two grandchildren felt uncomfortable around the talk of dying. Max was immediately more concerned about saying his goodbyes and making himself scarce before his father returned. Their relationship had been strained lately, since the *shit hit the fan* with Verity. *The damned bitch had his own parents in her callous little palm.*

'You've put on weight Maggie,' Grandma said, her social filter failing in her twilight days. Maggie shifted uncomfortably. If there was one thing that riled her it was someone commenting on her weight. However, Maggie tried to remain stoic. 'Yes well, Grandma, it's all paid for.'

'Paid for!' Berenice coughed a laugh. 'Must have cost a fortune.' The old woman had a lightbulb moment talking of money. 'That husband of yours got a full-time job yet?'

'You know he works at the nursery; he did thirty hours last week.'

Berenice huffed. 'Doing what, arranging flowers. When's he going to get a proper job paying proper money?'

Max cut in trying to defuse the negativity brewing in the room. 'Fishing's going well Gran.'

'Good. Glad someone's making money.' She looked Max in the eye. 'You are making money, aren't you?'

'Yes Gran. Life's good,' he lied.

'What about Vanity?'

'You mean Verity?'

'Yes yes. How is she? Still high maintenance I expect.'

Max so wanted to rip Verity's reputation to shreds but for Maggie's sake he said, 'Fine. She's fine.'

'She'll leave you one day that one will. You mark my words.' Now it was Maggie's turn to grin. 'She'll run off with another man. I know her type.'

Max wanted to add, you are so correct, but said, 'She'd never do that Gran.'

Maggie rolled her eyes. The conversation continued for twenty minutes when Berenice tired, and spoke of rest. The siblings stood, bid their farewells with promises to return soon, when suddenly Berenice had an urgency about her. Like she had just remembered a moment in time and wanted to tell Max something important. Maggie turned away and went to speak to the nurse outside the room when Berenice saw her opportunity, calling Max back in a hoarse whisper.

'What is it Grandma?'

'That ship your grandfather gave you some years back.'

'Ship, you mean the whalebone ship model?'

'Yes, what else would I mean? You should know that there is a bundle of old pound notes hidden inside.'

Max felt a sudden hot flush. What was the woman saying? She was talking about the antique whalebone ship he had given the corrupt magistrate, to keep him out of gaol.

'What are you saying?'

'Your grandfather Charlie won the money gambling years and years ago playing cards at the Italian Club. I was really mad at him for gambling, he could have lost money.' Berenice snatched Max's arm, her long thin cadaverous fingers gripping like talons. 'But no, he won that night. I warned him, gambling with those foreigners, those wogs. It would lead to nothing but moral destruction. Gambling's the devil's work I told him. So, when he was asleep, I hid it in that ship and told him I had taken it all to the bank. He never knew any better. Never dared ask me about it ever again. All pound notes they were, before decimal currency. We never needed the money, so I left it there. The devil's money I say.'

'No one ever told me. Why didn't you say something earlier?'

'Why should I? I didn't know the silly man gave you that ship when you took up fishing, until it was too late. *Give it to a seaman*, he said. *Seaman my foot* I told him.'

Berenice must have caught Max's unsettled reaction. 'I was going to donate it to the maritime museum where it belongs. If you had any decency, you'd do just that. Take it to Tom Dowling at the museum. I went to school with Tom. He's the man that should be looking after it, not you.' Berenice smacked her lips and remembered the nurse had removed her dentures. 'Anyway, you should know there's a lot of money hidden inside, over one and a half thousand pounds as I recall.'

'Pounds?'

'That's what I said. Why don't you listen, you're nothing like your father? Now he was a listener. One and a half thousand pounds, that's three thousand dollars in decimal currency.'

Max sat back heavily in the chair, dumbstruck. Max wanted to cry. Why did life have to be like this? He felt such a loser.

CHAPTER FIVE

Police Inspector Maddison Lovett was off duty this evening. Having been invited to the opening of the Tasmanian Museum and Art Gallery's new indigenous exhibition, the inspector entered the gallery with her elderly mother, Rosemary Wise, clamped on tightly to the crook of her arm. Museum director, Ms Charlotte Fysh, was working the room where over a hundred people had turned out to meet aboriginal elders of Tasmania, to listen to the director's introductory speech, sip champagne and eat nibbles. Now, out of the blue, Charlotte caught sight of an old friend – an old acquaintance really – whom she hadn't seen in years.

'Maddison!' Charlotte wasn't certain at first, and she certainly didn't mean to gape open mouthed. 'Maddie Wise? Is that really you?'

'Charlotte!'

The two women hugged. 'I haven't seen you in ages,' Charlotte said. 'How are you?'

'I'm excellent.'

'You look excellent. It's been … what? Twenty years?'

'More like twenty-five girl,' Maddison nodded.

Charlotte took a moment to hold Maddison at arm's length and give her the once over. Her old friend had aged well and looked most attractive in a light-yellow trouser suit with fawn turtleneck. Her straight dark shoulder length hair was pulled back in a ponytail with wisps escaping over her ears.

'And yellow really suits you.' Although Maddison was of European background, clearly there was an additional element; Moroccan, Maltese? Something Mediterranean Charlotte always thought. Her face was thin, her features sharp, with gorgeous dark brown eyes and unquestionably fit. Charlotte noted the ring.

'And you're married I see.'

'Yes. I'm Maddison Lovett now.' Maddison was quick to steer the subject away from marriage. 'I heard you had left the Powerhouse Museum to take this position,' she said. 'And I was hoping to bump into you here tonight. How's the new job?'

'Stressful,' Charlotte let out a deep sigh. 'But I'm getting there. I didn't know you were in town, let alone aware you were one of the *Friends of the Museum.*'

'I'm not, Mum is,' Maddison nodded to her eighty-one-year-old mother chatting to an aboriginal elder. 'I've been transferred to Hobart as well. I'm in the police force, did you know that?'

'I had heard that, somewhere.'

The policewoman alluded once more to her mother. 'Mum's not getting any younger and she's awfully lonely since Dad died, so when the position of inspector was offered here in Hobart, I thought what the hell, and snapped it up to be close to her.'

'Inspector huh?'

'Yep. Three stars.'

'Good work. Sorry about your dad.'

'Thanks. Cancer.'

There followed the briefest of silence as if that insidious word cancer demanded reverence. 'It's great to see you though.'

Charlotte had met Maddison Lovett, nee Wise, at a basketball event decades earlier when they were in their early twenties and the two had become close friends. Then careers intervened and their lives went off in different directions.

'Is hubby here?' Charlotte surreptitiously looked about the room.

'No, Stephen's still in Sydney, work keeps him there at the moment. He's in the aluminium business. The plan is for him to move to Hobart and open an outlet for his firm here.'

'Oh, all alone eh?'

'For the moment.' Maddison was once again evasive. She wanted to explain that her relationship with her husband was strained after accepting the transfer to Hobart and that they were having a temporary separation. 'I turned forty-six this year,' she switched subjects. 'How about you?'

Charlotte never liked talking about her age or her weight. 'Hmm, tell me about it. I'll be joining you in November.'

Charlotte scanned the room. It appeared all invitations that were sent out had been accepted for a change. 'Look, I have to make a speech in a minute. Then we'll catch up.'

***

The speech went a treat – Charlotte was a natural orator. After mingling to the best of her ability, something Ms Fysh was an expert at, she caught up with her friend.

'Interesting crowd,' Maddison said, taking her second champagne offered by the waiter. 'You clearly like what you do.'

'Love it.'

'And an interesting line-up of Hobart citizens here tonight I see.'

'Yes. They're a nice crowd in Tassie, not so pretentious as Sydney.'

'I noticed. Who's the old man in the long coat?'

Charlotte didn't have to look. She knew her friend was asking about Stanley Smart who had come straight from the administration basement in his dust coat. He stood stooped over the table of refreshments; his pointed nose, drooping jowls, large ears and hooded eyes hovering over the food while his small mouth worked overtime on the sandwiches.

'Hmm,' Charlotte took her first champagne as the waiter passed by. 'That creature is Stanley Smart the museum curator.'

'He's an employee?'

'Yes. And a bit too *smart* I feel.'

'How's that?'

Charlotte Fysh looked at her friend a moment. *She's a policewoman,* she thought. *You can confide in her.* 'Actually, you might be able to help me.'

'Sure. Shoot.'

'Well I don't wish to talk out of school, so to speak, but ... look this is highly confidential okay?'

Inspector Maddison Lovett, ever the cop, grew serious. 'Absolutely.'

'Well I can't prove anything, right. But I have reason to suspect he may have misappropriated an item or two in the past.'

'Item? You mean museum property?'

'Yes. From the collection.'

'No!'

'Coins to be specific. He is the resident numismatist.'

'Jesus Charlotte. You've got to nip this in the bud.'

'Well as I said I have no proof. But there is a chance ...' The museum director suddenly felt inadequate. 'There is a chance it's been going on a while. He's worked here for decades.'

Charlotte went on to explain everything as she knew, in detail.

'Jesus Christ Charlotte. You need to catch this bastard out.'

Like a sixth sense, Stanley sensed he was the subject of the director's conversation with the attractive businesswoman, whoever she was. The two had been talking some time and he had caught them looking in his direction once too often. Uncomfortable with the situation, he abruptly departed.

'Would you like me to do some snooping around?' Inspector Lovett suggested.

'Could you? I mean, I have no evidence but ...'

'I'll make a few enquiries; you'd be surprised at the extent of records kept on the good citizens of Hobart that are available to me.'

***

The next morning around ten...

Simpleton Rory Benetti stood at the front gate to *Salon Rouge* Bordello at the top end of Liverpool Street. He held a posy of pansies and an official letter of introduction. Finally, he was to meet his maternal mother, Mareike.

Twenty-eight-year-old Rory – at least he thought he was twenty-eight – was a man of simple means and in fact a simple man. IQ tests over the years had consistently placed him at less than seventy. He had been adopted out at birth, but his adopted mother became ill with MS. He ended up being cared for by his adopted grandmother. Eventually taken from her due to her old age he was again fostered, but the new *father* mistreated him and the *mother* was caught shoplifting. He was eventually sent to an orphanage at eight years of age and remained there until he was eleven. During this period he was abused mentally by the nuns and fostered again for a short period. He was sent to a new school at fourteen but ran away before finally being placed in another foster home at sixteen. This is when Rory settled down with Mr and Mrs Benetti of North Hobart, neighbours of antique restorer Jacopo Moretti. Now, as an adult, Rory lived alone in a granny flat at the rear of the house behind the retired Benettis. He found employment where he could, working with charities like Salvation Army and Vincent de Paul. He loved gardening and carpentry, enjoying watching Jacopo in his workshop and helping the old man deliver furniture when he was needed; for a little pocket money.

***

Now Rory stood anxiously at the front gate to the Mareike's bordello. Recently he had located – through Mamma Benetti's help and some legal assistance – his maternal mother. Mareike watched the man a moment from a front window. She had agreed to meet him and had reservations of her own. But after speaking to Mrs Benetti and eventually her estranged son on the phone, three times over the past fortnight, curiosity and some semblance of maternal love encouraged her to go ahead. Or was it guilt?

'Rory?' Mareike called ahead as she walked along the front path to the gate bordered with brilliant red roses. 'You must be Rory.'

'M–Mumma.' Rory didn't flinch but held up the posy. Mareike opened the gate and ushered him in.

'Let me look at you.' Mareike stared into Rory's dark brown eyes, dampening any doubt that this was not her boy. He had his father Ray's smooth skin, dark eyes and build. She felt her eyes moisten, but this would not do for the hardened madam. 'Come inside.'

Mareike had been warned of Rory's mental status by the institution that contacted her. She had been prepared, or thought she had. She took him through to the formal office where one of the girls brought tea. They both relaxed a little and talked for the next for three hours. Much of the time conversation was difficult and now and again a tear escaped. But only now and again.

It was early afternoon by the time Mareike ended the meeting; after all early clients were starting to appear. With her newfound son's employment situation established – albeit unemployed – and the fact that Mumma ran a brothel, Mareike offered her son work as gardener for the one-and-a-half-acre property. For all her coarseness and Rory's naivety, they shared a common bond, the garden.

Rory stood to leave when he remembered something. He'd nearly forgotten to give his Mumma the gift he had brought along. He handed her the small package tied in brown paper with string.

'For me?' Mareike was touched. She had managed to keep emotions at bay until now. The slightest of tears welled in the corner of her left eye. She unwrapped the present and let out a gratified gasp.

'Oh Rory, it's beautiful. Thank you so much.'

She stood and gave the man, her only flesh and blood, a peck on the cheek, before placing the antique glass paperweight in a prominent position on her desk.

***

Rory started work as gardener the next morning; three days a week, one hundred and twenty dollars, cash in hand. That way he could still claim his disability benefits. Rory settled in smartly, throwing his heart and soul into the new position, and as dim-witted as he was, his good looks meant he was popular with the girls. Hell, he even received occasional pleasuring when Mumma wasn't about.

***

Days later...

Drink wasn't Max the fisherman's best friend. With Verity like a white pointer circling for the kill, he frequented the Lindisfarne Motor Yacht Club bar more than he should. For him the club bar seemed safer than any of the ex-wife's drinking holes over at Salamanca Place. Occasionally Big Bill the Maori would call over and join his skipper for a pot or two. Max usually dominated the conversation – mostly bitching about the wife.

When Max drank, he tended to talk too much, and some conversations circulated more than others. So it was that fate would interfere when Max spilled his guts to Bill, in a rather loud slur, the story of his granddaddy's gambling habit and his grandmother Berenice's confession that she stashed thousands of dollars cash inside the whalebone model of an old whale ship. Most in the bar, within earshot this night, took no notice of Max's ramblings.

However, a young deckie called Mick listened with interest; for the simple reason he was best mates with young Mason Swinburne, Max's ex-deckhand whom Max had fired.

'I know that ship,' Mason told Mick later. 'I've seen photos of it. Max showed me once.'

'Yeh, and I heard the stupid bastard tell Bill that he swapped it.'

'Swapped it?'

'Yeh, he gave it to some magistrate what got him off the hook for the abalone shit he was doin'.'

Mason shook his head. 'What a stupid bastard eh?'

'So this magistrate bloke wouldn't know about the money, would 'e?'

'I doubt it.'

'You thinkin' what I'm thinkin'?'

'What, bust into this magistrate's joint?'

'Why not?'

'Gotta find out who he is first.'

'Can't be that hard. You up for it?'

'Jesus Mick, I dunno. A bloody magistrate?'

'Think about it.'

***

The next morning…

At 8AM, as arranged, antique restorer Jacopo Moretti called in to see Stanley at his Harrington Street address, before the curator left for work at the museum. He was here to show Stanley the *doctored* Duterrau painting, *Wild Man of Van Diemen's Land*, before he took it to the auctioneers for the house sale in Bellerive tomorrow. Stanley was impressed. Jacopo had touched up the valuable artwork with light watercolours, easy to remove later revealing the original oil. This of course was to disguise it, make it look like an average painting by an amateur. In the process it would be legally assessed by the auctioneers and placed in an auction with other framed pieces of *general tack* for a legitimate sale. Jacopo would buy the items, collect a receipt, *et voilà*, they would legally own what was a stolen painting.

'Good luck,' Stanley collected his coat, ready for work.

'I have sometheen interesteen here,' Jacopo took the folded pound note found in the model ship from his wallet. 'What ees thees? Ees it worth moneys?'

Stanley held up the green one-pound note. 'Hmm, where did you get this?'

Jacopo explained the model ship and how he came to be repairing it. 'Three hundred and forty-four moneys all together I count.'

Stanley whistled. 'You've hit the jackpot my friend.'

'Jackpot?'

'You're rich my friend. Well sort of. Let's go see what this one is worth.'

The Italian wore a broad smile and followed his friend to his study, housing his extensive library.

'Now. Let me see,' Stanley cast an eye over his coin catalogues. 'Here, Renniks Australian Coin and Banknote Values, the latest issue 1995.'

'Will it be in there?'

'Of course. Here we are.' Stanley ran a finger down the page and cross referenced with the catalogue. 'My, you have chosen a beauty Jacky.'

'Si?'

'There.' Stanley pointed to the page. '1953 Type 32S, HC Coombs, Roland Wilson one pound … and yours just happens to be a star note.'

'Star note?'

'Yes. Any note found faulty in the mint was replaced by a new note but using the same serial number. These notes had a star after the serial number and guess what?'

'What?'

'They are rare and sought after by collectors.'

'How much moneys? Does book say?'

'There, read it for yourself.'

'Five hundred dollars!'

'In that condition yes. If it wasn't folded and creased it would be worth more. Condition is everything to collectors.'

'I fold thees.'

'Oh Jacky, Jacky, you must never do that. You must look after them. Look, I've got to get to work, come over later with the lot and we'll go through them. I'm guessing you have twenty or thirty thousand dollars' worth.'

That evening the two men pored over the cache of stashed notes together and, for a reasonable commission, Stanley agreed to *move* them through the better numismatic auction houses in Melbourne and Sydney. Moral ownership was discussed briefly. Very briefly. Both men agreed they needed the money more than the dodgy magistrate. However, this was a windfall for Jacopo in particular and he wanted time to consider his prospects. Both men were wily, and shrewd and Stanley decided it best to give his friend time, and then together they would make a small fortune.

Jacopo returned home around nine. He listened at Eleanora's bedroom door. She snored. If Mrs Benetti next door was unavailable to look after Eleanora, Jacopo only left the house for short spells at a time when she slept or, rarely, he locked her in her room. Jacopo felt pleased with himself. He returned to the living room where the ship model was being restored and, taking Stanley's advice, he stacked the old banknotes methodically, placing them in a plastic sheath and returned them to their hiding place; hidden at the bottom of a stack of outdated Italian magazines where the banknotes would be pressed neatly, like his wife would press wildflowers in the old days.

***

Next day early afternoon…

Jacopo waited in the side lane of the weatherboard house in Bellerive, an Eastern Shore suburb of Hobart, where the house contents auction was held. He was biting his nails; a stupid habit he knew, but since he gave up smoking some time ago, he often found he was subconsciously chewing his nails to the quick. He had arrived at the house auction well before item 876 was due to go under the hammer and at a hundred items per hour being the auctioneer's average, he had plenty of time to enjoy the vista across the River Derwent to the city and its towering Mount Wellington backdrop.

Jacopo pulled his flat cap down over his eyes, anxious that no one working with Howard's Auction House would recognise him as the man bidding on items that he himself had entered in the auction. Looking about he hadn't recognised any of the administration staff who were there on the day he dropped off five boxes; except for one of the young attendants. Four of his boxes were antique carpentry oddities, like turned chair legs surplus to requirement and one was the box of odd framed family portraits, junk really, the sort of box one would expect to find in an abandoned attic; excepting this box contained the touched up (disguised) Duterrau portrait of the Tasmanian aboriginal.

Jacopo tore a fingernail free and cursed his painful habit. It was time. His boxes were at the tail end of the auction, with all the other junk. It was also where dealers knew there were bargains to be had. Looking about nervously, Jacopo joined the thirty odd punters remaining, standing shoulder to shoulder on the back porch.

'Lot 871,' the auctioneer called out. 'Box of sundries. Do we have ten dollars?'

'Two,' someone started the bid. Within seconds it was knocked down for six dollars. *Good* the Italian thought. *Everything's going to plan.*

Lot 876 sold for fourteen dollars. Jacopo couldn't have been happier. Pushing back through the crowd he paid cash at the auctioneer's cashier desk set up in the living room and returned for his box. But Lot 876 was a box of sundry crockery, china and a mantel clock!

'Where ees 876?' he asked the attendant, who cleared his receipt.

'That's it.'

'No! This ees …'

'876. It says so on the label.'

'But this ees not 876. This ees rub-bish.'

'It's all rubbish mate.'

Jacopo was starting to panic. 'But 876 … eet was frames and pictures.'

'Look. That box there is marked 876. You must have made a mistake.'

'No!' Jacopo shouted before realising he was drawing attention to himself. 'No,' he repeated softly through grinding teeth. 'There has been mix-up. The numbers … they have been mixed. Or switch even.'

'Now why would anyone want to do that?'

Jacopo had a sudden thought. 'Where's 875 or … or 877?'

'Gone mate.'

'What you say, gone?'

'Some bloke took them.'

'When?'

'When you were at the office I reckon.'

'Who was this?'

'I can't say. You'll have to ask the office. But they won't tell yer. It's a privacy issue mate.'

What's the big deal anyway? Say, aren't you the bloke that brought those boxes here the other day?'

Jacopo rushed to the office desk. At first they flatly refused, but when they saw how upset the old Italian man was, and the fact that it was a dealer who had bought lot 876, they relented. 'Birdwhistle Antiques,' the cashier said. 'In ...'

'Si si,' Jacopo called over his shoulder rushing off down the front steps. 'I know eet.'

***

Earlier that morning...

Magistrate Christian Winterbourne stood at his Mona Street, Battery Point letterbox. He wore his tartan wool dressing gown, matching slippers, and studied the two photos of himself with Chastity, naked and compromised. He was horrified ... No! He was mortified.

He felt his face blush like a steaming towel had smothered him. His heart rate rose and he had a sick feeling in the pit of his stomach with the taste of bile in his mouth. He sensed anxiety and then anger. The photos were of outstanding professional quality and there was no arguing that it was he, 'respected' magistrate Christian Yardley Winterbourne, who was thrusting Chastity hard from behind, with his mouth open, tongue protruding in ecstasy and eyes rolled back in his head in his moment of gratification. And it was not even a flattering image of himself. He looked old, short, fat and desperate. With the camera hidden behind the bed head the shot was National Geographic quality.

Chastity! How could you?

Truth was, Chastity was unaware the camera was there also.

But Chastity was only a tiny part of his problem. Some time ago Christian had let his guard down and – blaming alcohol – he had had a liaison with a younger girl. 'She is eighteen,' Mareike assured the magistrate. He knew better.

Why, the young woman had been before him a year earlier on soliciting charges and he knew her to be sixteen, then. Now, looking red-faced at these photos, he was certain Mareike had others of him and the girl.

At 9AM on the Monday Christian checked the up and coming court hearings, knowing he had no choice but to comply with Mareike's demands. He must be the magistrate to hear her case and smartly give her a slap on the wrist with a minimal fine.

**

Bribing Magistrate Ashley Hensley was fraught with danger. Christian often played cards at Hadley's Hotel in Murray Street with Hensley and other magistrates in their longer lunch adjournments. Hensley was good company, great for making legal contacts, offering favours for a favour, keeping Christian in the loop. So, Christian didn't have a problem exchanging bench appointments in the courtroom over the Mareike hearing. It only cost him dinner for two at the Revolving Restaurant at the Wrest Point Casino. Citing an awkward schedule as his reason for swapping hearings, Hensley seemed unperturbed. But the man wasn't stupid, and he graciously accepted the dinner for two; Hensley's wife would be thrilled.

**

Late that afternoon…

Two things occurred in antique restorer Jacopo Moretti's life. He had turned sixty-two today and now he had to face Stanley Smart's blistering rage when he explained that he had lost the painting.

'What do you mean, someone else bought the painting?'

Jacopo couldn't stop biting at his fingernails, tearing at them like it was self-flagellation, punishing himself for failing his friend. Although the friendship was being seriously tested right now.

'How could you? Such a simple task? You idiot.'

Jacopo twitched. 'The dealer … he swap numbers on the box.'

'Damn it, didn't you tell the auctioneers?'

'He had already paid and left with the boxes.'

'Boxes?'

'He bid on two.'

'He must have seen the Duterrau for what it was. Jesus Christ Jacopo! What dealer?'

'Birdwhistle Antiques in …'

'Yes, yes I know Birdwhistle Antiques in Campbell Street … Jock Birdwhistle … dodgy beggar, always has been. What did he pay for it?'

'Eight dollars.'

'Eight dollars! Jesus Christ.' Stanley turned on the cabinetmaker who was a similar height; five-feet-five inches. He stabbed the man in the chest with his finger. 'You get to Campbell Street, now. You hear me. Now! Do whatever it takes to get that painting back …'

'But …'

'Now I said.'

***

Jacopo sat in his Ford one-tonner flat tray and brooded. Never had he been so humiliated. And to make matters worse he had a parking ticket slapped on his windscreen for overstaying the meter directly outside Stanley's home. Harrington Street was like that, always parking inspectors creeping about near the CBD.

Mamma Mia. He sensed someone watching him and looked across at the front window of the old Funeral Directors Mortuary. Stanley was watching him from the window, saw the parking ticket and grinned. Angry with the world, Jacopo pulled out into the traffic and headed for Campbell Street.

***

Birdwhistle's Antique shop had been a paint wholesaler from the '50s, now converted into a retail shop. The original shop itself hadn't changed much in layout, with a solid sliding fire door between the showroom and the storage room at the back where originally volatile oil-based paints were stored. The sign on the front door of the antique shop read *Open.* Jacopo locked his one-tonner, fed the meter (with extra coins) and approached the antique shop.

But in that short time the sign had been reversed to read *Sorry, we're closed.* It was still swinging on its string. Jacopo pushed his face against the glass, shielding his eyes from the reflected late afternoon sun, just in time to catch movement at the rear of the premises. The back door opened and closed. Jacopo hurried around the corner to a side lane that led to the rear of the shop.

'Signor Birdwhistle!' he called out as the hundred and twenty-kilo dealer squeezed behind the wheel of his own vehicle, a Kombi van he used for delivering furniture. Jacopo noted more rust patches than paint.

'Can't you see I'm closed?' the dealer shouted back, short of breath.

'Un minuto Signor.'

Birdwhistle slammed the driver's door shut and twisted the key in the ignition. The 1975 Kombi coughed to life and a black cloud of exhaust drifted wraithlike by Jacopo. Jacopo stepped in front of the van.

'I told yer I'm closed, now bugger off.'

The dealer was a rough beggar who graded himself up the social ladder from second-hand dealer to the more elite title of antique dealer.

'Ees important Signor.'

'Are you deaf? I'm closed.'

'I just want to talk, si … about two boxes you buy at auction today.'

'Dunno what yer talkin' about.'

'Two boxes of pictures and frames.'

'I haven't been to no auction …'

'No true Signor Birdwhistle. You buy two boxes at Bellerive auction today.'

'Listen mate, move it or I'll run yer over.'

'That box you buy is my box.'

'Piss off out of it!' Jock Birdwhistle revved the engine. Another nimbus of black floated down the lane.

Jacopo pushed out his chest. 'I want my box!' Jacopo, ever stubborn, wasn't shifting from in front of the van. 'You change numbers on box. I know this true.'

The dealer revved the engine and released the brake slightly. The van jerked forward enough to frighten Jacopo who jumped back but stubbornly held his position in front of the Kombi.

Jacopo fired up. 'I get police, I tell you true bastard!'

Jock Birdwhistle wasn't to be threatened by a five-foot five Italian almost old enough to be his father. He pulled on the handbrake, slipped the gears into neutral and climbed awkwardly out from behind the wheel, taking Jacopo by the lapels. He slammed Jacopo's back against the grill. 'Listen yer old fart. Don't you dare threaten me.'

'I pay!' Jacopo managed to gasp meekly, two giant fat hands securing him. 'I buy box and all inside from you. Give back moneys. I give you one hundred dollar.'

Jock swung the Italian bodily, throwing him against the rear wall where Jacopo slid into a pile of pizza boxes and McDonalds packaging amongst other garbage awaiting pickup. 'You crazy wog,' he wheezed, short of breath. 'Stay out of me way.'

Birdwhistle squashed back behind the wheel and revved the engine. 'Go!' he yelled out the driver's window. 'Piss off before I really lose me temper.'

Jacopo was no match against this giant man's aggression, physically. But mentally, well that was another game altogether ...

Fat bastardo.

Brushing himself down he shot the angry dealer one last look and returned to his pick-up on the main street. Seconds later he heard the Kombi bounce out of the rear lane, into the side street and drive away. Certain all was clear Jacopo returned to the backyard. He tried the door. Locked, naturally. Cupping hands over his eyes he pressed up against a rear window. The solid sliding fire door had been left open in the dealer's haste and Jacopo could see into the showroom. He ran a keen eye over the stock. The antique shop's wares were eclectic; everything from Victorian porcelain to enamel signs, old relics from the whaling days to Nazi memorabilia. Sure enough, he could clearly see the two boxes just inside the door – boxes he had dressed up and put up for auction himself – but there was no sign of the Duterrau. Further along the lane Jacopo removed the glass louvres from the toilet window, fetched boxes for support and with a measure of difficulty, he climbed inside.

Jacopo had entered a workshop storeroom with its long work bench, shelves of cleaning fluids for French polishing, tools for restoration work, and even a generator with drums of petrol. The wily Italian hurried to the boxes – his boxes – and yes, the Duterrau *was* missing. With the nose for such endeavours, Jacopo started searching the shop; opening cupboards, looking behind furniture, after all, it couldn't be too far away and if it was here, he would find it.

CHAPTER SIX

Earlier in the day…

Max the fisherman's estranged wife Verity Shreeve sat behind the wheel of her XJ-S grand tourer Jaguar sports car and observed the rather choice hunk of eye-candy weeding around the rose bushes in the front garden of Liverpool Street's *Salon Rouge* bordello. *Typical I suppose,* she thought to herself, *for a brothel to employ some stud to do the garden.*

She checked the torn sheet of note paper on which friend Pammie had jotted down the address and a name. *Yes, this was definitely the right place. Such a lovely old home too, what a pity.* Verity knew the business to be called *Salon Rouge* but there was no sign swinging in the breeze. But from where Verity sat out front in her Jaguar, she could just read a brass nameplate of the old family home, *Currawong.* And Verity didn't need to check the slut's name written on Pammie's notepaper. How could she forget *Barbie?*

'*Currawong,'* she hissed under her breath, 'should be *Slut Palace.'*

Verity laughed at her little joke, speared a Dunhill gold tip from packet to mouth, clamping it tightly with candy apple red lips and hit the automatic window button for fresh air.

Rory was aware he was being watched and looked up in time to see an attractive woman, a peroxide blonde, a little older than him sitting in a Jag. As he looked on, she sparked a cigarette with a gold lighter and drew in a cloud of smoke … when their eyes met. Rory was hardly subtle, staring back. The woman jerked her head in a fashion that ordered, *get here.*

'Can I help you?' Rory asked from the gate.

'This is *Salon Rouge,*' Verity asked. 'Right?'

'Yes.'

'You work here? Stupid question, course you do.' Verity hooked her cat-eye framed shades to her forehead, showing off over-done mascara. 'Do you know if a Barbie works here?'

'Sure.'

'*Sure,* she does work here?'

'What do you mean?'

It was about now Verity recognised the man wasn't the brightest star in the galaxy. 'I mean … handsome,' and Verity flashed a smile flickering long eyelashes, 'does a girl named Barbie work here?'

'Barbie. Sure she does.' Rory stepped through the gate. 'You lookin' for a girl … for company like?'

Verity thought a moment. This might work in her favour. 'Maybe.'

Rory started to pull off his gardening gloves. 'I'll go see what time she starts,' he said, looking towards the mansion.

'No!' Verity said sharply, before softening her tone again. 'Not yet. What's your name?'

'My name?'

'Yes. What – is – your – name?'

'Why, I'm Rory missus.'

'I'm Pam.' Verity threw her cigarette onto the footpath and offered Rory her hand. He shook it limply. *Soft cock,* Verity judged the simpleton. *Soft cock and dumb fuck rolled into one. He could be useful.*

'Cool car,' Rory ran his un-gloved hand on the roof.

'You like it?'

'Very much. How much does a car like this cost?'

'A lot. Say, want to take a ride?'

'You're kiddin' me, right?'

Verity looked the hunk up and down, dropped the shades back into place and said. 'Hop in big boy.'

***

That evening in Harrington Street…

Museum Curator Stanley Smart carefully picked up the workings of the yellow gold ladies pocket watch from the crowded coffee table in the living room. The attractive Victorian solid gold half hunter style watch was in too many pieces for Stanley's peace of mind. He had always fancied himself as a watch repairer, and had actually successfully repaired a few, but this little gem was causing him grief and he knew he would have to put it aside; take this one to a watchmaker, if he wanted it in saleable condition.

With the pieces stowed in a cigar box under the table, Stanley lifted his coin albums onto the glass top. He had six in all, and each album was almost full of coins in *fine* to *very fine* or preferably *mint* condition. Thanks to his ruse at the museum. *Fools*, he thought. He had covered all bases. He could never be caught. It had been so easy over the many years. Scour the auction catalogues for rare coins in average condition – albeit rare and valuable – for up and coming auctions, purchase said coins, and exchange with the same coins in the museum's collection in better condition. It took audacity and determination, and Stanley had both.

He opened his folder dedicated to gold coins and studied his collection of Australian sovereigns and half sovereigns. The gold put a sparkle in his eye. What was it about gold that had such power over mankind? He loosened the opening of the empty top left sleeve; one of thirty–six coin sleeves per acid free plastic page in the folder. From his shirt pocket he took the tissue wrapped Adelaide One Pound coin, unwrapping it and holding it reverently by the rim only, so as not to pollute the gold with body oils. He closed one eye and lowered the coin expert's Loupe magnifier over the coin's date. 1852. Superb. Rare. In *very fine* condition. Value … oh … say eight thousand dollars at the right auction. The one in poorer condition Stanley had purchased at a Melbourne coin auction three years ago cost him a fraction of that. Content with the inspection, the coin was delicately wriggled into its pride of place; first coin in the page of Australian gold coins. Only now did Stanley dare pick up his glass and drink his Lindeman's Shiraz, or Chateau de Cardboard, as his contemporaries joked when they caught him ordering the cask house wine when he was out.

'Cheers!' Stanley saluted the albums.

Suddenly the front doorbell shrieked.

Hastily the albums were put into a cupboard. The curator moved to the front room where he pulled back the curtain ever so slightly to peer through the barred window. He could barely make out the back of a man standing at the front door.

The bell shrieked a second time.

Stanley opened the door to a tall thin man in his sixties. The man was wearing a false hairpiece that did nothing to improve his already unfortunate appearance. Dressed in tweed with a tweed trilby hat, he appeared *terribly* English.

'Stanley!' the man said in an undeniable cockney accent and broke into a huge grin. 'Stanley Smart ya old rascal. Look at yer. Same old puppy dog eyes. Yer shrunk a bit with age but.'

Stanley pinched his lips, accentuating his hush puppy jowls even more. He narrowed his eyes cautiously.

'Yer don't remember me huh?' the stranger said. 'I'm 'Ryan.'

'R-Ryan! Oh Christ … Ryan!' Stanley realised he never did know the man's other name or whether Ryan was his Christian or family name.

'Aye,' Ryan laughed. 'It's me, mate, Oh-Christ-Ryan.'

Immediately the connection between Ryan and the stolen Duterrau portrait of the Tasmanian aborigine slapped Stanley in the face. Hard.

'Well are yer gonna invite me in or let me stand outside like a stale bottle o' piss.'

'Sorry … yes … ah, come in.'

The old art thief pushed past Stanley and stood agape while Stanley jerked the door free of loose carpet to close it.

'Jesus mate, have yer got enough junk?' the visitor chuckled, gaping about.

'I'm a bit of a collector, well you know that, always was.'

'Bit of a collector! This place is a tip.' Suddenly Ryan realised his humour sounded like an insult. 'A nice tip that is.'

Stanley showed his visitor through to the living room and cleared him a chair. 'Sit.'

Ryan hooked his trilby over the back of the chair and sat heavily.

Stanley asked, 'Drink?'

'What'ya got?'

'Red wine, Shiraz.'

'Fine.'

'I heard you were gaoled in Cairo.'

'I was mate.' Ryan pulled a suitable face. 'Not an experience I would recommend to me worst enemy.'

'I should imagine'

'Fifteen fuckin' years.'

'Then I haven't seen you for … it must be twenty years.'

'More mate, more.'

Stanley poured drinks and Ryan sculled his like it was nectar of the gods. He leant forward in his chair and, holding his glass under the plastic tap, he squirted himself another glass of cheap wine, right to the brim. 'Look Stan, I'll not beat about the bush. I'm short o' cash. Real short.'

'I'm not exactly flush myself …'

'Don't panic mate. I'm not here to squeeze yer. I've come for me painting.'

'P-painting?'

'Yer, me Duterrau. It's time to sell. It's been well over twenty bloody years and I have a fence who'll give me sixty grand for it.'

'Sixty gr … thousand!'

'Yer. Not bad huh. He's got a buyer for it already, a collector what collects Australian Colonial art. He'll probably get a hundred for it. But truth is I'm skint. I spent me last two grand flying out here to collect the painting and do the deal. Then I'm off back to Blighty.'

Silence.

'Well?' Ryan was edgy. 'Where is it?' Stanley looked at this art thief, a man who had spent fifteen years in one of the world's toughest prisons, a man street-wise in London with underground contacts world-wide … and panicked.

Ryan became wary of the silence. 'Well?'

Stanley sucked a deep breath in. His chest rose and he exhaled nervously. 'I haven't got it.'

'What? What do yer mean you 'aven't got it?'

'I haven't got it. I did have it … up to recently I had it. Then I gave it to a colleague to sell …'

'You what?'

'You left it here over twenty years ago,' Stanley blurted. 'For all I knew you were dead.'

'Dead! You'll be fuckin' dead in a minute mate. So where is it now? Who's – got – my – painting?'

Stanley wanted none of it. Jacopo lost the painting; he could deal with this … this angry Englishman Ryan. He gave him the name Jacopo Moretti and mentioned the auction mishap, the name of an antique dealer named Jock

Birdwhistle and how as far as he knew the Italian may have retrieved the painting.

'This 'ere Jocko … Jacopo, whatever his fuckin' name is. Where can I find him?'

Stanley didn't hesitate. He gave Ryan Jacopo's North Hobart address immediately and hooked the security chain on the front door lock the moment he departed.

***

Sometime during that same day…

Phoebe Crow, bordello Madam Mareike's competitor, was livid when she heard the news. Mareike was set free. *She destroyed my cottage and got off with a fine.* Her residing Magistrate, Christian Winterbourne, threw the case out of court for lack of evidence. Would her rival never be punished?

***

A day later…

Magistrate Christian Yardley Winterbourne felt vulnerable. Deceived. Especially by Chastity. And he felt awkwardly alone. He also felt anger and vindication. He wanted retribution. But for the moment he decided to dabble in art, make some serious money.

The first chance he had, Christian crated the Tom Roberts, now framed, and flew to Melbourne where he presented the Australian masterpiece at Shadlocks, art auctioneers.

Mr Robert Singer, the appraiser for paintings, was impressed. The Tom Roberts, titled The Miners, was unrecorded in any previous sale, the true owner having purchased it privately twenty years earlier. After much deliberation Singer suggested the painting should be put up for auction at a starting price of fifteen thousand dollars, adding that he was confident it would sell for over twenty thousand. Christian was happy. Art dealer Goldman in Hobart had been right on the money (also suggesting it may sell for as much as thirty thousand) and Christian only paid ten thousand for it.

With the next big art auction scheduled for only weeks away, Christian flew home with hand luggage only.

A few evenings later

The magistrate took a call from art dealer, Neville Goldman. 'Have you been watching television?' the dealer asked him.

'No. Why?'

'There was advertisement on TV for the upcoming *Crime Stoppers* and I'm certain the Tom Roberts you have in your possession is being featured as stolen property.'

'What?' Christian knew of the television series *Australian Crime Stoppers*, but he had never watched the show.

'I think your painting is stolen.'

'Impossible.'

'Look, I called the television studio and they said the show is scheduled for Friday night at seven. I think you better watch it.'

Christian was dumbfounded. How could he be so gullible? He thanked the dealer and asked him to keep this news to himself. Neville Goldman agreed, for the meantime at least.

Crime Stoppers, Friday at 7PM.

Today's only Monday.

Christian took a card from his wallet. He read A. B. Kenning. Chartered Accountant and phone number ...

He dialled the number. '*Thank you for calling Alfred Kenning ...*'

'Now listen here Kenning ...' Christian barked into the receiver before realising it was a recorded message.

'*I cannot come to the phone right now but please leave a message after the beep.*'

Beep.

'This is Winterbourne here, call me ASAP. It's urgent.' Christian flipped the card to where Susan Kirby's phone number had been handwritten by Kenning. He dialled.

This is a Telecom announcement; this number has been disconnected.

Christian felt a sudden chill. Buying stolen property, especially valuable masterpieces, would not sit well with his already shaky reputation.

And it was not just the one we're talking about. It's eight!

The magistrate picked up the phone and made a third call; this time to Qantas reservations.

Next morning back in Melbourne …

Art appraiser Robert Singer of Shadlocks Art Auctioneers wasn't happy. Not happy at all. 'Look, the catalogue is at the printers,' he lied. 'It is too late to withdraw your painting from the auction.'

'At the printers? Already?'

'Yes. We need to get catalogues out to prospective buyers early, you must understand.'

'Well that's just too bad I'm afraid. I have flown over to collect the painting. Now. So if you would kindly fetch it I shall be out of your way.'

'Even if I suggest such a sought-after piece might go for as high as thirty thousand?'

'Yes. It must travel home with me, now.'

'May I ask why you are doing this?'

'Personal reasons I would rather not discuss. Now would you please fetch the painting.'

Robert Singer sent staff for the crated painting, but alarm bells were ringing in his head. He had been around art and sales for two decades and knew when he smelt a rat.

***

That Friday evening around 7PM…

Christian sat in front of the telly in his Mona Street mansion. He couldn't eat any dinner. To make matters worse art dealers Kenning and Kate Kirby had disappeared off the radar. It looked like he had been the victim of an elaborate con. Then, as plain as the nose on Christian's face, the stolen Tom Roberts on the television show *Crime Stoppers* turned out to be the same painting he had smartly recovered from Shadlocks. Christian switched off the television and poured himself a large cognac. He was sickened, yet he wasn't totally surprised.

Although content in his own mind that he had retrieved the painting, he knew he wasn't out of hot water yet. After all, he was still in possession of stolen property. If Singer at Shadlocks watched the television show, then he was in trouble, for he harboured no doubt, the art expert would call the police.

***

Several evenings earlier that week in his North Hobart workshop…

Antique restorer Jacopo Moretti was busy and deafened by the buzz of his wood lathe. The earmuffs helped, but the shadow that twitched across the wall in front of him had him turn sharply, startled. A man dressed in tweed with a matching tweed trilby and with his hands stuffed into his pockets had been watching the Italian cabinetmaker spinning his magic with a length of cedar, with undeniable interest. Ryan – the man looking to retrieve his missing Duterrau portrait *Wild man of Van Diemen's Land, Wurragunna* – always appreciated watching a professional at work.

'Who are you?' Jacopo said sharply.

'Sorry, didn't mean to startle yer mate, but yer gate was open, and I heard the lathe. And I was standin' here mesmerised by yer talent old boy.'

Old boy? Who is this?

'What you want?'

'You've been a hard man to catch mate. I've been trying to find you 'ere for a day or so.'

Jacopo felt uncomfortable with this intruder. 'What you want I say?'

'Oh, I was just admiring yer work … Signor Moretti is it not?'

'Si. And you?'

'Ryan.'

'Well what can I do for you Signor Ryan?'

'I'm here to collect me painting.'

'Painting?'

'Yes. An oil painting titled *Wild man of Van Diemen's Land, Wurragunna*, by the artist Duterrau. You have it put away safely for me I have been told.'

Jacopo had had enough malice for one day. He studied Ryan briefly and saw nothing but trouble. 'I have not got thees painting.'

'Oh, but that's not what I was told by Signor Smart.'

'I tell you true. I have not … thees painting.'

Ryan sighed, took his hands out of his pockets, picked up a hammer and walked towards the worried Italian. 'Is true, yes,' Jacopo said anxiously. 'I no have painting …'

The hammer came down hard on the workbench. 'Our mutual friend Signor Smart said you went to fetch the painting back from this dodgy geezer, what's 'is name, Jock, yeh that's it, Jock fuckin' Birdwhistle. So where is it?'

'Signor Birdwhistle difficult man, he still got it …' The hammer came down fast connecting with Jacopo's thumb. The Italian screamed out in pain.

'Oh, that's gotta hurt,' Ryan said, his face now close to Jacopo's with breath stinking of cheap wine. 'You fuckin' carpenters should be more careful. Now where's me painting?'

'Please, I don't know Signor.' The hammer crashed to the bench once more, but Jacopo jerked his hand free just in time.

'Thees man Jock is trouble. He say he no have painting. He say he no change numbers on boxes at auction. He tell lies and more lies. I tell you true Signor.'

The fear in Jacopo's eyes was real. Ryan knew when a man was lying or not. He had plenty of experience in an Egyptian prison. He leant over the short Italian and stared into Jacopo's eyes with piercing intensity. Finally, he said, 'Where is this bastard, Jock Birdwhistle.'

'Birdwhistle Antiques,' Jacopo spoke through tears and sweat. 'In Campbell Street near fire station.'

Ryan was pleased with himself as he walked down Jacopo's drive. Who says violence doesn't pay? He learnt the hard way in the Egyptian prison. Jacopo looked at his thumb. The hit was either a bad shot or carefully aimed, he wasn't certain. But with any luck, all he would lose was his thumbnail. He'd had enough for one night. Jacopo switched off his equipment, slid the workshop door closed, locking it. Before retiring, he checked down the driveway, there was no sign of the intruder, but as he turned to walk towards the back door a red Jaguar sports car pulled into the curb, across his entrance. Thinking this was his assailant's ride, he crept around the opposite side of his house and hid in the front garden. The driver was an attractive blonde, early thirties, smoking a cigarette and apparently waiting for someone. Seconds later Rory appeared. The passenger door opened, and the simpleton slid into the car. Jacopo couldn't believe what he was witnessing. *Rory you … how you say in English, dark horse … or gigolo, si si, gigilo.* Jacopo never thought he would see this day.

***

Verity, Max the fisherman's wife, watched Rory hurdle the picket fence with a spring of anticipation in his step and the hot flushes returned; that delightful shiver that started below terminating in crimson cheeks. Rory looked great; tight black jeans, black t-shirt hugging his toned body, oiled slicked blonde hair, black boots. For a simpleton he dressed well this evening. Although, to be honest, Verity wasn't sure about the makeup and homemade jewellery. The door slammed shut and the high heel stamped on the gas. 'You're all dressed up,' Verity said over the throaty motor changing first gear to second. 'Where do you think you're going? Out to dinner?'

Rory tightened his seat belt and tried to smile. He never thought he'd see this day. Riding in a XJ-S grand tourer Jaguar with a beautiful woman, like a model from a Bond movie. Yeh, that was it, she was out of a Bond movie … *And he was James Bond.*

***

Not long after…

Antique dealer Jock Birdwhistle sat in front of the telly in his flat above his Campbell Street antique shop. He was accompanied by a family sized Domino's Pizza, one with the lot, no anchovies, extra bacon and triple cheese. The box sat open, steaming, on his large portioned lap. His favourite television show, *Starsky and Hutch,* had just started airing on TV. Jock vacuumed half his litre container of coke in one slurp and was thinking he should have bought two litres when he thought he heard glass breaking, downstairs in the shop. He shut down the volume on the TV remote with a greasy thumb and listened. Nothing. His natural state of general laziness enticed him to continue eating; his *pizza was getting cold for Christ's sake.* But the thought of that crazy wog earlier in the day hounded him. For starters he had a suspicion the bloke had climbed in through his downstairs toilet window, but nothing seemed to be missing. Besides he had hidden the Duterrau painting in a blackwood wardrobe in the saleroom where no one would ever look.

Would they?

Damn it! For peace of mind he thought he had better check downstairs.

Jock pulled on his slippers, tightened his dressing gown cord about his mammoth girth and descended the stairs; the creaking treads heralding his passage. On the ground floor he rolled back the fire door to the shop and squeezed by chests of drawers and a pine dresser and entered his display room. The shop was in darkness. Yet early evening streetlights leaked through gaps in the blinds, casting a weak illumination over his stock. He looked to the windows first and the glass panels in the front door. Everything seemed in order, but for a man of huge proportions he had the nose of a truffle hound. He sniffed the air. Yes, there was a stale smell of body odour and cheap wine. Jock turned to retrace his steps and switch on the lights when he trod in broken glass.

Jesus!

***

Elsewhere, that evening…

Conman Alfred Kenning thoughts led to him packing his suitcases in his Moonah short term rental. *Be ready to scarper.* He had seen the advertisement for the upcoming television show, *Australian Crime Stoppers* but chose not to watch the program, knowing he would have to move interstate, again, ASAP. But he had one other problem to sort out first. *Cat burglar to the rich*, Ivano Stipanov, was on his way to Hobart to see him personally and Kenning owed Ivano two thousand dollars from the paintings deal, to be paid when the magistrate paid. Now he had the cash and knew better than to rip off a colleague thief. Besides, Kenning's contacts back in Melbourne also informed him that the police were looking for Ivano. Kenning would just have to sit it out a few days, and this made him most uncomfortable.

***

Back in Melbourne…

Ivano Stipanov worked on Plan B. He checked out of his motel and into a cheap pub, The Greyhound in Williamstown. He would have to careful, very careful. The Andrea Mancini apartment job had gone extremely well, and it was tempting to do more work in Melbourne. But clearly it was too risky. The cops would have him profiled by now. He would be able to lay low for a few days at the most. Ivano only went out after dark. He bought himself a pastrami sandwich and a bottle of scotch before retiring to his twenty-seven-dollar room at the pub with its tacky and sticky red shag pile carpet and stained bedspread.

***

Munching hungrily on his supper, he studied the jewellery from the Mancini heist, spread out on the bed. It was too hot for now; he would have to let it cool a year or so before fencing it. After his third scotch he reminisced on how far he had come. He remembered his early jobs with a wry smile. It was discipline that had put him at the top of the game. He recalled working for a parcel delivery firm and how simple it was to case properties legitimately. On delivery he would ask to use the bathroom and while inside he would unlock the window for later or ask for a glass of water while checking the layout. Sometimes he would put pizza flyers in letter boxes and return three days later. If the flyer was still in the letterbox, then there was a good chance the owners were out of town. Always knock first. If someone opened the door just ask for directions or pretend you have the wrong house. When inside always check the bathroom cupboard, the freezer, sock drawer and bedside tables. People thought they were clever hiding their cash, but Ivano knew better. Watch for dogs and nosey neighbours. During the day carry a clipboard or better still dress like a gardener and carry a rake. Ivano smiled at his past work and took another stiff drink.

During the day Ivano learnt through a few phone calls that Alfred Kenning had earlier managed to move eight paintings from the total of thirteen he stole from the private collector Benjamin Braithwaite, the wealthy industrialist from Toorak – living less than a kilometre from the botched *Stoneville* job.

Multi-millionaire Braithwaite was an avid collector of quality Australian art, with over forty masterpieces decorating the walls of *Ville de Braithwaite*, as he called his ten-bedroom mansion. One year earlier, to the week, Ivano had relieved the man of thirteen of these works of art, including the Tom Roberts, immediately fencing them to his contact Alfred Kenning, working for the moment from Tasmania. And Ivano's own spies had recently informed him that Kenning had finally moved several of the stolen paintings to a gullible magistrate in Hobart.

It was time to collect.

Ivano paid a visit to his safe deposit box in South Melbourne where he had an account under the name Joseph Bevan. Here he had stashed nearly four thousand dollars in cash for such an emergency. He took one thousand cash to tide him over until he collected from Kenning. Although Ivano lost several pieces of silverware from the Toorak job when groundsman Saunders slashed his backpack with the poker, Ivano still had some choice pieces to move – including jewellery. He left this behind in the safe deposit along with the Mancini *Highview* heist, before purchasing a one-way ticket on the Empress of Tasmania. Confident that the police would not suspect that he would travel south across Bass Strait, Ivano sailed for Tasmania on the ferry.

Plan B. Melbourne to Devonport. An overnight sail.

Ivano chose the cheaper ticket, sleeping upright in a deckchair in the lounge. It was comfortable enough, except for the Browning Hi-Power 9-millimetre pistol he smuggled on board, poking him in the ribs. Ivano dreamt of sanctuary in Tasmania a few weeks, a month even, with the two thousand dollars owed by Kenning he could live well, albeit incognito. Hell, he might even do a job or two on the island, and then it would be *Plan C,* probably move to Brisbane.

On arrival at Tasmania's northern shore Ivano phoned Mr Kenning from a phone box in Devonport. His fence, Alfred Kenning, wasn't keen on meeting Ivano in person since the word was out that the police were looking for him, but too bad ... it was too late for that.

***

Two evenings earlier at Birdwhistle Antiques in Hobart...

Obese antique dealer Jock Birdwhistle trod on razor-sharp shards of glass. The glass penetrated his cheap slipper and he felt blood soak his foot. From what he could tell in the dark he had stepped on a broken cut-crystal fruit bowl. So, *he did hear glass break.* Suddenly Jock felt vulnerable. He reached for the light switch when a metal object slammed his wrist.

'I wouldn't be doing that mate,' a voice came from the shadows. 'If I was you.'

'Jesus Christ!' Jock shook his arm free; the pain was excruciating. Ryan stepped into the soft light and Birdwhistle recognised the intruder had one of his SS Nazi officer's dress daggers from the Nazi memorabilia cabinet. Although the blade was blunt, the point was like a needle.

'Who the hell are you?' Birdwhistle cried.

'It don't matter who I am mate. All you need to know is why I'm here.'

Jock recognised the accent as English, Cockney maybe. He turned to face his assailant, a tall slim, older man but with a sturdy build.

'I haven't got any cash,' he whimpered.

'I'm not here to rob you mate. I'm here to take what's mine.'

'What?'

'You have a painting that belongs to me.'

Jesus Christ! Not that bloody painting again, surely.

'I believe there was a little Italian geezer here a day or so ago looking for the same thing. Now I know 'e ain't got it and it's 'ere somewhere, so where is it?'

'Painting?' Birdwhistle smelt money. *That bloody painting's more valuable than I first thought.* 'What painting?'

Ryan grew impatient. 'Don't fuck with me pal,' he prodded Jock with the dagger. 'I'm not in any mood to stuff about.'

Stubbornly the antique dealer was evasive.

'I don't know what you …' he never finished the sentence. Ryan pressed the point into the flab of his grossly obese belly. 'Shit!' the dealer squealed. 'Please.'

'Where-is-me-fuckin'-painting?' Ryan articulated, prodding the fat man with each word. Jock panicked. Lashing out he took the dagger by the shaft, but he wasn't quick enough for the angry Englishman. Ryan pulled the blade free before thrusting it forward once more. What he intended as a threat to put the fear of god into the fat bastard turned out to be a savage and fatal stabbing straight into the heart. The needle-sharp point easily penetrated flab. Jock Birdwhistle squealed once more, expelled a last gasp and collapsed to the floor, his massive body instantly pooling in a widening puddle of his own blood.

'Oh Jesus!' Ryan watched on helplessly as the fat man bled profusely. He had never killed anyone before. He'd seen plenty of bloody violence in the Cairo prison, but nothing perpetrated by himself, not like this. In a state of panic, he checked the front door and window. All were secure. He listened at the bottom of the stairs where he noticed a television light flickering without sound but nothing untoward. There appeared to be no one about. Ryan crept up the stairs to the flat. *Starsky and Hutch* was on the telly and a fat tabby cat guarded a huge pizza, otherwise he was alone. Ryan searched the flat for the painting. Nothing. He hurried back to the shop and searched through cupboards and boxes. He checked the artworks hanging on the darkened shop walls. Nothing. There was no trace of the Duterrau. Ryan hurried back to where he had broken in through the jemmied back door near the workshop and storeroom, when he almost tripped over the generator. *Petrol! Yes, Jesus there was heaps of it, fifty litres at least.*

With great difficulty Ryan dragged the dealer by the feet to a clearing on the cement floor in the back room. Panicked by his action, he doused the body in petrol and splashed it about the rear of the premises, but flustered as he was, he had the peace of mind to slide the fire door closed, the better to concentrate the fire and destroy the body. Hopefully it would look an accident. Ryan poured a trail of the volatile fuel out the back door and down the lane, like he'd seen a trial of gunpowder in a pirate movie. For the first time in sometime, he was glad he was a smoker. Clicking his Zippo, he sheltered the flame with his hands, lowering it to the spillage. With a loud whoosh the flame ignited, shot the length of the driveway and exploded just inside the door. Empty handed, Ryan bolted into the night, horrified that everything had suddenly gone so pear shaped.

***

The morning after the antique shop fire…

Police Inspector Maddison Lovett stooped below the police barricade ribbon cordoning off the crime scene at Jock Birdwhistle's Antiques, stepping into a fug that stank of old sooty chimneys, petrol and burnt meat. '*At last,*' she thought, '*something I can sink my teeth into.*' Maddison had started to believe that returning to Hobart to live had been a mistake. Hobart was a little too tame for her liking after the rat race of Sydney she had left behind. But she had made the transfer south for her mother. The shop fire looked like an unfortunate accident until the firemen called the police with the news that burnt remains had been found in the wreckage of the burnt-out shop and an accelerant had been used. Petrol. Although the majority of the main shop showroom survived, the fire had been fierce at the rear.

'Good morning Inspector,' Senior Detective Landon Finch approached from the main damage. If anyone was keen to have Maddison back in town it was forty-nine-year-old Landon. He'd finished the police academy one year after Maddison and as young cops they had hit it off back then; even had a romance, as short lived as it was. On one occasion they went to Victoria together for the Sunbury Pop Festival; Landon dropped acid and vowed his undying love for Maddie, even to the point of proposing marriage. That had been over twenty years ago. But those were memories blurred with time. Now here they were, working together once more in middle-age.

'Morning Senior Detective,' Maddison returned the formal greeting, but their exchanged smiles were warm and familiar. Landon hadn't changed a great deal, so it seemed to Maddison. The quintessential tall, dark, handsome Aussie with the life-saver's physique and a jaw like a building block. Sure, he'd put on a couple of kilos, but Maddison guessed he'd still be buff with his shirt off. Maddison on the other hand had lost any puppy fat of the early seventies and had grown into a model mature woman. The chemistry lingered, like the essence of an expensive perfume hanging in a bedroom.

'Welcome to your first major crime scene in the big smoke,' Landon said.

'Big smoke, yeh right.'

Maddison pulled plastic covers over her Doc Martens and slipped her hands into skin-tight latex gloves. 'So, it's definitely a crime scene?'

'Definitely.'

'Walk me through.'

'Well, we have a rather unusual murder.' Landon stepped aside for Maddison to take her first look at what little remained of the body, a pile of ash between what appeared to be an incinerated workbench and the collapsed brick wall. The upper torso was barely identifiable as human, where the fire must have been at its most fierce. The belly and legs however, were recognisable, like a bloated cow destroyed in a bushfire. The remnants of a bladed weapon were recognisable, still in situ where ashes of ribs remained.

'First up,' Maddison asked, trying awkwardly to avoid standing in the sludge of body fluids doused by the fireman's hose. 'Is there any chance he fell on that blade? What is it anyway?'

'It's a Nazi officer's dagger,' Landon said. 'You can just make out the swastika on the cross guard. And no. There is no way he fell on it … and you can rule out suicide also.'

'Oh?'

'The back door's been jemmied.'

Maddison looked at the totally destroyed door frame and ash that was once the back door. 'Jemmied? How can you be certain?'

'The metal lock has fallen out into the laneway, blown out with the initial explosion, I'd say. And there's enough timber adhering to the lock to identify the break in. It's been bagged as evidence.'

'Right. We have a murder then.'

'The coroner's on his way. I told him to bring a dustpan and shovel to sweep up the victim,' Landon shared a wry smile. 'That fire was ferocious.'

'The knife,' Maddison asked. 'Obviously out of the shop?'

'Yep. That thing's got a twenty-centimetre blade. Check that out.'

Landon led the inspector back into the shop – all exposed by the fire, but saved from destruction by the fire door – to a cabinet full of Nazi memorabilia including other daggers and bayonets.

'That's the case where the perp got the weapon. I checked. There's a similar dagger in there.'

Maddison was about to cross to the cabinet when she saw the blood on the floor sprinkled with broken glass. The small area had been cordoned off.

'Too much blood for a cut foot,' Maddison said. 'If, that's what happened here.'

'Exactly. I'd say the victim was stabbed here and dragged back into that storeroom.'

'Was the fire door closed?'

'Yes, the firemen opened it.'

'Then that's what concentrated the blaze. The confined space.'

'Exactly.'

Maddison moved to the cabinet taking note of the Nazi stiletto style dress dagger. It was a formidable weapon in its day and even more sinister now. Maddison noted the price. 'Two hundred dollars! Who buys this stuff anyway?'

'Collectors.'

'Think I'd rather collect stamps.'

An unseen voice appeared from back out amongst the burnt ruins. 'Morning Inspector.'

Maddison looked over her shoulder where forensics had already spent half an hour dusting for prints and searching for other clues. Luke Farrell peered back at her over a burnt pyre of antique furniture. He appeared puppet-like with only the top of his head showing and holding a fine brush for dusting fingerprints.

Luke was the rookie assistant to Coroner Barret Griffin, with only a year on the job and loving every minute of it. Farrell was a nerd, a scrawny twenty-four-year-old fresh out of his studies, but headstrong with a taste for gore and glory. Accepted by his colleagues, the likeable young cop was naïve as he was clumsy, with a great sense of humour and nearly twenty years Maddison's junior. Luke was also clearly infatuated with their new inspector from Sydney.

'Morning Luke, how's it going? Any prints?'

'Well there's not much back here to dust. But I found heaps on the louvres in the dunny that somehow survived.'

'Okay. Keep at it … oh Luke.'

'Yes Inspector.'

'Is there anything, anything at all to get an I.D. on the remains of the victim?' Maddison thought how ridiculous that sounded the moment she said it. 'So, we can eliminate his prints.'

'No Inspector. But I've got plenty from upstairs.' With an obedient smile Luke's head disappeared once more.

Upstairs, the flat was like a smokehouse, the walls yellowed and the stink of fire and mayhem lingering. But the fire hadn't made it beyond the door from the shop to the stairs. The TV set was still airing morning television. A large coke had spilt onto the carpet and the remains of a family sized pizza sat open on the armchair. Landon studied the pizza a moment. There were only two pieces taken.

'Look at that,' Landon said. 'It looks like he's eaten all the topping and left the pastry.'

'There's your culprit.' Maddison nodded to a fat ginger tom cat cowering on an open windowsill, its soot-stained fur wet and matted. It hissed at the intruders. A closer inspection of the armchair showed paw marks of tomato and cheese.

'Christ no wonder the cat's fat,' Landon was distracted by the television and used a gloved hand to switch off the set.

'So,' Maddison surmised. 'My guess is he was eating pizza, watching telly, heard a noise downstairs, gone to investigate …'

'The back door being jemmied?'

'Sounds about right.'

'And there's that broken glass bowl on the floor in the shop itself,' Detective Finch said. 'It's possible the intruder knocked it off the bench in the dark, and that noise attracted the owner.'

'Possible.'

'There is also no sign of a safe, or a cash box and the till still has ninety dollars in it. I'm starting to think he knew his killer.'

'Or it was a crime of revenge maybe.'

'Possibly. Or the perp was actually after something specific in the shop.'

'Something valuable.'

'Maybe.' Senior Detective Finch made certain he and the inspector were alone. 'I haven't even had breakfast yet, fancy a coffee?'

'Sure, why not.'

***

Landon parked the unmarked police car in the side street next to Harbour Lights Café on Hobart docks. He even fed the meter, not wanting to draw attention to themselves by exposing a police sign on the dash. The two sat inside away from the window.

'How are you enjoying the job so far?' Landon asked his old flame.

'Quiet, until now. A lot quieter than I actually remember it.'

'Well murders here are rare, that's for certain.'

The waitress arrived with their order. One long black, one flat white, both double shots and hot. Landon watched as the young woman returned to the counter before plopping two sugar lumps into his long black. He turned his back to the wall crossing his legs.

'I heard you and Stephen split up.'

'God! That was quick. How did you know about Stephen?' Maddison spoke of her husband Stephen Lovett. 'You been checking up on me?'

'I'm a cop remember. I make it my business to check up on people. Well?'

'Well what?'

'Is it true?'

'No … no it's not true.' Maddison had an uncomfortable moment. It had been years since she had seen Landon and although it didn't seem too awkward to talk about her rocky marriage, it came as a shock. 'We're just having a break from each other.'

'A break huh?'

'Yes. A break. Is that alright with you?'

'Hey, I'm just trying to be friendly okay?'

'Well don't.'

Landon had a moment to check himself, Maddison was his superior after all. Two beats later Maddison broke the ice. 'So, I heard you split up with Bev.'

'Huh! Now it's your turn eh?'

'Well?'

'How did you ...'

'I'm a cop remember?'

'Touché!'

'What happened? Or should I shut up and mind my own business?'

'We fell out of love, pure and simple,' Landon said openly. 'Shit happens. So why are you ...ah, *just having a break?*'

'Stephen's the executive director in a large aluminium firm. He travels a lot and ...'

'He had an affair?'

'Jesus Landon!'

'Sorry. Am I right?' Maddison didn't want to admit it, but Landon was right on the money. 'I am right, aren't I?'

Maddison sipped her coffee in silence.

'Bastard,' Landon spat.

Maddison looked vague for a moment, stirring her sugar-free coffee for no good reason, lost in unpleasant memories. Landon tipped his head. 'Maddie?'

'Sorry?'

'I *do* understand.'

Maddison looked at Landon in a fresh light. They had fond memories in times gone by, the two of them. But she genuinely wanted things to work with Stephen.

Landon tried to cool the air. 'And you never had kids, did you?'

'We've been too busy with our own careers.' Maddison would have liked to have had children. Now it was too late. But there was no point regretting it. 'You had kids, didn't you?' she asked Landon.

'Yeh, Bev and I had two kids, a boy and a girl, both in their early twenties now thank god. We went separate ways last year.'

'What is it with marriage in the 90s?' Maddison had a hint of exasperation in her voice. 'Every one's divorcing.' Realising she sounded a little harsh Maddison said, 'Sorry.'

'Don't be. As I said we just fell out of love.'

Maddison knew the feeling. 'Got a girlfriend?' she asked.

'Pardon?'

'Girlfriend? Come on, I should imagine a good-looking rooster like you would have a string of new girlfriends.'

'A few dates, nothing serious.' Landon swung his legs back under the table, leant forward, elbows on the top, entwining fingers. He lowered his chin onto his hands. 'And you?'

'*And you*, what?'

'Come on, a sexy middle-aged woman like you,' he said returning the flattery.

'I'm still married I told you.'

'Yeh, but you said you're having a break from each other. Surely you've dipped your toes in, testing the water and all that.'

'Certainly not.'

Landon sat upright, almost as if he was relieved. 'It's not much fun is it?'

'What, being lonely?'

'Yes.'

'I've grown accustomed to it. Doesn't bother me anymore.'

But that was a lie and Landon knew it; he was after all, a cop.

CHAPTER SEVEN

Late that night…

Seraph heard the whispers in his ear. The same whispers that encouraged him to disguise his voice on the phone when he called the escort from a lonely phone box in Taroona. The very same muted tones inside his head that told him *to kill* was a natural thing to do. *The bitch needed to die.* It was easy. Nothing to it. *You've killed cats and dogs before, it's time to man up and take the slut's life. And then claim your reward?*

***

It was late, after midnight. The night was still. Not a breath of air. Being a weeknight everyone in Taroona, a suburb south of Hobart, was tucked into bed. Seraph waited in the carpark at the end of the bush road; the carpark for bushwalkers to leave their vehicles while they hiked or jogged the coastal walk in a four-and-a-half-kilometre loop, popular, he knew, with the fitness fanatics. *Goody-goodies in lycra jogging off for a café latte.*

It was dark. There was little moon.

This is how Seraph liked it; dark and moonless. It matched his dark heart, and tonight, especially, his depression further darkened his ever-dark thoughts. Seraph had waited thirty minutes. Now he was about to be rewarded for his patience.

Meredith slowed around the bend, after passing by bus stop twenty-three. Her lights were full beam, yet it was still difficult to read the street signs this dark moonless night. On the twenty-minute drive down from the city her thoughts had turned to Max the fisherman. They had grown close and she had a strange sense of guilt going to work like this, having sex with another man. A guilt she had not experienced since becoming an escort seven months earlier. But Max seemed to be practical about the situation. She had to work, right?

Then again was he simply using her? He had become more passionate lately, in a deviant sense; simulating strangulation whilst climaxing. But Meredith enjoyed their times together. Their pillow talk had become personal, each sharing intimate secrets.

The headlight bounced off the street sign snatching Meredith from her thoughts. *Ah, there it is. Gumtree Lane.*

Half a kilometre along the dead-end road after the main road turn off, Seraph caught a glimpse of headlights blinking through the thick bushland. He shrank back into the trees feeling the invincible chameleon dressed all in black; just like the whispers suggested he dress. Black skivvy, black track trouser, black belt, black runners, black gloves and the pièce de résistance … the black balaclava.

I'm fucking invincible.

The car approached slowly. Apparently, the driver was searching for house numbers in the dark. *Christ it was dark.*

Seraph felt his depression lift. He started fantasising about his sexual reward, the sexual favours that would be lavished upon him for ridding the world of this bitch, this whore! He felt himself becoming aroused. No, not now. This wasn't the time or the place. *Save it for your reward.*

Meredith drove off the bitumen onto the unsealed road, Gumtree Lane. The sound under the wheels made a satisfying crunch reminding Meredith of her childhood, walking on the gravel path to the front door of her home in Ulverstone where she grew up. She thought about her parents and had a hot flush. If they only knew what she was up to, having sex with strange men to put herself through university. But then she blamed her father, that's right, shift the guilt. If father hadn't gambled the family fortune, for what it was, she wouldn't be here right now. Embittered, Meredith counted numbers: *eighty-two, eighty-four, there it is, eighty-six. Oh brilliant! The lights are off.*

The older model Ford Falcon parked under a streetlight fifty metres away at the end of the carpark. As Seraph watched from the blackness of his bush hide-out, he watched the tall slim figure, wearing a tight red miniskirt and revealing blouse to match, step from her car. She stretched and straightened her skirt, staring at the last house in Gumtree Lane, number 86. But it was in darkness. Seraph's plan was going smoothly. Stealing through the night, dressed all in black, black as his thoughts, Seraph slipped a large wrench from his trouser belt and approached the car, as the woman walked to the front of the house.

There were definitely no lights on in the house. Meredith checked the number on the standard iron letter box. *Eighty-six. Yep. This was it.* Meredith ascended the wooden steps up to the veranda, walked to the door and tapped a salute with her knuckles. Waited. Knocked again. No answer. *Jesus! You're kidding me, all this way for nothing.*

Annoyed, Meredith returned to the front garden and looked through the only window without a curtain in the hope that her client had just fallen asleep on a couch. But there were definitely no lights on, no telly flickering; If she didn't know any better, she would say the property was vacant.

Seraph watched silently from the cover of darkness. The bait had worked. He watched the hooker peering in dark windows and smiled under the hand-knitted balaclava.

No one home is there? Now his mark was alone and vulnerable.

He slipped silently through the shadows and knelt behind her car, watching through a side window as she returned towards him … and waited.

Meredith hooked her keys from her bag and rounded her car. Without warning she was confronted by a man in black wearing a balaclava. In that first instant, that very first split second, she thought it must be her client. She even cracked a smile. A '*we have a kinky one here*' smile. But the smile shredded into a look of utter fear as the figure leapt towards her swinging a large wrench. There was no time to scream. The killer made certain of that. Meredith's skull was bludgeoned with such force it shattered bone like toffee. Meredith crumbled to the ground. Seraph didn't waste a minute, gathering her handbag, he dragged the body through bushland in the black of the night, dumping her off the bush track under trees. Briefly the moon appeared from behind heavy cloud and the killer had a chance to admire his handy work.

Looking at the body he had sudden lustful thoughts. *She's yours if you want her*, the whisper purred in his ear. *Go on, you know you want to*. Seraph pulled at his trousers, the belt was tight. In a moment of sexual depravity he tore his belt from his jeans, throwing it aside. Instantly something came over him. Guilt? He had killed animals before but never a human. He wanted to vomit. Now he heard voices approaching. A fine line had appeared between sanity and madness. Voices screamed inside Seraph's head and he stumbled away, finally breaking into a sprint back down the country lane to the main road where his reward would be waiting.

***

The next morning. A new day…

Information was accumulating at Hobart Police Headquarters. Obese antique dealer Jock Birdwhistle, it transpired, was hopelessly in debt. It was soon discovered the man was a gambler, and had anyone known, the Duterrau's painting would have been his ticket out of debt. He must have fancied himself the luckiest bloke in the world when he discovered it in a box of junk, albeit disguised amateurishly, with watercolour paints. Prior to this, neighbours in nearby businesses told police, Birdwhistle spoke of being suicidal.

Coroner Barrett Griffin thought of the family-sized pizza the victim was eating before his demise. 'Well he was trying hard to eat himself to death.'

But Birdwhistle had also confided to one friend that he had considered staging his own death. And fire was one of his suggestions. Inspector Maddison Lovett listened to the report in silence.

'Well we ruled out suicide because the back door was jemmied.'

'Could have been a ruse by Birdwhistle.'

'But there's a body Barrett. Someone died.'

'Yes Maddison, I know, which makes it even more bizarre. If Birdwhistle did do a disappearing act, it would make him accessory to murder, or at the least, the improper use of a cadaver, should he have acquired a body somehow.'

'Which is ridiculous.'

'Yes, it is. But it can't be ruled out.'

'Then we need to establish, without doubt, that those remains are Jock Birdwhistle.'

***

Short time later…

Rookie coroner Luke Farrell stared at the pile of human ashes, preparing himself for the task ahead. The twenty-four-year-old had been surrounded by death ever since starting his traineeship; whether death be laid out before him, packed in boxes on shelves, frozen solid in freezers or sitting in formalin displayed in bell jars and phials on the shelves all about the laboratory. Standing at a stainless-steel bench beneath an exhaust hood, sifting human remains, albeit cremated remains, was a picnic after, say, sorting through the decomposing mass of gooey residue of a victim dissolved in sulphuric acid, while searching for a finger knuckle or maybe a wedding ring. It had taken Luke longer to acclimatise to the stink, rather than the actual sights, of decaying bodies, and, as the coroner explained to Luke, butyric acid, methane gas and the other organic odours are all manufactured naturally. But today was just burnt bones and ash.

Luke liked his boss and the man had taken the enthusiastic fast learner under his wing.

Barrett Griffin, *Tiger* to his mates, had been in the business a long time, was strong as hemp and intolerant of fools. He was branded the sobriquet *Tiger* after he was attacked by a four-hundred-pound tiger in the rain forests of the South Western Ghats in India. *Wrong place, wrong time* was all Griffin would say; for the tiger, not him.

Luke sifted the fire victim's remains through a tripod-mounted fine screen, first five-millimetre mesh and a second time through two-millimetre mesh.

'That's mesh about as fine as a flyscreen door,' Coroner Tiger Barrett told Inspector Lovett when he handed her his report.

'What was the point?' Maddison wanted to know.

'Glad you asked. I acquired the antique dealer Jock Birdwhistle's dental records and the man had a gold filling in an upper molar. Luke found it in the end.'

'What, the filling?'

'Yes.' Tiger held up a small zip-lock sandwich bag. 'Et voilà!'

Maddison recognised the glint of gold with two tiny pins protruding, one bent.

'Good god. That survived the blaze?'

'Pure gold melts at 1062 Celsius. Dental gold is a stronger metal. Even the hottest of fires fuelled by petrol only reach 1200 Celsius. I've seen aluminium tea pots and kitchen utensils melt in house fires, but dental gold is more resilient.'

'Fascinating.'

'Yes. Besides after all that sifting, we did find a portion of jaw with three teeth intact and it matched the dental records perfectly, including the gold filling that is.'

'Good, then we can sleep tonight, rest assured it was the antique dealer who died in the fire and not another unsolved death.'

***

The next day…

Inspector Maddison Lovett parked her car in the multi-storey car park and walked the two hundred metres to the police headquarters. That's another thing she loved about Hobart – everything was so nearby. Passing the Lansdowne Café, she cast an eye over the patrons inside. *Charlotte!* Museum Director Charlotte caught her attention at the same time. Although for Charlotte it was the woman in uniform outside that caught her eye before she recognised her old friend. By then it was too late.

Maddison walked into the café where Charlotte sat at a corner table, hidden mostly by low hanging indoor plants. It was then she realised Charlotte had company, a younger woman wearing a striped sweater, holed stonewashed jeans over black leggings with Doc Martens and homemade jewellery.

'Hello there.'

'Maddie,' Charlotte was genuinely pleased. 'Join us for coffee, we just ordered.'

'Oh, I don't won't to interrupt. I saw you in passing and wanted to talk to you about what we discussed at the exhibition, but I see you have company. Another time.'

'Nonsense … Ah Maddison, this is Stella Bathe, colleague of mine.'

'Stella. Nice to meet you.'

Stella stood. 'I'll get my coffee takeaway. You guys have business to discuss.'

Maddison felt awkward.

Stella stood with her hand on Charlotte's shoulder. 'Seriously, no problem. I have heaps I should be doing.'

'Okay, thanks.' Maddison took Stella's seat.

'See you back at work,' Stella told Charlotte. Maddison noticed the hand squeeze on Charlotte's shoulder before Stella walked off.

'What is it with this place and all these plants?' the inspector said.

'It's called atmosphere,' Charlotte smiled, remembering her friend always preferred the sterile.

'Okay, I'll believe you.'

The waitress was at their table before Maddison could continue. She ordered coffee. 'Sorry I didn't contact you sooner,' Maddison said as the waitress walked away. 'But we've had a murder in Taroona.'

'Yes, I heard it on the news. Awful business.'

Maddison lowered her voice. 'Now ... this Stanley Smart at the museum.'

Charlotte. 'You've found something on him?'

'Not a thing. He has no record. He's clean I'm afraid to say.'

'Hmm. I've tried to get to know him the past few weeks and he's a shrewd one. Doesn't say much. But what does bother me is that he is a known hoarder. Collects *everything* apparently. I've heard this from some of the staff he has confided in.'

'That doesn't make him a thief though, does it?'

'I don't know. I just don't trust him, neither does Stella.'

'This Stella, what does she do?'

'Conservation. She's been promoted. She's off to Launceston soon to work up there on a new travelling exhibition.'

Immediately Charlotte was transported back to the late '60s when they were basketball mates. Somethings never changed and she read Maddison like a book. She was judging her. 'Okay, spit it out.'

Maddison. 'Spit what out?'

'Let's address the elephant in the room.'

'What elephant?'

'You know I'm gay don't you?'

'Wh ... what ... no. Gay! What are you on about?'

'Cut the crap Maddie.' Charlotte's face was fixed on her friend's. Maddison stared back. Of course, Charlotte was right, there was no point denying it.

'Okay, so you're gay, who cares?'

'I thought you would have guessed earlier.'

'Well no Charlotte. Not until your friend gave you a squeeze on the shoulder, a familiarity not the norm from staff, huh?'

'Yes I know,' Charlotte tensed her lips. 'I don't know what the board will think if they find out.'

'Don't tell them.'

'It's a bit hard to keep it quiet. Being gay is one thing, but fraternising with the staff is another.'

'And she is twenty years your junior.'

'Don't use that word.'

'What, junior?'

'No. Look don't judge me Maddison. It's hard enough without that. It just happened, that's all I can say.'

'Hey, I'm not judging you, okay? Let's just catch this thieving bastard, that'll make the board happy.'

***

Late evening, same day...

Burglar Ivano Stipanov wasn't surprised to find Alfred Kenning's rented apartment in the Hobart northern suburb of Moonah vacated. But he *was* pleasantly surprised when his accomplice in crime made their pre-arranged rendezvous under the Tasman Bridge at 10PM that night.

'I must confess I had doubts you would be here tonight,' he told the sixty-five-year-old Kenning as the men dissolved into the blackness and shadows guarding their nefarious meeting.

'Oh ye of little faith. Of course I would be here.' Kenning pulled an envelope from his pocket. 'Here. Two thousand I owe you.'

He lit a long thin cheroot with his lighter, allowing the light from the flame to spill onto the contents of the envelope for Ivano's benefit. Ivano gave the fifties a cursory glance and pocketed them without counting.

Honour amongst thieves and all that.

'You've a few more pieces,' Kenning blew smoke rings upwards. 'Jewellery and silverware, you said on the phone.'

'Back in Melbourne.'

'Oh, I was under the impression you were bringing them here.'

'Thought about it, but changed my mind.'

'I trust you used a different name on the ferry.'

'Do I look stupid?'

'No. No you don't, but the police *are* looking for you.'

'Yes. But they wouldn't expect me to sail to Tasmania, now would they?'

'Oh, I don't know. Tassie's been good to me. Now I have to leave also. The man I sold the paintings to, who I knew as a collector, decided to try and make a quick profit and took the Tom Roberts to Melbourne's Shadlocks and the next thing you know it was on *Crime Stoppers*. You wouldn't read about it.'

'Look, Alfred,' Ivano had known Alfred Kenning some time now, they had had many dealings together and he felt he could trust the man. 'I'm going to lay low here a week or so, before heading to Queensland. If you hear of any work going, leave me a message at the Wagon and Horses in Argyle Street.'

'Sure.' Kenning took a long drag on his cigarette. He didn't smoke often, but when he did, he enjoyed the sensation of the nicotine coursing through his veins. He exhaled a poorly executed smoke ring, and watched the smoke whisked away in a sudden breeze.

'May I suggest you extend your wardrobe,' Kenning said. 'Especially now you have the money. The police in Hobart could quite well have your details and if you left Melbourne post haste, like I suspect you did, you have limited clothing.'

'Great minds think alike,' Ivano said. 'It's on my *must do* list for tomorrow.'

Keening made to leave. 'Alfred,' Ivano said softly. Keening turned. 'Don't forget, I could use some work. I've got a bit of cash with me, but I left most of my money in Melbourne for safe keeping.'

'If I hear of anything, I'll leave a message. Wagon and Horses, isn't it?'

Ivano nodded and watched Kenning disappear into the darkness returning to the carpark, where he assumed Kenning had parked his car. Ivano had walked. Hobart was like that, a great small city, and easy to walk most places. Ivano smiled to himself, he was reasonably cashed up. Well he had two grand plus the grand he brought with him, and he was incognito, so no one knew where he could be found. *Wagon and Horses?* Ivano had already paid the publican – an ex-con recommended by a like-minded contact in Melbourne – several days rent in advance. Sure, he would drop in occasionally to see if he had messages, but his real address was a small rented boat house at Cornelian Bay, a twenty-minute walk from where he stood under the bridge at this moment. The hundred-year-old boat shed had been converted into a living space some years back and was perfect for Ivano Stipanov, *burglar to the rich.*

CHAPTER EIGHT

Next morning. 10AM sharp…

Inside the Collins Street menswear shop, **Sophie Smart** – museum curator Stanley Smart's daughter – unlocked the self-opening sliding glass doors to her place of employment, Menzies Menswear. Stooping low to lift the locking latch from the tiled floor, she became aware she was under observation. The unintentional voyeur and first customer stepped inside offering a cheerful morning's greeting. Sophie liked what she saw immediately. The man was in his early thirties, average height, strong build, dark hair and looked remarkably like the actor Mel Gibson.

'Just browsing or can I help you? Sophie asked.

For the first time in this brief encounter their eyes met and Ivano sensed an instant connection. In the past Ivano had always attracted women. He was a good-looking rooster who played the field; however, his chosen profession caused him to keep his distance. Short romances were best. A thief who worked alone without partners was a lot harder to catch. But today Ivano felt a rare kinship with this curvaceous redhead with her green eyes, collar-length hair with green highlights and cordial smile.

Was it the Tassie air?

'Pardon? Sorry, what was that?'

'Can I help you or are you just browsing?'

'Oh, browsing.' They stood looking at each other for another three seconds that felt a lifetime. 'Sorry,' Ivano said. 'I don't mean to stare, but have we met before?' *That old chestnut.* 'I know,' Ivano suddenly felt like a sleaze. 'Sounds corny. But seriously I felt like I knew you,' Ivano was bumbling.

Jesus!

'No, I don't think so,' Sophie held her smile.

Ivano took a sharp breath and checked himself. 'Actually,' he said, his voice suddenly serious, 'you can help. I'm looking for slacks, jacket and maybe two matching shirts. Oh, and a pair of tight-fitting leather gloves.'

Ivano Stipanov left the store twenty minutes later wearing a Barney black biker leather zip-up jacket ($480.00), with a white T-shirt underneath and new denim jeans. Three shirts, one pair of brown slacks and new black gloves accompanied him in a store bag. (Total $595) For the first time in his life his confidence had deserted him. Ivano cursed himself for not pursuing his instinct. That shop assistant was a doll. *Damn it!* He hadn't even found out her name.

***

Two hours later...

Ivano had shopped well for a man who rarely shopped. After Myers and a stroll through Cat and Fiddle Arcade he was weighted down with bags; clothes, sunglasses, shoes, shirts and slacks. Pleased with his new wardrobe, Ivano sat at an outside table at *The Coffee Bean,* a café in Centrepoint shopping centre.

Sophie Smart walked through the shopping centre on her lunch break and noticed Ivano sitting alone. 'Nice jacket,' she said in passing; a throwaway line in a familiar manner to her first customer that morning.

Ivano's confidence flooded back. 'Hey! Hi there! Say, would you like to join me for coffee?' Sophie was rather taken aback. 'Ah ...'

'I've only just ordered.'

What the hell. 'Okay. Thank you.' Sophie sat on the chair directly opposite and Ivano could hardly believe his good fortune.

'I'm on an early lunch break,' she said. 'I often come to the food court here for a sandwich.'

'Then let me buy you a sandwich.'

'No! I mean ... no ... thank you ... I ...'

'I insist.' Ivano caught the waitress's eye. 'I'm starving,' he told Sophie. 'I missed breakfast this morning.' Ivano wasn't taking no for an answer. They ordered toasted ham and cheese bagels and coffees. 'Geoff Wright,' Ivano lied about his name and already hated himself for it.

'Sophia Smart. But everyone calls me Sophie.'

They spoke for nearly an hour. Sophie explaining her love for sports and in particular Aussie rules football. Ivano told Sophie he was an auctioneer in Geelong, down here in Tassie for a short break, and spoke of visiting the antique shops while he was here. 'I love history and have an ongoing love affair with antiques,' he told her.

'Then you'd get on well with Daddy.'

'Oh?'

'He's the curator at the Tasmanian Museum.'

'Really?'

Yes. And he's also a mad collector. Museum staff aren't supposed to be collectors, conflict of interests and all that.'

'Understandable.'

'My god!' Sophie saw the courtyard clock. It was right on 1PM. 'I'll be late.' She made to fetch her purse from her bag.

'It's my treat,' Ivano insisted. 'Remember.'

'Oh ... really?'

'Really.'

'No, I can't.' Sophie felt awkward.

'Buy me a drink when you finish work.' Ivano's words were spontaneous and unexpected. But he just knew it was right. Sophie looked at him surprised. But to be honest she had really enjoyed the man's company. He was so genuine and interesting, not to mention a bit of a hunk. Sophie looked at the clock.

'I won't take no for an answer,' Ivano had taken her by the wrist and held it firmly. 'Throw caution to the wind.'

'Alright.' Sophie astounded even herself. 'I really must hurry.'

'I'll be outside the store at five.'

At Sophie's suggestion the two took drinks at Hadley's Hotel around the corner from Menzies Menswear, in Murray Street. Sophie insisted on buying the first round; two gin and tonics, mint and lemon. Ivano sipped his gin, placing the glass on the coaster before him, on the glass top table.

'You were saying your father works at the museum,' he started, leaning back in his lounge chair and crossing his legs.

'Yes. Curator.'

'How interesting. And he's a collector you said?'

'Yes.' Sophie used her straw and nursed her drink. She had been looking forward to this moment. It was certainly impetuous for her, she was normally more guarded. But this man with the film star good looks, hot body and charming new leather jacket just seemed so … well, so right. Now she threw caution to the wind. 'Yes, he collects all sorts of stuff. I say stuff because Daddy's a bit of a hoarder.'

'Hoarder?'

'His home is packed with antiques.'

This was music to Ivano's ears. Suddenly he felt this chance meeting with a pretty redhead might bear more than just one kind of fruit. 'I'm crazy about antiques myself. I'm an auctioneer as I said, but I do manage to keep the odd piece that takes my fancy.'

'Like what?'

'Jewellery.'

'Jewellery!'

That grabbed her attention.

'Daddy doesn't have any antique jewellery, but he has an amazing coin collection, many of them gold.'

If Ivano's eye twitched slightly he hoped Sophie hadn't notice, because *there's some things you shouldn't be telling a professional burglar.*

'Gold huh?'

'Yes, do you know sovereigns and … guineas I think they're called?'

'I've heard of guineas, yes,' Ivano said in a disinterested tone. 'And how about you? Do you collect anything?'

'Only clothes,' Sophie giggled. Her smile was infectious and Ivano was struggling not to become too attracted. 'You'd like my dad,' Sophie said, drawing Ivano from his musings. I should imagine he would like to meet you.'

'Where does he live?'

'Nearby actually.' Sophie took a long drink before saying, 'I've got to tell you, you don't look like a Geoff.'

'Pardon?' Ivano had to be wary, reminding himself his name tonight was Geoff Wright.

'You don't look like a Geoff.'

'Oh, so what do I look like?'

'More a Mel … yeh, Mel Gibson, that's who you remind me off.'

Ivano so wanted to tell Sophie that he knew Mel Gibson quite well, that he had been a stuntman doubling for the famous actor on the Mad Max films, for starters. But it would only complicate his web of lies. Tonight, he was the mundane antique auctioneer from Geelong, Geoff Wright. He bought a second round of gins. 'Say, how about dinner?'

'Tonight?'

'Yes.'

'I can't. I've other plans,' Sophie lied. Things were moving a little too fast. She had only just met the man. But god only knows she was keen.

'What about tomorrow?'

Oh, he was keen also. A night to think about it. Sophie finished her second drink and, determined to play hard to get, sort of, she stood. 'Where and when?'

Ivano couldn't disguise his pleasure. 'Great. You tell me. I'm from out of town remember? What sort of food do you like?'

Sophie didn't hesitate. 'Seafood's my favourite.'

'Me too.'

'Then the Drunken Admiral down on the wharf is the only seafood restaurant worth dining at.'

'Drunken Admiral?'

'Yes. It's in an old warehouse on Old Wharf, you can't miss it. I'll meet you there, say seven?'

'Seven it is.'

Without hesitation this cute redhead had shown her mettle. Ivano, aka Geoff Wright, Stipanov liked that.

***

A week or so earlier...

When bordello madam Mareike started demanding favours from Magistrate Christian Winterbourne for her girls – to see that their charges for prostitution were dropped when they were caught soliciting on the streets – Christian was naturally nervous, and rightly so. Now Mareike was insisting he preside over an upcoming assault case, where one of her girls had slashed a difficult patron with a broken glass. This was a serious offence.

'I can only do so much,' he complained on the phone. 'My activities in court are raising suspicions amongst my colleagues. People are talking.'

Mareike's green eyes narrowed into cold orbs. 'You should have thought of that before you shagged Mia.'

Mia – the liaison with the young lady of debatable age. What a fool he'd been.

Christian always suspected there were other photos, and now Mareike's comment confirmed it. There could be only one answer; he would have to steal the photos. But how? *Chastity?*

Mareike placed the phone receiver back in its cradle. Staring ahead into a huge mirror with a carved gilt frame of naked cherubs canoodling with nymphs, Mareike saw the reflection of a crucifix directly behind her. It gave her comfort. Blackmail wasn't something she really wanted to do but occasionally …

Well … if you want to stay on top of this pile of shit, sometimes you have to break the law.

Looking Jesus in the eye, Mareike crossed herself for forgiveness but smartly looked away from the crucifix. For the moment she had other pressing business. Her son had made contact. After all these years he had somehow found out her name and wanted to meet his mother. Mareike was curious also, but she had chosen to push him from her mind the day he was born. Now she had reservations. Maybe he knows she's worth a few bob. Maybe he just wants money, or maybe he is a vindictive mongrel after retribution for deserting him. A chip of the old block. If he's anything like his father, he'll be a good-looking boy she thought.

So she had agreed to meet him. It was a week or so ago now. Mareike told no-one. They met at *Salon Rouge* and he was certainly handsome although he seemed a little shy. She recognised instantly he was a six-pack short of a carton. But then his father wasn't that bright either. He was tall, dark and handsome and had his father's gorgeous dark brown eyes. But most importantly he carried a letter of introduction from the adoption agency. He told her he lived moderately and only when she insisted, did he take the hundred dollars she gave him, suggesting he buy some new clothes. Mareike had discovered a soft spot she didn't know existed within her. Then, days after their meeting, Rory took up Mareike's offer for position as gardener at 'the business'.

Meanwhile…

Magistrate Christian had stewed over his dilemma all day. *Blackmail!* He never thought it could come to this. It was only as he lay in bed that night that the thought came to him. His English lass Chastity, her of the hazel hair, large breasts, button nose and blue eyes. Chastity had been Christian's regular at the bordello in Liverpool Street. He had a soft spot for her. Chastity was good company, intelligent. Recently he had felt betrayed by Chastity but soon learnt she knew nothing of the photos. Chastity felt betrayed also and would have left Mareike's employment, but the truth was apparent – she could not afford to go anywhere. She had recently turned forty-six, well past the retirement age for a prostitute. But Mareike had an older, professional clientele who enjoyed mature women. Now, Christian knew Chastity's movements well. She too was a creature of habit.

***

Next day. Midday…

Christian waited near the corner of Goulbourn and Molle Streets where he knew Chastity would have to pass by on her regular visit to her aged mother, living alone in a small cottage at the top end of Melville Street.

Christian stepped from the cover of a healthy wisteria spilling over a cottage fence onto the footpath. 'Chastity.'

'Christian!' Chastity instinctively looked about to be certain she wasn't being observed, especially by one of Mareike's thugs. This was the first time she had seen her elderly client outside of work.

Christian. 'I need to talk to you.'

'I'm on my way to …'

'Your mother's. I know. It won't take a moment and …' Christian's voice lowered and now he too looked about surreptitiously, 'I'm desperate Chastity.

I have no one else I can turn to.' The magistrate's eyes were moist and red, he looked tired and scared.

Chastity immediately guessed the gravity of the situation. 'We can't talk here.'

'No, no … of course not.' The magistrate had already thought this out. 'There's a café just down the street … coffee?'

'Thank you.'

Christian had a moment to observe Chastity on their brief walk. Dressed in her day clothes, there was no outward sign that the woman was a sex worker. Certainly, her skirt was short for a forty-six-year-old, but it was all the fashion. *Mutton dressed as lamb huh?*

Over a cappuccino and a long black coffee Christian explained the situation; which came as no surprise to Chastity.

'I'm sorry it's come to this Christian, But Mareike has had other young girls working lately, she never used to you know. But I think she's up to no good.'

'And I've been caught up in the middle of it,' Christian said.

Chastity had her own thoughts on the situation. *Dirty old men and young girls.* But then again, she was a young prostitute once and decided she was in no position to judge. Sex work over the years had toughened her but she did underneath it all have a soft heart.

'How can I help?' Chastity said from behind a moustache of cappuccino froth.

Christian smiled. For the first time in days he smiled. Chastity was such a sweet lass really and he had grown fond of her over the five years since they first met. Christian wiped her lip with his paper serviette. This intimate act caused Chastity to loosen a smile.

'Look, Chastity. I'm desperate. Those photos … with Mia …' his voice lowered even further. Suddenly he felt the guilt on mentioning the young girl's name. 'Ah, those photos with Mia could see me …' Christian's voice broke. He cleared his throat. 'Could see me sent to gaol.'

Chastity sighed. She felt awkward, like she was between *a rock and a hard place* as her mum would say. 'But what can I do?'

The magistrate's tired eyes darted about. The café was near empty and the room quiet. 'Where does she keep the photos? Does she have a safe?'

'She has a safe, yes. It's an old-fashioned iron safe bolted to the floor under her desk.'

'A key safe?'

'No. It's combination.'

'In her downstairs office?'

'Yes.'

'And you've seen it?'

'Several times. I'm one of her trusted girls and on more than one occasion I have helped her balance the cash after a busy night.'

CHAPTER NINE

Three days after the murder of escort Meredith Kendall...

Bushwalker Freddie Cuthbertson was walking Toni, his fawn female whippet, when the dog ran off the bush path and into the scrub behind Taroona. First thoughts, rabbit or a wallaby? But of greater concern were the black snakes, the venomous Tasmanian tiger snakes, prevalent in the bushland this time of the year. One bite and Toni would undoubtedly not survive. It was 6.20AM and the sun had risen over the hills on the eastern side of the River Derwent, heralding another warm day. But in the still air of the warming morning Freddie caught an unpleasant whiff – the redolent stink of death – and the last thing the owner wanted was his beloved dog rolling in the carcass of a dead roo. 'Toni!' he called out. But the excited dog, which lived for her morning walks, was having none of it. 'Toni, come here.' Already Freddie heard the ominous rustle in the long grass. Damned snakes! They were a real worry to the owner of a pedigree show dog like Toni.

'Toni!' This time Freddie was rewarded by barking. 'Toni, come here girl.' The barking grew urgent. 'Where are you Toni?' Although Freddie Cuthbertson always wore long socks and boots in the bush, he dreaded walking through the grass. 'Come here girl, damn it … Oh, sweet Jesus!'

Now the dog owner sensed an urgency, his voice grew deep with authority. 'Toni, get away. Toni!' Toni sniffed the cadaver from several angles. Freddie immediately recognised the body was that of a young woman. She had lain there hidden in the undergrowth a day or two; her twisted body semi-naked with her knickers stuffed into her mouth. Maggots squirmed hungrily. Freddie involuntarily retched. Placing a handkerchief over his mouth he snatched the dog by the collar, reattached its lead and hurried away to call the police.

Inspector Maddison Lovett was taken aback. 'And here's me thinking little old Hobart was a quiet and peaceful place.'

If the situation wasn't so serious, Maddison looked comical dressed in her PPE, her solemn face framed in a hood of plastic. She stared down at the body amazed at the horrific scene. But no one ever really acclimatised to scenes of brutal, senseless murder. It seemed so out of place with the serenity of the bushland setting and the magnificent view across the river. It was now 7.30AM and the sky clear, promising another delightful summer's day; although Maddison had been warned by her colleagues at the station not to be complacent with the clear sky. This was Tasmania and the weather was notoriously unpredictable. Only yesterday she overheard one cop say to another, 'If you don't like the weather wait ten minutes.'

Luke Farrell, the young forensic assistant was with his boss, Coroner Griffin. The scene had been thoroughly secured and the two men were taking photos, making extensive notes and waiting Maddison's appearance before bagging evidence. Griffin didn't wait for the inspector's question.

'Been two days,' he said as Maddison approached, fitting a face mask over her nose to stifle the stench where the body was already bloating with methane in the warm summer weather. 'Two days at least. I would say.'

'Oh.'

'Yes, as you can see fly eggs hatched out a day ago and those maggots are having a field day.'

As Maddison looked on, fully-grown maggots hopped about the orifices like popcorn. If Maddison was shocked at the viciousness of the victim's attack, she didn't show it. One side of the head had been bludgeoned.

'Any identification?' Maddison asked.

'Yep,' Griffin pointed to a small brown leather hand bag with faux gold clips thrown aside with some of the contents, including credit cards, strewn loosely. 'Bank card there says Meredith Kendall. She was twenty-two and lived at Forest Road'.

'West Hobart?'

'That's it.'

'Clearly it's not a robbery.'

'No. She was knocked unconscious with a hard object, but it wasn't enough to kill her outright. I'll have a better idea when inspect her at the lab. Then she was strangled with her own pantyhose and suffocated with those.' Griffin alluded to the panties.

Maddison noted the panties stuffed into the victim's mouth, the victim's jacket lay next to her, her blouse had been pulled up and her bra torn. 'Sexually assaulted I assume?'

'Well yes and no. It's also a question of when she last had sex.'

'Oh?'

'Yes. She was a prostitute.'

'Really? How did you deduce that?'

'She had an address book in her bag.' Griffin nodded to young Luke who proudly held up a clear evidence bag securing a small black book. 'One of the first phone numbers inside is for *Salon Rouge,* a well-known brothel at the top end of Liverpool Street.' Griffin read the inspector's quizzing expression. 'And no, I have never visited the place,' he jested without smiling.

'Are you sure Tiger?' Senior Detective Landon Finch arrived at the crime scene in time to hear the coroner's last comment. 'I heard you held a gold card membership.'

'Look what the cat dragged in,' Griffin and Finch exchanged friendly smiles. They were old mates. It showed.

'I've located the victim's car Inspector,' Landon told Maddison, maintaining formality in front of his colleagues. 'And like we thought, it was one of the vehicles parked at the end of the street near the entrance to the car park.'

'Great.'

'White 1991 Ford E.B. Falcon.'

'So, we know how she got here. She was an escort right? I mean she didn't work at the brothel all the time?'

'That sounds about right.'

'So the perp has called the brothel, I'm guessing, giving an address in Taroona.'

'I'll have all nearby phone booths dusted for prints.'

'Good. Dust the car before it's towed back to the police garage also. Look for tire prints next to, or near the victim's car. What's the address for this brothel, I'm heading there first? From my experience the best people to ask about sexual deviants in any given area are the working girls themselves.' Maddison tried to focus, take in the surroundings. 'Any other clues?'

'Well she was knocked unconscious elsewhere and dragged here.'

'Yes, you said she wasn't killed outright.'

'You can just see the disturbed undergrowth there,' Tiger pointed to disturbed bracken and grass. 'And dragged by her feet. See the thick brown string used to bind her ankles. And her wrists were tied as well.'

'And we have this.' Landon held up a black leather belt sealed in a clear plastic sachet. 'Found right there.' He pointed to a spot in the long grass where a number had been pegged into the earth when the photographic record was being taken.

Maddison studied the accessory, a black belt with a simulated grain pattern and a brass buckle of a goat's head. On the goat's forehead was an engraved pentagram.

'Measures seventy-six centimetres. Suit a slim wearer.'

'Man's belt, obviously?'

'Definitely. If I was to hazard a guess, I'd say the perp was removing his trousers for a sexual assault but was disturbed by someone.'

'A sexual assault after death?'

'Huh-hu.'

'Sick bastard. But his fantasy wasn't fulfilled, right?'

'It appears not. I can't determine either way until I have examined the body back at the lab.'

Maddison studied the remote location a moment before asking about uniformed police door knocking the houses in the dead-end street, speaking to potential witnesses. 'You've got uniforms door knocking?'

'As we speak. The boys won't leave any stone unturned.'

'Good.'

They watched in silence a short while as the victim was zipped into a body bag, when Tiger broke the pensive silence. 'You know, this isn't too far from where another murder happened eight years ago.'

'Oh?'

'A female cyclist, twenty-three,' Tiger stared up into the eucalyptus trees deep in thought, as if searching the ghostly white branches for the macabre details. 'She was recently married and had just returned from her honeymoon, up the Gold Coast if my memory serves me correctly, when she went for a cycle after work, alone on the scenic path.'

'The one over there?' Maddison alluded to the coastal scenic loop.

'Yes. She was forced to dismount because someone had placed rope across the path.'

'Rope?'

'Like workmen had barricaded it temporarily. This caused her to take a shortcut through bushland where …'

'She was attacked?'

'Exactly. Where the perpetrator lay waiting for her. Her husband reported her missing when she failed to return home and I recall the police at the time gave him a hard time.'

'Why's that boss?' Luke Farrell asked.

'Well it's common knowledge that a large percentage of murders are committed by the next of kin and she wasn't found for ten days. She had been battered unconscious and raped, before he strangled her.'

'Really?' This sounded a little too familiar to Maddison watching two constables in PPE carry the body out of dense bushland back onto the path.

'The perpetrator then set fire to the body hoping to destroy evidence against him, however we found semen traces in her clothing. This later proved the killer was a secretor.'

'Secretor?"

'Yes. A secretor is a person who secretes blood–group antigens in body fluids such as semen or saliva. This meant we could test for his blood group.'

'And?'

'He was blood group A. Also, an enzyme called PMG,' Tiger looked to his young assistant. 'That's short for phosphoglucomutase and it enabled us to narrow the sample down even further.'

'But at least a third of the population are blood group A, aren't they?' Maddison asked.

'True, but these special factors meant they could eliminate four out of five suspects, if they had any, which they didn't at that stage.'

'So, was he caught?'

'Unfortunately, it's still listed as a cold case.'

'Hmm, there are similarities here wouldn't you agree?'

'I don't want to comment until I've thoroughly examined the body. The first thing that stands out is that this victim was hit on the back of the head first, the other victim eight years ago had her hands tied behind her back, but that's not ruling out it's the same suspect.'

'But you never found a suspect?'

'No.' Griffin shrugged, sighing heavily. 'I estimated the time of death at ten days prior to her discovery. The police conducted serious door to door enquiries.'

'And?'

'And the police had a description of a man seen loitering in the area over that period. A description from more than one witness, who claimed they saw a man acting suspiciously at the time. A short man, red hair, late thirties. But what sticks in my mind most is they all told of his piercing, staring, unblinking eyes.'

'Okay,' Maddison turned to Landon. 'I want that cold case file pulled out soon as you get back.'

***

That evening…

Burglar Ivano Stipanov, calling himself Geoff Wright, met the museum curator's daughter Sophie for their first real date. If ship figureheads, lanterns, anchors and old grog barrels in a century-old sandstone warehouse serving the island's freshest seafood was your thing, then the Drunken Admiral Restaurant was perfect.

Ivano met Sophie out front on the wharf. Together they left the problems of the world behind them to meld amongst the ambience of nautical antiques, oak beams, the bouquet of freshly sautéed garlic, crispy fried fish, char-grilled prawns and freshly poached shellfish.

Sophie started with steamed mussels, white wine, sour cream broth with spring onions. Geoff ordered a hot rock salmon; bar-b-qued salmon on a volcanic rock with wasabi mayonnaise. It was during the incredible seafood platter and over the last in the bottle of Tasmanian Bream Creek Pinot Grigio that Geoff, Ivano, broached the subject of Daddy once more.

Sophie speared a fat fried scallop with her fork, dipped it in her caper mayonnaise and allowed the morsel hover before her a moment. 'I told Daddy about you.'

'Oh. And?'

'He said he'd like to meet you.' Now this was a downright lie. Stanley avoided visitors. Sure, his daughter told him she was going out on a date, and with a stranger she just met for god's sake. But the truth was he loved his little girl to death and would do anything for her.

'Can I bring him to meet you?' she had asked him.

'But you just met.'

'Well that's how dates work, Daddy. How else am I going to meet Mister Right if I don't go out on dates? Well then?'

'Well then what?'

'You didn't answer my question.'

'What question?' Now Daddy was acting evasively.

'Can I bring Geoff to meet you?'

'But why?'

'Well you're a good judge of character that's why. I trust your judgement. Besides he loves antiques for god's sake. He's an antiques auctioneer. You'd get on like a house on fire.'

'I don't know Sophia.'

'Well I'm bringing him anyway.'

And that was the end of the matter.

***

Over a shared dessert of Pistachio Crème Brûlée, two spoons, a Tasmanian sticky muscat and strong black coffee, Sophie suggested she take Geoff to the Antique Centre in North Hobart. Ivano couldn't be happier. But forever careful not to let his guard down, he played his cards low.

'Are you asking me on another date?' he asked, trying unsuccessfully to keep a straight face.

Sophie's wide green eyes stared into his. The wine had made her a little incautious. She felt she was falling for this man. He was different and she liked different. Their hands reached out across the table and Ivano placed his warm fingers on top of hers. '

You have soft hands for a man.' Now Sophie was being evasive.

'Well I'm an auctioneer, not a lumberjack.'

'Ha, ha. Well?'

'Well what?'

'I have tomorrow off. Do you fancy going to some antique shops, maybe a bite of lunch and after, we can meet Daddy?'

'So, you *are* asking me on another date?'

'If that's what you want to call it,' she said softly, a corkscrew of orange-red hair springing over one eye. 'Well then yes, I'm asking you out on another date.'

For Ivano this went against all his own rules. Never date your target and whatever you do never, ever, fall in love. 'I'd love to,' Ivano answered. Smitten.

After Sophie's finger mopped the remaining brulée, and licked it clean …

After short black coffees and sticky muscat …

After a short stroll to the cab rank, holding hands …

Ivano stole a kiss. Sophie was at first taken aback. But it felt right. She had been wary of suitors lately, but this Geoff was a gentleman, smart and funny and great company. The second kiss lasted longer. Sophie's heart was beating faster and Ivano was softening. Ivano bundled Sophie into a taxi.

'See you tomorrow then,' he closed the door and headed off on foot towards Cornelian Bay.

***

Early evening the next day…

Stanley Smart stood on the pine library chair with its turned stiles supporting a cross rail, wrap around to form armrests. Carefully balanced, resting one knee on a tall four-drawer iron filing cabinet and placing one foot on the left armrest, he barely had enough elevation to reach the wooden boxing concealing the track for the hand-drawn curtain. The heavy braided cord hung loose and pushing it aside he managed to reach behind the boxing. This is where he kept his spare cash. In his study, come library. Who would ever guess?

Stanley didn't trust banks and besides he wheeled and dealed occasionally in antiques and coins, and all transactions were, where possible, in cash. No paper trail and keep the Australian Taxation Office in total darkness. That's the way it was. *I wasn't named Mr Smart without reason,* he chuckled away, feeling behind the rail cover.

Hearing the back door open and close Stanley quickly climbed back down to floor level and stuffed the two fifty-dollar notes into his wallet. He closed the study door and made his way as best he could through his myriad of *stuff,* to greet his daughter.

'Daddy!' Sophie clearly loved her father. Ivano stood back in his new leather jacket and watched them hug. Finally, Sophie introduced her friend.

'Daddy,' she smiled cheerfully. 'This is Geoff. Geoff Wright.'

'Hmm,' Stanley looked his daughter's date up and down with a sharp eye. The man was a few years on Sophie and that bothered him for starters. Ivano stepped forward giving Stanley little choice, arm outstretched. 'Nice to meet you sir.'

'It's Stanley,' Sophie said. 'Isn't it Daddy?'

Stanley barely nodded, forcing himself to share the slightest of smiles, just to appease his daughter. Ivano realised immediately the man would take some effort to win over and searched the room smartly for something, any damned thing, that he knew enough about to strike up a conversation.

'Huh, I see you collect Satsuma,' Ivano admired the metre-tall vase with its raised gilt motifs of Japanese mythology.

It worked. 'Yes. Do you like it?'

'Magnificent. I've handled a few pieces through the auction room. Meiji Period, 1860s to 1912, I believe.'

'Very good.'

Ivano had misappropriated a few choice pieces of Satsuma only a year earlier and knew enough to fool Stan. But Stanley was keen for an evaluation. 'What do you think it's worth?'

'Oh, a piece like that?' Ivano knew his fence would pay no more than three hundred, so he doubled it. 'Six hundred.'

'Lovely. I paid eighty dollars for that ten or so years ago. Care for a drink?'

'Thank you.'

'I've only got wine I'm afraid, and red wine at that.'

'Red wine's fine.'

'Don't get too excited,' Sophie said. 'Daddy drinks cask wine.'

'Nothing wrong with cask wine Sophie,' Ivano said, keen to continue winning over the old man. With tumblers of cheap wine in hand, Stanley gave Ivano a little tour. After all Sophie's friend *was* an antique auctioneer. Ivano managed to keep his head above water, careful to comment only on items about which he knew at least something. And surprised even himself how much he did know about antiques and art.

Sophie poured more drinks. 'Show Geoff your coin collection,' Sophie said, her innocence lost on *Daddy* who never showed anyone his coins, and for good reason. 'Daddy?'

'Oh, they're put away. Bit hard to get to right now.'

'Nonsense, they're in the safe in your bedroom.'

Ivano saw the look Stanley shot his daughter. Sophie acted ignorant, albeit embarrassed. Ivano feigned disinterest in her request, observing a collection of porcelain figures in a showcase. An awkward quiet veiled the room, briefly. Sophie realised she had overstepped the mark. 'We better be off I guess.'

'Yes, I expect you must.'

'Well it was really nice meeting you, Stan.'

'Yes, yes, likewise.'

***

The Veal Marsala was ordered by Ivano and Sophie the Spinach and Ricotta Ravioli. The waiter at the Mona Lisa Italian Restaurant, in Liverpool Street, checked the order in the kitchen and returned to their table with a bottle of Chianti.

'Chianti?' Sophie mused.

'Why not, we're in Italy tonight.'

Sophie was taken by the traditional *fiasco,* straw-wrapped wine bottle. The food was superb, the wine, well better than Daddy's cask, but the company was … bellissima. Sophie had already made up her mind she was going to give herself to this handsome man, this Mel Gibson look-a-like who wandered into her life two days ago. He was everything a girl could desire.

'I'm sorry about Daddy,' Sophie said, her green eyes in the glimmering light of the candle reminding Ivano of a pair of Brazilian emeralds.

'Sorry? Why?'

'Oh, the coin collection business.'

'Oh that. Don't worry about it.'

'It was embarrassing.'

'No, not at all. He just wanted to be private, that's all. I understand.'

'You do?'

'Sure I do. He doesn't want to show off things like that to strangers.'

'But you're not a stranger.'

'To your father I am.' He held up his glass. 'Salute.'

'Cheers.'

'What sort of coins has he got anyhow? You mentioned he collected gold coins.'

'Yes. He has quite the collection. But not just gold, he specialises in rare Australian coins. Do you know much about them?'

'Yes, a bit. I have a few myself.' What Ivano should have said, if he was honest, was, '*I have handled lots of rare coins, after I stole them and sold them on, to a receiver of stolen property*

'Then you know the 1930 penny?'

'Yes.'

'Daddy has three.'

Well there's nearly twenty thousand dollars right there.

'Three, wow.'

'He has a large collection of Australian sovereigns, including the Adelaide pound.' *Another five thousand for that sought-after gem.* 'And bank notes and tokens and war medals. He even has a Victoria Cross, one of the few in private hands Daddy told me.' *Victoria Cross, a hundred thousand if sold legitimately, Ivano knew. But impossible to sell if stolen.*

However!

'Why does he keep them in his bedroom? Why doesn't he keep them in a bank vault?'

Sophie was oblivious to Geoff's fishing for information. 'I know, I've told him that, but he keeps them in a wall safe bolted under floorboards beneath his wardrobe. It's just an old safe he picked up at a sale years ago.'

Once again, this was music to Ivano's ears. It was time to celebrate. Dinner arrived and they ordered a second bottle of wine. Ivano had all the information he needed, including when Daddy would not be at home.

Monday to Friday, nine till five. Perfect.

***

Sophie shared a flat with flatmate Julie, a cute brunette on the cuddly side judging by the photo on the sideboard, and with a fetish for toe sucking, according to Sophie. Tonight, she was staying with her boyfriend at Seven Mile Beach and Ivano couldn't help thinking Sophie had planned this.

The love making was intense. Ivano tried to distance himself from the romantics, as he knew only too well how badly he was about to betray this young lady. But Sophie was committed, she had fallen in love, while Ivano struggled with both his conscience and his feelings.

CHAPTER TEN

Hours after Meredith's body was found...

Madam Mareike answered the doorbell of her *Salon Rouge* bordello. She wasn't pleased to see a cop on her front step. Her first thought was that *that bloody magistrate had dobbed her in for blackmail* but then she thought, *nar, he's got too much to lose.* When she discovered the cop was enquiring was about one of her girls and not Mareike herself, she coughed a laugh.

'Killed!' she said, fingering her crucifix. 'Whadya mean Meredith was killed?'

'She was murdered.'

'Oh dear god no.' Mareike crossed herself. 'By whom?'

'That's why we are here, to find out.' Inspector Maddison Lovett took an instant disliking to the short overweight madam. She could tell the woman had been a pretty young thing in her day; what with green eyes, long black hair and a trim figure. But now at fifty-three she appeared a ruthless bitch with silver hair – fat and angry. 'Can we talk somewhere private?' Maddison asked.

Mareike grunted for the policewoman to follow. She led Maddison into her office; not her inner sanctum mind, her faux office for visits from people like the cops. First room down the hall, on the left. Maddison made a brief copper's reconnaissance. The room was the size of a large bedroom with a high ceiling and a shuttered window overlooking the city lights. A modern copy of an Edwardian blackwood desk was the main attraction, with a leather swivel chair, its back to the wall. Watching over the desk was a large figure of Jesus on the cross; cast silver on dark wood. Maddison wondered to herself what *the man* himself would think today in 1995, presiding over the administrations of a house of ill-repute.

'I run a clean, honest house here,' Mareike snapped, noticing the cop looking at her crucifix.

'I'm sure you do …' Maddison was about to say 'madam' but thought better of it. 'I'm sure you do.'

Mareike fell heavily into the swivel chair and pointed to an old library chair in front of the desk for the policewoman to take a seat.

'Alright then,' Mareike said. 'Tell me what happened.'

Maddison explained where Meredith Kendal's body was discovered, in what condition it was found and what the police had figured out so far.

'Dead two days yer say?'

'Yes.'

'I wondered why I hadn't seen her lately. We had a bit of a tiff, but the girls that go out make their own hours any'ow.'

'Tiff? About what?'

'Money. Them girls always want more. They think they's better than the working girls what stay under me roof. I took that call for Barbie meself,' Mareike said. If there was any remorse, she was bottling it.

'Barbie?'

'That was 'er workin' name.'

'I see. You took the call you say, so you have an address?'

'Yeh, it's in me reservation book here.'

Madison wondered if it could be this simple. The perpetrator's address. No one is that stupid, unless it was a spontaneous killing.

'Here,' Mareike twisted the reservation book to face the inspector, open to the respective night's page. 'Eighty-six Gumtree Lane.'

Maddison knew that to be the last home before the nature park's carpark where the victim's car was found. The last house was a convenient ruse, a false address. *So, it was a planned murder.* Now Maddison imagined the killer waiting in the shadows while the unwary call girl stood in the dark wondering what to do next. For Maddison knew 86 Gumtree Lane was empty, on the market, because the lads had door knocked the area that morning. That's why the killer chose it.

'What did this client sound like on the phone? Presuming it was a *he?*'

'From what I remember 'e sounded normal. A regular sort of bloke.'

'Voice? Deep? High?'

'Like I said, normal. Although 'e spoke slow like.'

'Slow?'

'His words were paced. Like 'e was thinkin' carefully what he was gonna say next. And he asked for Barbie, specific like.'

'Oh? Is that normal?'

'Sometimes, the regulars like to stick to favourites.'

Maddison made a note. *Meredith was singled out for the call.* 'Do all the girls have working names?'

'Of course. They don't want dirty old men or perverts knowing their real names.'

'Perverts!'

'Some of them.'

'Then that brings me to my next question. I'm new in Hobart …'

'Yeah I know.'

'Oh?'

'Small place.'

'Yes well, when I've dealt with similar cases in Sydney I found the working girls to be a valuable source of information. They know the nuances of their customers, like the rougher deviant types. I'll need to talk to your staff, your girls.'

'Nar. I can't 'ave you sniffin' about,' Mareike bristled. 'The ladies what work here demand privacy. No. Sorry.'

'I'm not asking Mareike, I'm ordering you.'

'Piss off. No one tells me what to do.'

'Oh. If you don't give me access to them, I'll get a warrant and strip this place bare. Do you understand?'

***

The very next morning…

Museum Director, Ms Charlotte Fysh, couldn't believe her luck. Bequeathed collections were few and far between in this modern age; what with beneficiaries aware of the value of rare coins, medals or banknotes collected by dad or grandad, they preferred to sell on the open market and share the spoils rather than see the valuable collection donated to the museum. So when Harry Button's widow walked into the director's office with a shoebox of old documents, banknotes, colonial promissory notes, coins and medals to donate to the museum, Charlotte saw a solution to her dilemma with Stanley Smart. She called her old friend Inspector Maddison Lovett with her plan.

'Perfect,' Maddison agreed. 'Set a trap. But make certain you record and photograph everything in that box. You must detail everything exactly, the condition, and blemishes, anomalies or foreign markings on the banknotes. Take macro shots of the coins.'

'Consider it done.' Charlotte felt good about herself. Now she was bent on catching a thief. She looked at the clock. It was after five.

It was time.

It had been two days now since she had thrown caution to the wind. Charlotte wasn't certain who made the first move; her or Stella. She was certain it was her, but then again … it didn't matter.

With the cache safe within its shoebox and nestled under her arm, Charlotte made her way to the basement to the conservation lab.

'Charlotte!' Stella said, delighted as the director walked in. Charlotte looked about the conservation lab. 'We alone?' she barely whispered. Stella didn't answer. Her presumptuous grin said it all. Stella closed the door and as she fancied herself to be the dominant one in their new relationship, she locked the door from the inside pushing Charlotte against the tiled wall and started undressing. Charlotte jiggled out of her suit coat. Stella couldn't wait. She clamped her hands about Charlotte's cheeks, forcing her lips onto the director's. The kiss was steamy and wet.

'It's just you and me babe now,' Stella purred. Charlotte's glasses fogged and fell to the floor.

Jesus! Charlotte knew it to be so wrong, but this relationship ticked all the boxes for all the wrong reasons;

She was forty-eight, Stella was twenty-six. *Tick.*

She was Stella's boss. *Tick.*

They were carrying on in the workplace. *Tick.*

And she had fallen in love with the young woman. *Tick.*

***

Stella unbuttoned Charlotte's skirt. It fell to the floor leaving nothing but laced panties. She ran warm hands under her boss's blouse, loosened the bra with an experienced hand and, while Charlotte hooked one leg up onto a stool, Stella dropped to her knees.

***

Down the passageway Stanley was certain he heard that busy body Stella Bathe call the Museum Director by her first name, *Charlotte*, a familiarity unprecedented in all his decades at the museum. He may be a little hard at hearing, but he was an intelligent man and he was certain this wasn't the first time. Then there was the time only two days earlier when he thought the young conservationist was standing a little too close to the boss when he entered the staff room. Yes, there was something afoot, and Stanley thought it may be in his best interests to make it his business to find out.

He peeled his ear away from the locked conservation lab door. He had heard enough. He knew the two women were alone in the room, but he could not hear voices. Well nothing intelligible anyhow, just murmurings and an unnatural commotion, foreign to the environment.

***

Charlotte fell into a swivel chair sated, her springing curls in disarray, her lipstick and mascara in need of a touch-up. She leant back with mixed feelings of guilt, slaked lust and adventure. *Stolen love was the best*, she giggled to herself as Stella tidied herself.

'What's this?' Stella finally asked. Her attention was drawn back to the shoebox.

'We have been bequeathed a small private collection of banknotes and coins, all Tasmanian related.' Charlotte said. 'I need you to give it to Stanley tomorrow.'

'Why?'

'We are going to catch that bastard red-handed, that's why.'

'Okay,' Stella said in a questioning tone.

Charlotte explained the sting as she got dressed. 'But first thing in the morning we need to record everything in that box, take photos and detailed descriptions. And then I want you to take the shoebox to Stanley, tell him you just spoke to me in my office and I asked you to give it to him to prepare an inventory.'

Stella's face relayed the pleasure it would give her. 'Inventory huh. You mean *one for the museum, one for me, one for the museum, one for me.*'

'That's about right. Coming for a drink at Maloney's?' Charlotte asked of the pub across the street from the museum.

'I can't. My brother Mason's in a spot of bother. He's lost his job on a fishing boat and I think he's in some sort of trouble.'

'Fair enough. I'll see you first thing in the morning.'

***

That evening, late…

Max the fisherman was feeling sick in the gut. It had been several days since Meredith was murdered by some deranged killer and he was having difficulty coming to terms with her death. Not to mention being grilled by the cops as a suspect until he proved he had a solid alibi. Everything in his pathetic life lately seemed to turn to shit. Now he missed her so much, whether it be the meaningful conversations, cooking her bar-b-queued fish dinners on the deck or the great sex that followed. Max finished his seventh can of beer and contemplated an eighth. This was easily managed as he only drank mid-strength these days. It was cold and wet. The only downside was it made him piss a lot, especially on an empty stomach. Max contemplated bed, but somehow the fond memories of Meredith below kept him on deck. And he sensed her presence, like her spirit watched over him.

Max wrestled with his conscience. The fact that he did not tell the cops everything sickened him. He did not tell the police he was in love with a prostitute who was murdered out on a job, on an escort call.

He didn't tell the cops what a decent person Meredith really was.

Max pulled back the ring top to the satisfying hiss of carbonated beer and sucked the froth before he lost too much of the brew. *I better turn the fridge down a bit,* he thought. *The beer's a bit warm tonight.* Max looked across the water from his mooring to the club. He heard the last revellers leave the bar over an hour ago, their noisy cheer clear across the water in the calm of a warm night. And Terry the manager locked up and drove away, the last to leave the carpark, not that long ago. Max noted he had Tammy the brunette barmaid with him. *Giving her a lift home I should imagine,* Max guessed. *At least I hope that's all he's up to, he's married to a lovely lass from Devonport and she's pregnant I believe … Married!*

Thoughts turned to his estranged wife Verity. The latest news was she wanted him to sell the boat or pay her half its value. *Bitch! Where can I get money like that?*

Suddenly mid-strength beer wasn't cutting the mustard. Max remembered he had half a bottle of rum below. *Yeh rum, that'll make you sleep.*

With a tumbler full of rum Max transferred negative thoughts brought on by Verity into positives. He fancied how nice it would be to have Meredith by his side right now. She was fun, she was young, but she *was* an escort. *Jesus!* Max had weighed up his options. She had firstly been a university student paying for an education, *right.* She was studying for a Bachelor of Arts, wanted to do law she told him. *Hell, I'd only been with her a week but it just felt right.* Max remembered thoughts of taking her under his wing, she could live with him while she finished Uni. She only had the rest of this year to go and she would have had her degree.

But she was an escort. Max had thoughts of Big Bill his Maori deckhand and knew what he would say if he was here on board right now. 'Boss what were yer doin'? Yer've been thinkin' with yer dick again, eh.'

***

Seraph Stood in the shadows of the yacht club's rubbish skips and recycle bins. He was comfortable here. He liked shadows and dark places, dark like his wretched heart. He didn't even mind the stink of festering kitchen scraps. He watched the noisy pissheads leave the bar, all bantering their drunken bravado as they walked to a waiting taxi. One besotted fool crowing his attraction to the young barmaid with the long corkscrew hair. Then the manager locked up; Seraph assumed it was the manager, with the attractive barmaid the pisshead was boasting about. It had been close too; the manager was carrying two milk crates of empty bottles for the recycle bins on his way out and Seraph had to crawl between the skips to hide. *Bloody close that was.*

Seraph could see the fishing boat *Infinity* clearly, moored a hundred metres out amongst a dozen other craft, mostly yachts. And he could see the skipper was still sitting on deck; he could make out the stocky bloke's figure under the soft light of a low voltage lamp. Seraph also noted the jetty berths were all rented, and there were possibly other yachties on board their crafts. He knew he would have to be discreet. He could make out other lights amongst them. Seraph looked at his watch, it was 12.10AM. He would just have to wait. But the whispers were constant. *Do it, get it over with. Do it … do it …*

Max heard the subtle bump against the hull, centimetres from where he lay his head on his bed in the bow. His initial thought was it was Sammy the seal. The huge overfed bull seal, a resident in the bays around here, was fed regularly by locals. Then again it could be a bull shark. There were plenty of the mongrels in this area also. A second thump was slightly louder.

I best go and check. I need a piss anyhow.

Max rolled back the door into the wheelhouse and looked about. It was deathly quiet. It seemed the entire eastern shore had called it a night. As there was little moonlight the deck was masked in darkness. Max looked out the window towards the stern. Something wasn't right. The hold hatch was open, and Max knew he hadn't had that much to drink, not to know he checked it before retiring below deck for the night. Stepping out onto the deck Max saw the small eight-foot tender. It was tied up to his mooring cable.

'*Bloody kids!*' he thought. '*Thieving bastards!*'

Max slipped quietly back into the wheelhouse and fetched his marine torch. Besides being powerful, it doubled as a handy club. Returning back to the open deck he realised he was only wearing his underpants. *Shit! Bit late now.* He trod quietly barefoot to the hold. The hatch was open wide enough for a small person to enter. Max took a deep breath. Flooding the hold with light he saw sudden movement.

Max shouted. 'Who's there?'

There was no warning. Max felt a sharp pain in his chest. The speargun harpoon fired at close range penetrated his heart, protruding out the other side. Max's eyes rolled back in his head. He let out a dying gasp and, clutching at the bloodied shaft of the spear, he collapsed to the deck.

Seraph couldn't believe how easy the kill was. The balaclava appeared above deck and looked about. The coast was clear. Seraph rose from the hold like a wraith from the grave. He checked the fisherman was dead. He cut the line with a pocketknife and threw the speargun over the side before fetching a fishing net from a locker. Within minutes he had rolled Max's body into a tangled mess of netting and, burdened with lead diver's weights, he eased his kill over the side and watched the corpse sink into blackness.

***

Earlier that afternoon…

Magistrate Christian Winterbourne had the information he needed from Chastity. Now all he had to do was act upon it.

Tyron Maynard was eighth generation Tasmanian aboriginal. He had grown up around racehorses and it was this background that brought him to Christian's attention. Fortunately for Christian he had tipped more winners than losers and Christian had seen minor charges dropped, like drunk driving, in exchange for the tips. But Christian knew Tyron had contacts with Hobart's underbelly. He had heard rumours that Tyron and his mates – many of them dock workers – dabbled in items that had '*fallen off the back of a truck*' or been pinched from cargo ships. Tyron also mentioned he knew thugs for hire, should the magistrate want someone *slapped*.

'I need a job done,' Christian told the twenty-eight-year-old. This was music to the young man's ears.

'What sort of job mate, want someone *slapped*?'

Christian looked along the length of stables at Elwick Racecourse where Tyron worked. Other stable hands went about their business; no one seemed particularly interested in the old cove talking to Tyron. 'I need someone to break into a house and remove something specific from an old safe.'

'Jesus!' Tyron laughed. 'Go Mr Winterbourne eh!'

'Please, keep it down Tyron. This is no joke.'

'Aye, I can see that. I've never seen ya so serious mate.'

'Can you help or not?'

'Well break and entry ain't my gig mate, me or me mates. We deal in a little contraband, but hey. You want a burglar.'

Christian looked exasperated. 'Look forget it. Forget I was even here.' He made to leave.

'Wait, wait.' Tyron was always eager to help, and he particularly liked having a magistrate in his little black book, so to speak. 'Leave it with me will ya? Can I call ya at home?'

'Have you got my number?'

'Got it somewhere,' he smiled, knowing very well he had it locked in his memory.

***

That same day…

At Police Headquarters Inspector Maddison Lovett dunked the English breakfast tea bag robotically. At work she liked her tea strong and black, no sugar, yet her focus was on the cork board pinned to the wall in front of her. The photo of the remains of the obese dead antique dealer Jock Birdwhistle was in the centre. The charcoal orbs remaining in what was left of his skull where the eyes once were pleaded with her.

Catch the bastard that did this.

The inspector had seen plenty of violent deaths in Sydney, but a fifty-year-old Nazi dagger for a weapon? *Jesus!*

Constable Lachlan Harlow, a good-looking constable with the whitest teeth Maddison had ever seen, had been sitting at his computer for hours, gazing at finger-print records. Suddenly he jumped to his feet. 'I've got a match,' he yelled across the room.

Maddison turned from the notice board. 'From the antique shop?'

'Yep, I mean yes Inspector.'

'Well?

'Jacopo Moretti, Italian immigrant came out here in 1974 from Naples. Listed as a cabinetmaker. Born 1934 so that makes him … ah …'

'Sixty-one'

'Yes, sixty-one.'

'Crime?'

'Receiving stolen goods. Arrested 1983 when his prints were taken. Suspended sentence of twelve months.'

'Only one offence?'

'Yes.'

'What goods?'

'Pardon?'

'Receiving stolen goods. What goods?'

'Oh, sorry.' Lachlan ran an eye down the screen. 'Antiques.'

'Antiques! Yes, that sounds about right. Address?'

The rookie wrote down the address on a sheet of paper and passed it to the inspector. 'It's in North Hobart.'

Jacopo wasn't surprised to see the police car. He had caught the early morning news the day before and was dumbfounded that the dealer he had paid a visit to, the thieving mongrel who *stole* his painting, was dead. And he just knew they would find his fingerprints at the crime scene. The police car crept slowly, crunching over his gravel driveway, blocking in his pickup.

Due to the seriousness of the crime, Jacopo was to be driven to the police station and interviewed there; although they assured him he was not under arrest per se. The officers listened to his pleas concerning his wife Eleanora's dementia, and he was escorted to the neighbour directly next door, where an elderly and helpful Mrs Benetti agreed to watch Eleanora until he returned.

Before entering the interview room at the police station Inspector Maddison Lovett observed the short, wiry, old Italian through a one-way mirror. Jacopo looked nervous, but he was no fool, he knew he was being watched, and sat uncomfortably chewing his nails.

Maddison and another policeman sat opposite Jacopo at the interrogation table with its stainless-steel restraints for shackling prisoners. However, Jacopo was spared this humiliation. 'Good morning Mr Moretti. I'm Inspector Lovett and this is my colleague Sergeant Highlander.' Maddison then spoke for the benefit of a tape recorder. 'For the purpose of this interview I am recording Mr Jacopo Moretti of North Hobart. Is this correct?'

'Yes,' Jacopo was nervous, his voice very soft.

'I must ask you to speak up Mr Moretti.'

'Si. My name … eet is Signor Jacopo Moretti.'

After the usual preliminaries Maddison tackled the serious questions. 'Where were you last Tuesday evening between the hours of 7PM and nine?' Maddison had given herself a two-hour window here. After enquiries at the nearest Domino's Pizza kitchen they had ascertained the murder happened shortly after the pizza was delivered, which was around 7.10pm.

'At home.'

'Anyone with you to verify that?'

'I live with wife, Eleonora, but she sick. She have dementia. She know nothing.'

'What were you doing at home?'

'Watching television. I watch *Wheels of Fortune.*'

'Wheel of Fortune huh?'

'Si, I like these television show. People win moneys.'

Sergeant Ray Highlander had an idea. 'Who is the compere?' he asked.

'Burgo and Adriana,' Jacopo answered the question with the zeal of one of the shows contestants.

'Yes, John Burgess and Adriana … what's her name?'

'Xenides.'

Highlander looked at the inspector who clearly didn't have a clue who ran the show. The sergeant nodded.

'What was the *surprise wedge*?' Highlander asked of the winnings pool for last Tuesday night's show.'

'Two-thousand-dollar,' Jacopo answered without thinking. The sergeant made a note to check this, but truth was someone could have told the Italian the results the following day.

'What did you do to your thumb?' Jacopo's bruised thumb had not been bad enough to bandage.

'I hit eet with hammer.'

Jacopo finally had the courage to ask the police a question. 'Why you ask me these things?'

The delay in him asking had made Maddison suspicious. Any innocent person would be demanding to know why they had been detained the moment they were brought in. Maddison leant across the desk and eye-balled the Italian cabinetmaker, hoping she looked as menacing as she felt. 'Mr Moretti. Do you know an antique dealer named Jock Birdwhistle?'

'Jock Birdwhistle, si, si, he has a shop in the city somewhere I'm theenking, but I don't know him.'

'Have you ever visited his shop?'

'No. Never.'

'Are you certain Mr Moretti?'

'Si, si. Never have I been to thees shop.'

'Well then, how do you explain your fingerprints all over the glass louvres in the toilet at the back of his shop?' The look on Jacopo's face said it all. *So they did find my fingerprints.* 'You see Mr Moretti; Jock Birdwhistle was murdered Tuesday night. Stabbed to death in his own shop and the premises set alight.'

'Si, I see these things on television.'

'So, Mr Moretti, would you like to change that last answer?'

Jacopo buried his face in his hands. Finally, he looked up. 'I tell you true, I home watching *Wheel of Fortune.*'

'Then how do you explain your fingerprints all over the glass louvres? Every single one of them in fact.'

There was no point lying further. 'I tell you.' Jacopo went on to explain *exactly* what happened; from the switched auction numbers on the boxes to confronting the dealer in his shop; everything except the existence of the Duterrau painting.

'Are you trying to tell me you broke into Mr Birdwhistle's shop when he was away simply to steal back some rubbish prints and pictures that weren't rightly his?'

'Si. Si.'

'Why?'

'Was … ah … how you say, principle.'

'Then why lie to us in the first place?'

'I theenk, Jacopo, you in trouble.' Jacopo wanted to tell the police about the man called Ryan who threatened him. He was probably the killer, Jacopo thought, but then the truth about the painting would be exposed.

Maddison looked at Highlander and shook her head. She wasn't buying any of it. However, the police didn't have enough to hold the man in custody. She terminated the recording and turned back to the Italian. 'You may go Mr Moretti, but you are not permitted to leave Tasmania. Got it?'

'Si.'

***

The police car drove Jacopo back to his residence only to be greeted by an angry Mrs Benetti, now joined by her husband, the elderly Giuseppe, still holding a gushing garden hose. Insidious smoke and the steam from a doused fire crept down the laneway to greet him.

'Mamma Mia.' Jacopo jumped from the police car and hurried up the lane as fast as his scrawny legs would take him.

'Quello che e successo?' he called out to the animated Mrs Benetti. The police driver followed.

'What you do?' Jacopo switched to English for the benefit of the police officer. Mrs Benetti's short plump animated arms waved about, accentuating her anger. 'I no look after your wife Jacopo. She should be in hospital, si.'

'What happen?' Jacopo now saw Eleanora cowering near the back door, her tiny hand clenched about the Zippo lighter that appeared to be of so much amusement to her lately.

'Il mio amore, Eleanora … what you do?'

'She start fire to your … your … wood there.' And now Jacopo saw the source of the fire and subsequent smoke. His drum of Huon Pine shavings had caught fire and if it wasn't for Giuseppe and his garden hose the outcome could have been a lot worse.

***

The next morning…

Police Inspector Maddison Lovett arrived at *Salon Rouge* bordello for her appointed meeting. It was 10AM.

Uncharacteristically, Madam Mareike was accommodating. The brothel keeper made her office available for the police interview and ordered the girls, whom she had rounded up for the purpose, to cooperate with the cops.

Maddison stepped into the office and smiled. If the large gilt mirror with carved cherubs looked out of place, the crucifix *definitely* did. 'Thank you, Mrs …'

'Mareike. Just call me Mareike.'

Maddison ran a hand along the brass-studded, leather inlaid desktop. The desk had been cleared except for a glass paperweight Maddison recognised as antique.

'Nice. French isn't it?'

'Yes, I do believe it is. My son gave it to me recently.'

'Oh, you have children?'

'Just a boy.' Mareike looked pensive. 'Actually, he has only recently come back into my life.'

'Oh?'

'Yes, he was adopted out at birth.' Maddison suspected she recognised a hint of guilt, which vanished smartly. Mareike, in turn, studied the policewoman for a sign she was being judged. 'Girls are ready,' the madam said, and, suddenly blunt, 'Don't delay them longer than necessary.'

Each woman was asked to recall any particularly strange requests in the bedroom. And there were plenty. For most of the lawmen, including Maddison, it was an education.

Poppy Fellows, a gullible blonde with trusting eyes, had a regular client who liked to be whipped. Jacinda Maisch spoke of being urinated on. Her peer Savannah spoke of another man whose fetish was to wear the girl's panties and bra while he watched her pleasure herself with a vibrator. Ginger told of one kinky customer who paid extra when she dressed up in a schoolgirl's uniform, while Candy and Ivy told of another who liked them both at once, a threesome, while they shocked him, literally, with a low voltage electric current on his genitals, attached with alligator clips.

None of the men seemed violent until Maddison talked to a young woman who looked stunning in a long black hairpiece. She introduced herself as Billie. 'I had a guy here a few weeks back who tried to choke me the moment he ejaculated.'

Maddison leant forward on her chair. 'What happened?'

'Well, the moment he climaxed he wound me stockings around me neck and tried to choke me.'

'What did you do?'

'I screamed out and he stopped. Then he was real apologetic like, going on and on saying how he couldn't help doing it and how sorry he was. Gave me a fifty-dollar tip.'

'Can you describe him?'

'Stocky bloke, late twenties, early thirties, short dark hair slicked down with hair oil and a trimmed beard. He could be good company, quite charming when he wished to be, but behind his joviality he could be dangerous.'

'Dangerous, as in trying to choke you.'

'Yeh well that too. But I've been with him twice now. He didn't do it the first time. He liked to chat a bit first, paid for an hour, so why not? I'm happy with the talking, gives Sally a break.'

'Sally?'

'Yeh.' Billie pointed to her groin.

'Oh, right … what did you talk about?'

'Well that's the thing, right. He told me he had a record, that he was born into crime, caught thieving when he was twelve, robbed a tobacconist when he was fourteen, stabbed another boy with scissors when he was fifteen, and he was put into a boys' home for that. At sixteen he was a burglar and by twenty he knew how to crack safes. I took it with a grain of salt, thought he was just big noting himself. Many do. But then he fuckin' choked me … excuse the French.'

Maddison fought a smile. 'Anything else?"

'Said his favourite food was Indian.'

'Do you remember his name?'

'Hank, I think.'

'Isn't there a record kept?' One of the cops asked. 'Of the clients here that is.'

'Are you kiddin'? Some are reservations, others walk in off the street and the ones who do tell you their name are usually bullshitting.'

The police were comparing notes when Candy knocked on the door. Her pretty round pale skinned face accentuating her bright red lipstick, appeared around the door. 'Just had a thought,' she said.

'Yes.'

Candy walked back into the office, removing spearmint gum from her mouth and squeezing it into its wrapper before continuing. 'Meredith wasn't like the rest of us. She was a university student.'

'Yes, we know that.'

'Just earnin' money to get a better education. Lots of girls do it.'

'Sure,' Maddison said. 'What was that thought of yours?'

'Well she told me she had a crush on a client, a fisherman called Max. Said he was real keen himself, and that his wife was a real bitch and Max was in the process of a divorce.'

'Max. A fisherman?'

'Yep. Said he had a boat down the docks, and she went and stayed with him a coupla times at his shack.'

'Shack? Where?'

'Cremorne, I think she said.' Candy grew teary-eyed. 'Jesus, I miss her, Meredith was a good sort, she never deserved what she got, poor thing.'

***

Maddison had barely sat at her desk when Detective Landon Finch bowled into her office unannounced. They were alone. 'Maddie.'

'Landon.'

'This was just pointed out to me by one of the juniors downstairs,' he tossed a folder report onto her desk. 'It arrived while you were interviewing the *ladies* at the bordello. How, by the way, did that go anyway?'

'You should have joined me,' Maddison said with a pert grin. 'Might have found yourself a date.'

Landon stood in front of Maddison's desk. Leaning forward, arms at full length and resting his knuckles on the desk, he pretended to be insulted. 'Come now Maddie, you know I'm not that sort of bloke.'

Enough foolery. Maddison picked up the folder. 'What's this then?'

'It's a report made to the police by a Sylvia Brandt, who came forward and said she had been approached by a man a few weeks back, in the area of the murder. It was in the carpark and he whistled her and she said *you whistling for a dog* and he said no, *I'm whistling to you love.* He then approached her and she hurried down the bush path into the open and back to her home nearby. This bloke followed her. Not long after her husband returned home from work and he was mad as hell and went looking for the guy but no show.'

'Description?'

'Man of average build, good looking, late thirties, wavy red hair combed back over his ears and with piercing, unblinking eyes. Like lasers she thought. It made her feel most uncomfortable.'

'That sounds similar to the suspect from the cold case murder we were reading about recently, in the same area.'

'That's what I thought.'

'And she just reported it?'

'Well yes, when she read about the recent murder.'

'You have an address?'

'Right there.'

***

An hour later…

Taroona resident Sylvia Brandt stood in her doorway, hesitant to let the police inside her flat. The problem was she had just changed the baby's nappy and … *well the flat could use a good airing.* Feeling embarrassed, she quickly reiterated what she told the police HQ front desk over the phone.

'Did you see the colour of his hair?'

'Red I think. He wore a hood.'

'And he threatened you?'

'No, I said I felt threatened, he didn't actually threaten me.' Sylvia wanted to help. She thought hard. 'There was one thing though.'

'Oh, what?'

'He had a small birthmark or tattoo on his neck under his right ear, shaped like a jellybean.'

'Jellybean?'

'Yeh, sort of foetus shaped. I could just make it out when he approached me. That's when I took off. Bloody creepy he was.'

'You had time to notice a small birthmark?'

'Yeh, well I worked at a mole clinic before Robbie came along,' she said of her baby. 'And a dark mole like that would catch my attention.'

***

That evening…

7PM. Vivaldi's Four Seasons percolated through the Mona Street mansion from the magistrate's Pioneer stereo system. Christian had the music louder than usual and sat back in his favourite armchair nursing a generous balloon of Hennessy VSOP cognac. The newly arrived 1995 *Miller's guide to antiques* sat open on a side table at a page on clocks, but was neglected in favour of a recently purchased book on nineteenth century Australian artists resting on his lap. Christian found it hard to concentrate. His eyes grew heavy and he fought sleep, but his phone in the hall had other plans.

'Christian Winterbourne,' the magistrate's official voice resonated. 'With whom am I speaking?'

'It's me boss.'

'Me? Oh, Tyron?'

'Yer mate. I got you a … what yer asked for.'

'Oh.'

Talking openly on the phone was not wise. 'Meet me in the mornin', Princess Park, say nine?'

'Very well.'

***

Meanwhile, out on the street…

Antique restorer Jacopo Moretti parked his Ford pickup in Battery Point's Francis Street. He scanned his surroundings surreptitiously, as if he was looking for a certain address. Paranoid that he was being watched by the police, he sat in silence a moment, cursing daylight saving for keeping evening light so late. He guessed the time to be around 7.30PM. It was dusk and he thought he caught a flash of lightning off towards the horizon south. A thunderstorm was brewing and no wonder, Jacopo thought, after today's balmy weather. There were few people about. One old dear who didn't look a day under ninety hosed her roses, otherwise the streets were deserted. It was dinner time after all, and most residents would be inside or having a summer bar-b-que out the back. This he was certain of, for he could smell meat grilling and now realised how hungry he was himself. *But first things first.*

Taking the package wrapped in an old sheet, he locked his Ford and walked the two hundred yards from Colville Street and along Mona Street to magistrate Winterbourne's property, looking about constantly to be certain he wasn't followed.

***

Christian Yardley Winterbourne had lost his appetite lately, and with good reason. He stood at his kitchen table picking at some cold meat left over from the night before when his doorbell beckoned. Instantly the magistrate felt vulnerable. It was time to renew his home security. Have a lock put on the iron gate at the footpath for starters. Why, only recently Christian was missing a valuable glass paperweight. He had noticed the Georgian mahogany glass bookcase ajar and one of the paperweights was missing; a rather delightful Murano millefiori Bacchus style paperweight with a fleur-de-lis in the centre. Date 1900–1910. Value one-hundred-and-fifty-dollars. But he had two dozen in his collection, or was it twenty-three? He couldn't be certain. But he also couldn't ignore his nagging suspicion that that halfwit neighbour of Jacopo's, *what was his name? Rory, yes that was it, Rory,* had snooped about when he asked to use the toilet that evening; the evening they delivered the Huon pine chest of drawers. The doorbell called a second time.

Suspecting Tyron had been in the area all along when he phoned earlier, Christian prepared to remonstrate with the lad for visiting him at home unannounced, when he opened the door to the Italian cabinetmaker Jacopo Moretti.

'Buona sera signor.'

'Monoochi!'

'Signor Moretti signor Winterbourne.'

Christian considered asking the Italian about his neighbour, the halfwit, when he glanced at the parcel under the man's arm, stepped out onto the veranda, looked about smartly and quickly ushered the Italian inside.

'What are you doing here at this hour Moretti? Is my chair finished?'

'No. Sorry signor. But I have something to show you. Sometheen I theenk you love, si.'

Christian sensed the thrill of being in the presence of fine art, maybe something that had never been discovered before. Something rare. A bargain preferably. 'Follow me.' Christian returned to the kitchen and signalled for the Italian to place his parcel on the pine kitchen table. 'It's a painting, yes?'

'Si.' Jacopo unwrapped the framed oil he so masterfully retrieved from that *fat bastardo antique dealer, Birdwhistle.* He had spent the afternoon carefully removing the water colour disguise he had painted on the portrait before the auction. Now *Wild man of Van Diemen's Land, Wurragunna,* stared back at the two men.

Christian was in awe. He had been reading extensively on historic Australian artists lately; especially early colonial artists of Tasmania, the likes of William Gould, John Glover, Robert Hawker Dowling and Benjamin Duterrau, and recognised Duterrau's style immediately. The Tasmanian aborigine stood before the artist dressed in a cloak of animal skins – quoll, platypus and pademelon. His matted red-ochre coloured hair hung over his eyes, almost hiding them, with two shell necklaces adorning his neck. About his waist he wore a belted lap-lap and he held a shield and spear. Christian could just make out a date, 1833. It was magnificent, early and rare and the magistrate could barely disguise his interest.

'Where did you get this?'

'I have home, many, many years si. Eet was given me for payment for fixing table,' he lied.

Christian reigned in his enthusiasm. 'Yes, I've seen similar work,' he said trying to dampen his fervour.

'Is Benjamin Duterrau, Engleesh art-teest with Frenchman name, si.'

If Christian was put off by the fact this Italian cabinet maker knew his art, it did not faze him. He simply had to have it. 'How much?'

Jacopo rubbed his chin as if contemplating his asking price. Whilst he wanted to rid himself of the luckless painting, he did not wish to be greedy; then again, he did not wish to undersell such a rare piece of art. 'I am wanting fifteen thousand.'

'Fifteen! That's a lot of money Mr Monoochi.'

Why can't this old fool get my name right? Jacopo thought. But let it slip. 'Ees worth it signor, I theenk you know thees.'

Christian had never been a great negotiator. Life had been generous to his purse over the years and he pretty much purchased whatever took his fancy. 'I'll tell you what my friend.' *My friend? I don't think so.*

'I'll give you ten.'

'No signor. Ees worth four times that. I theenk you know thees things.'

'I'll tell you what I do know. I know a man who needs the money when I see one. And I'm looking at one right now. I'll give you eleven and that's my final offer.'

Rude bastardo, what a cheek.

'Twelve,' Jacopo shot back, and his hand darted out just as quickly. Christian ran another assuring eye down the rectangular painting in its walnut veneer frame. 'You have a deal.' He took the Italian's hand and they shook to seal the transaction. 'I can write you a cheque now or you come back in a day or so and I'll have the cash.'

'I come back, I'm thinkeen.' Jacopo rewrapped the painting. 'I no want cheque, si.'

'You can leave that here. It's quite safe.' Jacopo hesitated. 'You *can* trust me you know. I'm a magistrate for Christ's sake.'

'Si … si … but I …' Jacopo had not prepared himself for this scenario. He thought a moment. *The man was a magistrate, si, he had plenty of money, si,* and Jacopo convinced himself it would be safer out of his hands if the police came to his home with a search warrant.

'Give me a couple of days and I'll have your money,' Christian said. 'Alright?'

Jacopo returned to his pickup satisfied with the outcome. The evening was now growing dark with storm clouds rolling in. Sheet lightning grew closer and now Jacopo felt drops of rain.

***

About three kilometres north under the Tasman Bridge and not too distant from Cornelian Bay…

Ryan wrestled with his conscience. *Everything had turned to shit.* He had killed that antique dealer in his own shop. *But it was manslaughter for Christ's sake. The fat bastard attacked him.* But the cops wouldn't see it like that, *you broke and entered his premises.*

Shit!

Ryan had nowhere to go. No money. And the irony was if he had the Duterrau painting he could be sixty grand richer at the snap of his fingers.

He moved about in the dark only. Fetching a day-old Mercury newspaper from a waste bin he read the headlines. The murder was big news here in little old Hobart. Christ, if it was Melbourne or say … London, it'd hardly rate a mention. But the good news was the cops didn't have any leads and the paper hinted that the antique dealer had surprised a random burglar. With this in mind Ryan felt he could stay in town and pursue looking for his only chance of a future. *Find that fuckin' painting.*

Ryan had spent two nights sleeping under the Tasman Bridge. As it was late summer the weather had been considerate. It wasn't the sort of camping out a man would try in winter, not with only a stolen blanket. But he was never really alone; he derived some pleasure in spying on the odd car parking at the water's edge in the dark beneath the bridge. Young lovers. Fogged windscreens. Rocking vehicles. Glowing cigarettes. Driving away, dissolving back into the night, returning to their homes. *Ah youth! How it's wasted on the young.*

The first night Ryan slept under the bridge he thought he was spying on two gay men, meeting in secrecy under the Tasman Bridge on a balmy summer evening. But as he watched on, well hidden in the dark shadows behind a pylon, he noted the men were engaged in some different clandestine activity. One had driven to the site in an early eighties Ford Escort, parking out of sight. The other arrived on foot. The older man, who smoked and attempted blowing pathetic smoke rings, passed the younger man something, an envelope maybe. Money? Was it drug deal? They spoke briefly, words Ryan could not hear, and parted ways.

Tonight, it threatened to rain. Distant lightning threatened a thunderstorm heading upriver from off the Tasman Sea. Ryan had been casing the waterfront during the afternoon and only half a kilometre from the bridge in a cove named Cornelian Bay, he had discovered two dozen or so old shanty–like boat sheds backing up against an embankment. But these weren't any old boat sheds. Ryan had randomly peeped in a few windows and noticed most of these brightly coloured huts had been turned into tiny shacks, most with a veranda over the water where a person could fish, feet up and enjoy a beer. And to make them even more inviting they all seemed unoccupied. Privacy was secure. Ryan waited an hour until it was dark; well after 9PM with the daylight savings time in summer. There were no lights on in the sheds. They all seemed empty. Now Ryan heard the thunder approach. What did he have to lose, he thought? And broke into the first shanty that took his fancy.

It was barely sunrise and Pacific gulls were already fighting over food on the roof of the boat shed. Ryan woke groggy, early. The birds were bigger and heavier than normal gulls, with large red beaks and huge webbed feet. Pacific gulls he seemed to recall someone naming them. Ryan lay awake on the old wicker couch where he had crashed for the night. He had barely made it inside when the rains came. Torrential rain like in the tropics, with loud thunder overhead and strobe lightning Ryan fancied would wake the dead. And with Cornelian Bay Cemetery only two hundred metres away across the cove, waking the dead was the last thing he wanted; haunted as he was by the violent death of the antique dealer.

Ryan took in his surroundings. It had been pitch dark the night before and he dare not turn on the lights. Now in dawn's golden hue he could make out the interior of the shanty. The weatherboard boat shed had been re-roofed with iron and a skylight fitted. The interior walls were painted yellow and blue; very '80s by the look of it. Not much else had happened. Inside was cosy with an open fireplace added back in the '40s. The owners had gone with a fisherman's theme, and why not, it *was* on the water with its own wee jetty. The walls were hung with old cork life buoys, enamel signs, glass fishing buoys, driftwood, fishnets, and the mandatory shell decorations. Not Tasmanian you understand, the type of nautical tack one finds in tourist souvenir shops in Bali or Phuket. Half a dozen fishing rods hung across the open rafters; fishing rod styles that spanned generations. From where Ryan lay, he could see through a sliding glass door onto the bay. It was going to be a beautiful summer's day.

The gulls grew louder.

Noisy bastards!

Ryan stood groggily and stretched. From where he stood, he could see across the bay to the cemetery. Wary of early morning risers he approached the sliding door to see what all the noisy avian fuss was about. At the end of the jetty, only six metres away gulls were now going crazy. *Jesus! There must be thirty or forty of the big fat bastards.*

Without warning something fell from the apex of the roof outside the sliding door. Something heavy. It landed with a meaty thud. Squabbling birds dived bombed the object. Ryan caught a flash of red and pink and yellow, when he recognised sinew.

Oh Christ! They've seized a large fish and the bastards are butchering it right here. Why here? Damn it!

Ryan wrenched the sliding door open. Frightened birds rose en-masse, flailing and squawking, and Ryan recognised human flesh immediately. It looked like belly with some intestinal organs intact.

Fuck!

Ryan slammed the door shut and jumped back.

What's going on?

Careful to remain unseen, he looked along the row of sheds. As the shanties were built side by side, they had no windows, except vista windows looking over the bay. Satisfied he was alone, Ryan opened the door once more. The birds were wary and circled overhead, but half a dozen bolder gulls were still feeding at the end of the jetty. Ryan made a scene of shooing them away and looked over the edge of the jetty.

Christ!

Just as he feared, the shredded and pecked body of a man naked except for underpants, floated near the surface. He was bound in fishing net, like he had tangled in it. *Maybe he drowned that way,* Ryan was thinking, when he saw the spear gun harpoon through the body. *Oh Christ! It's a murder victim!* Ryan could make out the face of a man much younger than him, about thirty but it was hard to tell. His eyes sockets had been pecked clean leaving hollow black orbs framed in rings of purple red blood. Ryan couldn't believe his bad luck. Of all the shanties. Of all the areas in Hobart. Why here? Why me? The place will be crawling with cops when this news comes out.

***

About three hours later...

Inspector Maddison Lovett climbed down the embankment to the row of neat shanties the southern water's edge of Cornelian Bay. The Cornelian Bay boat sheds, unique to Hobart and so close to the city, looked so inviting early morning. Not the expected scene of a murder. Maddison had looked forward to a later start today and even cooked herself a hot breakfast. Now it looked like breakfast would be a cold omelette for lunch instead.

Senior Detective Landon greeted Maddison, 'Morning Inspector.'

Landon maintained formality in front of colleagues, although all those close to the detectives knew the two shared a distant past.

'Are you certain this isn't a job for the waterfront police?' Maddison asked Landon – already suited up in protective gear so as not to pollute the crime scene. He waited for the inspector at the shanty door. 'How do we know it's a homicide?'

'Follow me,' was all Landon said.

Maddison caught the look in his eye before he turned and walked away. 'Something tells me this is going to be nasty.'

'Sorry, I thought you'd been briefed.'

Maddison followed Landon through the shack, nodding a morning's greeting to police colleagues present, including rookie Luke Farrell and the Coroner Tiger Griffin, who passed her PPE plastics. Suited up, Maddison continued out through the sliding doors and onto the jetty. 'Oh Christ!' The body, what was left of it, had been hoisted from the water and placed next to a body bag on the deck. A recreational diver's spear from a spear gun penetrated the body, all the way through the heart.

'If that's not a homicide I don't know what is,' Landon said. He didn't mean to sound sardonic, but to those standing by he sure did.

Maddison let out a deep sigh. 'Any I.D.?'

'Not yet. Sarah has taken a damaged driving licence to the car, she's radioing in to have the number I .D'd.'

'Water damaged, or otherwise?'

'No, more like seagull damage. The bloody things have been pecking at him for hours.'

For the first time Maddison noticed the great black and white gulls with their bright orange beaks and feet, crying overhead as they circled; annoyed that their repast had been disturbed. Maddison looked into the hollow eye sockets and imagined the birds pecking out the eyeballs. 'Christ. Okay then, clues?'

'The shack owner's on his way here,' Landon checked his note pad, 'Daven Taylor. Draftsman at the council, designs roads, I think. He was really pissed off that someone broke into his shack.'

'Ah, that was my next question,' Maddison said. 'How did you get in?'

'Door was left open. We have a witness also. A man was seen leaving here.'

'When.'

'Bit after six.'

'Description?'

'Slim, early sixties, fit for his age.'

'Squatter?'

'No. Not the homeless squatter type, wore tweed and a trilby hat ... oh yes, she thought his hair looked fake.'

'Wig?'

'I guess that's what she meant.'

'So, who reported the body?'

'The same witness who saw the bloke leave. Her name's Lexi McMahan and she owns one of the sheds further along. She came to check her property after the storm last night and saw this codger leaving. As she knows Daven Taylor, the owner of this place, she knew the perp wasn't him so she came to investigate. She called out to him, but he ran off. As he left the door open, she entered, saw the remains.' Landon alluded to the blood and viscera left by the seagulls on the deck.

'And where is she now?'

'She had to get the kids to school. But I've got all her details here,' Landon slapped the notebook in his hand. 'Why ... do you want to talk to her?'

'Later.'

A commotion drew attention back to the front door where a civilian was arguing with the duty cop keeping people away. 'That'll be the owner.' Landon pushed by his colleagues in the cramped space. 'Daven Taylor?'

'Yes. What's happened? Any damage?'

The detective nodded to the young policeman to let the man through. 'Everything looks pretty well in place to me,' Landon said.

The shack owner barrelled angrily through the living area and looked about. To be honest, Landon and Maddison thought, there was very little to damage or steal in the boat shed, suffice to say, unless vandals broke in and trashed the joint. Taylor noticed the body. 'Oh Jesus!'

'If you're up for it,' Maddison said. 'Please have a closer look at the victim, tell me if you recognise him.'

There wasn't much to recognise. The cadaver once had a reasonable physique, a strong looking man in his thirties with short dark hair and a trimmed beard. Now it was almost unrecognisable.

'Is that a ... a ... spear? From a spear gun?' Taylor asked.

'Yes. It's not from here I take it?' Maddison said looking at fishing rods stored horizontally up near the ceiling.

'No.'

'When's the last time you spent time here Mr Taylor?'

'Weeks ago. But I can tell someone's been here.'

'Oh?'

'Yes. Unless your boys have been moving stuff around?'

'Certainly not sir, this is a crime scene. The police have touched nothing. What's been moved?'

'Well the cupboards have been opened ...'

'Someone looking for food.'

'And the day bed's been slept on; all the cushions are up one end. I always spread them out.'

'Well we're in the process of dusting for prints Mr Taylor. You've had a visitor alright, but I don't think he had anything to do with this murder. That cadaver has washed here and snagged on the jetty, probably during the storm last night.'

'Oh!'

'But we'll need your fingerprints.'

'My fingerprints! Why for Christ's sake?'

'So, we can eliminate your fingerprints and isolate the prints of your mystery guest.'

'Guest? Not likely.'

A voice caught their attention from behind. 'Inspector Lovett.'

Maddison turned. 'Ah, Sarah, isn't it?' she said to the attractive young constable.

'Yes Inspector, Sarah Reinhold.' Sarah had a winning smile, the tell-tale look of success. 'I have an I.D. on the victim.'

'Great. And?'

'Max Shreeve, crayfish fisherman. He has his own boat, *Infinity*.'

***

A short time later

With *Infinity* towed to a nearby Lindisfarne Motor Yacht Club jetty, police divers searched the seabed around the fishing boats mooring. They found the speargun in eight metres of water, thrown overboard, but after its night in water there would be no pulling fingerprints. Landon returned from interviewing the club manager and other staff available.

'No one has seen anything suspicious,' he told Maddison, joining her on board at the crime scene. 'The manager said he saw Max Shreeve's lights on two nights ago but not last night.'

'Oh.'

'And it seems he moored over here several days ago, moving from Victoria Dock, citing privacy issues.'

'Oh, like what?'

'Wife issues. Apparently, he was going through a bad divorce.'

'Well there's a motive right there. Do you have a name?'

'Valery ... ah ...' Landon flipped pages in his notebook. 'No, Verity. Verity Shreeve. The manager told me she lives in the family home in Sandy Bay. Poor old Max was given short shrift. That's why he was living on this boat.'

'Poor old Max eh?' Maddison tutted. 'Typical male, take the husband's side.'

'Well, the boys over at the club reckon she's a piece of work, especially when she's been on the sauce.'

'There you go again, *the boys,* I rest my case.' Maddison caught Landon winking to an officer standing within earshot. 'Let's settle this once and for all,' Maddison ordered Landon. 'You go find this Verity Shreeve and form your own opinion.'

Maddison watched Landon fetch his driver and the two men left in an unmarked police car. Physically Landon hadn't changed all that much in the past decades. He looked after himself, regularly exercised and watched his diet; most of the time. A little like Maddison, although she wasn't managing the gym as much as she would have liked. And she liked Landon's lack of vanity; he was content to turn grey gracefully. There was no dyeing of hair for this man.

'Good man, that Landon,' Coroner Griffin broke Maddison's reverie on his approach, clumping down the dodgy gangplank like a boy scout.

Maddison. 'Sorry?'

'I said he's a good man … Landon.' Tiger had followed Maddison's eyeline across to the car park. 'He's dedicated to his work.'

'Yes … yes of course.' For a moment Maddison thought Tiger was alluding to their distant past as lovers. Then again, maybe he was.

'Any chance of you two … you know …'

'You know …?' Maddison knew very well what the coroner was suggesting and tried to look affronted. But she had grown to like Tiger since she started back in Hobart over a month now. 'You know … *what,* Tiger?'

'Come now, I might be old but I'm not blind. I've seen the way you two look at each other.'

Now Maddison looked affronted. 'I'm a married woman Tiger.'

'Are you, really?' Tiger queried. 'Be honest with yourself Maddison, life's too short. Are – you – really – still – married?'

'Okay Mr Griffin,' Maddison stood erect, puffing out her chest, hands on hip. She turned back to face *Infinity.* 'Enough playing Cupid. What have we got?'

'Well there's no fingerprints, the perp clearly wore gloves. And there's little remaining of the blood spills either.'

'So the perp cleaned up?'

'I doubt it. The storm last night would have done that.'

'Of course. So, the victim was tied in fishing net and dumped overboard?'

'It wasn't just fishing net,' Tiger said. 'The victim was bound hands and feet with particularly thick string. Unusually thick, like string used by the postal department. And, I might add, it looks like the same string as that used on the Taroona victim.'

'You're kidding me?'

'Nope. I'll know when we've compared it with the other. The divers also found lead diving weights on the seabed below. The body was weighted, to be certain it'd sink. But it appears they became unattached.'

'And the storm and tides had other ideas eh?'

'That's about it. One stormy night and our dead friend floated across the estuary to the bay opposite where the netting got tangled on the wooden jetty at high tide …'

'And the gulls had a feast.'

***

Back at Police Headquarters…

Maddison walked into the conference room filled with chatter and a fusty male-dominated atmosphere of testosterone, perspiration and freshly brewing coffee. She poured a full mug of the brew. That omelette lunch was still a good hour away. She eyed the Harvey's Deli party pies someone had seen fit to bring along, thought briefly of her battle to retain a slim waistline, smelt the fresh buttery pastry, weakened and added two to a plate before sitting at the head of the table. *They were after all, small pies.*

'Right.' The chatter softened. Maddison managed a quick head count. Two female police, one female psychologist, eight men. *Typical.* 'Okay then, ladies and gentlemen. Be seated please.' All present took up seats around the conference table.

'First up, we have been informed this morning by the fisherman's wife, Mrs Verity Shreeve, that her husband was in a relationship with the escort murdered at Taroona.'

'Really?'

'Yes, she knew all about the two of them,' Landon said, walking in late. He parked himself in the empty seat next to Maddison. 'Isn't that right Harlow?'

Constable Harlow verified that he and another constable paid Mrs Shreeve a visit that morning to notify her of her husband's demise. 'And from what he tells me she was not at all that upset about the news.'

Harlow gestured in agreement, adding, 'Yes. Although I must say the news of her estranged husband's death *did* seem to come as a total surprise. That's in my view anyhow, and I think I'm a pretty good judge of character.'

'You say victim and the escort were in a relationship,' another cop asked. 'You mean lovers?'

Maddison. 'What else would I mean?'

'But she was a hooker.'

'Sex worker. Yes,' Maddison chose to be politically correct. 'Prostitutes can fall in love too you know.'

'She only charged him for the first few,' some smart-arse quipped.

'Alright,' Maddison silenced the sniggers. 'Keep focussed thank you.'

'We are also fairly certain they were murdered by the same perp,' Tiger Griffin said. 'As both bodies were secured with exactly the same wide brown string. It's quite distinctive and mostly used by the postal service.'

'So, Max Shreeve was a fisherman living on board his boat at Lindisfarne Motor Yacht Club. The second victim was Meredith Kendal. Yes, she was a sex worker, but it appears the two got a little more involved with each other than originally intended. So, motivation for murder? Suspects? Any ideas?'

'The fisherman's wife.'

'Logical. But they *were* separated.'

'It was getting nasty by all reports, I checked with her lawyer, she was about to take him to the cleaners.'

'Well that's more motivation for *him* to kill *her.*'

'Yes. But he had a million-dollar insurance and with the husband dead she gets the lot.'

'No children?'

'No.' Maddison twisted about to the coroner off to her right. 'Now, Dr Griffin here has joined us to give you novices an idea of profiling a murderer and the use of DNA.'

The coroner explained deoxyribonucleic acid, reading from a textbook. 'Deoxyribonucleic acid is a self-replicating material which is present in nearly all living organisms as the main constituent of chromosomes. It is a carrier of genetic information.'

'Is DNA conclusive?' one officer asked.

'Absolutely. There is no arguing with DNA.'

'DNA is the hereditary material in humans and almost all other organisms,' Tiger continued. Tiger went on to explain the complexities and how DNA points to the truth, especially in criminal investigation.

'It is also helpful in solving cold cases, of which we have a few on the books here in Tasmania.'

'That's correct, especially cold cases where the victim's clothes are still in storage with blood or sperm samples etc left by the killer.'

***

Next the police psychologist, Doctor Jennifer Macintyre, was asked to speak on psychological offender profiling; a method of sifting through all the evidence looking for repetitive patterns, particularly in mass murders, to create a portrait of the perp from clues found at the crime scene.

'This includes behavioural analysis,' she started. 'With which psychologists can produce a remarkably accurate description of the criminal, often nailing his home area, marital status, possible occupation, and even the type of car he drives,' Dr Macintyre said. 'Armed with this information I deduced the murderer lived in the Taroona district, was married but experiencing a turbulent marriage, childless, employed in a semi-skilled position in an occupation that brought him into contact with the public. I also deduced he had few friends.'

'Fascinating.'

'That's all very well,' an older cop stated. 'But you're talking about a cold case that is still unsolved.'

'Yes, but when he is caught, and I say *when*, I guarantee he will fit my profile.'

'Yes,' Maddison backed the psychologist. 'We have a forty percent success rate.'

'Have you met many sex murderers?'

'A few. I've worked in Melbourne, Perth and Sydney,' Macintyre said. 'And spent four years in London. But even the most skilled psychiatrists have a limited access to the mind of any sexually motivated murderer. The mind of a sex killer is a complex and convoluted intellect of evil and cruelty. They display a lack of empathy and a complete lack of morality or inhibition.'

'This is what makes them so difficult to catch is it not?' Landon said. 'The fact that they kill at random, there is rarely any link between the killer and the victim. They strike without warning.'

'But we have DNA,' Luke Farrell said. His face immediately flushed, aware he had attracted attention to himself in the busy room.

'If we are lucky … Luke Farrell isn't it?' the psychologist asked. Luke smiled weakly.

This earned Luke an elbow from the officer directly next to him.

'Yes, if we're lucky they will leave behind their DNA in sperm, blood, hair or something like saliva,' the police psychologist continued. 'But if they are not previously in the criminal database, then the search is as difficult as ever.'

'Why are these sex crimes becoming more frequent in the 20st century?' asked one of the female cops.

'Interesting question. And I've read up on it. In the 19th century prostitutes abounded. Sex was cheap. Rape was rare. It seemed absurd to our ancestors to want sex so desperately as to murder for it. So yes, it is true that the sexual serial killer is a relatively modern phenomenon. One of the early offenders was the French Ripper, as he was nicknamed. In three years, he murdered eleven young people, male and female, inflicting horrific injuries on his victims.'

'French Ripper,' Landon said. 'That was Joseph Vacher wasn't it?'

'Yes.'

'I read about him recently.'

'Well he was caught in 1897 and studied for five months by a pioneering psychiatrist on the subject, a Frenchman called Lacassagne who determined the man was sane and not the insane killer as the prisoner tried to portray.'

'He was an evil bastard,' Landon said. 'Pure and simple.'

'What happened to him?'

'He was guillotined.'

'That's right,' Macintyre said. 'In 1898. The next early mass murderer who comes to mind is a German, Peter Kurten, whose gruesome crimes saw him dubbed, Monster of Dusseldorf. Like many serial killers, he started by killing animals …'

'They often do, don't they?' one officer said. 'Kill animals, that is.'

The police psychologist nodded. 'Many do, yes, often committing bestiality before or after the cruel act. Kurten once beheaded a swan just to drink its blood from the stump of its neck.'

This piece of information had hardened cops shaking their heads.

'Kurten derived sexual satisfaction from arson, masturbating in the shadows as his handy work went up in flames. But this wasn't enough, he progressed into murder, committing sodomy and necrophilia. He was eventually caught and when interviewed, confessed to practising bestiality with sheep, pigs and goats from the age of thirteen; progressing to killing the animals, as I just said, a common trait with psychopaths. I tell you of this man, because the disturbing thing is, as evil and despicable as he was, he appeared outwardly normal and was apparently happily married.'

'And what happened to him?'

'He was put to death by decapitation. '

***

Later that day…

Maddison took the call. 'There's an Officer Nathan Irons asking to see the officer in charge of the dead fisherman case. Said he has information.'

'Officer? Is he one of ours?'

'Fisheries.'

'Okay, excellent. Where is he?

'Front desk.'

'I'll be right down.'

***

Nathan Irons waited with Constable Harlow in an interview room on the ground floor. The Tasmanian Fisheries inspector started as an inland fisheries enforcement officer before joining the police force to become a marine and rescue officer. It had been thirteen years now and he loved his work. Catching poachers had been a highlight of his career and arresting Max Shreeve the cray fisherman for poaching abalone and selling them to the Chinese restaurateur Tom Chung of the Smiling Dragon Restaurant in Moonah had been one of his more memorable arrests. But when Max was let off with a small fine and a 'slap on the wrist', Nathan was determined to keep an eye on the man.

Maddison and Landon exchanged introductions. 'You have some information for us ... the Max Shreeve case.'

'Yes. Did you know he's a convicted felon?' Irons asked.

'Oh? Please tell.'

Irons told his story, how he and his colleagues kept Max and *Infinity* under surveillance, finally acquiring the evidence they needed and making the arrest. Maddison and Landon were surprised to hear of the punishment after the guilty verdict.

'It reeked of corruption,' Nathan said sourly. 'After all the resources and expense to catch them, and for what?'

'You were saying you have further information.'

'Well yes. A few days ago, we were watching him, that's a colleague and myself, from a parked fisheries car on the wharf. Quite openly you understand. You might even call it harassment, but I just wanted him to know we are watching. Well a young man turned up, I'd seen him before – a deckhand who we found out goes by the name Mason Swinburne – and an altercation broke out.'

'Mason Swinburne,' Landon looked to Constable Harlow, who left the room to do a record search. 'Please go on ... an altercation you said?'

'Yes. Arguing. Voices raised. I should mention here that Mr Shreeve has an off-sider, a big Maori man, who's been with him for years.'

Landon made notes. 'Do you have a name?'

'Bill. I don't know his surname.'

'Was he a part of your arrest?'

'No. At the time we had no proof he was involved in the poaching, although I'm certain he was. But we got Max Shreeve, and that's what mattered.'

'So, Bill was there during this altercation huh?'

'Yes. They started shouting and Max, the deceased, attacked the young deckhand, Mason.'

'Attacked him. How?'

'Went for him, throwing punches. He knocked him to the ground, or I should say the jetty, and Bill the Maori broke up the fight.'

'Then what?'

'Mason left but he was very angry, and I heard him threaten Mr Shreeve.'

'How?'

The fisheries officer took out his own notebook and flicked to the suitable page and read aloud. 'Ah, he said … *you're crazy.* Max told him *piss off, I never want to see you again around here.* And the young man yelled back, *Oh, you'll see me again, don't you worry, when you haven't got that bloody gorilla to save your arse.*'

'Gorilla!'

'He was talking of the huge Maori.'

'Have you any idea where we can find this Maori, Bill?' Maddison asked.

'I don't know where he lives but I have seen him drinking at the Custom's House several times over the past year.'

Maddison remained seated on the edge of the desk. She looked across at Landon, closing the door after the fisheries officer left. 'What do you reckon?'

'Do I think it's enough to want to kill someone after an altercation? No, not really.'

'But it's a lead nonetheless.'

A knock at the door had both cops turn. 'Ah!' Landon took a folder from Constable Harlow in the doorway. 'You found something?'

'I think you'll be pleased sir,' the young cop said before closing the door behind him. Landon ran a rapid eye over the file.

'Guess what?'

Maddison. 'What?'

'This Mason Swinburne bloke has a record for violent assault.'

'Oh, does he now?'

'Certainly does.'

'Okay, so he might have had a motive to kill Max but why would Mason kill Meredith Kendall?'

'Possibly it was a love triangle. Maybe Mason was in love with this Meredith as well and when he couldn't have her, he killed them both.'

'It's unlikely but possible.'

'Well that was what the altercation on the jetty was all about, when the fisheries boys were there. There was all this shouting about a hooker.'

'Please Landon, call her a sex-worker, not everyone has a cushy job like yours.'

'Cushy!' Landon looked at his watch. 'Well, will you look at that? It's after five. Fancy a drink?'

'I assume you are suggesting we pay the Custom's House a visit?'

Landon nodded.

'Sure.'

***

Warm weather induces a thirst only a chilled frothy headed beer can quench and Maddison, a *sauvignon blanc girl* usually, was keen to join Landon in a beer. The Custom's House Hotel bar was filling with after work nine to fivers and the atmosphere was convivial. Landon paid for the first round, passing the barman a fiver while asking about a tall, solidly built Maori called Bill.

'Big Bill,' the barman – a middle-aged, grey-haired, hard-faced, no-nonsense barkeep – said without hesitation. But then he stopped short, to consider the man and woman before him at the bar. Plainclothes or not, they *smelt* like constabulary. Landon showed his badge. 'Thought so,' the barman said. 'What's Bill done then?'

'Nothing,' Maddison said. 'We just need to ask him a few questions.'

'Is this to do with Max Shreeve's murder?'

'You've heard about it?'

'Who hasn't around here? Max was a regular.'

'So,' Landon persisted. 'This Bill bloke?'

'Forget Bill,' the barman bent below the bar to attend the glass washer. 'It's Mason you need to talk to.'

'Mason? And he would be?'

'An angry young shit,' the barman shook his head. 'He was deckhand on Max's *Infinity* for a few months. Bloody troublemaker … came in here causing fights. I've barred him twice.'

'So where can I find him?'

'Bill knows. He used to pick him up from his flat himself, in West Hobart, I think. Bill used to say it was the only way they could be certain he'd turn up for work …if you went and fetched him like. And I know Max was sick of his bullshit.'

Maddison. 'So, where can we find Bill?'

'Boots'll know.' The barman opened the glass-washer, slipping the tray free, temporarily engulfed in a cloud of steam. 'Boots is Bill's drinking buddy. That's him in the corner with the pint of Guinness.'

Boots was wary. He never liked coppers and was evasive until the barman caught his eye and gave him a reassuring nod. *It was in Bill's best interest after all.*

Armed with an address Maddison and Landon agreed their day wasn't finished.

'My shout when this is all over,' Maddison said, slipping behind the wheel of her sky blue '93 Ford Capri convertible. 'Buckle up!' she grinned, squealing rubber on the carpark's polished concrete.

If this was work, Landon was loving it. He stole a glance at his boss, with her work chignon unleashed, her hair whipped free in the wind. They had been lovers back in the day – back in their early twenties. Then they were in love, then they were young and reckless. But fate had other plans, they went their own separate ways, married, followed their ambitions. But now?

Maddison sensed Landon staring and looked across at her passenger and together they shared an adolescent moment of let loose fun. Maddison pumped the accelerator and Landon felt himself sink further back into the seat. On Cascade Road heading south-west the sixty k's road sign flashed by at ninety. Maddison showed off her driving prowess. A hundred metres from Big Bill's cottage Maddison dropped back through the gears and stopped abruptly. 'We're here.'

'So I see,' Landon grinned, catching his breath.

***

Both cops knew immediately how Big Bill had earned his sobriquet. Big, tough, tattooed; the quintessential indigenous New Zealander. But they were also quick to learn the man could be a huge marshmallow inside, when his two beautiful offspring joined them at the door to see who dragged daddy away from the dinner table. Clearly the police had arrived halfway through their evening meal.

'Sorry to bother you during dinner,' Maddison said.

Being a single woman, she was thinking who eats at 5.30PM? Big Bill seemed to read her thoughts. Bill could have done without the intrusion but was amicable enough.

'Hey,' Bill turned to his kids and, stooping, he shooed them back inside waving his giant hands, palms open, as if to shovel them back down the passageway. 'Get inside you two, go finish yer tea,' his New Zealand accent still strong.

Bill stepped onto the porch of his 1840s stone cottage and closed the front door behind him. 'This about Max?' he asked.

'Yes,' Landon started.

'What can you tell us about Mason?' Maddison asked.

Bill's eyes narrowed. 'You don't think 'e killed Max do yer?'

'We don't know …' Suddenly Maddison realised they didn't know the Maori's surname. 'Mister?'

'Bill. Just call me Bill.'

'Bill … we just want to ask Mason a few questions at this stage. We were told he had an altercation with Max a few days back.'

As much as Bill didn't like young Mason, he never thought him capable of killing someone.

'Christ! Who told yer that?'

Maddison. 'We have a witness.'

'Two actually,' Landon added.

'Ah, them fisheries cops. Bloody hell, they don't miss much eh, and they came runnin' to you. Jesus.'

'Well? What happened exactly?'

'It was nuthin' really, although Mason did start it, and besides he should never 've hit the boss anyways.'

'Why did they fight?'

'Mason was givin' the boss stick over his new lady friend.'

'Oh? Why?'

'Well.' Suddenly Bill felt awkward talking of the dead. 'I'd rather not say.'

'Look Bill, everything you tell us is confidential and could be very important. Do you want the killer to be caught or not?'

Bill looked back to the front door. It was closed. 'This bird the boss was hangin' out with was a hooker.'

'And Mason knew?'

'Yer. And Mason used this information to wind the boss up eh? Called out to him, loud like for all the world to 'ear, said 'e was fuckin' a whore.' Bill reddened and looked to Maddison. 'Sorry love.'

Maddison shrugged off any modesty. 'This sex worker, do you happen to know her name?' Maddison asked, just for the record.

'I heard 'im mention 'er as Barbie, but that were 'er hooker name.'

'And the argument became physical?'

'Yer. The boss flew 'im, knocked Mason to the jetty an' punched the shit out o' him. I had to pull the skipper offa him, I thought Jesus, he's gonna kill the little bastard.'

'Then what happened?'

'I told Mason to piss off like, and 'e called me a gorilla,' Bill laughed at the memory. 'A fu' ... sorry, a bloody gorilla.'

'And that's when Mason threatened to come back and see Max again, is that right.'

'Yep, that's about it.'

'Okay, thanks Bill. So where can we find this Mason?'

'He lives in a flat at 40 Pine Street West Hobart. Flat five, double-storey white joint with a bright yella front door.'

'Does he have a car?'

'He shares a car with his flat mate, Terry, an old HD Holden sedan.'

'Colour?'

'Bluey-grey.'

***

6.35PM...

Mason's twenty-two-year-old flatmate opened the apartment front door with hooded bloodshot eyes staring through a fug of burning weed to be greeted by two suits who clearly looked like cops. He sobered, peering around the half-opened door gaping like a deer trapped in the headlights. His words were suddenly croaky high notes. He cleared his throat and managed a meek, 'Can I help you?'

Landon and Maddison showed I.Ds. 'We're looking for Mason Swinburne.'

'He's not here.'

Maddison thought otherwise, noting a bluey-grey HD Holden parked out front. 'Terry, isn't it?'

This opened his eyes. These cops knew his name. This can't be good, no good at all. 'Terry. Yes, how did you ...'

'Can we come in?' Without waiting Maddison shoved past the stoner. Inside, the two-bedroom flat, one central lounge room, kitchenette and bathroom, was a tip site. Crap everywhere. Maddison shook her head. An empty orange juice bottle bong still smouldered on a coffee table accompanied by a bag of weed and other smoking paraphernalia. 'Where is he?'

'I told you he's not here.'

Immediately a commotion came from the backyard. Maddison rushed to the back door in time to watch Mason trip over a bin, pick himself up and disappear around the side of the block of flats. 'Front door. NOW!' she yelled at Landon. Maddison hit the back steps three at a time. Landed on the concrete and rushed after their suspect.

Mason leapt the neighbour's fence. Twisting back he saw he was being pursued. He bolted through a vegie garden. Maddison closed in. Mason booted fence palings from an aligning property, squeezing into a right-of-way. Maddison leapt for Mason's foot, but he kicked it free and sprinted up the lane.

I'm too old for this shit! Maddison cursed.

At the same time Landon had ejected from the front door into an empty street. The perp's car was still parked where he left it.

Dog barking. Screamed profanity. The sound of splintering wood.

Landon followed the sounds. Three properties distant, Mason hurdled a fence. Landon rushed down a steep path, ploughed through someone's garden and crashed into another fence. He saw Maddison in pursuit. Landon cut across a flower bed. Hit the fence at a run. Leapt into the laneway and careered into Maddison.

'Shit!'

'Where is he?'

Up on the road a car started.

The two cops scrambled back to the roadway in time to spot the HD Holden cornering to the sound of squealing rubber.

'If that's not a sign of guilt,' Maddison said snatching breaths. 'I don't know what is.'

A short time later…

Mason ditched his car in bushland three kilometres from the Lindisfarne Motor Yacht Club, at Gordon's Hill Reserve. Now he hid beneath a jetty on Lindisfarne Esplanade. And waited, watching the club rooms with interest. The night was pleasantly mild but from what he could ascertain the club house wasn't overly crowded. It seemed since Max's murder in the nearby bay, and with the killer still on the loose, members were keeping clear. When Mason felt it was safe he walked around the shoreline, keeping to the shadows. At the club and marina he easily found a small rowboat. Sourcing oars nearby, Mason rowed out to *Infinity*. He had nowhere else to hide and with the fishing boat impounded as a crime scene for the moment, he figured he would be safe until he could work out a plan. With Max's tender tethered to *Infinity* Mason set the stolen dinghy adrift and slipped below deck.

The stale aroma of Max's last fry-up hung in the galley mingling with raw diesel fumes, engine oil and the inescapable essence of stale fish from the holding tanks below. Familiar with his surroundings, Mason taped up the windows with newspaper and afforded himself a low wattage reading lamp for an ambient light. In the cupboard he found tinned beef casserole and a packet of Vita-Weat biscuits. Dinner was served. The Nirvana album, 1994 live tour was still in the tape player and the half empty bottle of rum was right where he saw it last.

CHAPTER ELEVEN

A new day…

Just before 8AM, Jacopo Moretti twisted Stanley Smart's front doorbell and stepped back into the open so Stanley could see it was him, as he knew Stanley always peeped through the front room curtains before opening the door. Stanley cracked the door ajar enough to glare out. 'You better be here to tell me you have my painting,' was all he said. No greeting.

'You know I no have painting,' Jacopo lied. *Well technically speaking he didn't have the painting, not in his possession anyhow.* 'What I want to know ees why … why you send that man Ryan to my workshop?'

'Ryan. What Ryan?'

'Don't lie to me. Ryan … he say to me Signor Moretti, Stanley Smart say you have my painting. What painting says I? And he attack me.'

'Attack you?'

Jacopo held up his purple thumb. 'Now thees man dead.'

'Ryan? Dead! What do you mean, dead?'

'No Ryan, thees Birdwhistle.'

'Birdwhistle! Dead?'

'That what I say. Morto … dead … the police, they come to see Jacopo. They take me to police … how you say? Police station …si … and ask questions.'

Stanley's eyes darted about. Up the street … down the street. 'Get inside.' He lent out and took Jacopo by the shoulder, dragging him in through the door. 'You say Jock Birdwhistle is dead?'

'Si, si, you no listen.'

'How?'

'He dead in shop. Shop burn. Police ask me questions … questions … questions …'

'What sort of questions?'

'They think I kill these *bastardo*, Jock Birdwhistle.'

'So Jock's really dead?'

'Si. He were stab dead in his shop and shop put to fire'

'Stabbed! Jesus!'

'It was these Ryan man who kill him. I know thees thing. Ryan looking for painting si.'

'How would Ryan know about Birdwhistle?'

Jacopo looked sullen a moment.

'Jacopo! How did Ryan know about Birdwhistle?'

'I tell him. He come to workshop. He angry. I tell him Birdwhistle swap boxes. He say, who Birdwhistle? Jacopo say Jock Birdwhistle antiques man. I tell him everything.'

'So you killed Birdwhistle.'

'No. No.'

'Effectively Jacopo, you killed the man. So you got the painting back, is that right?'

'No. Painting disappear. Jacopo knows nothing.'

***

Later that morning…

Verity Shreeve seethed with anger. Her venom was almost palpable. Holding her front door ajar with her left hand, she used her right hand to support herself on the door jam. She smelt of booze. Landon snatched a discreet glance at his watch, it was only 11AM. Verity had learnt of Max's demise earlier that morning; two other cops came to her home at 7.30ish and told her. That's when she pulled the cork from a celebratory Veuve Clicquot. Sure, Max's death came as a shock. Sure she was upset. But that was then. Now it was three and a half hours later.

'I know the prick's dead,' Verity sounded as remorseless as Lindy Chamberlain when interviewed on television fifteen years ago … *a dingo killed my baby and* some people had struggled to understand her lack of empathy. That sort of reaction had made police arrest the wrong person. But this attitude didn't bode well with Landon or Maddison right now. 'Mrs Shreeve, may we come in?'

'Why?' Verity made no effort to rein in her slurred speech.

'Well,' Maddison threatened, 'unless you want us to ask personal questions out here on public view.'

Verity sighed and opened the door wide. Inside smelt of stale booze, cigarette smoke and something else familiar. *Was that sweating bodies? Sex?* Maddison wasn't certain.

Verity flopped backwards into an armchair and her night dress lifted. Landon was certain she wasn't wearing underwear. Verity wasn't drunk enough to not notice the cop gaping, and folded her negligee about her. 'Sit,' she ordered.

'I'll stand thank you,' Maddison fired back. '*Besides,*' she thought, '*what bacteria's laying in ambush amongst the expensive upholstery of this woman's lounge suite'?*

'Where were you two evening's ago, Tuesday, say dusk until midnight?'

'Straight to the point huh?' Verity reached for the champagne bottle when Maddison moved it out of reach. 'I'd prefer you don't drink Mrs Shreeve until after this interview.'

Verity scowled.

'Well Mrs Shreeve?' Landon asked.

'Well what?'

'Where were you on Tuesday evening between dusk and midnight?'

'Oh Tuesday.' Suddenly Verity was coherent and clear-headed. 'I was at the State Cinema in North Hobart.'

'At the movies?'

'Well why else would I go there, to read a book?'

'What did you see?'

'Babe.'

'Babe? You mean the film about the talking pig?'

'That's the one. Why, don't you believe *pigs* can talk?'

If the recent widow was having a dig, the police weren't biting. 'Were you with anyone?

'Of course. I went with my dear friend Pammie and her husband Wilbur.'

'Can they verify this?'

'Well what do you think? Then we went to the Casino Grill Room after for supper. I had a Club Sandwich. And I got home about eleven thirty.'

'How did you pay?'

'Pay for what?'

'Supper. Do you have a credit card receipt?'

'Wilbur shouted. He used his Diner's Card.'

***

'She was too ready with her answers,' Landon told Maddison when they were back in the car. 'Too rehearsed.'

'I agree. However, you have this Pammie's number so we can check her out along with the supper receipt. But I can't see why she'd lie and surely those friends aren't going to lie to the police in a murder investigation.'

'True. But she's our prime suspect at this stage.'

Instantly a ringtone broke the silence. Landon fumbled awkwardly finally fetching a Motorola from his trouser pocket. Plugging one ear with his finger against the surrounding interference, he spoke briefly.

Maddison was impressed. 'That's the new Motorola huh?

'Yep. You going to get one?'

'I've been thinking about it. I'm suggesting that the force makes them standard issue for all officers but I'm not having much luck at the moment.'

'This is great,' Landon passed Maddison his new mobile phone. 'It's the latest Motorola flip phone.'

'Nokia 101,' Maddison read the brand.

'Yep. Candy bar design, extendable antenna and a phonebook that stores ninety-nine phone numbers.'

'Ninety-nine huh?'

'Yep. It also offers a SMS text service.'

'What's that?'

'Short Message Service.' Landon proudly demonstrated the set up.

***

Same day, around lunch time...

Maddison took the call patched through to her office from the main desk switchboard. 'Inspector Lovett.'

'Maddison, it's Charlotte.' The two hadn't spoken since Charlotte confided in her plan to catch Stanley Smart with the bequeathed coin collection. 'Charlotte. Hi. Good news?'

'Yes. We've got him.'

'Your curator?'

'Yes. Stanley Smart.'

'Really?'

'Reeled him in hook, line and sinker.'

'So he took the bait.'

'He certainly did.'

'Okay then,' Maddison looked at the wall clock. 'It's nearly lunch time. Want to meet for a quick bite?'

'Sure. Where?'

'How about Café Avec Vue. It's near Myers in Liverpool Street. They do a great smoked salmon salad.'

'Sounds good to me.'

***

Burglar Ivano Stipanov had decided to burgle Sophie's dad, Stanley Smart. How could he not? And relieve the old magpie collector off his coin collection. It sounded too good to be true – *one more little haul before I bugger off to Brisbane.* But he wanted to be certain of her father's movements during the day. As a professional burglar he covered all angles; *I mean for instance, the museum is only a few blocks from his home in Harrington Street, what if he ducked home for lunch?*

Ivano called Menzies Menswear and Sophie answered the phone. 'Soph?'

'Ivano? I thought you'd forgotten me.'

'Don't be silly. I've been really busy that's all. Work related.' Now that wasn't a lie. 'It's your lunch break soon, meet for a bite?'

'Absolutely. Where?'

'Do you have somewhere in mind, close to the shop?'

'Café Avec Vue. It's near Myers in Liverpool Street, you can't miss it. I go there often.'

Ivano looked at his watch, 12.50PM. 'See you in ten minutes then.'

***

Café Avec Vue. Twenty minutes later…

The evidence was damning. Museum Curator Stanley Smart had taken the bait in one greedy grab. There were seven coins missing, one alone – an Australian Steam Navigation Company token – Museum Director Charlotte knew to be very scarce. After a phone call to a peer at the Powerhouse Museum in Sydney, she discovered that particular coin was worth several thousand dollars.

'There were fourteen early Van Diemen's Land promissory notes. Three were duplicates and all rare and highly collectable which makes them valuable …'

'And?"

'One each of the three duplicates is missing and a fourth, a John Weavell Hobart Town shilling note has disappeared. I checked and one sold at Downie's coin auction last year for $835.'

'Christ! He's not bad is he?'

The museum director's face grew ashen. 'It terrifies me of what he may have misappropriated in the past. It's frightening. His position is one of utmost honesty and trust and he does … does this!' Charlotte slapped her notebook. A waitress hovered.

'May I take your order?'

Charlotte looked at her friend once again. 'You know what, I'm so annoyed I've lost my appetite. Just coffee for me thanks.'

'Pot of tea, no milk or sugar,' Maddison said. 'So, you have proof he's a thief, now's the hard part. We need to catch him with the stolen property, preferably at his home. Where does he live?'

***

The café was full but Ivano managed the last table, a small table for two with bentwood backed chairs squeezed beneath the stairs in the old chemist shop, converted to a café back in the '70s. Ivano, looking very European this day wearing his new leather jacket, caught the eye of two middle-aged businesswomen sitting in intense conversation four tables away. Ivano, accustomed to attracting the eye of women, shot Maddison a smile. Maddison felt herself blush slightly. *Caught staring! Damn.* The act did not go unnoticed by Charlotte.

'How is your love life anyhow?' the museum director asked, edging their conversation away from the negatives.

'Ah, so, so.'

'So, so. What does that mean?'

'Well … I don't know if you remember Landon Finch?'

'Vaguely. He was at the academy with you, wasn't he?'

'That's him.'

'And you guys hung out together for a while.' Charlotte thought a moment. 'Jesus! That's fifteen … twenty years ago.'

'Thereabouts.'

'And?'

'Well we're back working together.'

'And?'

'We're both single.' Maddison had to chew that one over briefly. 'Well sort of single.'

'And you're getting back together?'

'Who knows?' Maddison finished her tea. 'You know I might have a quick bite after all. Smoked salmon salad you reckon?'

They ordered two salmon as an attractive young redhead squeezed between the tables to join the good looking European.

'Damn, he's taken,' Charlotte said on Maddison's behalf. Maddison looked at her friend bemused. 'I saw you staring Maddie. He is cute.'

Maddison. 'What?'

'Couldn't take your eyes of him from the moment he walked in.'

'It's not like that at all.'

'Oh?'

'I just feel I've seen him somewhere before,' Maddison said.

'That's what they all say.'

***

Ivano stood as Sophie approached the table, almost cracking his head on the stairs. They kissed like new lovers before Sophie sat and Charlotte recognised Sophie for the first time. 'Speak of the devil.'

'What's that?'

'That redhead. She's Stanley Smart's daughter.'

'Well, Hobart was always a small place.'

The waitress, efficient as ever, took Ivano and Sophie's orders and moments later Ivano sipped a glass of Shiraz while Sophie drank an iced coffee as the professional thief weaved his magic and extracted the information he so desperately needed.

***

That evening...

Maddison decided to handle this one personally. Stanley Smart certainly didn't notice the unmarked police car parked down the street when he walked home from the museum at 5.15PM. The driver radioed in.

'He's home Inspector.'

'Good. I'll be there shortly. We'll let him settle in a bit.'

6.40PM. One police car parked in Victoria Street behind the old morgue and another parked out front. Stanley heard the doorbell, went to the window and froze.

Cops!

Cold shivers came over him. The doorbell shrilled a second time followed by heavy, determined knocking. He heard his name called and imagined neighbours gathering to watch. He went straight to the door.

'Mr Smart?' the policewoman asked. 'Mr Stanley Smart?'

'Yes.'

'I'm Inspector Lovett and this is Senior Detective Finch. We have a signed warrant to search this property.'

'Warrant! S-search? Why?'

'We have reason to believe you are in the possession of coins stolen from the Tasmanian Museum, misappropriated recently during your employment there, as numismatist.'

'Namely the Harry Button collection,' Landon continued. 'Bequeathed to the museum.'

Stanley was lost for words. He stood in the doorway red-faced, his mouth opening and closing like a freshly landed bluefin tuna.

Maddison pushed past followed by Landon and eight well trained police officers. The two senior police stood in the passageway and looked down the hall. It was daunting. Stuff everywhere. *Yes stuff,* Maddison shook her head. *There was no other word to describe it.*

***

It was after 8PM when Maddison and Landon returned to Police Headquarters…

Maddison walked into her office, threw her coat on the peg and slumped into her desk chair.

The smirk on Stanley Smart's face when she had to admit defeat, leaving emptyhanded, haunted her. She was angry and annoyed that she may have let her friend Charlotte down.

'Did you see the smug look on his face?' Maddison said.

'We'll get him, don't worry.'

'God! It's after eight,' Maddison sighed. 'Well past cocktail hour. Go for a drink? I need one.'

'Why not.'

Maddison moved a stack of files aside to tidy her desk before retiring for the night when she spotted a faxed memorandum from colleagues in Melbourne C.I.B. 'What the hell!'

'What?'

Maddison picked up the file and studied the mug shot. 'Ivano Stipanov,' she read aloud. 'Have you seen this man? Wanted for questioning about several high-end burglaries in Melbourne and believed to be in Tasmania.'

'No. Why, should I have seen him?'

'He was in the café where I had lunch today with Charlotte.'

'You're kidding.' Landon studied the photo. 'Are you sure?'

'Hell yes. And guess what?' Maddison took back the photo shaking her head slowly.

'Well, don't keep me in suspense.'

'This man … this criminal …' and the inspector flicked the fax with the back of her hand, 'this burglar was with Stanley's daughter, Sophie.'

'Stanley. As in Stanley Smart?'

'How many Stanley's do you know?'

'How do you know her, Stanley's daughter?'

'Charlotte the museum director recognised her when we met for lunch today to discuss the curator.'

'Well we need to talk to her.'

'No, she'll warn Stipanov and he'll run. We need to find out where Sophie lives and works and put a tail on her.'

***

The next morning…

Maddison Lovett had good reason to smile. For the moment the inspector had at her disposal enough officers to conduct surveillance on the dodgy curator and the murder suspect, Jacopo Moretti, and to watch Sophie Smart. The more evidence she could accumulate on her museum thief, she figured, the harder it would stick and the tougher the sentence. One outcome she did not expect however was the Italian Jacopo seen visiting the curator at Stanley's home in Harrington Street. Constable Lachlan Harlow, given the responsibility of surveillance, delivered the news. The two men were photographed by the police, they were in heavy conversation on Stanley's front doorstep.

'Now that *is* interesting,' Maddison shared a moment with her team. 'Convicted receiver of stolen antiques is on friendly terms with alleged museum thief.'

'Alleged?'

'Yes, I know Lachlan,' she said to the rookie. 'But until he is charged, we are not legally permitted to say the accused.'

'I'm not certain though inspector, that they are overly friendly. They spoke at the front door several minutes before Stanley Smart dragged him inside suddenly.'

'Dragged?'

'Yes, real quick like. Smart looked about, up and down the street dodgy like, as if he was looking for someone and they quickly closed the door.'

'I wonder if the word police came up in their conversation. That's what spooked them.'

'Possibly.'

'So, we also have Stanley's daughter befriending a wanted felon, a high-end burglar from Melbourne no less, while Stanley befriends Jacopo Moretti, an Italian once convicted for buying stolen property, namely antiques.'

'It's turning into a den of thieves,' Landon said.

***

Stanley was paranoid, and with good reason. Certain he was being watched by the police, he attempted to maintain as normal a life as possible. More disturbing was the phone call he received from his new director Charlotte, ordering him to take leave until further notice. He was beside himself with worry; worried what his work colleagues were thinking, or worse, wondering how much they actually knew. He checked his safe one last time in the bedroom, hidden under floorboards beneath the wardrobe. He had built it himself and it was impossible to see once the wardrobe was jiggled over the top. Even fooled the cops! And no one else knew about it, except of course his daughter Sophie.

With time off, Stanley walked through the city centre and headed north three blocks to the Hobart Country Women's Association shop. Being a creature of habit, the curator made this short journey once a week for home-made pies and cakes. After the gentle incline leading up Elizabeth Street to the shop, Stanley stood to gather himself briefly, always admiring the premises; one of several original shopfronts remaining from the mid to late 19th century. He made a cursory inspection of the window display; hand knitted teapot cosies; cloth sachets of freshly dried lavender; hand–knitted beanies and all those other home comforts for the elderly. But Stanley was here for the pastries and cakes and to lead the cops astray.

'Mr Smart, good morning.'

'Layla.' Stanley offered his warmest greeting. Layla was in her mid-seventies he surmised, but life had been generous to the woman. She had a fine figure, long loose silver hair and all her own teeth by the look of her smile. 'Do call me Stanley.'

'Oh yes, I keep forgetting. Well then Stanley, what can I get you today?'

If Stanley didn't know any better, he was certain she had taken a fancy him. Or was it motherly love? Stanley had lost his wife of thirty-eight years, eleven years ago; to pancreatic cancer. The museum was his mistress now. (At least it had been until today) Volunteer Layla worked Thursday and Fridays at the CWA and it had not gone unnoticed by the woman that Stanley always visited the shop on a Thursday, usually in his lunch hour. Stanley took a discreet peek out the window and was certain one of the parked cars across the street was an undercover cop.

'Stanley!' Layla repeated herself. 'What can I get you?'

'Sorry.' Stanley stroked his chin, as was his want when he was undecided.

'The cream sponges are Barbara's today,' Layla knew Stanley liked Barbara's cakes because she used more cream than the other ladies and her passionfruit icing was always rich and creamy with the right amount of tart.

'Then I'll take one of those thank you … and … ah … a lemon coconut square, one peppermint slice …' Stanley ran a keen eye over the glass cabinet of home-made cakes. 'And two vanilla slices please.'

'Two?' Layla didn't mean to question Stanley, but it was spontaneous. 'Having a visitor, are we?'

The little minx he thought. She's checking me out. 'I have a friend who visits, and he likes the vanilla slice.'

He? 'Oh, I see. And here's me thinking you were trying to sweeten a lady friend,' Layla said in a throwaway fashion as she leant into the cabinet armed with tongs and a cake box. And then had an embarrassing thought; I shouldn't be presumptuous; the man might prefer the company of his own gender.

'Yes, he is an old friend whose wife has dementia and he visits me when he has the opportunity.'

'Oh, how sad.' Suddenly Layla remembered, 'Oh, I nearly forgot.'

'What's that?'

The CWA volunteer fetched her handbag from under the counter. 'I was hoping you would be here today, and I brought this along.'

She passed Stanley a gold fob watch. Stanley recognised it immediately as an early Victorian Baume Mercier man's pocket watch with its original gold fob chain. But what was so special about it was that a gold sovereign had been set into the casing at the back behind the workings. 'It works,' Layla said enthusiastically.

'Oh, I'm sure it does.' Stanley tried not to show too much interest. But this antique watch was magnificent, and the truth was; he wanted it badly.

'But why did you bring this to show me, Layla?' Stanley asked, knowing only too well that she had brought it along to sell, as she had done with the odd item in the past, like the time he purchased her grandfather's Boer War medals, for a song.

'Well,' Layla appeared a little disappointed that Stanley wasn't showing more interest. 'I was hoping you might buy it from me. I'm a little short at the moment and behind in my bills. The Hydro alone was a hundred and five dollars this quarter. I'm way behind to tell you the truth.'

'Mongrels,' Stanley muttered. 'Well I suppose I could get you out of a pickle. How much?'

'I was hoping you'd make me an offer,' she said.

Stanley preferred the seller to make the first move. Now he was in a situation where, if he offered too little the seller might rescind or, if he offered too much, the seller would think it worth a lot more, and again rescind. He would have to find a happy medium.

'Oh … I don't know,' he breathed quietly, studying the watch like he was beastly careless whether he purchased it or not. 'Two hundred,' he finally said and put the watch on the counter as a sign he wasn't fussed one way or the other.

'Oh,' Layla couldn't hide her disappointment. 'I thought it would be worth a little more than that.'

Stanley sighed and pinched his lips before tapping two fingers on the glass top bench in an act of further consideration. 'I suppose I could go to two fifty.' Now, knowing the antique watch was worth over one thousand in anyone's money, Stanley had a damned cheek. But that's how he was. He loved a bargain and if it meant ripping off an old lady, then so be it. Layla finally agreed. She was desperate for the cash. Stanley slid the watch back across the counter towards her. 'Are you here tomorrow?'

'Yes.'

'Then I will be here in the morning with the cash.' But Stanley changed his mind. 'I tell you what. I'll go fetch the cash now. Back in a bit, alright?'

***

At that moment downtown…

'Finding Sophie Smart, Stanley's daughter, proved easy,' Landon told Maddison. 'Phone book easy. And we know where she works also, at a menswear outlet in Collin's Street.'

'Keep a tail on her,' Maddison ordered.

'Done as we speak Maddie.'

***

Over on Battery Point's Princess Park…

A sprinkling of young mums with their eight or nine squealing infants and three dogs with their owners shared the public gardens. Besides this lot, Magistrate Christian Winterbourne and Tyron the dodgy stable-hand had the park to themselves. They sat, well apart, on a park bench watching the play area and in particular the antics of young mothers.

'I don't remember me mum ever takin' me to the park,' Tyron started. 'Dad neither, 'e was always at the pub … or in gaol.' Christian remained silent. Tyron caught the message. 'So then, I made a few calls yesterdee and there is this 'ere bloke in town what's lookin' for work.'

'Oh.'

'Pretty good too from what they say.'

'How can I get in contact?'

'Yer don't need to boss. I took the liberty of givin' this contact your number.'

***

Tyron left the magistrate and walked along Salamanca Place back towards the CBD. Had he taken notice of the police car and ambulance over on Waterman's Dock in passing he may have learnt that one of Hobart's notorious brothel-keepers was being fished out of the water.

Phoebe Crow, Madam Mareike's rival, had been found floating face down in the docks. The incident looked an accident, there were no suspicious signs. But many of those close to the fiery madam suspected otherwise.

Meanwhile Mareike rejoiced. *Until* the police came to her first asking questions. Of course, Mareike had alibis aplenty, albeit all on her payroll. One or two patrons of her Liverpool Street address came forward also and she was struck from the list of suspects.

***

While this new drama was unfolding, back at Harrington Street...

Stanley was unnerved by the less than discreet cop car following him. He hurried inside, locked the doors and drew the curtains. He felt he needed space, time to think. But first he needed to fetch two hundred and fifty dollars from his curtain rail cash stash and return to the CWA to purchase the rare gold fob watch. Minutes later he balanced on his library chair, stretched out with his right arm and felt blindly behind the rail.

***

Moments later, a little after 10AM...

Burglar Ivano Stipanov arrived at Stanley's front door confident in the knowledge Stanley would be at work. Ivano had managed to misappropriate a council smock coat complete with an employee lanyard identification to hang about his neck – not to be inspected at close range mind – and armed himself with a clip board. He donned false beard and moustache and wore false reading glasses; all standard in his travelling kit. Today he would portray a public servant on a survey. Knocking on Stanley Smart's front door, Ivano waited. He knew Stanley should be at work, but one could never be too careful. He knocked a second time. No answer. Ivano skilfully picked the door lock in seconds. This is what he did for a living and he was bloody good at it. His heart raced, that part never became easier, but once inside with the door closed behind him, he could breath.

'Mr Smart,' he called out, another standard ruse. If the man was home, he could make some excuse – like I'm looking for Sophie – after all he was known

to the homeowner, and then make another excuse to leave. 'Mr Smart ....
Stanley,' Ivano called a second time.

Nothing. Silence. Brilliant.

Although he was alone Ivano moved about silently. He made his way
through the cramped home. The stairs to the first floor and bedroom were at
the end of the passage.

Work fast. Get out.

Ivano padded quietly past downstairs rooms. Passed the living room. By
the study…

Shit! The study door was open. Sophie had told him Daddy always kept
the study door locked. Ivano glanced inside. *Fuck!*

Stanley Smart was gaping blankly in his direction. Eyes wide open, lower
jaw dropped open, tongue protruding to one side.

Fuck! Fuck!

Ivano was about to flee. But something wasn't right. The museum curator
looked stretched; head drooped, feet not touching the floor.

Shit! The man's dead. No!

Ivano approached, his heart racing, his mouth parched. What the hell!
Stanley had hung himself from the curtain cords. Ivano reached out cautiously.
He touched Stanley's neck.

He felt a pulse! He was still warm.

Oh, sweet Jesus! Ivano pulled a pocketknife from his belt and hacked away,
severing the cord. Stanley fell free. His dead weight into Ivano's arms sent both
men tumbling, before Ivano managed a hold and lowered Stanley to the floor.
He laid him on his back and immediately started CPR. It took less than two
minutes, but Stanley Smart was sucking breaths. Ivano rolled the man onto his
side and when he was certain Stanley was breathing rhythmically, yet barely
conscious, he went searching for the phone. Knowing the ambulance service
was only blocks away at the Royal Hobart Hospital in Argyle Street and assured
they were on their way, Ivano made to leave.

But the safe! *So near. So close.* Ivano's slipped into overdrive. *You can do
this, yes. Hurry man, hurry …*

Ivano took to the stairs three treads at a time. He found the master bedroom
and, shoving the wardrobe aside, he located the safe under loose floorboards
just where Sophie happened to mention it was.

Forty seconds.

With years of practice, a tension wrench and a lock pick Ivano had the safe cracked open in just under a minute. It was after all an eighty-year-old iron accounting office clerical safe.

One minute twenty seconds.

Inside he found six heavy coin albums. '*Gold was like that,*' he smiled inwardly, '*heavy that is.*' He dropped the lot into a light backpack alongside his council worker clipboard and pen. He zipped up and hurried back down the stairs ...

Two minutes forty seconds.

He looked in on Stanley. The man was breathing and showing signs of regaining consciousness ...

Twenty seconds.

Ivano rushed to the front door, left it ajar and made good his escape. In less than seven minutes since calling 000 he was walking with a casual swagger away from the property. Only a few blocks away a siren approached.

Never in all his years of crime had Ivano experienced anything more bizarre.

***

Later that morning at police headquarters...

Inspector Maddison Lovett dropped the phone receiver heavily into its cradle turning to Senior Detective Landon Finch, deep in concentration studying witness reports.

'Well, if that isn't a sign of guilt,' she said, 'I don't know what the hell is.'

Landon ran a rake's eye over the inspector's shapely legs as she sat, her skirt seemed shorter today. 'And what would that be Maddie?' he asked.

Maddison caught the wandering eye and tugged at her hem as she swivelled her chair to face him. 'Our light-fingered museum curator, Stanley Smart, tried to hang himself.'

'What? When?'

'This morning.'

'No! How?'

'That was Charlotte Fysh on the phone, from the Tasmanian Museum.'

'Yes, I know Charlotte.'

'Well she put him on indefinite leave this morning, pending our investigation, and he was found hanging in his study shortly after. Attempted suicide by all accounts.'

'Admission of guilt?'

'Looks that way.'

'Attempted you said?'

'Yes, he's in hospital. Get a new warrant. Send some boys to the address. Have a really good look about while he's in incapacitated. Check out the suicide angle, it might just have been attention seeking.'

'So who found him?'

'Well that's another weird thing. An ambulance was called, they were there in minutes, the front door was left open and they found Stanley lying on the floor, critical. But he had been cut down, given CPR by all accounts and rolled onto his side, as if someone knew what they were doing. But there was no one else at the address.'

'Could it be someone had tried to kill him?'

'Apparently not. There's a police presence there now so get over there ASAP, I'll join you shortly. And find out why I wasn't notified earlier by our boys.'

***

Less than an hour later...

On foot, Ivano Stipanov, arrived at Cornelian Bay. He waited amongst bushes on the shoreline embankment leading up to the cemetery on the opposite side of the bay to his boathouse. Two days earlier he couldn't believe his incredible misfortune. When he returned to his boat shed, cops had been everywhere. He thought his time was up. But then he learnt there had been a murder and a fisherman's body had been washed up near his shed. It was an incredible coincidence and not a sight he wanted to see again in a hurry. Satisfied he was alone once more, Ivano returned to his rented boat shed and locked himself inside.

It was time to freshen up and go back to work. A message had been left from Kenning, at the Wagon and Horses. *One last job for a desperate magistrate who was being blackmailed apparently, couple of extra grand, then back to the mainland and drive to Brisbane. Selling the coins in Sydney on the way.* He inspected the six–coin albums, plastic sheet after sheet of rare coins in excellent condition. But he had no doubt he would be the prime suspect. Ivano loosened boards in the ceiling above the kitchen bench and stashed the coins in a cavity before making himself a cup of tea. He would rest up a few hours and then set off on foot once more, to the affluent inner city suburb of Battery Point.

***

Late that afternoon…

The police contacted Stanley Smart's daughter Sophie and told her about her father. Assured that he was out of danger, Sophie checked his property was secure and made directly for the Royal Hobart Hospital. It was out of visiting hours and the ward matron had other ideas, but Sophie Smart was tenacious. She would not take no for an answer. Daddy was in recovery, sitting up in bed and feeling rather foolish.

Stanley dozed but was relieved to see his daughter who immediately noticed the red cord mark about his neck, and, looking rather ominous, Sophie felt tears well up.

'Now, now,' I'm okay,' Stanley took her hand in both of his. 'It's not what you think Sophie. I slipped off the office chair and hit my head.'

'And nearly died hanging yourself, Jesus Daddy. How on earth did you manage to do that?'

'I don't know love. I just don't know. Clumsy I guess.'

'What were you doing on the chair in the first place?'

Stanley looked his daughter in the eye and knew he would have to confide in her. 'I need you to do something for me.'

'Anything.'

'Well,' Stanley remembered the company surrounding him in the other hospital beds. He motioned his daughter to come closer. 'I need you to make certain my house is secure,' he said in a soft voice.

'I've already done that Daddy.' Sophie thought a moment. 'You know the police had another warrant, don't you?'

'Mongrels, but I'm not surprised.'

'Well they searched the house for a second time …'

'And?'

'Found nothing.' Sophie looked at her father with a worried look. 'Why, should they have?'

They've just got it in for me. They reckon some coins went missing at the museum. It's the new director, Charlotte Fysh. She's been making accusations since the day she started.'

Sophie sighed. She had overheard the police talking and hoped there was no truth in what they said. 'They found money,' she said.

'What?'

Sophie whispered, 'Daddy. They found four thousand eight hundred dollars hidden behind the curtain rail in your study.'

'Bastards!' Stanley checked himself. 'Sorry love. Mongrels. Did they take it?'

'No, they counted it and put it back.'

Stanley let out a sigh of relief.

'Why have you got money hidden?'

'I always hide some cash. Always have done Sophie, you can't go trusting banks all the time.'

'Yes, but …'

'Don't you worry yourself, it's all legal. And they found nothing else of interest?'

'They found your safe under the wardrobe.'

Now Stanley's eyes narrowed. Suddenly the hospital ward felt oppressive. It was a warm day outside. He sat upright and beads of sweat formed on his forehead. 'And?'

This was the information Sophie dreaded telling her father. 'It was open Daddy.'

'What!'

'The wardrobe was moved aside and the safe door was open, and your coin collection has gone.'

'Gone! The police took it?'

'No Daddy. Someone got there first. And it could only be the person who saved your life.'

Stanley had momentarily forgotten someone was in his house shortly after he fell and hit his head. Whoever it was had cut him down, called an ambulance and then scarpered; but not before opening his safe. 'How?… I mean who?

Who knew the safe was there? Only you Sophie. You're the only one who ever knew about it.'

'Not your friend Jacopo?'

'No. Besides, Jacopo's not strong enough to move the wardrobe or to have cut me down and lowered me to the floor.'

'Then whoever it was has had a quick look around before leaving, and in doing so they have found the hidden safe.'

'Impossible. The police never found it the first time they searched my house,' Stanley was devastated. He stared at the hospital wall opposite, racking his brain. 'But it was locked. They opened it somehow without a key. It must have been someone who knew what they were doing, a professional. Who?'

'It was an old safe daddy, a key lock. Whoever broke into your house had a key or picked the front door lock. Someone that smart could easily pick the safe lock as well.' As Sophie said this, she had a nagging sense that she knew who it was.

***

Lying in his hospital bed Stanley had time to think. The colonial painting by Duterrau of the Tasmanian aborigine would be his financial ticket, his saving grace, and the more he thought about it the more he suspected his Italian friend Jacopo of double dealings. *He wouldn't look me in the eye when I asked him about it, he looked sneaky, I know he did.*

***

That same evening about 10PM…

Ivano Stipanov, *cat burglar to the rich,* walked the backstreets of Battery Point. He had made up his mind to leave town and he was annoyed with himself for breaking one of his own golden rules, he'd fallen in love. Now after the weirdest experience at Sophie's father's house he could have been caught. No, Hobart wasn't for Ivano. But he *did* have one last commitment … *So, execute the job and get out of town.*

Ivano earlier had made a visit to the Wagon and Horses Inn at the top end of Argyle Street to collect any messages. If the publican thought it strange that his guest never slept at the inn, although paying a couple of weeks rent in advance, he asked no questions. Men with criminal pasts respected other like-minded felons.

Ivano had the phone number and a name. Christian Winterbourne. With that information and a phone book it was easy to find his *mark's* address. Mona Street Battery Point. Approaching the address from the darker side of the street Ivano slipped silently through the front gate and made a brief reconnaissance. Whoever his mark was, he wasn't short of money.

Perfect.

Ivano heard the music before he saw the old man sitting half asleep in an armchair listening to classical music. Pleased with what he saw, he walked to nearby Hampden Road where he located a phone box. It was now 10.15PM.

'Mr Winterbourne?'

'Yes, who's this?'

'Call me Pete. I believe you need assistance. Would you like to meet with me?'

'Yes. When?'

'Now.'

'Now?'

'Yes. I'm nearby.' Christian instinctively looked out through his living room window and into the night. 'Yes or no Mr Winterbourne?'

'Y-yes.'

The line went dead. Within minutes Christian heard a noise in the kitchen. Warily he walked the passage to the rear of the house, flicking on every light switch until the house was lit like a hospital. He entered the kitchen. 'Good god man!' Christian felt his heart thump. The intruder was dressed all in black; jeans, roll neck skivvy, gloves. 'How did you get in here?'

'It's my business to enter where I want, isn't that what you're going to pay me for?'

'So you're Pete?'

'Christian ... isn't it?'.

Christian nodded. He seemed to have lost his air of authority. Ivano sat at the kitchen table, helped himself to a banana in a wooden fruit bowl. The fruit was over-ripe, with streaks of black forming at the stalk.

'You know you shouldn't keep bananas in a bowl with other fruit, it ripens them too fast,' Ivano said.

Christian ignored the comment. He looked distant and impatient.

Ivano said, 'Sit.'

Christian sat obediently. He certainly would not normally have arranged to meet the stranger in his home, but here he was. And the man's confidence was reassuring.

'You need something retrieved from a house I believe?'

Surprisingly Christian was beginning to feel comfortable with this stranger. He wanted to know all about him but dared not ask. Instead he explained his situation in detail.

'I want a thousand up front and a thousand on delivery. I keep any cash in the safe, you get the photos.'

'No problem. I can only assume the negatives will be in the safe also.'

'I'll need a day or two to case the property and assess this Mareike.'

'How can I contact you?'

'You can't, I'll contact you when the job's done. Now, do you perchance carry one thousand dollars in cash?'

'No.'

'I guessed not.'

'But I'll have it at ten in the morning when the banks open.'

'Fine.'

Of course, Christian did have cash on the premises but thought that fact was best kept to himself.

'I'll be here at 10.30.'

No goodnight, see you tomorrow. One moment he had company, the next Christian was alone once more and pouring another Hennessey.

***

The next morning…

Stanley Smart checked himself out of hospital. No signed discharge papers. He simply dressed in the clothes he had arrived at hospital in, folded in a ward cupboard, and took off down the fire escape, unaware of the vivid red and purple bruising around his neck, from his near death by accidental hanging.

Stanley let himself inside as discreetly as possible and looked about to see if the police had disturbed much. But the house was so busy with possessions one would never be able to tell. Stanley closed his curtains, preferring to move about in semi-darkness, and then phoned his mate Jacopo Moretti.

Under Stanley's instruction Jacopo used the side gate in Victoria Street, where the short Italian could barely reach the latch. The old gate squeaked open and he hurried to the back door. Although the sun shone warmly in a clear blue sky, inside was gloom and shadows. Jacopo found Stanley sitting on the sink in the kitchen nursing a large glass of red wine. He appeared paranoid, his eyes darting about. Jacopo looked at the kitchen clock, it read 10.40AM. He noted the wine in his friend's hand. Stanley wanted to say *hello my friend, thanks for coming at short notice*, but he was miffed. He suspected his friend knew where the Duterrau painting was and was keeping the information from him. He harrumphed instead and said, 'Help yourself to a red.'

Jacopo considered the situation. Something was wrong. Stanley looked pre-occupied. Angry even.

'Grazie.' Jacopo had a feeling it would be considered rude, an insult even, if he didn't at least have a small glass. He found a glass on the sink and rinsed it. The cask of Yalumba Shiraz was near empty, but he managed to half fill a small glass. 'Salute.'

'Salute.' Stanley gulped his glass as if quenching a thirst. There followed an awkward silence.

'Your neck, my friend,' Jacopo asked. 'What you do?'

Stanley didn't acquaint his friend with the last crazy twenty-four hours. Not yet anyway. He took a slurp draining his glass and slid off the sink to front Jacopo face to face. Jacopo smelt Dettol, anxiousness and cheap wine.

'We've been friends a long time, me and you, Jacky, haven't we?' Stanley's voice sounded deeper than usual.

Jacopo was feeling decidedly uncomfortable. 'Si, si. Of course. Long time.'

'Then I want you to look me in the eye and tell me you honestly don't know where the Duterrau painting is.'

Jacopo fumbled. He swallowed hard and took a gulp of wine to disguise his guilt, before his eyes wandered.

'Look at me Jacky,' Stanley's voice grew louder. 'Tell me the truth.'

'I … I don't know notheen Stanley. Notheen.'

'Don't lie to me.'

'The paint-een, she disappears.'

Stanley had had enough. 'You're lying Jacopo,' he yelled. The curator's face grew red, demonic. His near-death experience gave him muscle. 'I can read it in your eyes.' He salivated, taking a step closer, centimetres from the Italian's twitching face.

'How would you like a neck like mine?'

Jacopo was sprayed with spittle. Stanley threw his glass aside shattering against the wall. He grabbed the little man's scrawny neck.

'No! Stan-ley. No. I tell you true, si?'

'True! You tell me true!' Stanley mimicked the Italian's accent. 'I'll tell you true you thieving bastard!'

Stanley hooked the cord over Jacopo's head, the same cord that had almost choked him to death. He pulled it tight and dragged the antique restorer along the passage to the toilet.

Jacopo squealed. 'What you do?'

Stanley forced Jacopo to his knees and shoved his head in the toilet. Jacopo's face was centimetres from the water when he capitulated in a terrifying shriek.

'I tell you … please … no do thees. I tell you true …'

Stanley yanked the man's head out of the bowl where Jacopo fell into a corner on the lavatory floor, tears streaming down his cheeks. Stanley smelt success. Jacopo's shoulders sagged. He started spilling the truth, Stanley listened, relishing success. The malice had evaporated, and Jacopo's words flowed freely. Almost like a weight lifted from the little man's shoulders.

He related how he had sold it to the magistrate Christian Winterbourne for twelve thousand dollars and how he was yet to collect the money. Stanley decided then and there that he would never trust his friend again. However, he wasn't going to make a scene. *Not right now anyway.*

Stanley took a generous flab of Jacopo's jowl between finger and thumb and, pinching hard, he gave the flab a good shake. 'See, telling the truth wasn't so bad, was it now?'

Stanley went on to explain how he nearly killed himself. How he lay unconscious with the noose around his neck. How someone, persons unknown, cut him down before calling an ambulance.

Jacopo listened in bemused silence. 'Who call ambulance?'

'What? Are you deaf? I told you I don't know. But whoever it was broke into my safe and stole my coin collection.'

'Your coin collection,' Jacopo mused. He had other ideas.

'Who could do thees things?'

Stanley took a deep breath. 'I don't know how.' He turned on Jacopo again, still sitting on the toilet floor, and his eyes darkened.

'Do *you* happen to know by any chance,' Stanley said in a low accusing voice, 'who stole my coins?'

'No Stanley … It no me. Jacopo never do thees things.' Jacopo's bottom lip quivered, he looked about to burst into tears again. Truth was Stanley didn't think his old friend capable either.

'I'll find out Jacky, you mark my words.' Stanley smacked his lips. So what if it was still morning, he wanted another glass of red. He offered Jacopo his hand and jerked the antique restorer back onto his feet. 'But first things first. Where can we find this magistrate?'

Immediately Jacopo panicked. Stanley's near-death experience had made him gung-ho.

'Why you ask?'

'We're going to take back what is ours.'

'Take back? But I sell to thees man.'

'What? For a piddly twelve thousand dollars and I might add, twelve thousand you haven't got yet. That's chickenfeed. It's worth fifty, sixty thousand, so he can keep his twelve thousand, we'll get double that on the black market. No, we're going to take the painting back. He can keep his flamin' money.'

'But I know thees man. He never let us take painting, and he magistrate Stanley, powerful man. He get police.'

'He won't even know we've taken it,' Stanley said with a brazen grin. Jacopo's shoulders sagged a second time, defeated. 'Another red?' Stanley asked.

'The cask of vino, she finito I'm thinking.'

'No.' Stanley stomped back into the kitchen moving one pile of junk to another pile. 'I've got a half full one here somewhere … ah, there you are.' The wine cask was hidden behind a pile of empty egg cartons. Stanley filled their glasses taking a generous gulp. 'We'll be crafty,' he muttered, swiping his lips with his sleeve.

'Crafty? … what ees thees, crafty?'

'Well, you've got an old chair you restored for him, an oak carver you told me.'

'Si.'

'Well you and that half-wit neighbour's boy of yours, what's his name, Rory, you deliver it early in the evening, when the neighbours are inside eating their dinner. You distract this magistrate while I search the house and take the painting back.'

Jacopo looked at Stanley like he was loco, and maybe he was ... *The near-death thing and all that.*

'Have you got any idea at all where he may have put it?'

'He put it in office, he tell me thees things when I was there last time. For safe keeping he says.'

'Well there you go Jacky. Well done. Piece of cake.' Stanley gulped the remaining wine in one mouthful and squeezed the cask tap squirting another *Chateau de Cardboard* into his glass. 'Is that chair finished?'

'Is near si. I need one day ... maybe two I'm Thinkeen.'

'Then finish it. We go day after tomorrow in the evening.'

***

Police Headquarters. A couple of hours later...

Landon wrapped a knuckle on Maddison's door and entered without waiting, stopping at her desk. He held an evidence bag. 'We managed another search at that hoarder's property and still found nothing to pin on him regards museum property, unless you include Museum stationery.'

'What?'

'Well we found a TMAG pen.'

'Really? Nothing huh?'

'Not a loose penny, let alone a collection of stolen gold sovs. But we found something far more interesting.' Landon held the bag high.

'Okay, what have we got?' Maddison stared at the evidence bag with Landon's excited face in focus directly behind it.

'This.' Landon's grinning white teeth and a winning smile showed clearly through the plastic.

Maddison noted the red-handled pocketknife. 'And?'

'Well it was on the floor near where Stanley hung himself. It was lost under a chair. But here's the thing. I don't think Stanley Smart tried to top himself. It was a weird accident. He was balancing on a chair, he's only short as you know, and he's toppled, smashed his head on the corner of a filing cabinet, knocked himself unconscious, fallen, his head hooking through a curtain cord and bingo, he is hung like a crooked curator.'

'A bizarre accident.'

'Yes, I'm certain of it.'

Then what was he doing on the chair in the first place?'

'A-ha, glad you asked. The boys found a cash stash on the first warrant remember, hidden inside a custom-built hidey-hole in the curtain rail.'

Maddison read the report, but this fact seemed irrelevant to the suicide investigation. But now. 'Hidden in the curtain rail, how?'

'I mean the surrounding boxing.'

'It was several thousand wasn't it?'

'Four thousand eight hundred to be exact, mostly fifties.'

'Where's the cash now?'

'Left it there. It's hardly illegal. All old people stash money, don't they?'

'Probably, but for this old person, it's suspicious.'

Maddison nodded to the pocketknife in the evidence bag. 'And this?'

'Someone's cut him down. The cord was severed, and they called the ambulance before making themselves scarce.'

'Why?'

'For some nefarious reason, that's for certain.'

'Now there's a word.'

'Nefarious?'

'Yes.'

Landon pushed the evidence bag across the desk. 'Check the handle.'

Maddison picked it up and read aloud the carved initials. 'I.S. Well, well, our good Samaritan left a calling card. But who the hell is I.S.?'

'Any prints? Or is that a stupid question?'

'No prints. No blood. Clean as a whistle. But …' Landon was grinning like a panda in a sugarcane field.

'What?'

'Do the initials I.S. Ring any bells?'

'No.'

'What was the name of Stanley Smart's daughter's liaison in the café the day you were there for lunch? The same bloke wanted for high-end burglary in Melbourne.'

Maddison snatched up the folders of faxed notes and found the one she wanted. 'Ivano Stipanov!'

'Yes ... I.S.'

'It's too much of a coincidence, isn't it?'

'Absolutely. We need to find this bloke.'

'Any developments on his daughter leading us to this Ivano Stipanov?'

'We've been on her for days now. Not a thing. That meeting at the café may have been a one-off.'

'Stay on her for another seventy-two hours.'

***

Two days had passed since Stanley hung himself when, at 1.40 PM bordello madam Mareike turned up at St Joseph's in Macquarie Street for the funeral of her rival madam Phoebe Crow. Mareike had insisted all her girls attend the funeral out of respect for the industry if nothing else. *It'll look good for our public image.* There was standing room only. Mourners lined up out onto the street. It appeared Phoebe Crow riled Mareike even in death and Mareike's last words were immortalised as she was heard muttering on arrival at the church, 'God rest the old bitch's soul.' Phoebe Crow had always commanded more respect than her rival around Hobart. People liked her, as rough as she was.

Burglar Ivano Stipanov did his homework. He read of the funeral details in the Mercury Newspaper. The timing was perfect. He would commit his theft at 2PM. *Day light robbery.* It couldn't have panned out better.

***

The Liverpool Street Bordello was an easy target. Ivano navigated the outside of the property first, noticing only one staff member in the backyard, a gardener in his late twenties weeding lazily in the sun, his Walkman headphones playing tunes while he was humming to himself.

The challenge was too easy. Wearing a delivery driver's smock (although he arrived on foot) and carrying an empty beer carton sized box wrapped in brown paper as a prop, Ivano picked the front-door lock. He stepped into the hallway and called out.

'Hello.' No answer. Great. He was alone. Knowing the layout as detailed to him by his client, the magistrate, Ivano hurried to the office. He found the safe built into the desk with faux drawers for a face over the safe door. This information came via Chastity. Excellent. It was a Watson and Son early combination iron safe.

Christ it must be a hundred years old. The mechanism was clumsy, and the same combination used over and over. Ivano dropped to his knees and with one ear pressed to the tumbler he listened as each number sounded with an ever so subtle click. Ivano had the safe open in just over one minute. He pulled the solid door open ... and gasped. *You're kidding me!*

The old bat didn't believe in banks, or more likely she didn't want to declare her loot to the Australian Tax Office. Ivano counted twenty grand before giving up. Clearly there was double that. With so much to lose, urgency tapped Ivano on the shoulder. He crammed the bundled notes into the prop parcel before finding the photos. The photographic negatives had been buried under more cash. He made a brief inspection, enough to be certain he had the right photos, and was about to retreat when he noticed an antique glass paperweight on the desk. If there was one thing besides antique jewellery and fine art that appealed to Ivano, it was antique paperweights.

French, 1900–1910 Murano millefiori Bacchus style paperweight, if I'm not mistaken. Nice. I'll have that thank you very much.

It had all taken him less than fifteen minutes.

Two blocks away Ivano flagged a cab. At Cornelian Bay he noted a parked police car. Two cops appeared to be drinking coffee, but he felt uncomfortable. It wasn't worth the risk. Ivano decided he would retrieve the coins at night when he thought it safe. He ordered the cabbie drive directly to the Wagon and Horses instead, where he had paid for a room in advance, his temporary safe house. Ivano spread the cash on the bed. Forty-seven thousand three hundred and sixty-five dollars in mostly fifties and twenties. Ivano flicked through the portfolio of compromising photos. His client, Christian Winterbourne was there all right. But so were several others. *The blackmailing bitch.*

Ivano made his mind up to leave town the next night. He would collect from the magistrate and get the hell off this island before the shit hit the fan. But as he studied the photos, he thought Winterbourne wasn't getting off that lightly. Ivano figured the photos were worth more than two grand. Five grand at least ... *Yeh. Five grand, then I'm outa here. For now, though, I'll let him sweat.*

CHAPTER TWELVE

Earlier in the day...

Rookie cop and coroner's assistant Luke Farrell sat on a bench outside the retail shop Charles Davis in the Elizabeth Street Mall, in Hobart's CBD, chatting to his new love Tammy Gilbert. It was lunch time and the crowds were out. The two ate lunch, a burger each and shared a bag of chips. The food was cold and the thick-shakes warm, but who cared? Love was in the air. Tammy, a nineteen-year-old brunette from the eastern shore suburb of Howrah, worked in the account's office of Coles Department Store in the mall. The two met six weeks earlier at the New Sydney Irish Pub on Bathurst Street on a Friday Guinness and Craic Night. Tammy was easily impressionable and loved Luke's usually embellished stories to do with his often-gruesome work.

Five metres away, towards the Liverpool Street entrance to the mall, a homeless man – by all appearances – approached two women in their thirties who were smoking and minding their own business. 'Can yer spare a smoke?' he asked the one with the dyed black hair – white at the roots – still holding a packet of Marlboro and her lighter. Her friend, the strawberry blonde, chewing gum and twirling her permed corkscrews, studied the man briefly. He was late thirties and quite good looking, average height with a hood pulled over his head. Her friend capitulated and without saying a word she flipped open the packet and tapped a cigarette free. With not so much as a *thank you* the vagrant took a cigarette. 'Light?' he more demanded than asked. The faux black-haired woman huffed, shocked at the man's audacity, but sparked up a flame and held the lighter out before him. The vagrant cupped his hands around the flame, puffed a cloud of smoke and took the opportunity to caress the young woman's hand.

'Piss off!' she said, loud enough for anyone nearby to hear.

Luke Farrell heard and turned with a dozen other heads. The man didn't budge and stared at *faux hair* with cold dark eyes.

'Fucking creep!' She stepped back while her friend stood defensively. The man snatched the cigarette packet and lighter and bolted in Luke's direction.

'Hey!' the woman screamed out.

The vagrant weaved between bodies. He was nimble, fast … and he rushed by Luke.

Luke didn't hesitate. He struck out, fast as a spitting cobra. One boot between the man's legs while snatching an arm. The mugger tripped and fell heavily, cracking his head on a mall bench. Luke pounced while the man was down, one knee in the back and a twist of the arm behind his back.

'We've got it, we've got it!' Two beat cops, one swinging handcuffs, appeared from nowhere.

'Cuff him!' Luke ordered, pumped with adrenalin, and offering the cop two wrists pulled tight behind the man's back.

'We'll take it from here.'

'I'm a cop,' Luke said loudly, and Tammy Gilbert's chest swelled.

The thief fought furiously, but with three men restraining him he finally surrendered, his cheek flat against the mall paving stones. It was at that moment, as the cuffs were locked into position and his hood fell free, that Luke had a sudden recognition. This man resembled the identikit portrait assembled after the police interviewed Taroona resident Sylvia Brandt. The cops hoisted the man onto his feet while one radioed for a paddy wagon.

'You're under arrest on suspicion of murder,' Luke barked in the suspect's ear.

'Hold on …' one of the officers started.

Luke finally managed to reveal his badge. 'Coroner's office,' Luke said with a wide grin. 'And this man is wanted on suspicion of murder.'

It was then the prisoner turned to face the rookie cop. Luke fixed the man with a stare; gazing back into those dark, piercing, unblinking eyes. Luke swallowed hard. There was no denying it – he felt he was looking into the eyes of Satan himself.

***

One hour later…

Luke Farrell stood legs apart, arms crossed and feeling pretty proud of himself. He watched his prisoner through a one-way mirror where he sat, handcuffed to restraints at the interview table staring at the wall before him. It was almost like meditation.

'He's been like that for twenty-three minutes,' Luke said to Senior Detective Landon Finch as he joined him.

'You did a great job Luke,' Landon said. 'Well done.'

'You could very well have caught our murderer single-handed,' Sergeant Highlander said.

Luke was too chuffed to speak. He knew he would have to pull his head out of the clouds, but it was difficult with all his superiors complimenting him. 'You'll get an medal for this.'

Now Luke chose to speak. 'Do you really think so?'

'You'll need a chest to pin it on first son,' another cop said. Luke felt his face flush.

Inspector Maddison Lovett appeared in the doorway. 'Good work Luke.'

'Thanks Inspector.'

'Go easy on him,' another cop added. 'He'll never get his head back through the door.'

'Alright then,' Maddison took a long hard look through the two-way mirror. 'What do we have so far?'

'We swabbed him for DNA an hour ago, wasn't happy. Says we have the wrong person.'

'Naturally, they all say that. Do we have a name?'

Landon. 'Ronny Smith.'

'Ronny Smith?' Maddison eyeballed Landon.

'Yes I know, sounds like bullshit to me too.'

'How long before we get DNA results?'

'Tiger reckons it'll take a day.'

'Okay.'

Sergeant Highlander took the clipboard from under his arm and pulled the pen from behind his ear. As a wily criminal interviewer, he had read up on the recent murders and had all the material he needed. Now it was time to do his best. He looked to the interviewee waiting in the lockup. 'So, who's joining me?'

'Me,' Landon said.

Maddison turned on her heels. 'Keep me in the loop,' she said as the door swung closed behind her.

***

A short time later...

Landon threw open Maddison's office door. He didn't knock. Never did. 'We have a problem,' he blurted.

Maddison looked up from her paperwork allowing a wry smile. 'No *excuse me*, Senior Detective?'

'Sorry In-spector,' Landon accentuated the title, returning the sarcasm. 'But excuse me … we have a problem with Ronny Smith.'

'Oh?'

'That's his real name by the way. We've checked.'

'And?'

'Well he was difficult to interview. He refused to answer questions and tried to intimidate by staring with those wide, unblinking eyes. He admitted nothing.'

'Well then, what's the problem?'

'I found out he's been in prison the past three years.'

'In Risdon?'

'Yep.'

'And?'

'Well he was only released two days ago so it's impossible, he could not have committed those murders.'

'And you checked his alibis?'

'Of course. He was still in prison when Meredith Kendall was murdered and consequently, he was in Risdon when the fisherman was killed.'

'Well that's thrown a spanner in the works. He fits the description of our perp … and we've got DNA from the crime scene, when is the ETA of the DNA results?'

'Well Tiger said twenty-four-hours so …' Landon looked at his watch. 'About noon tomorrow I guess.'

'What was he in prison for?'

'Ah, well, that is interesting…'

'Well?"

'Sex crime. Rape. Second offence.'

Inspector Maddison shook her head. 'You've got to find something to hold him here until the DNA results come through.'

'Well the thing is, he fits the description of the cold case killer back in '88. And he has a tiny jellybean birthmark under his right ear.'

'Is the witness that reported him back then still around?'

'I'll look into it.'

'Because if they are, we need to bring them in for a line-up.'

'Got you.'

'Then we can hold Ronny Smith on other charges.' Maddison had another thought. 'We need a warrant to search his home.'

'Already happening. I also have the address of his ex-wife. I'm on my way there now.'

***

Coroner Griffin joined Maddison in her office to hear Landon relate his findings from the cold case interview. 'Ronny Smith's ex-wife didn't have one kind word to say about the man.'

'I can believe that.'

'Ronny used to drive the school bus for Taroona High School, casual like, that's how he knew Taroona so well. He was arrested for loitering originally. Acting suspiciously. He gave false information to police and was found in possession of a large kitchen knife that he made some silly excuse for. The ex-wife said when the police searched their house three years ago, they took away sixty pieces of Ronny's clothing, all to be minutely examined.'

'I did the work on that case,' Tiger said. 'And I found seven fibres that matched the material in the victim's tracksuit top on a woollen jumper of his.'

'The rape victim's track suit you say?'

'Yes.'

'That was as good as a fingerprint.'

'Certainly was. That's what convicted him.'

'His wife also told me Ronny was also linked to an attempted rape two years before that in the same area, Taroona, but down near the shoreline. And more interestingly she told of him wanting rough sex, where he would tie her up. The more she struggled, she said, the more aroused he became.'

'He has to be guilty of the 1988 murder,' Maddison shook her head slowly. 'So let's hope we can prove it.'

CHAPTER THIRTEEN

That night, late…

Seraph had read of the killings in the papers and he'd watched the news. The cops hadn't a clue, never would. *Stupid bastards.* But now he heard the whispers in his ear once more. *His* reward had been slow in forthcoming. There had always been a promise of intimacy. He read the signs, there was no doubt in his mind. The woman wanted him.

She craves me … Seraph just knew it. The voices assured him. Seraph had been totally seduced by the siren of death, but one excuse after the other started to unhinge him. He suspected he had been exploited, manipulated. Had this woman read his weaknesses from the day they met? He was after all a killer. Always had been. Did she recognise this and take advantage?

After much investigation he discovered where the woman lived. Now that Seraph was parked outside the woman's two-storey home in one of Hobart's more affluent suburbs he felt a mixture of trepidation and anxiousness, yet a fear of rejection. He felt his bowels rumble.

It was late, after midnight. But Seraph hadn't a clue what time it was, he never wore a watch. Time meant little to him. Standing alone in the dark he studied a soft light burning in the bedroom on the upper floor. *She's home.* Seraph heard music. Faint music. Soft like the light. He listened carefully, padding silently across the front lawn. It was the theme from *Cats*, the musical. *I think.*

Without warning the front yard flooded with light. *Shit!* Sensor lights. Seraph pushed his back hard against the lower floor wall. Masked by the canopy of the healthy green leaves of a tamarillo tree, Seraph froze. On the floor above a woman's face appeared at the window. From here the woman could see all the front of the property out onto the street.

There was no one there. *Damned wildlife.* The woman made a mental note, *must get the electrician to readjust those lights.* She faded from sight, but not before Seraph caught a glimpse of his Medusa. She looked wonderful in her Paris red negligee, her long silky hair loose about her shoulders. Seraph felt the arousal so long denied him. He imagined her hair trickling through his fingers. He imagined he could smell her perfumed body, her feminine scent. Lust stirred through his loins. With the sensor light on a five-minute timer still flooding the front garden, Seraph crept around to the side of the house. Quietly and carefully he trod the exterior steps to the upper floor balcony where he prowled along the decking to steal a peek in the bedroom window…

The bitch! The fucking bitch! The woman lay on her bed, propped on one elbow sipping champagne. Lying with her, Seraph saw the back of a man, naked. They were barely covered by a sheet. *Clearly … fucking clearly, they had just had sex!*

The voices returned. The *word salad* in his head tossed jumbled and confused thoughts, all symptomatic of Seraph's schizophrenia.

***

6.50AM. In an affluent suburb of Hobart…

Camila Harper left her front door ajar, stepped onto her front porch and looked about, up and down the street. Satisfied neighbours weren't out and about, she checked her pink dressing gown was secured, not exposing anything it shouldn't, and hurried across the lawn, damp from an early morning shower. Today her Mercury newspaper, rolled in plastic, was amongst the daffodils where it had been sent spiralling onto the garden by the passing delivery boy. She fetched up the paper and prepared to scurry back inside when something rather strange caught her attention. Was the woman across the street blatantly staring at her? She hadn't known the neighbour long, having only moved into the area five weeks earlier herself, and to be quite honest she thought her rude, the odd times she had encountered her. 'Up herself', husband Frank had said. But here she was, it's 6.50 in the morning and the woman was staring wide-eyed at her from her ceiling-to -floor bedroom window. And even worse she appeared to be making faces at Camila; lying bodily on the floor with her head pushed hard against the glass, her mouth open wide. Wide as in a circle 'O', like she was drunk or something. Camila looked away shaking her head in disgust, but something compelled her to look back once more. She was still there. She hadn't moved. Camila's eyes weren't that great at the best of times but now the sight seemed comical; like it was a sex doll with its mouth beckoning oral pleasure, its distorted face pushed against the glass.

Camilla fetched Frank, who was by now late for work. Frank too, stood on his own lawn, narrowing his eyes in uncertainty. But Frank recognised something his wife hadn't. The lifeless head appeared to have hit the glass and slid to the floor. And Frank recognised blood streaks down the window.

'Jesus Christ!'

'What?'

Frank didn't answer but ran across the street. Closer inspection standing on the neighbour's front lawn confirmed his suspicion. 'Call an ambulance!' he yelled to his wife.

Maddison donned PPE plastics at the door to the double-storey house crime scene and stepped into that ever-familiar cloying coppery effluvium of spilt blood. Of course, Maddison had been to this house only days before, to interview the dead fisherman's wife, Verity Shreeve. Now the wife too was a statistic, her face pancaked against the glass of the scenic window like a contorted portrait an infant would draw.

'The victims are the owners I'm presuming?' Senior Detective Charlie Smite, the first responder at the scene only twenty-five minutes earlier, asked the inspector.

'The woman is Verity Shreeve,' Maddison sighed. 'I don't know who the male could be. It certainly isn't her husband. He was murdered a few days ago.'

'Jesus! Really?'

'Yep.'

'Shreeve,' Detective Smite asked. 'You're talking about Shreeve as in Max Shreeve the dead fisherman.'

'Very same.'

'Christ! Now what?'

'The male and Mrs Shreeve were lovers.' Maddison walked through the upstairs passageway to face body number one. The mystery male victim. A naked man sprawled down the stairs headfirst, arms splayed awkwardly. Blood had oozed from several stab wounds in the neck and back and the carpet saturation continued for six steps. 'John Sparkes, solicitor with Bollman and Marsh in Murray Street.' Another officer held up exhibit number nine in its clear protected sheath. 'The solicitor's wallet including driving licence. And the address is Lenah Valley.'

Maddison nodded. 'So now we have a name. Married?'

'We're checking on it.'

'It appears he has put up a fight,' Smite said. 'Chased the killer to the stairs before succumbing to his wounds.'

Maddison entered the bedroom where the coroner, forensics and four other officers were already hard at work. 'Morning inspector.' The coroner was in fine spirits. 'You got the brief on the way up I take it?'

'If you mean do I know it's Max Shreeve's ex-wife, then the answer's yes. This will either make it easier to solve or harder.'

Maddison's attention was immediately drawn past the coroner to the female victim. From where Maddison stood the body reminded her of a female contortionist at a circus performance she had seen years ago. The figure was twisted, whilst the face was pushed hard against the floor to ceiling window. It appeared she had fallen against the glass and slid down, leaving a smear of blood. She was clearly naked, yet a sheet had been thrown over her lower body. Luke Farrell was busy printing the woman's fingers. 'Morning Inspector.'

'How's it going there Luke? You've had a time of it lately.'

'Sure have. But I'm learning heaps.'

'Well that's one way to look at it.'

Griffin looked down at his young assistant and jerked his head. Luke understood immediately and peeled back the sheet. Maddison bunched her lips, shaking her head slightly, involuntarily. The victim had her hands tied behind her back. Dark bruising had formed around the inner thighs, barely visible the way the body was twisted, but a lot of blood had been lost from the groin. Maddison had only one word. 'Rape?'

'Well I won't know for certain until we get the body back at the morgue, but yes.'

'So the male was murdered first it seems.'

'Looks that way. The male has made to defend himself and been killed in a stabbing frenzy in the process. Then the killer has tethered the female and sexually assaulted her, presumably while she was still alive. Although it could have been after death.'

'You recognise the ties?' Luke asked.

Maddison took a closer look. The binds were blood-soaked but resembled the wide brown string of the other victims. 'It seems we have a serial killer on our watch,' Luke offered.

'I'd have to argue that one. The victims are known to each other. It still might be a crime of passion.'

***

Later that day at Police Headquarters…

Maddison, Landon, Tiger, Sergeant Highlander, young Luke Farrell and Constable Harlow stood about the pin-board trying desperately to join the dots. They had photos of suspects and victims; they weren't pretty.

'We now know we don't have a serial killer,' Maddison started. 'The recent killing of Verity Shreeve we know is connected to the murder of fisherman Max Shreeve …'

'Mrs Shreeve's husband?'

'Ex-husband.'

'Yes, and Max was connected to the sex worker, Meredith Kendall.'

'Love triangle?'

'In a sick sort of way, maybe.'

'So who would want the three of them dead?'

'The Shreeve murder scene at Sandy Bay,' Landon said. 'There was no sign of a break-in.'

'No, that's because Mrs Shreeve's backdoor lock was picked,' Griffin said.

'Oh, I wondered about that.'

'I've had the advice of a locksmith. He was in no doubt that back door lock was picked, a little clumsily he said by the signs of scratches. All the same, it was picked by someone who knew what they were doing.'

'And the broken pick,' Luke Farrell noted.

'That's right,' Tiger agreed. 'We found the remains of a broken lock pick on the path near the back door.'

'Mason the deckhand,' Highlander said. 'We know he was an apprentice locksmith before he became a fisherman.'

'That's right. And he chucked it in.'

'Got sacked you mean.'

'Is that true?'

'Yes, he did a job under supervision at the fire department in Campbell Street and it was discovered later that while he was there, he picked the change-room lockers of a couple of firemen. Nicked wallets and a few other valuables. Got caught. Got fired.'

'They didn't press charges.'

'Bloody well should have.'

'And this Mason worked for our other murder victim, Max the fisherman, who he assaulted.'

'Okay, so that connects Max and Verity with Mason. But what's the motive to kill the wife Verity?'

'I'd say he's a prime suspect.'

'But where the bloody hell is he?'

'We have a search warrant out for him, but he's slipped through the net.'

'Oh shit!' Lachlan Harlow, the young constable, suddenly came to life. 'Excuse me Inspector … ah, sorry. I nearly forgot to tell you. The traffic boys put in a report. The blue HD Holden, license plate …' Harlow checked his notebook. 'Ah … KW 9406, has been located parked in bushland at Gordon's Hill Reserve.'

'Deserted?'

'I guess so. It's been there a few days the boys reckon. A local bush walker said it had been there the last three days that he knew of.'

'Gordon's Hill Reserve,' Maddison thought aloud. 'That's over Lindisfarne way isn't it?'

'Sure is.'

'Now humour me a moment. Isn't that near the Lindisfarne Motor Yacht Club?'

Landon. 'Yes, a couple of kilometres away, so?'

'Well that's where *Infinity* is moored, the boat that Max the fisherman was murdered on. The very same boat our HD Holden owner, Mason, was a deckhand on?'

Landon leapt from his seat. 'Ray,' he ordered the sergeant. 'Get a car out the front. Now.'

***

Call it intuition, a sixth sense, a psychic visitation, Mason felt the law were closing in. He'd spent a couple of nights on board *Infinity,* but had this gut feeling the cops were onto him. And he was scared. Damned scared. He packed a kit from Max's wardrobe, a few cans of food, waited until the bay looked deserted, and rowed ashore.

***

Also, that afternoon…

Charlotte took the flute of champagne offered and pulled the single sheet up over her naked body to the breasts. Museum conservator Stella Bathe sipped her rather full glass before it spilt and sidled back into bed next to her principal.

'To us,' Stella saluted. Charlotte said nothing, chinked glasses and sipped. 'You okay?' Stella asked.

Charlotte forced a smile. The guilt was tearing her apart. She had broken her own rule and become involved with a staff member, and one twenty years her junior at that. Stella sensed the tension. 'Charlotte? You okay?'

'Oh,' Charlotte let out a great sigh. 'I just feel so … so damned guilty.' Stella's face grew serious. 'Sorry Stella, it's not you. It's not your fault. I, well, it's just wrong on so many levels.'

Stella was in love. There was no denying it. For her it was bona fide, real, true love and, until this moment, she was certain Charlotte felt the same way.

'This has got nothing to do with my brother Mason has it?' Stella asked of her brother, who she discovered was wanted for questioning by the police after officers came to her workplace only days ago.

'No,' Charlotte was quick to answer. 'Nothing like that. I just … well … it's just that I …'

The shrill of Stella's apartment front doorbell severed the conversation. Charlotte shot Stella a sideways glance. 'Are you expecting someone?"

'No.' Stella looked suddenly pale.

The door shrilled again impatiently.

Stella dressed quickly, closed the bedroom door and padded quietly to the main entrance. She squinted through the spy hole.

Jesus, Mason!

Mason rapped the front door with bony knuckles the moment Stella opened it. 'Do you know the police are asking about you?' Stella said bluntly.

'Yeh, yeh.' Mason pushed past his sister into the hallway. 'I need a favour.'

Stella looked up and down the street and closed the door. 'You can't stay here.'

'Why not?'

'Are you deaf? I said the police are looking for you. They're watching this place.'

'It's bullshit.'

'No. It's not bullshit Mason. This is serious.'

'I didn't do it for Christ's sake.'

'That's all the more reason you should hand yourself in, tell them the truth.'

'Bugger that! The bloody cops are looking for a scapegoat. One night okay, that's all I ask.' Stella was torn between family, doing the right thing by the police and then this crazy affair she had started. 'One night sis.'

Suddenly something seemed alien. 'Who's here?' he asked.

'What?'

Mason's face broke into a cheeky grin. 'You've got someone here haven't you? Some lucky bloke eh?'

'Mason ...'

Mason didn't hesitate. He rushed to Stella's bedroom throwing the door open. 'Oh Christ!' Charlotte sat on the edge of the bed pulling on pantyhose. For once Mason was speechless. He gave Charlotte a licentious grin before closing the door.

'How long's this been going on?'

Stella had been meaning to *step out* for some time. But she never thought it would be like this. 'Stella,' the brother urged. 'How long?'

'Hey,' Stella said defensively. More embarrassed for Charlotte than herself. 'I'm twenty-six, okay. What I do is none of your business.'

'Hey, it's alright sis. I already knew.'

'You what?'

'Well I suspected anyway. You haven't had a boyfriend since high school.'

Stella looked sheepish. 'Really.'

'Really. Hey don't worry about me, I'll keep your secret.'

'It's telling Mum and Dad that bothers me.'

'Just suck it up, tell 'em, they'll be fine.'

'You think so?'

'Yes, I think so. Listen, I ...ah ... ah, I'll stay with Mick. But can you lend me some money?'

***

Meanwhile…

Sergeant Highlander in the lead police car radioed in from the carpark of the Lindisfarne Motor Yacht Club. Senior Detective Landon Finch took the call patched through to his office.

'Hey,' Highlander started, but Landon sensed the news wasn't good. 'Do you want the good news or the bad first?'

'Bad.'

'I'll give you the good first then. You were right. He was hiding on board the victim's boat.'

'Cheeky bastard. And the bad news? He's cleared off?'

'Yep. He was pretty discreet too, no one here saw or heard anything.'

***

A short time later…

Deckhand Mick's girlfriend Cassandra barely heard the crack at the window. In her befuddled state under the influence of THC she thought a bird had flown into the glass. The second sound she realised was a rock. She called out to Mick. From the second-floor window of their conjoined house flat in Glenorchy, Mick immediately recognised his mate Mason waving up from the backyard.

'That's Mase,' Mick yelled out over *Pearl Jam* pumping from the stereo.

'What's he doin' chucking rocks at the window?' Cassandra yelled back.

'What?'

'I said what's he …'

Mick couldn't hear a thing. 'Hang on.' He tweaked down the volume.

'I said what's he doin' chuckin' rocks at the window?'

'Dunno, let him in and ask 'im.'

Cassandra unlocked the back door and Mason was already on the top step. 'What's happenin' dude?' Cassandra's eyes were running mascara, her cheeks flushed, and her mouth remained open sucking air. She held a cigarette high.

'Gotta be careful, the cops are after me.'

'Shit.'

Mason shoved past Cassandra to Mick, who'd flopped back onto a stained well-worn couch that harboured more germs than a Petri dish. 'I need a bed for the night. The cops are lookin' for me.'

'So I heard mate. You're a regular Ned Kelly yer bastard. Close the door Cas.'

Mason headed to the couch. The place was as much tip as his own flat. 'Make yourself at home mate.'

'That's easy,' Mason joked, stepping over last night's pizza box and skittling an empty stubbie across the sticky carpet. 'Your joint's a bigger mess than mine, and you've got a girlfriend.'

'What's that s'posed to mean?' Cassandra took offence. 'Typical bloke, reckon the women have to do all the housework.'

'Yeh, well.' Mason decided to shut it. He could never understand how a good-looking bloke like his mate Mick ended up with this scrag. But he never told him to his face.

'Wanna bong?' Mick asked.

'Why not?'

The hours passed, the bong changed lips half a dozen rounds and Mick slipped out to buy fish and chips, dim sims and potato cakes, a tub of chocolate chip ice cream and another six pack of Fosters; using Mason's sister Stella's money. Cassandra was cooked by 11PM and hit the sack, but the boys sat up another three hours *floating around the lightbulb* and plotted how they would rob this dodgy magistrate of the cash hidden inside the old model ship.

***

Late afternoon next day…

Burglar to the rich, Ivano, found a phone box one street from the Wagon and Horses Inn and made two calls. One to Qantas where he booked the last flight to Melbourne at 9PM, and another call to the magistrate he was blackmailing.

'Five grand!' Ivano demanded, calm and determined.

'What?' Christian exploded; his anger fuelled by an early cocktail hour to calm his ever-increasing anxiety. 'We had a deal …'

'I don't give a shit. I have what you want, plus negatives. Five grand. I'll call in on you this evening. Deal?'

'The deal was for two thousand. One before, one after. I was expecting you here yesterday.'

'Yeh, well I got waylaid didn't I. Like I said, I don't give a rat's arse about the deal. It's five grand now. The banks close in forty-five minutes. Do we have a deal or not?'

'This is robbery!'

'I can't hear you?'

'Yes. Yes. You have a deal.' Christian slammed the receiver back onto its cradle and balled his fists in a silent scream. He snatched his car keys and drove to Westpac in Magnet Court shopping centre, five minutes away.

The clock was ticking. Ivano checked out of the Wagon and Horses and decided to walk to Battery Point, after all he didn't want to arrive too early. After fleecing the magistrate, he would taxi to Cornelian Bay, collect Stanley's coins and go directly to the airport; many thousands of dollars richer than he could ever have imagined.

CHAPTER FOURTEEN

Sometime around 5PM...

Deckhands Mason and Mick – looking to steal the model ship full of cash - found the magistrate's Mona Street Battery Point mansion after looking in the phone directory. And their timing seemed perfect, there was no one home. Although they were both stoned off their faces, they had the sense to conduct a recce from the fruit trees and overgrown garden at the rear of the property.

'There's no car here,' Mick noted. 'So, there's no one home, right?'

'Who knows, your guess is as good as mine mate. Let's take a look in the windows.'

'Jesus!' A haze of paranoia brought on by good quality home grown weed threatened. 'You sure about this?'

'For fuck sake Mick, we're here now. Let's get it over with.' Mason left his cover and hurried to the back porch.

Mick joined him. 'Watch out for neighbours. They looked about, but a large walnut tree obscured the house north and fruit trees gave them reasonable cover to the south.

Mason moved from window to window on the porch, then tried the back door leading into the laundry. 'Locked.'

'Well what did you think?'

'Smart-arse. It means there's no one home.'

'Yer can't be certain. Hey,' Mick had a thought. Fumbling awkwardly in his tight jeans he finally managed to remove a Motorola from his pocket. 'Did you jot his phone number down with the address?' Mick flipped open the mobile. 'We'll call first. Make sure no one's there.'

Mason was impressed. 'That's a Motorola flip phone.'

'Yeh. It's the latest model.' Mick held the phone out for Mason to inspect.

'Nice, where'd yer get it?'

'Nicked it. So have yer got his number or what?'

'No idiot, course I haven't got it. Go around to the front door, act natural like, and ring the doorbell.'

'Are you crazy?'

'No. It'll make certain there's no one home.'

'What if someone is home? What if *he* opens the fuckin' door?'

'Then make some excuse, say you looking for … for Terry. And when he says there's no Terry living here, say sorry to bother you mate, and piss off up the street.'

'And what if there *is* a Terry living there?'

'Jesus you can be a fuck-knuckle. Seriously. What are the chances eh? Fuck all.' Mason found a secluded window to what appeared to be a storeroom at the end of the porch. He pulled his jumper tightly over his arm and was about to smash the window with his elbow when. 'Wait.'

'What?'

'What if he has a dog?'

'Can you see a kennel, a water bowl outside, dog-shit on the lawn?'

'No.'

'Well there's no dog. Now keep a sharp eye out.'

With the windowpane smashed it was easy to gain entry. Mick aided Mason to slide on his belly over the exposed sill, and somersault inside. The room smelt musty. It was a junk room. Mason unlocked the back door for Mick.

'Here, put these on.' Mason passed Mick a pair of latex surgical gloves and entered the hallway where he started up the stairs. 'I'll do the top floor, just look for the ship right, don't fuck around, you got it?'

Three minutes later they met downstairs in the passage. 'Anything?'

Mason. 'No.'

'Christ, where is it?'

'It's made of bone right. It's all white. Not wood.'

'Yeh, yeh, got it. There's a room off to the left with ship paintings and stuff in it but I didn't see no ship.'

'Where?'

'Second door on the left.'

The Haughton Forest seascape caught Mason's eye the moment they walked into Christian's Maritime Room.

'Jesus!' Mason blew out his cheeks. 'I wouldn't mind that on me wall.'

'You, mate,' Mick chuckled. 'Haven't got a fuckin' wall!'

***

Stanley had walked the one and a half kilometres to Mona Street from his Harrington Street address. It was a pleasant evening and a pleasant walk, and he appreciated the exercise after his hospital stint. But wearing a full-length trench coat – the plan being for the coat to hide the Duterrau portrait – Stanley was sweating by the time he arrived. He patrolled the street at the front of the property and hoped he didn't look too suspicious in his coat with his exposed neck showing off his distinct hangman's lesion. Stanley did not realise just how dodgy he looked. He checked his watch. It was 5PM. There was no car in the garage. With Jacopo's sketched plan of the mansion's interior in his hand Stanley took a side path along the southern side of the property and stepped onto the back porch. He waited, hoping he hadn't been spotted. *Jacopo should be here any minute to distract the magistrate*, he told himself. But the magistrate wasn't home. And that's when Stanley noticed the back door was ajar. He entered, locking the door behind him, stood silently and listened. When he thought it was safe, he hurried to the study.

***

By the time Christian returned from the bank it was just after five. A sudden bout of wisdom suggested he park his Mercedes in the next street, where he walked back to his home hoping this action would not attract suspicion from nosey neighbours. He slipped in the front door. Once inside, for some uncanny reason, Christian felt he was not alone. There was a hint of lingering body odour for one thing. Yet he put his suspicion down to drink. Besides he always suspected he shared the property with a ghost, albeit a friendly one. *But the body odour?*

***

Stanley found the Duterrau propped on the floor with other paintings in the study. 'Hello you,' he whispered. 'We're back together at last.' He was admiring the handsome portrait a moment when he heard the owner arrive home.

Jacopo should be outside watching for him, waiting. Stanley told himself. *I'll hear the doorbell in a minute and make good my escape while Jacopo distracts the magistrate. Too easy.* Stanley secured the portrait beneath his coat and waited behind the door.

***

'Oh Christ, he's home,' Mick hissed. 'Now what?' They waited, listening anxiously.

'He's gone upstairs,' Mason whispered in his mate's ear from where they had crawled under the dining table.

'Let's get outta here while he's up there.'

'No way.'

'What?'

'I'm not leaving without that money.'

'But we can't find the bloody ship.'

'Then I'm going to nick something else valuable. Fuck it Mick, we're here now.'

'Jesus … listen. He's on his way downstairs again.'

***

Christian had changed out of his suit, placing the bank envelope containing five thousand dollars in his smoking jacket pocket and, returning to the main lounge room, he poured himself another cognac. His hand was unsteady. Although he had dabbled on the wrong side of the law for some time now, he was not suited to this clandestine lifestyle.

***

Ivano crept through the fruit trees at rear of the Mona Street mansion and stood silently, wraith-like, at the back door under the porch. As always, he was dressed in black, his attire of choice, and just in case this bloke Winterbourne tried anything, like bounce him with hired thugs, he secured the 9-millimetre pistol down the back of his jeans under the belt. *Just like Mel Gibson would in the movies.*

Ivano used his set of lock picks to enter the Mona Street property via the rear door. He stepped through the old scullery, now a laundry, and stood quietly. Listening. Outwardly, the house appeared unoccupied. Being summer late afternoon sun spilled through the windows, so there were no tell-tale lights burning in the hallway or in any rooms that he could tell. Also, as the magistrate's car was not in the garage. Ivano suspected Winterbourne was still making his way back from the bank. He called out, his usual ruse to be certain he was alone … and a sound behind him had him turn sharply.

Christian stood in the doorway, a brandy balloon in one hand and an envelope in the other. He had changed into a Japanese-style smoking jacket and appeared slightly drunk. 'Why don't you knock like any normal person?'

'Cos I'm not a normal person,' Ivano answered. He had been asked this before.

'Well, where are they?' Christian asked impatiently. 'Show me.'

'Show me the money first.'

Christian threw the envelope onto the kitchen table. 'There's your blood money. Now give me the photos.'

Ivano unhitched his backpack, landing it on the table and unzipped his cache. He pulled the portfolio free, but the stolen paperweight fell from where the burglar had shoved it in his pack in haste. Christian recognised it immediately. 'Where did that come from?'

'France,' I believe.

'No you idiot! Where did you get it?'

Ivano was taken aback. Why the sudden interest in his paperweight? 'What? That?'

Christian didn't hesitate. He dived forward snatching up the Murano millefiori Bacchus style paperweight. Christian rolled the piece over in his palm and identified a small nick in its base. 'That's mine.'

'What?'

'This paperweight was stolen from me.'

'Don't be ridiculous.'

'It's mine I tell you. It's a Murano paperweight, circa 1910. It's Italian yes, and it went missing from here recently. Where did you get it?'

'Look sport, it isn't exactly unique you know.'

'Oh, isn't it?' Christian pointed out the chip. 'See that. That's unique. Where did you get it?'

Ivano's profession was hardly a secret to the magistrate so he told him. 'I took it from Liverpool Street,' Ivano stabbed a finger at the portfolio on the table. 'When I was retrieving those photos.'

***

Mid-forties sex-worker Chastity couldn't believe what she was witnessing. She stood with her back to the wall outside the kitchen window and carefully, slowly, twisted about to take a second peek. Her favourite client, her benefactor, her often lover Christian Winterbourne was clearly shaken. And now she knew the man in black pointing to a folder on the table must be the man who broke into Marieke's safe while they were all at Madam Phoebe's funeral.

'*Good for you Christian,*' Chastity thought. '*You went ahead with your plan. But unfortunately Mareike knows that you did get someone to break into her property and steal the photos.*'

Chastity cheered silently. After Phoebe's wake Chastity had arrived back at *Currawong House* in Liverpool Street with some of the other girls ten minutes after Mareike. Now the brothel-keeper was in her office screaming blue murder. Chastity had been the first to enter Marieke's office. The safe was left open and empty. 'I've been robbed!' Mareike wailed. 'All me savin's, all me life's savin's.' Chastity tried to console the woman who was a fountain of tears ... when suddenly Mareike turned nasty. Her eyes darkened. Her brow tightened into battlefield furrows. The tears vanished; she wiped her nose on her sleeve and uttered two words of revenge … *Christian Winterbourne.*

Chastity had to warn Christian. Now.

***

'That's crazy,' Christian, dumbfounded, studied the paperweight in the palm of his hand. 'Simply crazy … I …'

'Listen, keep the bloody thing, alright.' Ivano picked up his envelope, checking the contents.

'There's a coupla nice shots there,' Ivano sneered at the photos on the table. 'Quite professional.'

Christian reddened. He pocketed the paperweight before stepping forward snatching the binder. He quickly inspected the photos. 'Where's the negatives?'

'In the back.'

Once he eye-balled the negatives Christian was relieved. Happy even. 'Take your money and get out.' Confidence had returned. Christian embraced the folder of incriminating photos. With such tension and loathing surrounding the two, neither heard Mareike. Ivano had left the back door unlocked after picking it. Now Mareike crept along the passageway, searching out their voices.

Suddenly Ivano saw the Tom Roberts, The Miners. It was leaning against the pantry wall where Christian had placed it since bringing it back from Melbourne. 'Where did you get that?'

Christian turned warily to look at the painting. 'None of your business.'

Ivano stepped forward to look more closely. 'It's framed!'

'So?'

'Well … ah …' Ivano realised he couldn't say anything without incriminating himself.

'Where did you say you got it?'

'I didn't, now leave. You've got your money …'

'And much more thanks to you.' Ivano had had a most lucrative day.

But now he was fascinated by the very presence of a painting he stole a year earlier along with others, and the curiosity was too much. '*You!* It's you who bought the paintings, isn't it?'

'What on earth are you talking about?'

'You're the buyer in Hobart.'

Instantly it occurred to Christian that this man was affiliated with Alfred Kenning the conman.

'You know Alfred Kenning?'

'A-ha, so it is you.'

'Do you know where I can find this man?' Christian saw a way out. If he was to be arrested for buying stolen property at least he could take Kenning down with him. It would lighten any sentence. 'Look,' Christian's tone mellowed. 'I'll pay you.'

'For what? For Kenning? Not likely.'

'I'll pay you ... two thousand.' Ivano shook his head. 'Three ...'

'Forget it. I scored big at your girlfriend's brothel, got enough loot to last me a lifetime.'

Mareike came through the door armed with her pepper spray, her furious eyes on stalks. She stood with her arm outstretched, an arm's length from Ivano, safety catch off, finger on the trigger.

'Well, well, well. How convenient, I come 'ere to face this bastard,' she said oscillating the canister of spray at the magistrate and back to Ivano, her trigger finger shaking with fury, 'and I find the actual scum who broke into me house.'

Mareike turned slightly to the magistrate. 'I didn't think an old fat prick like you could do it alone.'

Ivano dropped his hands to his side, palms out and open. 'Easy lady, I ...'

'I ain't no lady shithead.' Mareike shot a glance at the backpack. 'Is that me money?'

Ivano was desperate to distract her a moment. This wasn't the first time he'd been threatened with capsicum spray and from experience, he didn't want to cop a face full at close range.

Do as she says, distract her, disarm her, run with the money.

'Yes,' Christian said with great pleasure, his chubby fingers tight around the photos. 'That's your money, now leave, the both of you.'

Mareike reached for the backpack with her free hand.

'Leave that!' Ivano lurched forward, shouting.

Mareike pulled the trigger.

'Jesus!'

Christian Winterbourne panicked. He jumped sideways, shielding his face and dropping his photos, which scattered across the floor. He pressed against the wall as far from the capsicum mist as possible; trapped in the corner ... like a rat.

'That's right,' Mareike spat. 'Your – fucking – Honour.' She put a handkerchief to her mouth to try and filter the spray. 'You stay right there. I'll deal with you in a minute.' She turned the spray once more on a writhing Ivano.

***

Outside Jacopo and Rory pulled into Christian's driveway and began untying the restored oak Jacobean style carver from the pickup tray. Glancing across to the rear of the house Jacopo was pleased to see the backdoor ajar. *Good, the man is home.* Once again, he had forgotten to phone first.

***

'Jesus! Oh god ...' Ivano floundered, blinded by the spray. His eyes were burning. The pain was unbearable. He slapped the back of his trousers blindly feeling for his gun. 'Jesus Christ!' he coughed and shrieked.

'Shut yer gob yer thieving' bastard.' Marieke's eyes narrowed. She shook the backpack to inspect the contents.

Money! Yes ... all me money and more!

Christian had avoided the worst of the spray, but copped enough to sting his eyes and make him cough. But he saw his opportunity and heaved the paperweight with all his strength. At such close range he could hardly miss.

Bullseye!

The seven-hundred-gram mass of solid glass hit the madam on the temple. 'Shit!' Marieke dropped the canister and grabbed at a welt erupting on her brow, rising like a raspberry soufflé.

***

Jacopo and Rory carried the heavy oak carver to the flagstones of the back porch where the laundry door was ajar. Instantly they heard cursing. A woman's voice.

'Wait here,' Jacopo told Rory in a loud whisper. Nervously, he entered but the simpleton followed.

Ivano found his pistol. Jamming the heel of his right hand into the grip the pistol automatically loaded. Ivano aimed at the cursing blur before him the moment Rory recognised his mother's voice.

'Mother!'

Mareike jerked about, one hand clutching the money bag, one hand on her pounding head. 'Rory!'

Ivano didn't hesitate. He pulled the trigger. Twice.

'Mother!'

Mareike took both nine millimetre bullets in the heart. Her arms flew in the air. The open pack spiralled, and rolls of cash scattered across the floor. Jacopo bolted. Rory leapt for his mother, collapsing to his knees beside her.

'No!' His scream was guttural. Wild. 'Mother!' he cried lifting her head from the floor. But it was clear she had died instantly.

In commando mode, Ivano rolled across the floor. He took cover under the table firing a wild shot towards the wailing shape. Rory dived into the laundry for cover. Christian was panic-stricken. Why? How could the day go so wrong?

Ivano was desperate. Christian saw his chance. He made to escape. Ivano saw movement through his impaired vision. He fired another two shots. One piercing the magistrate's belly like cheese. Not life-threatening but for an old magistrate it was enough to make him collapse to the floor ... where he feigned death – a wise move.

Rory dropped to his hands and knees, crawling across the laundry floor. Ivano crabbed out into the hallway. Rory caught sight of Ivano and unwisely leapt after him. Ivano rolled onto his back and through a peppery haze he fired. The blur closed in. Two more rapid shots.

Rory took one slug to the right thigh ... another creased his shoulder tugging at his collar. Both were superficial. Both hurt like hell. The simpleton exhaled a manic howl. Fearing a fatal bullet, Rory back tracked into the kitchen ... into the laundry ... in time to hear distant police sirens. Instinctively Rory ran.

Outside, neighbours had heard the shots. Someone had called the police. Now alone in the kitchen and lying face down on the floor Christian looked over at Marieke. She was clearly deceased. Blood continued to pour from her wound. Christian gathered up his photos and negatives stuffing them into his pockets. Terrified that Ivano was still nearby with the gun, Christian checked the passageway. He heard the distant sirens. Although his wound was superficial, he bled like a pig. His eyes stung like hell. Sweat mingled with his blood. The wound started to sting … survival was paramount.

The coast was clear. Christian made for the front door. He stepped onto the veranda in time to catch Jacopo reversing his Ford Pickup down the drive. Rory appeared from the rear of the property. He too was bleeding.

Bastards! Christian's mind screamed. *What's going on here?*

Jacopo saw Rory. He braked. Reached across, opened the passenger car door. Rory climbed awkwardly into the cabin. Seconds later the Ford Pickup disappeared around the first corner, the moment blue flashing lights strobed the neighbourhood.

***

Ivano crawled back into the kitchen, desperately trying to compose himself. Hyperventilating. Rubbing his eyes. Frantically rinsing them under cold water. He was suffering shortness of breath and nasal and sinus discharge. Looking like a drowned rat Ivano dropped to his knees in the kitchen groping for spilt cash through blurred eyes, when two things happened … he heard the sirens and he remembered the Tom Roberts painting … *twenty grand easy!*

Outside sounded like the entire police force had descended on Mona Street. Whipping the bread knife from the knife block Ivano cut the painting from its frame. He rolled it faster than a meatball Subway on a Saturday night. With the cash in his pack over one shoulder, the Tom Roberts under arm, Ivano stumbled into the hall.

'You bastard!' Christian came down the passageway wielding a bronze figure of a ballerina. 'You thieving rotten bastard.'

Ivano still had the gun. 'Whoa there big fella,' Ivano stifled coughs. He aimed towards his assailant, his eyes a kaleidoscope of pain. 'Stop – right – there.'

Christian was close. He stopped dead. Although his own vison was still impaired, Christian recognised instant death clean down the barrel of the nine millimetre. Ivano had killed once, another death wouldn't matter.

'Now then,' Ivano managed a sneer from behind the weapon, twitching with involuntary eye closures. 'What were you planning to do with that?'

Christian was gobsmacked. Had an angel appeared?

'Chastity!'

Christian didn't mean to call out, but the sight of Chastity suddenly appearing behind Ivano with a large vase raised over her head was just too much. Ivano's face was blistering red and his skin painful.

'Chastity,' Christian's pained face broke into a forced smile.

Ivano suspected a ruse. 'You're not getting me with that old chestnut,' the burglar barely finished his sentence when ... a Motorola ringtone broke the awkward silence.

Christian's jaw dropped. 'Now what?' Mason and Mick appeared from the Maritime Room. 'Who the hell are you?'

Mick tossed the ringing phone aside and the deckhands bolted. Ivano swivelled about as the Motorola slid between his legs and Chastity brought the vase to bear, shattering the porcelain over Ivano's skull.

All went black. Ivano's feet collapsed beneath him and he crumpled to the floor at the same moment half a dozen police officers crashed the hallway.

***

Christian sat, groggy from his wounds. But he was alive. *Alive!* Minutes earlier he thought he was a dead man. Refusing to be taken to hospital, his superficial wound was attended to by Chastity with a first aid kit while the police crawled about his house like a scene in a Hollywood crime movie.

'That ... that dead woman came here to kill me,' Christian told the first responders on the scene. 'And others came to rob me ... me! A magistrate. They started arguing, shouting at each other,' Christian ranted on. 'One had a gun, the other pepper spray. It was terrifying.'

'You're a very lucky man sir,' one policeman said. 'Very lucky indeed. Your bullet missed any important organs or arteries.'

'And you're lucky miss ... ah ... Chastity was here,' another officer said. 'Otherwise you could be lying on the floor dead.'

'Why would they attempt to rob you?' the officer asked. 'I mean this woman Mareike was a well-known madam around town and I believe wealthy in her own right?'

'They were in this together,' Christian lied. 'And they started arguing and … well … you can see the result. I can't help you there I'm afraid. Only to suggest it's greed. Plain and simple. Greed.'

Chastity sat next to Christian holding his hand. He had lost all inhibitions. Lost caring. *So this woman is a sex-worker, so what, she saved my life.* He squeezed Chastity's hand and she squeezed back.

Two officers eventually brought Ivano back to the world of the living and, pulling his wrists tight behind him, they placed him in handcuffs and sat him in an armchair in the library for the moment. With the swelling of Ivano's mucous membranes in his eyes, nose and ears, and a crack on his skull from the vase wielded by Chastity, his discomfort trebled, but no amount of protests would free him until he was at the police lockup.

'Sit still and keep quiet until the detectives arrive,' a senior constable ordered.

***

Twenty-five-minutes later…

Maddison was amazed. She had taken the call at home around 6.10PM and now she stood in the kitchen of their latest crime scene. The kitchen was crowded. Coroner Griffin and assistant Luke Farrell were already taking photos and dusting all surfaces for fingerprints. Luke was snapping photos of blood splashes on the wall and recording splatter measurements when Landon entered the room.

'Who said police work in Hobart was slow?' Maddison told Landon, mothering the senior detective by wiping sauce from off his chin with a tissue. 'They spoiled your dinner too did they?' she asked him.

'Yep,' Landon took out his handkerchief to finish wiping what Maddison had started. 'I was enjoying it too.'

Maddison studied her tissue. 'Spaghetti bolognaise?'

'Close. Lasagne.'

An officer brought Maddison and Landon up to speed while they slipped into PPE gear including plastic shoe covers, briefing them on what they knew so far. Of particular interest was the fact they had the of killer the dead woman on the floor. But he was refusing to talk until he had a lawyer.

'He's under guard in separate room to the owner,' the officer said. 'Whom, in my opinion, is not entirely innocent.'

'Who, the owner?'

'Yes. Now,' the cop waited for effect. 'The case gets even more interesting Inspector.'

'Oh, like how?'

'Well we caught two young thugs trying to escape.'

'Are they known to the shooter?'

'No mam. Just a couple of opportunistic thieves I'm thinking.'

'And they are where?'

'They've been removed to the lockup.'

'Good,' Maddison took a breath in. 'Lead me to the victim.'

'There's more.'

'Oh!'

'Witnesses saw a Ford Pickup leave the scene in a huge hurry seconds before we arrived. Driven by an older man with a younger passenger who had a limp.'

'Wounded?'

'Maybe.'

'Descriptions?'

'Here.' The policeman held up his notes.

'License plate?'

The cop tapped his notebook, looking particularly pleased with himself.

'Excellent.' Maddison's attention was drawn down the hall.

'One more thing,' the officer said as another perp, an older man in a trench coat, was ushered along the passageway in handcuffs, to be detained for questioning in a separate room. Maddison recognised Stanley immediately. The sad figure avoided eye contact and shuffling sheepishly, he was led from sight. Maddison was incredulous. She turned to Landon. 'What the hell?'

'He was found trying to escape over the back fence when we arrived,' Landon said. 'And he had *that* under his coat.' Maddison looked to a painting of a native propped on the hall stand.

'What's going on here?' Maddison leant closer to Landon and whispered. 'That man is no other than Stanley Smart, the curator at the Tasmanian Museum … and already under surveillance.'

Landon knew all about him of course, but hadn't a face to put to the name until now. 'Is that him?'

'Yep.'

***

An officer stepped around Marieke's body, her cadaver pretty much blocking the entrance. She was after all of large portion. Covered by a blood-soaked sheet she was sprawled half in the kitchen and half into the hallway. Maddison and Landon returned to the kitchen where the peppery aroma hung in the air. Coroner Griffin and Luke Farrell were still busy snapping dozens of photos and taking notes, looking for clues and evidence in this most bizarre crime scene.

Maddison and Landon recognised Mareike; even in death with a golf ball size welt on her forehead. 'First Stanley Smart and now Mareike the brothel-keeper?' Maddison turned to Tiger. 'She was shot right?'

'Twice.'

'Was she stuck on the head as well or did that lump happen when she fell?'

The coroner looked over the rim of his glasses to Luke who held up exhibit number six. 'What's that?'

'It's a paperweight, and a rare antique the owner told me.' Maddison studied the glass ball and noted hairs adhering to drying blood.

'The owner told you?'

'Yes. He threw it at her and hit her on the head seconds before she was shot.'

Maddison laughed. She couldn't help herself. 'What next?'

Landon. 'Good throw.'

'You may find exhibit four rather interesting to.'

Farrell passed the inspector a photo, also in a plastic satchel. 'Found it under the table.'

Maddison stared at the image and a smile crossed her face. She passed it to Landon, whose head tipped on various angles making sense of the image.

'We'll hang onto that for a moment,' Maddison said. 'If you don't mind.'

'Certainly. I thought it would be of interest … and this also.' Farrell presented another evidence package, a roll of fifty-dollar notes secured with a rubber band.

'My,' Maddison realised. 'A blackmail attempt?'

'That's what I was thinking.'

'How much there?'

'One grand at a guess I'd say.'

'Where was this?'

'On the floor also.'

'Dropped?'

'I reckon.'

'So we're talking thousands more.'

'I should imagine.'

'The owner'll talk to you now,' an officer told Maddison. 'He's in the front room.'

'He's a magistrate, and I believe he has a history?' Maddison queried.

'Yes Inspector. He has had a reputation in the recent past for lenient sentencing and there were some suspicions about why.'

Landon. 'Corruption?'

The officer nodded. 'And he's got attitude.'

'Attitude?'

'An arrogant stubborn son of a bitch, if you don't mind me being honest.'

***

Christian still wore his silk smoking jacket. He sat in a Victorian period cedar gentleman's chair nursing a large cognac and a sour face. He was in shock. Chastity was at his side. After introductions, Maddison suggested Chastity waits in another room while they asked Christian questions, but he flatly denied the request.

'This woman saved my life. She stays.'

'Very well. Let's get on with it.'

'Where do you want me to start?'

'At the beginning.'

Movement out in the passageway caught everyone's attention – two officers carrying Marieke's body out on a stretcher.

'She came here to kill me,' Christian started. 'That damned, madam, brothel-keeper came here to murder me.' He started to shake once more.

Landon. 'What would be her motive?'

'Damned if I know. She's crazy. Check her record.'

Maddison recalled Chastity being one of the girls she interviewed at the bordello. 'Sorry, I didn't catch your name,' she asked.

'Chastity.'

'Yes, Chastity. You worked for the deceased did you not?'

'Yes.'

'We spoke to you about Meredith Kendall.'

Chastity nodded. 'So could you explain your relationship with Mr Winterbourne?'

'I ... ah ... I, we ...' Chastity looked at Christian for support.

'We're close friends,' Christian said, chin high, defiant.

Landon wanted to say, *she's a prostitute mate, how close exactly?*

'Sex workers can fall in love you know,' Christian said irritably, his eyes still puffy and watery red from the capsicum spray.

'So you can't explain what the deceased was doing in your home?' Maddison asked.

'No – I – can't, inspector. I came home and minutes later she appeared, walked down my passageway as if she owned the place and seconds later that, that idiot with a gun turned up and shot her dead.'

'Come, come,' Landon shook his head. 'You don't expect us to believe that now do you?'

Maddison revealed the sachet containing the photo found in the kitchen.

'Would this have anything to do with why the madam was paying you a visit?'

Christian looked at the photo and instantly looked away, his face colouring a deep red. 'Well,' Maddison persisted.

Christian, angry that he had misplaced one of the blackmail photos, reached for his brandy muttering. 'I want a lawyer.'

'You had other visitors here this evening I do believe,' Maddison started. Christian remained silent.

'Well Mr Winterbourne?' Landon persevered.

'I said I want a lawyer.'

'And you'll get one sir. But these questions are hardly incriminating. The other visitors in your house tonight, people you weren't expecting. Can you shine any light on why they were here? For starters what are those two young men doing hiding in your dining room?'

'They must have come with the crazy woman.'

Landon. 'Nope. No relationship whatsoever.'

Maddison. 'They confessed they were opportunists, came to burgle you.'

'And you weren't known to them, or them to you?' Landon said.

'No.'

'Can you explain what the curator of the Tasmanian Museum was doing trying to climb your back fence with a painting of a Tasmanian aborigine on his person?'

'What?' Christian snapped to attention.

'Oh,' Landon straightened. 'That got your pecker up.'

'What are you talking about?'

'We have detained in the next room, a curator from the Tasmanian Museum, a Mr Smart, who was caught by our officers trying to make off with a painting that, by the looks of it, but I'm no expert, looks very old and possibly very valuable.'

'Of an aborigine you say?'

'Yes, indigenous Tasmanian I'm guessing.'

'That Jacopo,' Christian hissed. 'Thieving Italian.'

'Who's Jacopo?'

'Jacopo Moretti. An Italian antique restorer.' Now Christian saw an answer to his problem. A scapegoat. Someone to unload some blame onto.

'I commission him to restore antiques from time to time,' Christian spoke freely. 'I know he is friends with this Curator Stanley isn't it? Although I've never met the man.'

'So what was he doing with your painting? It is your painting is it not?'

Suddenly Christian thought there was a good possibility the painting was stolen. 'No.'

'It's not?'

'No, Jacopo brought the painting here for my perusal, so see if I would like to purchase it.'

'For how much?'

'Twelve thousand.'

Landon whistled. 'And does this Jacopo drive a Ford Pickup?'

'Yes.'

'And this Jacopo was here also was he not?' Maddison said.

'Yes.'

'So who would the younger man, about thirty, with the shock of blonde hair, torn jeans and leather jacket be? He was with this Jacopo.'

'That's Rory, he's a simpleton who helps Jacopo with deliveries.'

'So why were the two men here this evening?'

'They were delivering an antique carver, it's at the back door where they dumped it before running off. Christ! What a night.'

'Do you know where we can find this Italian restorer?'

'Yes, North Hobart. He has a workshop registered there in his own name.'

Maddison presented the plastic evidence envelope holding the fifty-dollar notes. 'This was on the kitchen floor. Can you explain how it got there?'

Christian shrugged.

'Are you certain?'

'Never seen it before,' he lied.

'I put it to you, sir, that this roll of fifties is a part of the cache the gunman was carrying when Miss Chastity here clocked him on the head with that vase.'

'I told you, I haven't seen it before.'

'Call your lawyer,' Maddison finally ordered the magistrate. 'Tell him to meet us at Police Headquarters.'

***

Maddison and Landon moved onto the library where the wounded gunman waited, hand-cuffed and guarded by an officer. Ivano was defeated. He had taken the full force of the capsicum spray attack at close range and had a painful lump on his head. Now he was being charged with murder, breaking and entering, possession of an illegal firearm and blackmail. Hell, when they knew the truth, Ivano worried, they'd throw extortion at him as well. His future was not looking bright. There seemed no point lying. *If anything, shift some of the blame*, he thought.

'It was self-defence,' Ivano started. 'She attacked me with the capsicum spray. I couldn't see, I tried to defend myself.'

Maddison hoisted a foot up, resting it on the corner of Ivano's chair, crossing her arms, showing she was in charge. 'Are you trying to say a fit bloke like you needed to defend yourself from a much older woman with a loaded gun?'

Ivano's head pounded. 'Can I have something for a headache? My head's killing me.'

Maddison nodded to the officer guarding to fetch Panadol.

'Tell me,' Maddison asked. 'What was your relationship with Mr Winterbourne?'

'Where do you want me to start?'

Maddison and Landon looked at each other. *That's the second time I've heard that line in the past fifteen minutes.* 'At the beginning.'

'How about telling us first, what were you doing here, and did you know the deceased?' The word deceased seemed to hit home. Ivano had killed another human being. His gut knotted.

'I have never met the woman before. However I was hired to break into her house while she was at a funeral and steal photos locked in her office safe.'

'We're talking lewd photos of Magistrate Winterbourne with prostitutes are we not?'

'Yes. The madam, Mareike I think they call her, was blackmailing the magistrate.'

'And that was your pay out was it, the cash in the bag.'

'Some of it ... five grand in the envelope. The rest I took from the woman's safe when I took the photos.'

'Her savings?'

'I guess so.'

A knock on the door paused the questioning. A pretty female officer, early thirties, long legs, thin face and with long auburn hair tied back in a bun poked her head around the door. 'We've got an address on those license plates.'

'And?'

'North Hobart.'

'Yes, we know that, have you the exact address?'

The young cop passed Maddison a note. Maddison concentrated, deciding which way to run with this. She turned to Landon over her shoulder and spoke softly. 'It's imperative we chase up this Jacopo and his mate Rory as soon as possible and bring them in for questioning also.'

'I agree.'

Ivano overheard the name Rory. 'Rory you say? I heard that young blond guy with the older Italian call the brothel-keeper mother.'

'Mother! Are you certain?'

'As certain as I know my headache's killing me.'

'It just keeps getting better and better.' Maddison called over the officer guarding Ivano. 'Take this man away and see he receives medical treatment.'

'Yes Inspector.'

'And don't take your eyes of him.'

The officer ushered Ivano out into the passageway just as Stanley was being led to another waiting prison van.

'Geoff!' Stanley was dumbfounded. 'Geoff Wright! What are you doing here?'

Ivano was equally shocked. 'Mr Smart ... I ... I ah, what's ...'

'Keep moving.' Both respective officers moved their charges apart.

Maddison stepped into the hallway. 'Did you hear that?' she asked Landon. 'Sure did.'

'This just gets weirder and weirder.'

CHAPTER FIFTEEN

Forty minutes earlier in North Hobart...

Mrs Benetti watched out the window with some reservation. Neighbour Jacopo had driven like a maniac up his own driveway and hurried into his workshop, while her adopted son Rory looked equally fazed and leapt the fence between their properties. Clearly, Rory was returning to his bungalow at the rear of her property. Both men looked anxious. Mrs Benetti had been keeping Jacopo's wife Elanora company while Jacopo delivered a large chair to a client in Battery Point. Now he was home. Jacopo hurried through his back door and saw the fire burning briskly in the lounge room fireplace.

'Why is the fire lit?' he asked his neighbour. 'It's a warm evening.'

'Eleanora, she insisted. And you know what she's like when she makes up her mind that she wants something.'

Eleanora stared vaguely into the flames, mesmerised by their devilish beauty. Rory hadn't replenished the firewood scuttle on the hearth during the warmer months for this very reason, but something was burning brightly. It was then he recognised the pile of old magazines. These were the fuel, burning fiercely, that had Eleanora so mesmerised. She ignored her husband and continued tossing periodicals onto the fire.

Jacopo noticed a banknote curl up and float up the chimney. 'No!' He leapt forward as dozens of similar banknotes exploded into flames.

'No!' he screamed out.

Jamming the poker into the flames the fire exploded into a million sparks while the action only succeeded to feed oxygen into the fire. The banknotes from the model ship were destroyed in seconds and Jacopo looked to where he had hidden the money under the pile of magazines. It had all gone, up in smoke. 'No!' he cried once more and slid to the carpet hugging his knees.

***

Twenty minutes later...

Maddison and Landon parked their unmarked police car four houses down from Jacopo's home. Landon checked his watch. It was twenty minutes to eight with dusk fading to night in a subtle hue left by a late sunset.

Maddison noted. 'Pickup's in the drive.'

The front doorbell went unanswered. A power tool buzzed somewhere nearby. 'Round the back.' Landon led the way. At the end of the driveway past the pickup, Maddison and Landon caught a glimpse of Jacopo through open workshop doors. He had his back to the officers, working on his lathe. Maddison knew better than to surprise anyone working with power tools. She called out. Nothing. The two approached. Jacopo jumped. He caught them in his peripheral vision. He recognised Maddison and Landon immediately and his face flushed.

Maddison. 'Mr Moretti.'

Jacopo looked nervous. Anxious. If Maddison didn't know any better, she'd say guilty. Jacopo killed the lathe and fiddled while the rotation slowed. He looked about for something to do with his hands.

'Now what you want?' Jacopo asked. But he knew damn well.

'We'd like to ask you a few questions.'

'I tell you before.' Jacopo swallowed hard.

'This is a new enquiry Mr Moretti. You were at Mona Street in Battery Point earlier this evening, were you not?'

Jacopo knew there was no point lying. 'Si.'

The stress had been too much for Jacopo. He felt a weight suddenly lift from his shoulders and made it clear to the police he was only too happy to co-operate. Jacopo explained he was there only to deliver a restored chair.

'We know that'.

'Why did you leave the chair at the back door and leave in a hurry?' Maddison demanded.

'I hear shooting,' Jacopo's face was strained with guilt and fear. 'I scared. I run, si.'

'So you know nothing about your friend Stanley Smart being on the premises at the same time?'

'No. No. I know notheen. The shooting. Is anyone ... ah ... is anyone ...?' his voice trialled away.

'One dead, two wounded,' Landon said matter-of-factly, hoping to frighten the Italian even more.

'Mamma Mia.' Jacopo crossed himself. 'Morto!'

'Yes.'

'M–Mister Winterbourne is he ...'

'Dead? No.'

The Italian allowed the whisper of a smile and Maddison read it as relief. Jacopo thought he might still be paid what he is owed.

'Mr Winterbourne told us that you were in the process of selling him a painting,' Maddison said. 'A painting by a colonial artist named Duterrau, we have been informed that it is a valuable oil of an aborigine and titled, *Wild man of Van Diemen's Land.*'

Jacopo shoulders sank. He didn't think Christian would tell the police about the painting because he was sure the magistrate suspected it to be stolen.

Landon. 'Is that true?'

'Si.'

'Do you own the painting?'

'No.'

'Oh! Then who does own it?'

Jacopo clamped up. *He had rights in this country*, he was certain of it. 'I ... I'd rather not say.'

'Well can you explain to us why your friend Stanley Smart was in possession of that painting and trying to escape over Mr Winterbourne's back fence with it?'

Jacopo. 'I don't know these things.'

'Oh,' Landon's tone became condescending. 'But I think you do know sir. We know he is your friend; we have seen you together on many occasions.'

'Old friends I believe,' Maddison added.

Have you been spying? Jacopo felt his brow sweat.

'So, who owns the painting?'

'And where did it come from in the first place?'

'I would rather not say,' Jacopo fidgeted.

'It doesn't work that way Mr Moretti, you either tell us what we want to know, *now*. Or we take you down the police station for more questioning until you *do* tell us.'

Jacopo looked decidedly uncomfortable. '

'An easier question for the moment Mr Moretti,' Maddison said. 'Rory Benetti, where can we find him?'

'Why? If you do not mind me ask?'

'We have to ask him questions also.'

Jacopo thought a moment. 'Ah, he live in house next door.'

'Next door! Well that's convenient, for us at least. Which way next door, left or right?'

Jacopo pointed right.

'I'll go and see if this Rory's home. You continue with Mr Moretti,' Maddison said, sharing the conversation with Jacopo. 'I'm certain Mr Moretti here will see fit to tell you what we need to know without being taken to the police station.'

Fancying she had persuaded the Italian to see reason, Maddison left Landon with Jacopo.

***

On older Italian lady with long salt and pepper hair opened the door. 'Police, si?'

'Yes. Are you Mrs Benetti?"

'Si.'

'Is Rory home?'

The Italian mamma held back tears. 'What he done?'

'Mrs Benetti, *is* Rory home?'

'What he done I say? Rory good boy …'

'Mrs Benetti, Rory was seen at the scene of a crime earlier this evening. Is – he – home?'

As Maddison asked this, she noted what looked like blood on the woman's sleeve. It appeared smeared, wet, like she was trying to clean it when she arrived.

'Is that blood?'

The old woman broke into tears.

'He's wounded, isn't he?' Maddison asked.

Mrs Benetti nodded.

'He was shot Mrs Benetti. This is serious. Is the wound bad?'

'No, is no bad. Is in leg.' And she pointed to her thigh.

'Where is he?' Maddison was looking into the darkening hallway either side of the woman, watching for any signs. If she didn't hurry he might run.

But running from what for god's sake, Maddison wanted to know? *He was only delivering furniture. Wrong place wrong time. Or was it?*

'He outside, in back,' Mrs Benetti sobbed. 'He live in flat in garden.'

Maddison pushed by the old lady and started warily down the darkening passage. 'Out the backdoor? In the garden you say?'

'Si. But Rory, he no like people go there. He not let me or Giuseppe in his flat. He no like visitors.'

Maddison passed down the hall. Few lights burned and Maddison suspected a frugal lifestyle. She passed the TV room where old man Giuseppe was watching some reality show with the volume high, oblivious to what was going on. Mrs Benetti followed Maddison to the back door.

'Please don't take my Rory,' she wailed. 'He good boy. It's that bad womans, Mareike, she make Rory forget god.'

Maddison let the fly wire door swing shut on its spring hinge and turned to face the woman. 'Mareike, his maternal mother, yes?'

'Si. She Rory's mamma. She adopt Rory out when he bambino.'

So it was true.

The dots were joining. Maddison nodded recognition and headed into a backyard of apple and apricot trees, once part of a large orchard in years past, subdivided into blocks decades earlier. Twenty metres from the house Maddison found the weatherboard granny flat, a shanty built in the 1940s, overgrown with vines and ivy and backing onto a neighbouring property. The sun had completely disappeared behind Mount Wellington now, and amongst the mature trees it grew dark rapidly. Overhead clouds gathered, threatening rain, maybe even a thunderstorm.

There were no lights on in the flat. The curtains were drawn. Maddison knocked on the door to the right of the shack.

'Rory. Rory Benetti, this is Inspector Lovett of the Tasmanian Police. Will you open the door please?'

No answer.

'Mr Benetti?'

Silence.

Maddison tried the door. Locked. Somewhere nearby dogs barked, large dogs. She moved around to the back locating a second door. The neighbour's old paling fence, two metres from the rear of the flat, was dilapidated to the point of collapsing. Only dense overgrown blackberry bushes kept the structure semi-erect. Maddison found a dead tree branch to fend off prickle bushes working her way to the back door when … she involuntarily gagged.

Now Maddison caught the smell – the stench of death. Unwittingly she disturbed a swarm of fat black blowflies. Maddison froze, throwing an arm in front of her face until the flies settled.

Oh Jesus!

Nailed to the back fence, half hidden by blackberries, was a dog. A black Labrador most likely. A long nail through the neck and one through the chest. Maddison was challenged to keep down her dinner. She took deep breaths. Disgusted, determined, Maddison shoved on towards the rear door. In the gloom she saw the remains of other animals lying on the ground in various states of decomposition. No wonder the stink was so putrid, so strong. She recognised one other dog and at least two cats. *Christ!* Someone's loved pets. *Sick bastard!*

Instantly the barking dogs over the fence grew closer, louder. Dobermans, the inspector could just make out over the fence, with angry snarling viscous jaws. Comfortable that the dogs were separated by thick blackberry bushes, Maddison reached the rear door. Clearly it was rarely used. There was no knocking this time. Maddison took a pencil torch from her pocket and tried the door. The lock was broken and the door opened.

Because curtains were drawn, she stepped into an abysmal darkness, panning the torch beam around the three-room flat, and entered. The smell reminded her of a public toilet.

Suddenly the torch blinked. *Damn, the batteries are low.*

Shaking the torch back to life, Maddison swept the beam around the room. The flat consisted of a main living area with a bathroom and a bedroom off to one side. The floor was strewn with refuse. Empty Gatorade bottles, empty beer cans, plastic takeaway containers, thick-shake cups, clothes and soiled underwear. Housekeeping was not a priority. A free-standing television stood in one corner. There was one only armchair with an Ottoman, a sideboard with missing doors storing a sparse collection of crockery and little else. Off to one side an open wardrobe; as in a metre-long hanging rail, held the tenant's spare clothes. At a glance Maddison noted everything was black, or leather.

Very Gothic.

This drew her attention to the walls where demonic black and white posters dominated the theme. One poster in black and red boasted *The Brotherhood of Satan*. Another was simply a large Pentagram. But a portrait photo taken at a concert was of immediate interest. The large print showed Rory wearing a simulated grain belt with a brass buckle of a goat's head. And what made it unique was the pentagram on the goat's forehead that Maddison felt she had seen before somewhere.

A kitchenette boasted a single sink filled with dirty crockery and a two-plate cooktop laminated with yellow solidified fat. In the bedroom a double mattress lay on the floor. It hadn't been made in months; the linen was stained, the bedside lamp broken, and clothes were strewn about. Pornographic literature was casually thrown aside. The bathroom stank of stale urine, the once white porcelain toilet pan was brown with filth, heavily stained and the shower bay black with mould. The sink matched the filth. The medicine cupboard, with its broken mirror, held basics like Aspirin, aftershave, cologne and a squeezed tube of toothpaste with its contents oozed onto the sink. Maddison noted nothing illegal – there were no signs the man used drugs.

Maddison stepped back into the living area. She stood silently and listened, not wanting to breath in the spores of filth longer than necessary. Outside the dogs protected their territory; snarling, barking, pacing up and down the fence. Maddison ran the torch over the kitchen buffet and froze. Amongst a half loaf of white slice on a wooden board with a serrated knife, Maddison saw a ball of string … *brown string and unusually wide.*

A chill ran the length of her spine. She recognised the unusual string immediately as the same string used to bind the recent murder victims.

Maddison sucked air. A sudden reflex of recognition. She sensed immediate danger.

Without warning the *wardrobe* exploded to life. Maddison swivelled sharply. A dark shape manifested from the wardrobe. Where there were Gothic leathers, an attacker materialised, just as her torch died.

Maddison had no time to defend herself. The blow came fast and hard. She managed a short sharp yell, but the strike sheared off the side of her head.

Maddison's legs buckled. She fell onto her knees, blacked out and fell forward onto the Ottoman.

Landon heard the yell and crashed through the front door like a rugby league bulldozer, splintering the door off its hinged jamb. The dark shape leapt for the back door as Landon swung his police issue torch towards the body on the floor.

'Maddison!'

Immediately the Dobermans over the fence went into a frenzy of vicious barking. Landon dropped to his knees next to Maddison.

'Maddie, Maddie ...' he shook her shoulder. Landon slapped her cheek. Maddison opened one eye, then the second.

'It's him,' she wheezed.

'Rory?'

'H– he's the killer.'

'What?'

'Rory. He's the killer. Back door. Quick.'

Landon sprang to his feet. He threw the rear door open but was stopped by the encroaching blackberries. Thorny vines threatened. They clawed at his coat. Prickles pierced his skin. Landon cursed. Holding his torch like a truncheon he hurled light towards the racket. The dogs were hysterical, snapping and tearing. Landon heard inhuman screams ... guttural repulsive squeals. Maddison appeared at Landon's side and together they gaped at the confusion.

'Oh Jesus!'

Rory Benetti was trapped in the blackberries. In his haste to escape he was hopelessly caught in the prickles. Like a hare in the brambles, Rory frantically tried to escape but the dogs had torn palings from the fence and were ripping the man apart. There was nothing Landon and Maddison could do but listen to the sickening crush of human bones. The tearing of flesh, the shredding of muscle and the deathly squeals of a man being torn apart and eaten alive. The Doberman dogs, Bruno and Barron, had their day. After years of torment from Rory, years of abuse and finally witnessing the recent murders of their fellow animals being crucified alive, the dogs took their revenge in the only way they knew.

Late next morning. Police Headquarters…

Mason sat looking sorry for himself, waiting for his interview to continue. He was alone and had watched enough cop television to suspect he was being observed through the huge one-way mirror to his left. Had he known, his mate Mick was sweating in another room.

'He doesn't look so smug now,' Maddison cupped both hands about her personalised coffee mug, given her by the crew the day she started. *Babe with the Power* the caption read. A little twee, she thought, but it kept a cuppa hot.

'So he runs from us, wanted for questioning about Max Shreeve's the fisherman's death and winds up hiding in the dining room where another murder has just taken place. Will someone please explain?'

Landon sipped his mug loudly. He was parched. The coffee was bloody hot.

'Reckons he ran from his flat because he was terrified we were going to stitch him up for Max's murder.'

'Too right we were.' Maddison thought carefully a moment and restructured her comment. 'Well we wanted him for questioning at least. He *was* a suspect at the time.'

'He does have a record for assault, and he did have a physical fight with Max down the wharves.'

'Well we know now *he* didn't kill his boss, Max Shreeve.'

'So what's his story? What, in god's name were he and that idiot mate doing in Christian Winterbourne's home?'

'Opportunist thieves. Said something about going there to steal a ship.'

'A ship?'

'Yep. Told us they broke in with the intention of stealing an antique model ship made of whale bone that apparently, the boys had heard, was full of hidden cash?'

'What?'

'Yes, a few thousand dollars was hidden in the model years ago by Max's grandmother.'

'Our Max the fisherman?'

'Yes. Dead Max.'

'And how, pray tell, did the ship end up at the magistrates?'

'That's what we need to find out.'

'Okay,' Maddison watched Mason fiddling, looking about anxiously. 'Let them both sweat a while. We've a meeting scheduled with the coroner and psychologist first.'

***

Maddison had plenty to be pleased about. Her smile said it all. She had only taken the position of Inspector weeks earlier, but the policewoman had cemented a great reputation, work ethic and camaraderie with her colleagues. The detectives gathered about in the meeting room, or the *engine room* as Maddison liked to call it. Freshly brewed coffee permeated the air, conflicting with the baker's box of assorted pastries someone sent out for, for morning tea. This morning was to be a celebration.

Maddison sat at the head of the conference table and took a moment to recognise each colleague as they poured mugs of the coffee and took up seats. Joining her was Coroner Griffin, his assistant Luke Farrell, Sergeant Ray Highlander, Constable Lachlan Harlow, Detective Charlie Smite and of course, Landon. Police psychologist Dr Jennifer Macintyre arrived minutes late.

'Morning. Have I missed anything?'

'No,' Maddison said. 'Just started.'

Maddison appreciated the female company in this predominantly male regime. Jennifer was a breath of fresh air in her dark suit and slacks with long wavy hair tied in a chignon.

'Well I've got to say we have had an extraordinary week.' Maddison's first words silenced the room. 'I think you'll all agree.'

Satisfied faces smiled back.

'Rory Benetti,' Maddison continued. 'Who would have guessed? A baby-faced simpleton manipulated by an evil woman to do her bidding, to kill her spouse and lover. A mentally handicapped man groomed into killing for the promise of sex. How sad is that.'

'Sex that was never honoured.' Landon said guilefully, leaning back in his chair. Maddison wondered if Landon was sending her a message.

'Yes well, she was a smart woman,' Maddison shot back.

'Hardly,' Griffin weighed in. 'She was murdered for her trouble.'

'Yes, but the simpleton was already a sexual deviant,' Dr Jennifer Macintyre said. 'Maybe it was fortunate he met that woman rather than molest joggers in the bush.' Landon suddenly realised what he had said. 'Maybe I should rephrase that. It's unfortunate that people had to die, but ... well I think you know what I mean.'

'True,' Highlander came to Landon's rescue. 'We found some pretty hard-core porn in his flat.'

'Yes, well.' Maddison turned to the psychologist. 'I know you've had a gruelling morning with our killer's adopted parents. I don't envy you at all.'

Jennifer Macintyre spread her notes before her. 'You can say that again. Mrs Benetti was difficult to interview. However, I have made extensive notes and can give you a preliminary profile at least, which I think you will all find interesting.'

'Fire away.'

'Rory Benetti was like two dissimilar entities living within the one skin; one irreproachable and one a depraved sexual deviant. Like so many other psychopaths he had an abused childhood.'

'You say psychopath,' Highlander said. 'But he killed four people, who were all known to each other, sort of.'

'True, but I have no doubt he would have killed again. These killings had given him a taste for it. They were the tip of the iceberg. I hate to say this but there is a possibility he had killed before and was never caught.'

'Yes, we're looking into cold cases that may have a connection,' Maddison said.

'He was adopted out at birth,' Macintyre went on. 'Now we don't know how this case slipped through the welfare net, but his adopted mother turned out a bad egg. She was gaoled for twelve months for third offence shoplifting and the assault of a police officer. During this time, Rory lived with his aged adopted grandmother. Released nine months later the mother fell into depression and became an alcoholic, cutting her wrists in the bath. Rory found her body. He was only four.'

'Oh Jesus,' someone muttered. 'There was no hope for him.'

'He never knew his adopted father.'

'How on earth was he ever adopted out to ... to such people?'

'As I said, we don't know how this slipped under the radar. He was then placed in the care of foster parents, but the foster mother developed MS and the father drank, so by the time he was eight he was placed in an orphanage. This was 1973 and he was already a difficult child. In the orphanage, run by nuns, crying was a sin punishable by a spanking, *to give them something to cry about.* Bedwetting was an even greater sin. A child who wet the bed was forced to stand for an hour under a cold shower while the other children went to the dormitory for breakfast. If the bedwetting continued, they were beaten before bedtime. If this failed, then Sister Agnes and Sister Marie, as Mrs Benetti recalled their names, made the boys stand in the playground holding up their soiled linen whilst calling out *I am a bedwetter.* Another punishment featured by the nuns was for the bedwetter to hug a tree while the other boys lined up and took turns kicking them.'

'I thought this was the 20th century!'

'No wonder hatred festered.'

'Where did you learn all this?' Landon asked. 'Not from Mrs Benetti, surely?'

'Some from her yes, but most I sourced from adoption files and police records.' The psychologist looked at Landon accusingly. 'I *have* been busy.'

'Oh, I don't doubt that.'

Macintyre continued. 'Occasionally relatives brought the children cake or sweets on Sundays. Rory was always denied this. *You are a bedwetter,* the nuns said, *you do not deserve sweets.* Once when his eighty–three–year–old adopted grandmother managed a visit, Sister Agnes took the sweets she had brought along, and divided them amongst the other boys, *because you are a bedwetter.*'

'Bitch!'

'At fourteen he ran away from the orphanage. Caught and placed in various foster homes, he was sent to school for nearly two years. He enjoyed a positive spell at this time, befriending a teacher who saw his intelligence for what it was, scoring top grades in his chosen subjects like carpentry. However, when a local church was vandalised, and he was blamed – although he was totally innocent, I was told – his attitude changed. Once more he became the angry young man, stealing, breaking and entering and shoplifting.'

'This is his adolescent period I take it?' Landon asked.

'Yes. He discovered the opposite sex at sixteen and recognised he had charisma. He was after all, a good-looking boy. The girls loved him. At this point he gained confidence. The girls found his shyness an attraction and he was discreet. Apparently he slept with plenty of girls before falling in love with

Amy Black. Amy worked as a shop assistant at a chemist in the local mall. They were best of friends for several weeks, but then one afternoon he saw her outside the movies with another boy, a St Virgil's prefect. They were acting extremely friendly his adopted mother told me. They appeared to have been intimate and he grew angry. He had never experienced such hatred and Mrs Benetti remembered Rory vowing to kill them.'

'Jesus,' Highlander said. 'What happened?'

'I've been trying to corroborate this, but I can find no evidence of Amy Black ever existing.'

'Did Mrs Benetti meet Amy?'

'No. I suspect Amy Black was a figment of Rory's imagination, that Rory was trying to impress mother.'

'Any questions so far?' Macintyre asked.

'This Seraph business,' Griffin asked. 'Why did Rory call himself Seraph?'

'A-ha, I was getting to that next. As Rory grew older, he disowned his foster parents, but in a subtle way they were simple-minded folk who didn't really notice any problems. He was easily influenced by others, saw the Benettis as inferior immigrants. But he continued to live his deteriorating life in a granny flat, a separate building at the back of the Benetti's North Hobart property where he could come and go at will.'

'And never let the Benettis inside, huh?'

'That's correct. He became very secretive.'

'You should have seen the flat,' Luke Farrell said. 'It was a tip.'

Young Constable Harlow blew out his cheeks in agreement. 'It was filthy. Dirty clothes on the floor, empty food packets and wrappers chucked anywhere, empty coke bottles, chocolate bar wrappers, sink full of dirty dishes, McDonald's crap, it was disgusting.'

'You would have felt at home then Harlow,' Landon squeezed off a smile.

'Rory got in with the wrong crowd,' the psychologist went on. 'He dabbled in the dark arts, eventually calling himself Seraph amongst his dark arts associates. We won't call them friends.'

'Seraph? Does it have meaning?'

'It means *the burning one,*' the coroner said. 'Doesn't it?'

'That's correct. Traditionally Seraph is placed in the highest rank in Christian Angelology and the fifth rank of ten in the Jewish angelic hierarchy.'

'What, like an angel?'

'Yes. But Rory and his gothic friends had a warped idea of *the burning one.*'

'As in Hell?'

'Exactly. The term is used to describe a type of celestial being or, as you said, an angel. Other uses of the word refer to serpents, a symbol of evil power and chaos from the underworld; a translation that Seraph's associates had a sick distorted understanding of. The fact that the serpent was also a symbol of fertility, life and healing in the Hebrew Bible went undetected by the group. In other words, the associates were all mentally disturbed, which had a powerful and evil influence on the simpleton.'

'Then he meets Verity Shreeve, wife of one of the victims,' Maddison said. 'She is a real piece of work. She works on Rory, encouraging his dark arts and grooms him to become a killer.'

'And he offers him love and sex if he kills Meredith and Max,' Griffin sighed sagely.

'I remember seeing Rory in the garden on the two occasions I visited Mareike's bordello,' Maddison said. 'She gave him a job as her gardener after they met some weeks back. You'd have never picked him as a killer.'

'You rarely do,' Macintyre said.

***

That afternoon, Maddison looked long and hard at the letter on her desk. It was unusual to have personal mail sent to the station, but she recognised her husband Stephen's writing immediately, with its sweeping, leaning italic letters and bold capitals.

***

Dear Maddison, it started. Dear Maddison! He never called her Maddison, so formal. Maddison knew without reading the rest that this was a letter of resignation. Resignation from their marriage. She skipped the few lines, searching for the name Lucie. Lucie had been hanging around for months. Maddison's spies in Melbourne had told her that much. But her name wasn't on the page. Just the *fallen out of love* bullshit that she knew was coming.

Disgusted, Maddison threw the letter in her wastepaper basket just as Landon walked into her office, without knocking. He saw the angst on his old flame's face.

'Okay …' he said. 'Already sorry I didn't knock.'

Maddison looked into Landon's kind blue eyes and memories of good times flooded back. She smiled. The smile turned to a huge grin, almost a laugh.

'What's up?' Landon asked warily.

'What's up?' Maddison sang. 'Is that offer for a dinner date still on the table?'

EPILOGUE

Stanley Smart's daughter Sophie was upset. Upset and hurt. She'd followed her heart *again*, and had been dumped, *again*. It seemed the story of her life. Just when she thought she had met Mister Right, she was *kicked in the guts*. There was no other way of describing it. *Kicked in the guts.*

But Sophie also wanted closure. What if Ivano had taken ill? What if something bad had happened to him, an accident maybe? What if ...?

She just needed to know and move on. The more Sophie replayed their pillow talk on the one occasion she slept with Ivano, the more information she remembered. And he did let it slip, once, that he had rented a boat shed. Now Sophie Smart knew enough about her hometown Hobart to know there were only the one set of boat sheds close to Hobart CBD and that was at Cornelian Bay. But not only did he mention the shanty, but he had commented how much he loved its red door, in contrast to the grey painted weatherboards of the boathouse itself.

***

Sophie finished work at five and by 5.20PM – that same afternoon her father was to be arrested at Mona Street – Sophie arrived by cab at Cornelian Bay. She tipped the cabbie two dollars, kicked off her shoes and walked along the beach towards the gaily coloured boat houses on the south of the cove. The sand felt great underfoot and the evening was pleasant. Sophie took to the communal right-of-way, a path onto which the thirty-six sheds backed, looking for a red door, when she came to the police barricade ribbons of boat shed number 17. It was too much of a coincidence. Sophie felt her heart quicken. She tried looking through a window when she was disturbed.

'Can I help you?' asked an older woman with the prying eye and a labradoodle.

'Oh! What happened here?' Sophie referred to the police tape.

'It's a crime scene. A body was washed up her a few days ago. But the victim wasn't killed here, so I don't understand what the hold-up is with the police tape.'

'Crime scene?'

'Yes. A fisherman was murdered over at Lindisfarne, so I believe, and his body washed over the river and was trapped under the jetty here. During that storm the other night.'

'Body? A fisherman?' Sophie looked relieved.

'Yes. Are you looking for someone in particular?'

Sophie described Ivano.

'No sorry. But some owners rent their properties out from time to time. He could be in any one of them.'

'Is there a boat shed here with a red door?'

The woman looked surprised. 'Why yes, it's the grey boathouse if you continue along this path, about six or seven further along.' And she pointed east.

Sophie watched and waited for the woman and her chocolate labradoodle to walk off in the opposite direction before seeking out the grey shack. As the woman said, the boathouse was the sixth building along. It looked deserted. Sophie managed to peer in one window, and it was clear someone had been here recently. She tried the red door. Locked. Looking about she was alone, the area quite deserted.

The tide was out. Sophie waded out between shacks until she was knee deep in water before climbing onto the small jetty that each property boasted. Sophie tried the sliding door on the waterside. Locked. Looking under the doormat seemed so ridiculously naïve. Under planters and outdoor furniture. Nothing. Sophie ran her outstretched fingers along the beam over the glass sliding door. Something dislodged, a key fell to the deck and bounced, before stopping at a gap in the decking. Sophie swooped, catching the key before it slipped to the riverbed below.

Inside was comfortable and still warm from the afternoon sun with the windows closed. Sophie sniffed the air. Ivano's Old Spice aftershave lingered; she was certain. *Was he returning?* She thought not. There were no personal items, no clothes, suitcase, toiletries. Nothing. *The bastard's scampered.* Run off with his *tail between his legs.*

Why? Sophie said aloud. *Why me?*

It was the story of her life. *Shit!*

Sophie slammed her handbag onto the kitchen buffet and was rewarded with a loose wooden ceiling panel dropping onto her head. Dust and detritus followed. Sophie jumped aside before she was assaulted by another panel, but only a dark space remained where the panel had loosened. The pine board sat on the kitchen buffet where it fell. Sophie dusted herself down, spitting grime and stared up at the opening. Something caught her eye. The corner of a brown folder looking somehow familiar poking from the exposed opening. And if she looked carefully there seemed to be boot prints on the laminated bench next to where she stood. Man's size boots. If Sophie didn't know any better, she would say someone had stood on the bench to stash something in the ceiling cavity. Sophie blinked dust before mounting a stool, climbing onto the buffet. Not tall enough to grope about, Sophie commandeered the firewood scuttle for an extra step-up. The first folder she recognised as her father's coin album. Sophie was ecstatic, horrified, shamed and furious all at once. She retrieved the other five. *Why you thieving bastard!* It became clear that the rumours about her father's acquisitions were true and the walk back to town along the foreshore gave Sophie focus. There could be only one outcome for the collection.

***

Hours later Stanley Smart, Museum Curator, was charged with being in the possession of a rare and valuable colonial painting, the Duterrau *Wild Man of Van Diemen's Land.* Suspected stolen property. However, this could not be proven, and magistrate Christian Yardley Winterbourne refused to press charges against Stanley for trespass.

The next day a parcel arrived at the museum addressed to Director Charlotte Fysh. It was delivered by courier from an anonymous sender. The parcel contained six albums of coins, medals and banknotes; all once belonging to the TMAG. Most were in mint condition and at least a hundred extra items were included, unrecorded. Charlotte assumed they were from Stanley's legitimate collection. Stanley never did return to the museum. He was retrenched and although his dishonesty went unpunished, he was ostracised by his colleagues. It took some time, but Stanley eventually forgave his daughter Sophie for returning the collection.

**

Stella Bathe never did take the position at the Queen Victoria Museum and Art Gallery in Launceston. The board at the TMAG promoted her to Museum Curator, the youngest ever to be appointed. On a more personal note her relationship with the director, Charlotte Fysh, was still going strong at the time of writing this saga about prisoners of fate.

**

Ivano Stipanov was charged with Madam Mareike's murder, a charge that was reduced to manslaughter. He would serve three years after good behaviour, in Hobart's Risdon Prison, before being extradited to Melbourne to face multiple upmarket burglary charges. Sophie never saw him again after the boathouse incident.

**

Jacopo's wife Eleanora died the following year in 1996. Two months later Giuseppe Benetti, Jacopo's neighbour, died of heart failure. The stress of the truth of their adopted son, Rory, a killer, was too much to bear. Mamma Benetti sold her property and Rory's granny flat was immediately demolished. Mamma Benetti, Bella to her close friends, moved in with Jacopo; although she swore they slept in different rooms.

**

The police could never find Alfred Kenning the art conman. It was believed he had travelled overseas.

**

Magistrate Christian Winterbourne was investigated by the art squad and the paintings in his possession confiscated. He was dismissed and forced to sell his mansion and downsize, eventually settling in a two-bedroom unit in Howrah. As Mareike's brothel was closed Chastity was forced onto the street. But in an act of kindness, weakness or just to make things right, Christian invited her into his home on the pretext she was his housemaid. A housemaid who slept in his bed. On the bright side, Christian no longer had to pay for sex. And maybe he overindulged, for he died eight years later of a stroke, leaving what was left of his fortune, the few antiques remaining and his unit, to Chastity. The day of the funeral Chastity purchased a kitten, a Siamese, and called it Desire.

**

DNA results proved that Ronny Smith was guilty of the cold case Taroona murder back in 1988.

As for Ryan the dodgy art thief from London, he disappeared into the history books; presumably back to the United Kingdom, never to be seen again.

ABOUT THE AUTHOR

Craig A. Godfrey lives in Tasmania, where he grew up. A chef by trade, Craig established and operates a popular sea food restaurant, The Drunken Admiral, since 1979. He also produced and directed films, enjoying a colourful life, and travelling extensively. This and his love of history, along with a passion for collecting antiques, shows in his writing, mostly historic drama, and action thrillers. He is currently working on his twenty sixth novel.

NOTE FROM THE AUTHOR

Word-of-mouth is crucial for any author to succeed. If you enjoyed *Prisoners of Fate*, please leave a review online—anywhere you are able. Even if it's just a sentence or two. It would make all the difference and would be very much appreciated.

Thanks!
Craig A. Godfrey

We hope you enjoyed reading this title from:

BLACK ROSE
writing™

www.blackrosewriting.com

Subscribe to our mailing list – *The Rosevine* – and receive **FREE** books, daily deals, and stay current with news about upcoming releases and our hottest authors.
Scan the QR code below to sign up.

Already a subscriber? Please accept a sincere thank you for being a fan of Black Rose Writing authors.

View other Black Rose Writing titles at www.blackrosewriting.com/books and use promo code **PRINT** to receive a **20% discount** when purchasing.

www.ingramcontent.com/pod-product-compliance
Lightning Source LLC
Chambersburg PA
CBHW010730100726
47899CB00009B/2998